CROSSED

LINES

P.A. Stockton

To Bonnie Gilbert, thank you for the kick in the pants
when I needed it most.

PROLOGUE

There was a good wind today, he'd been looking forward to this day for a week. The warm sand came squishing up between his toes as he raced along the beach letting the string out a bit at a time, until a gust of wind grabbed his bright red kite and drove it high into the sky. He could hear his parents cheering him on and his heart raced. This was a special day, his mother and father were happy with him and with each other. He turned to wave, saw them sitting in the sand next to the picnic lunch and they were both smiling. They hadn't smiled or spoken much to each other in months, now they sat holding hands. This was a good thing and his smile broadened as he looked at them.

The clacking sound startled him and he woke suddenly. He rubbed his eyes and looked around not knowing where he was. At first he saw nothing but slits of light dancing on the wood and then he remembered. He wished he could escape back into the dream and perhaps change the outcome of the reality he was living now.

Clack- clack, clack-clack, the sound was never ending, it seemed he had been listening to it forever. The endless sound of wheels on rails stretching on toward an unknown horizon. The smell in the boxcar was unbearable, he was sure the young boy next to him had died for he had dirtied himself and hadn't moved for a day. He was afraid to touch the boy for fear that once he did he'd start screaming and be unable to stop. He squeezed his eyes shut, drew his knees up to his chest and turned toward the filthy wall, trying to draw himself away from...everything, the smells, the noises and his own fear.

The boy who calls himself Ignacio nudged him, leaned down close to his ear and said, "Time to grow up."

1

The young boy struggled up the sandy, brush covered hill leading from the river. Behind followed his sixteen year old brother carrying a small pack with their meager belongings, an old shirt and two pairs of pants. His other shirt had been torn into strips to bandage their feet before putting their shoes on again, the man had taken their socks away, saying it would look better. They had ridden the train for two days and then had been driven to a spot near the river. They were hungry, thirsty, dirty and tired, having been denied very much food or water. The men who were watching over them had said it looked more believable.

The young boy stopped and looked back over his shoulder to the other side of the river, the other side of the border. The brown water in the river swirled under the small foot bridge they had used to cross the border. On both sides of the river the trees, if you could call them that, were thick and hung low over the water. Behind him, far behind him, was his home, his country, his life. He was not sure how far he had come, but he knew he had been moving toward this border for a very long time and if he lived long enough he would find a map, find his home and he would return. He turned back toward the top of the hill and as he did he saw his brother grab a handful of earth and scrub his face with it putting more dirt and scratches on his skin. This puzzled the boy, but he said nothing.

As they topped the hill they saw a dirt track and nothing else except scrub brush, small trees and more hot dry land. This was Texas, but it still looked like Mexico. The boy started to move forward to the road when his brother grabbed him, pulled him back and pointed to a thin line of trees. They walked parallel to the road, but behind the trees for a few hundred yards and then moved onto the road. They knew the border patrol or someone would come down this road and find them, an American would find them and help them.

It didn't take long before the white SUV with the green slash down the side found them. The agents gave them water and hustled them into the SUV where several other dirty, hungry people sat. They looked at one another, but there were no words spoken or heads nodded, not even a smile. The agents drove slowly a bit further down the road then turned around and drove faster to a new destination.

They soon stopped at a small bus where other agents and border crossers had gathered. The border crossers sat on the ground and their little group joined them. The agents were asking questions of everyone. Soon it would be their turn. The older boy turned, looked at his brother and said, "Recuerdo."- remember. The young boy looked at him with frightened eyes and only nodded. The older boy knew that this was the easy part, just never look up always look at the ground.

The agent walked over to them eyeing them for anything unusual and in fluent Spanish told them he only needed some information. The first thing he asked was if they spoke any English to which they shook their heads, the rest of the interrogation was conducted in Spanish. The only one to answer was the older boy.

"I have a few questions before we get on the bus," the Agent said. "I need to know where you are from, your first and last name and your age."

"I am from Honduras, my name is Ignacio Garza and I have sixteen years," the older boy said.

The agent turned to the young boy and asked, "What is your name?" The older boy answered, "He is Rogelio."

The agent looked back at the older boy and asked, "Can he talk? I need him to answer for himself."

The older boy, still looking at the ground said, "He can speak, he is only afraid."

The agent replied, "Alright, you may answer for him, but he must start speaking for himself."

"What is his name and age?"

"Rogelio Garza and he has seven years. He is my brother."

"Where are your mother and father?"

"Our mother is in Honduras and our father is with God"

"Why did you come here?"

"My mother sent us, she told us there was food and safety here."

"Why is your brother sweating and shaking so much?"

"As I told you, he is afraid and we have not eaten in a long time."

The agent stood, picked up the pack of their belongings, went through it and dropped it back on the ground. He looked at the boys one more time and walked to the bus. He pulled another agent off to the side, spoke to him and pointed at the two boys, the other agent nodded and then started to load everyone onto the bus. When they got to the door they were given a bottle of water and went inside and found seats apart from the others. As the bus moved forward Ignacio reached up to his upper left arm and pushed at a small scar as if to rub an itch. In reality what he had done was send a signal hundreds of miles to the south.

The agent looked over the two boys again and thought, "Sanchez is right they don't look related. The older boy was much darker in color, the bone structure is completely different and there's something about the eyes." He shrugged, turned and sat down.

The bus bounced down the dirt road and soon turned onto an old cement road, then picked up speed. Ignacio looked over and saw that Rogelio was asleep, but he couldn't sleep, he needed to take in his surroundings and think. He knew they would be held somewhere, asked more questions, be checked out by a doctor to be sure they were not sick or infested. If they had bugs on them it would take longer to be released. If things went as planned they should be free to get where they needed to be very soon.

On the seat beside him Rogelio only feigned sleep. Inside he cried for his mother and home. He did not want to make this journey, he was happy with his family and friends, he did not like being dirty and hungry.

Rogelio had been handsome for his age. When he looked in the mirror he saw his fathers' face and strength, when he smiled he saw his mothers' laughter and humor. He had the dark hair and eyes of most Latinos, but his skin was much lighter almost white. His once round face was now getting hollow with dark circles under his eyes, his eyes where the light was once bright now was dull. He was a seven year old who had the worries of an adult and a great weight upon his shoulders. As he drifted off into a light sleep, a small tear rolled down his cheek.

2

Ignacio suddenly sat up in his seat. They had been traveling for less than an hour, but the rocking of the bus had lulled him into a half sleep. Out the window of the bus he saw what looked like a prison, the buildings were sand colored with fencing around them, only one road leading in or out. "This isn't right," he thought, "It should be a school or church." He wondered if they were trying to keep people in or out, this did not look good, something must be wrong.

The bus pulled up to a gate in the fence and the doors to the bus opened. A Border Patrol Agent started moving everyone off the bus and into a narrow fenced walkway, even the top of the walkway was fenced. Another agent stood at a solid door at the other end, he was armed and kept his hand on the butt of the holstered gun. Even though Ignacio never took his gaze off the ground, his eyes took in everything. He kept his hand on Rogelio's shoulder applying a small amount of pressure.

They passed the second agent and entered a large room that was sectioned off by more fencing. "This looks like an old hangar or assembly building that is being used like a jail. It has to be as big as a soccer field." Ignacio thought to himself.

In front of them were long tables, a few chairs and people writing things down, this would be the next place they would want information. Ignacio again put his hand on Rogelio's shoulder, he watched as women with children talked with the people behind the tables. They all looked frightened or sad, some appeared as if they did not want to speak. Then some began to smile shy small smiles, one or two of them actually laughed a bit as they stood up and gave their thanks to the interviewers. He jumped as a hand tapped him on the shoulder, it was only someone directing him to the tables.

He sat looking down at this hands and answered the same questions he had been asked before. Suddenly the person across the table said, "Look at me." He glanced up and then back down again. The female voice demanded, "Look at me and don't look back down again!"

He looked up and for the first time noticed that this was not an agent, but just a woman who wore no uniform or badge only a name tag. He also saw some papers and two photos on the table. The photos, one of him and one of Rogelio had been taken at the border, he wondered if everyone had their pictures taken or just the two of them.

The lady behind the table asked, "What is your last name, your family name?"

"Garza," Ignacio answered

The lady asked, "Do you speak English and do you have relatives in the United States that we can contact?"

His face lit up, "Yes, yes. My uncle and I do speak some English," He responded.

"Do you know where your uncle lives?"

He replied, "Atlantic, Georgia."

She smile, "I think you mean Atlanta, Georgia. Do you know his name and address?"

Ignacio gave her the information and she told them they would be taken over to take a shower, get clean clothes and then see one of the doctors. Rogelio never moved, only looked at the floor.

The lady stood up, walked around the end of the table and stooped down to eye level with Rogelio.

Ignacio quickly said to her, "He doesn't speak English."

"Are you feeling alright?" she asked him in Spanish.

He nodded, but kept his eyes down cast.

"You must be hungry and tired." She placed her hand gently on his arm. "We will take good care of you while you are here, no need to be afraid."

She stood and motioned to an agent.

As they were led away Ignacio didn't notice the woman write on a note pad, gather the papers and walk over to an agent and a tall man in a dark suit. She looked at the men and said, "There is something not right here. The young boy never moves, all the other children that come through are animated. They are curious, they touch things, ask questions. He says nothing and never moves. When I asked the older boy their last name, the boy stiffened and looked at his brother oddly. We need to have the doctor spend a little time with him, without his brother around. My opinion only, but they sure don't looked related."

She then handed a copy of the name and address of the uncle to the man in the suit. "I thought I should let you know that this is the fourth time this week this name has been given to me as a relative. Nothing I can put my finger on, just an odd feeling. Too many kids coming across with a relative that lives in Atlanta."

The two men nodded, the agent took the file and headed in the direction the boys had gone and the man in the suit pocketed the piece of paper, turned toward one of the doors and walked out.

3

The showers felt good and the clean clothes were comfortable even if they didn't fit exactly right. As they walked over to see the doctor, Rogelio's demeanor stayed the same. The agent watching them thought the child walked like a zombie, he might be depressed or maybe even drugged. "It can't be drugs," the agent thought to himself, "Where would they hide drugs? Oh well, the blood test will answer that question."

There were three doctors and Ignacio watched what they were doing. The usual doctor thing, eyes, ears, throat, teeth, heart, skin, hair and in some cases they took a blood sample. He was not worried he knew he and Rogelio were clean in all areas.

When it was their turn the agent walked over to the doctor and said something to him, turned, walked back to them and motioned for Ignacio to move forward to the doctor, but he made Rogelio stay behind with him. Ignacio started to protest, but thought better of it. The doctor did all the normal stuff spending a little more time looking at his teeth and hair. When he got to examining Ignacio's arms he noticed a scar on his upper left arm, as he started to run this thumb over it, Ignacio pulled his arm back.

"What happened to your arm?" the doctor asked.

"It is nothing. I hurt my arm playing ball, a bandage fixed it," Ignacio said.

"Does it still hurt?" the doctor inquired.

"Sometimes." was the only reply.

The doctor wrote something else on the paper, took no blood sample and told Ignacio he was finished. Ignacio stood and waited for Rogelio, but the agent made him move to the end of the area and out of sight as Rogelio sat down.

The doctor, in a soothing voice, told Rogelio what he was doing as he examined him. He noticed that the boys' teeth and gums were in much better shape than his brothers'. He started to take a blood sample and ask, "Do you speak any English?"

Rogelio looked over his shoulder in the direction his brother had gone, when he didn't see his brother he very quietly said, "Yes."

While taking the sample the doctor said, "In the file it says your brother said you didn't. Why did he say that?"

Rogelio only shook his head no.

"Are you afraid?" the doctor asked.

Rogelio looked up and saw the kindness in the blue eyes that stared back him. He again said, "Yes."

"Why are you afraid?"

Rogelio only shook his head.

"Are you afraid to speak?"

Rogelio nodded.

The doctor put a label on the sample, and something fired in his brain, another question. He started to look through Rogelio's hair again and asked, "Did you want to come here?"

Rogelio looked over his shoulder again, looked back at the doctor and without moving his lips said, "No!"

The doctor showed no reaction to the half expected answer. He was an ex-military doctor, had worked in the Middle East with many children and nothing much surprised him anymore. What did bother him was to get an answer like that from an illegal border crosser. He put a smile on his face and told the boy not to worry, he said, "I am Dr. Phillips and if you need me someone will come and get me for you. I hope I will be your first American friend." With that he told Rogelio he could go find his brother. Rogelio stiffened for a moment, put his eyes back down to the floor and was led away. The doctor saw a few more children, picked up his files, dropped all but two of the files at the main intake desk and headed for the door.

Dr. Jake Phillips was six feet three inches of nervous energy, but he had learned to control it because of his profession. He had dark brown hair, blue-green eyes, the face of innocence and the angular body of a swimmer. His job was to be sure that the people coming across the border were not ill and he took his job seriously. Everyone coming across the border as an illegal was supposed to have a medical check, but some of the facilities didn't bother. He had only been at the facility for a few weeks and his favorite part of the job was the children. This particular child set off his radar.

He immediately went to a portable building outside the staging area, which was where the man in the dark suit had his temporary office. He knocked and was told to enter. The interior was typical portable building décor, wall paneling made of fake wood which was aging. The carpet was an institutional green, well worn down the center and around the desk. The furniture was two inexpensive chairs facing the desk, the desk was old, worn and covered with papers. A small table sat in the corner looking sad and misplaced. There were no wall decorations or personal items anywhere in the office. There was one window next to the door and one on each of the side walls, but none behind the desk, there was nothing behind the desk except the man he had come to see.

The dark suited man looked up, "Hey, Phillips. What ya got?"

"Well, hello to you too Brock. Got any coffee?" Phillips replied.

"Stale, but drinkable" answered Ed Brock.

Ed Brock was a 'Federal Mutt'. He was CIA with a splash of FBI, on special assignment, it was a complicated story. He was also six foot three, but on the more mellow side. He had brown hair, blue eyes and bulkier than Phillips, but it was all muscle.

He and Jake Phillips had known each other since they attended Harvard. Both were smarter than they looked and their IQ's were huge for their chosen professions. Both held law degrees with Brock also holding a degree in Criminal Psychology and Phillips holding a medical degree. Neither one could make up their minds as to what degree they really wanted so they chose both. They were driven men and had been since an early age.

Ed Brock had been raised in Northern California and wanted to see the world on his own terms. His parents were well educated attorneys one criminal the other corporate. His mother had taken a few years off to raise him until she came to the realization that he really didn't need her. She went back to the corporate world and he went off to Harvard at the age of fifteen.

Not to be out done by a left coast kid, Jake Phillips, without knowing Brock even existed, also left for Harvard at the age of fifteen. Jake had been raised in East Texas and felt that Texas was too small when you considered the size of the world. His father was also an attorney while mom was a microbiologist who dealt with communicable diseases.

Being fifteen at Harvard is a problem socially, which is the reason that brought Ed and Jake together. They soon discovered that they had the same goals, likes and dislikes. It was an immediate bond that held them together through hard times as well as good times and held them together even now. Personality wise they were mirror images of each other, mentally it was if they had known each other their whole lives. They did not finish each other's sentences, they considered that rude, but they usually knew what the other was thinking.

After they graduated from Harvard, Ed was courted by the FBI and after a few months decided that was not where he wanted to be. Shortly after his decision he was recruited by the CIA and soon felt he had found his niche. Jake had taken off for home at the request of his parents, but not before promising Ed that he would be back and to watch for a good job opening. At the same time Ed went to the CIA, Jake was sent to the Middle East at the request of the Pentagon. The CIA wanted a brainy operative and the military needed a super doctor for all the damaged children. It took a bit over two years before they saw each other again, but they never lost touch.

After availing themselves to a cup of sludge, as Brock called it, they got as comfortable as possible for two six foot three men around a small table. Phillips put the two files on the table side by side, he put his hands flat on each folder, looked at Brock and said, "I have something here that bothers me."

Brock gave him the go ahead nod. Phillips opened the first folder and turned it around so Brock could see it.

"This is Ignacio Garza, Honduran, age sixteen. The initial agent states that Ignacio answered all the questions for this brother because his brother was scared, he also mentioned that the boy didn't speak English per his brother. Ignacio is in good health," tapping the other folder he said, "so is his brother who is seven years old."

Brock pulled at his lower lip and said, "I got the feeling you may disagree with this information, the big 'but' so to speak."

"Yep, I do", responded Phillips. "First, when examining Ignacio his teeth told me he was older than he says, a few had been removed whether from decay or to hide his age. His other teeth showed no sign of decay, but not very good oral hygiene. Second, his hair. At sixteen the hair still has that childhood feel to it, his was coarser and had been dyed in places. Now, granted this could be due to contaminated water over the years and the dye job could be ego talking, but if contaminated water was the issue, his teeth would show more overall decay and gum irritation and is hair would be thinning. Third, was the health issue, they may have been thirsty, but they were not showing signs of dehydration and they were not starving."

"The older boy has a scar on his upper left arm, but he tossed that off as an accident while playing ball. The injury had been surgically taken care of, it wasn't just a band aide issue. When I reached up to touch it he jerked his arm away and said that sometimes it hurt. The only reason I was curious about it was because I had noticed another boy with the same scar this morning and another two days ago. Now I wish I had paid more attention to their names."

"Now to the younger boy, Rogelio," he moved the other folder over to Brock, "he has dark circles under his eyes, but I believe this is due to lack of sleep. He is healthy and his teeth and gums, unlike his brothers', are in very good shape. I know he is only seven, but you can tell he has had better oral hygiene. The most interesting thing is he does speak and understand English."

Brock looked up at him and said, "How sure are you?"

Phillips then recounted the conversation he had with Rogelio. He finished with, "The kid answered direct questions, but when I asked something that needed a longer answer he only shook his head. Plus he kept looking over his shoulder to see where Ignacio was before he answered and when he answered he tried not to move his lips."

"So what are you thinking," Brock asked, "child trafficking?"

"I don't know, they usually seek a different route, but with the huge amount of people we have crossing the border it could be a possibility." Phillips replied.

"That's what I was thinking as well." Brock said tapping his pen on the folder. "You've only been here a few weeks and this rush for the border has been going on for a while, so I wonder how many other older boys, or girls for that matter, are not what they seem. I also wonder if some of the other kids have this upper arm scar."

"Are you thinking tracking device?" asked Phillips.

"I'm not sure what I'm thinking except we need to interview those two kids again and soon, they will be moving them in about two days. I think all folders of older kids need to be checked to see if scars were noticed. I don't want to alert anyone unnecessarily, so I think we should do it." Brock said.

"How many are we talking about?" asked Phillips

"I have no idea, but we are about to find out. It would be a bit easier if we had all of this on computers, this may take a while." replied Brock as he picked up the phone. "Guess it's a good thing I stopped by and you volunteered."

4

Since they had to wait for files to be pulled they decided there was plenty of time to go in search for food. They settled on a barbeque place where their noses said it was the place to be and their body's, screaming for protein, could be satisfied.

Brock took a sip of his iced tea and said, "You realize a number of the files are no longer here. Busloads of these people have already left and tracking them down is going to be next to impossible."

"Hell," Phillips put in, "we don't even know if we really have anything yet. All I know is this little kid, Rogelio, acts like he's trapped. Maybe it is child trafficking, with the influx of this many people it would be an ideal situation."

"Ideal for anything, actually", said Brock. "Cartels, terrorism, human or drug trafficking. Crap what a mess, but we have to start somewhere with this kid. Maybe I'll have that initial contact agent talk to him again and if that doesn't work you can check him out again. You are the only one he has spoken to so far."

Brock took out his cell phone, "Laura, this is Brock. Do me a favor and get the name of the initial contact agent for the Ignacio and Rogelio Garza files, it should be on the copy of the field contact sheet, then get hold of him and have him run another interview with both boys. Tell him to try and dig a little deeper, especially with the Ignacio kid, but be subtle with his questions. Thanks."

Across the table Phillips was waving his hands and giving the time-out signal.

Brock said into the phone, "Hold on a sec." Then to Phillips, "What?"

Phillips said, "Tell her to have the agent do separate interviews and in a place where they can't make eye contact with one another."

Brock relayed the request, told her they would be back in an hour, thanked her and hung up as their food arrived.

Phillips mouth watered as the plates were placed on the table, then his eyes started to glisten. "Now, this is food!"

They had both ordered the Barbequed Brisket sandwich with the works. The sandwich was huge and slathered in sauce, all the extras on the side, plus an extra slice of the meat. The waitress noticed them looking at it and said, "You're pretty big hombres so I figured you might need a little more meat than most. I'll be right back with the Cole Slaw and beans."

Through a mouth full of food Brock asked Phillips, "Where are you staying tonight? You can bunk in my trailer instead of the Med. Office, unless you have a motel room somewhere."

"Nope, no motel room." Phillips answered using his second napkin. "I like staying in the Med. Office in case something happens and they need a doc. Anyway, I want to be on the floor after lights out, I want to see if Rogelio sleeps or just naps. By the way, why don't you have computers?"

Brock shrugged his shoulders, "Not enough immigrants coming through our area, the facility is huge, but we only use a fraction of it. We only get up to 120 a day and that is sporadic, DHS says it isn't enough to justify computers. Once the files get to McAllen they'll be put in the computer, which means some screw-up in the middle will lose files. Beats me how the hell they can keep track of anything."

They finished their food in hungry silence and went back to the facility.

Opening the door to Brocks' office they saw a stack of files on the desk and a box on the floor. Brock started a fresh pot of coffee while Phillips counted files.

"Hmm, looks like we have thirty files from today." Phillips said. "This box has a note attached that says these files are all the files that didn't make it out with the last transfer bus."

"See, I told you about screw-ups." replied Brock. "How can you match files to people arriving if you don't have the files? I didn't want to say anything in the restaurant, but I have a feeling that a lot of this paper will disappear as if it never existed."

They split the files and spent the next few hours going through them and making notes. Phillips stretched and yawned, "I only have six that noted a scar on the upper arm and several of the files are lacking in health information. The ones that noted scars also have stateside contacts and only a few of the others have contacts."

"Shit, I forgot," Brock said as he reached into his pocket and pulled out a piece of paper. He handed it to Philips, "This is the contact information that the intake person gave me. She also noted on there about the inconsistencies she saw concerning Rogelio."

"The contact info is in his file," Phillips said, "I wonder why she handed you a note about it."

"Maybe she didn't think I would see the file. I'll make a note to ask her." Brock grunted as he put the box back on the floor. "In this box I found five where a scar was noted and these five also have contact info." Brock thought for a moment, looked a Phillips and added, "I hate to do this, but let's go through these again and make a list of all the contact info even if they are women with children. I want to cover all the bases."

Phillips smiled, "Some agent you are. I'm way ahead of you," he handed papers over to Brock. "Here are names and contact info on everyone except the girls. I'm going to check on my little overnight project, see you tomorrow."

As Phillips left, Brock mumbled to himself, "I've lost my edge, been out of the chase too long."

5

After seeing the doctor, Rogelio had joined Ignacio outside the medical area and they were led passed women and children who were divided from the other people by high fences, the same with unaccompanied girls. They got to the area for the boys and were each handed a thin blanket and sleeping pad. The gate was closed and locked behind them as they were told they would be having dinner soon.

Ignacio found a place for them against one of the fence walls as far away as they could get from the other boys. There weren't as many boys as there were women and children, so it was easy to find a clear spot. Ignacio wanted to keep them apart from other people, he couldn't take a chance on one of them getting sick or infested with bugs.

As they started settling in, Ignacio looked around the enclosure and spotted two older boys. He would need to get the attention of each one and see if they had anything in common with him. One of the boys looked in his direction, then down, then back up again. Ignacio's arranged his blanket and wondered if they were being watched by cameras. As he started to sit down when he heard, "Hello."

It was the boy he had noticed only a minute ago. The first thing Ignacio did was glance at the strangers' upper arm, it was covered by the sleeve of his t-shirt. The new boy casually moved both sleeves up his arms showing the scar and said, "I'm Jorge. Warm in here isn't it?"

Ignacio took his new t-shirt off to get comfortable and to show his scar. Then he shook Jorge's hand and introduced himself, but not Rogelio. After the two had exchanged a few casual words Jorge went back to his blanket and Ignacio sat down. Rogelio had never moved, had never looked up.

Not long after this exchange the gate was unlocked and they were told it was time to eat. Ignacio took Rogelio's hand and led him over to get in line. Ignacio bent down and looked at Rogelio, "Are you alright? We are going to eat now so you stay with me. Don't worry little man," he said with a smile, "we will be out of here very soon." Rogelio only nodded.

Ignacio lined up behind Jorge and they walked into another room that had tables with benches. After they sat, a cart would come by and hand out plates of food, glasses of milk and a bottle of water.

Phillips had just entered the area and noticed the boys in the food line. He walked over to the agent who had helped him in medical. "How's it going?" he asked the agent.

"Not bad," the agent answered. "Better when I get out of this uniform and off my feet."

"Anything new come up with our two kids over there?" Phillips asked.

The agent, with arms still crossed over this big chest, replied, "Well, they met a new friend, the one standing in front of them. Nothing unusual, exchanged names, shook hands, a little chit chat and that was it. The one kid is here alone so he is probably looking for someone to talk to."

Phillips' brain hiccupped, then shifting his weight said, "Well, have a good one. I have stuff I need to sort through and get ready for tomorrows onslaught."

As he walked toward the medical section he thought about the brain hiccup he had and wondered what it was about. It was probably nothing, but the agent had said the loner kid was just looking for someone to talk with. "Hell, the place was full of kids for him to talk to." Phillips said to himself. "Why Ignacio?" He needed to get this other kids name and look up the file or see if he was on a list.

Phillips went back out of medical, but the agent was gone, he would have to do it himself. He grabbed a translator and went over to where the three boys sat. He pointed to the boy, told the translator to get his name and let him know they were working on his transfer.

Armed with the name, he located a place where he could later observe Rogelio and returned to medical to start a pot of coffee.

After the translator had left the table, Jorge had a big smile on his face. Ignacio asked him, "How many of us are there do you think?"

Jorge replied, "Hundreds maybe even thousands.

Phillips watched Rogelio sleep, it was a fitful sleep, a sleep with whimpering sounds, tossing and thrashing. Suddenly Rogelio sat up, mouth open in a silent scream, sweat had beaded up on his face, rapid breathing, eyes wide. While Ignacio slept soundly unaware of the movements and sounds beside him.

Phillips wanted to go to him, but knew he could not chance it. Instead he made notes and watched as the young boy again lay under his blanket and tried to sleep. Phillips slowly moved out of the shadows and walked back to medical and his cot, he too would try to sleep.

6

Rogelio lay under the thin blanket, he really didn't need the blanket, but he knew that even a thin cover while sleeping gave people the feeling of privacy, made them feel safer. Nothing would make him feel safer, he didn't think he would ever feel safe again. He thought back to the doctor he had seen when he first arrived and got his health check. He didn't know this doctor, but he trusted him because he had acted suspicious of Ignacio when he did the examination. When it was his turn the doctor made Ignacio go into another area, he had even waited until Ignacio was out of sight before starting the examination. He spoke in English and it was then that he decided to let the doctor know that he understood and could also speak English, maybe it would raise questions. He had to let these people know that he was in trouble, but he had to be careful. If Ignacio noticed that he was trying to get help it would mean death, not just his, but his entire family.

The boy who called himself Jorge was talking to Ignacio, Rogelio used this time to look at his surroundings and see if there was a way to get help. He saw nothing except more immigrants and walls. The only way, he decided, was to write a message and hope that the nice lady or the doctor would see it, but he had nothing to write with, he didn't know what to say or where to put it. His thoughts were interrupted when Ignacio made him stand up and told him they were going to eat. Ignacio didn't speak to him very much, so he would have more time to think while they ate. He knew that Jorge was one of the special ones who had come across and could not be trusted. He didn't seem as smart as Ignacio, but he was still dangerous. He would have to remember to watch everyone.

They walked into a large room with tables and sat down with Jorge sitting across from them. As people came to serve them food, he saw that it was hamburgers with enough fried potatoes to fill up even the hungriest among them. The burgers had nothing on them and looked very dry, this is when an idea came to him, ketchup. He started to get up and Ignacio grabbed his arm.

"Where are you going?"

"I need something to put on the sandwich, maybe ketchup." Rogelio pointed to a table against the wall, "Its right over there."

Ignacio looked in the direction of the table, "Okay you can go and bring back extra for us."

Rogelio walked to the table and picked up some packets of ketchup, then noticed the mustard. He thought, 'ketchup looks like blood, I don't want them to think I am bleeding'. He picked up some mustard and looked over this shoulder at Ignacio. Jorge and Ignacio were talking and laughing, not looking at him. He grabbed handfuls of mustard and put them in his pockets, walked back over to their table and placed several packets of ketchup in front of Ignacio. He put some on his hamburger and started to eat and think.

After brushing his teeth with his new toothbrush, he washed his face and went back to his bed with Ignacio close behind him. They both lay down, not speaking. Ignacio on his back staring at the ceiling, Rogelio turned on his side away from his brother and began to think again. This time he thought of home, of his room with the baseball and music posters on the walls, the view of the garden from his window. The thought of the garden brought fresh tears to his eyes, it was his mother's favorite place. She loved to work in the dirt and bring out the beauty of the flowers, other times she would only sit on the bench under the trees and enjoyed what she had created. Sometimes she would get this same look when she watched him or his brother, at these times, for no reason she would walk up to them and give them a hug or plant a big kiss on their cheeks. He shook his head and wiped away a tear, he could not think of this any longer, he was not a baby anymore. He had to find a place for the message.

He sat up in a silent scream, he'd had the dream again, the one of the train. He looked around, then lay down again and listened to the sounds of sleeping people, even Ignacio was still asleep. He closed his eyes and tried to think of something other than the dream, but he couldn't let himself fall asleep again. The message, he needed to think of the message, he needed to tell them that everything they had been told was a lie.

He heard a shuffling noise and his mind froze. Slowly he opened his eyes to no more than slits and looked in the direction of the noise, he saw a shadow move toward the door leading to the hallway. Someone had been watching. Were they watching everyone, did they watch every night and would they be back? He was torn between fear and elation, he had to leave the message and he had to write it now.

He waited until he felt it was safe then very slowly moved off the mattress and onto his knees. He took the top of the thin mattress and gently folded it down toward the bottom half. There was barely enough light for him to see what he was doing, but he did not need very much. He took the mustard packets out of his pocket, opened one putting a drop of it on the floor and using his finger started to print the letters. When he was finished he put the used packets back into his pocket, waited another minute for the mustard to dry a bit more and unfolded the mattress so it was in place again.

He lay down and realized he was shaking, he took a few deep breaths and tried to relax. On the other side of the big room a baby started to cry softly and Rogelio smiled. For some reason he found the sound comforting and soon was asleep again.

7

Phillips woke to the sounds of people moving around the facility. "More already?" he thought. He looked at the clock, "Holy Crap, 8:30am! Not only have I overslept, but I missed breakfast, coffee will have to do for now." He grabbed clean clothes and went to the small shower. "Okay," he thought, "quick shower shave, teeth, coffee and I will be good to go."

He stepped out of the bathroom and into medical, it was empty. He walked into the big room and there were a number of people missing, actually almost all of the immigrants were gone. He hurried over to an agent and asked what had happened.

The agent replied, "The bunch of them were moved out this morning. It happens every few days."

Phillips hurriedly walked to the area where the boys had been, no Ignacio, Rogelio or their new friend Jorge. "Shit, shit, shit!" He said under his breath and bolted for Brocks office.

He flew into Brocks' office and found him red faced and yelling into the phone, "I need one more day!" he listened then said, "I know that, but these guys have not been here 24 hours! We are on to something here and we can't follow-up unless we can talk to them." Again he listened, then said "But... well can't you at least..." the stopped mid-sentence and listened some more then said, "Got it, I guess that is all we can do for now. Okay, I'll keep in touch." As he hung up the phone he looked at Phillips and threw his hands in the air and growled.

Phillips held out his arms, "What the hell happened?"

"Someone decided they needed to move these people in a hurry. I've been on the phone since the buses pulled up trying to get it stopped. Hey, I'm just an observer here! There is no one who is going to listen to me, this is DHS and they don't listen to anybody." Brock's voice had a hard edge.

Phillips sat down as Brock continued, "Sorry, I'm just frustrated. The last time they moved a group out they gave us at least a days' notice." Brock started to pace, "This was too quick, someone wanted them moved."

Brock got them both coffee and sat down. "First things first. Did you get to watch the kid last night?"

Phillips filled him in on the events of the previous night, "I'm worried about Rogelio. Something is really freaking him out and it is so bad it is affecting his health. Also, Ignacio made a new friend. I'd like to check out this new friend, but I guess all those files are gone now."

"Actually, no. They moved so fast that the files are still right here behind my desk. Golly gee whiz, I must have forgotten about them. Tsk, Tsk," Brock said sarcastically.

"How about that second interview?" Phillips asked.

"Sanchez, the initial agent, had to be out on patrol, so to save time he and another agent did it. Sanchez took Rogelio and got a yes in English and then tears, but nothing new. The other agent, Addison, got nothing new. Here take a look," he said as he slid two papers across the desk.

Phillips read the papers, looked up and said, "Hell, you got a kid here who contradicts the 'no English' statement twice, gets tears in his eyes when asked if he is afraid and they let him go. On top of that, this other agent asked the same questions as before and didn't try to dig deeper. Why didn't Sanchez do the Ignacio interview as requested and let the other guy do Rogelio?"

"I don't know." replied Brock, "Let's go over to the radio room and see if we can raise him."

The radio room is not a busy place and they were able to contact Sanchez quickly. He only thing he said was that the other agent had said his size might be more intimidating to Ignacio.

"Who is this other agent?" Phillips asked.

"Addison," said Brock. "I don't know who he is, let's find him too." He turned to the radio personnel and asked if anyone knew him and where he was. One of the female agents reached for a clip-board and said, "Sorry sir, he's on one of the buses that just left."

"What are you talking about? The agents here don't go with the buses. Who authorized it?"

The female agent looked at Brock and said, "We don't have that information sir, but I will see what I can find out."

Another agent said from across the room, "Mr. Brock, a call for you." and handed him the phone.

"Yes, this is Brock."

"Mr. Brock, this is Julie I talked to you yesterday about the odd behavior of one of the children."

"I remember," said Brock, "sorry I didn't catch your name before. What can I do for you?"

"I think you need to come back over to the hold building, there is something I think you should see. It might be important." she said excitedly.

"On my way." replied Brock and headed for the door with Phillips close behind.

"Mr. Brock," the female agent called after him. He turned toward her and she said, "Sorry sir, but we can't find anything that shows an agent Addison assigned here."

The two men raced to the main building and found Julie standing in the holding area for boys. She had been watching for them and motioned them over to her. As they walked up to her Brock asked, "What's got you so excited?"

"This is the mat where the seven year old was sleeping," she replied. "He took the blanket, but left this." She folded the mat over and written on the floor below, in shaky letters was:

not igna not at

tam

Phillips took out his cell phone, took a photo and Brock asked Julie to get the big camera to get another photo.

The two men stooped down to look more closely. Brock said, "Looks like he wrote it in mustard."

"With his finger," added Phillips pointing to a perfect dirty yellow fingerprint. "They served hamburgers for dinner last night, looks like he took some packets of mustard. He must have written this last night after I left, smart kid. Look it transferred to the back of the mat."

Brock stood up, looked at Phillips and said, "We need to find those buses."

They thanked Julie and as they exited the building Brock tossed Phillips his keys, "Get my car, I need to make a couple of phone calls."

8

Phillips ran over to his car and opened the trunk. He looked inside a black bag, walked around to the rear door, pulled some things out and threw them in the bag. He lifted up the trunk carpet and took out two small black cases, placed them in the bag and zipped it up. He trotted over to Brocks car and pulled it around to the front of the small building.

Brock came out of his office, threw some files on the back seat, jumped behind the wheel and left a large cloud of dust as he headed for the highway.

Phillips asked, "Why didn't we take my car it's faster?

Brock took the corner onto the two lane black top and said, "Because mine has pretty flashing lights on the front and if I'm really pissed, a loud annoying siren. What you got to offer besides fast?"

"Well, maneuverability. This thing is a fucking barge."

"Hey," Brock cocked his head toward the back seat, "grabbed those files back there."

Phillips looked in the back seat and said, "What, take off my seat belt? Do you want me on the inside of your windshield?"

"You're too big to fit on the inside," Brock laughed.

Phillips grabbed the files and Brock handed him the note with the name and address that Ignacio had given Julie.

"Read me the file on that Jorge Ruiz kid, guy or whatever he is," Brock said.

Phillips shuffled through the files and said, "Okay, Jorge Ruiz from Guatemala, age 16, left in fear for his life. Maybe a gang member?" Phillips added. "His parents are deceased, lives with his grandmother and my, my look here."

"What?" Brock added.

"It seems that Jorge also has an uncle in Atlanta, Georgia, with the same name. What are the odds on that? How dumb do these guys think we are, I guess they think we were born yesterday," Phillips shook his head.

"Hell, they probably know the system better than we do, figured no one would catch it," Brock said without humor. "The buses are headed to McAllen then on to San Antonio. According to my info, this group is slated to be housed in the northeast. I made two calls, one to my boss to tell him we may have something hot and gave him a quick rundown. The other call was to see if there was a chopper in the area to find those buses, they have a head start on us even if they are slower. I have an itchy feeling and I could scratch that itch if I knew for sure where the buses are."

Phillips shuffled the files into a neat stack and said, "You're not wasting much time. I haven't seen you this animated in a long time."

"I can't waste any time. Last night when we were going through the files and making out those lists, you had written down info we needed before I even thought about it. You said you were 'way ahead of me' and that made me realize I was losing my edge, I've spent too much time 'stupid-vising'. Several of us were sent down here to check the people coming across, to see what kind of OTM's were coming across. There had been reports of Syrian, Pakistanis and all kinds of Middle East types getting across, so they wanted CIA down here. Kind of an eyes on, not that we can cover it all, but it was a start. No CIA personnel want to be down here, hell, you can't shoot anybody! Anyway, who would want to shoot a kid? The rest of the story you know, so no sense in me hashing it over again. These Border Patrol Agents do a good job when the government doesn't handcuff them." Brock looked over at Phillips and said, "Sorry, guess I got a bit worked up. What I'm trying to say is that I am CIA, I don't do work on American soil, or at least I haven't in the past. I am supposed to be out in the field after the bad guys, not behind a desk on the border. I like being in the field on a chase, it feels good and I will not give that up again."

"Come on Ed, it takes good CIA guys to see through the crap. That's why you're here," Phillips commented.

"Whoa, first name basis Jake? You must be really serious."

"I am." Phillips sighed, "I hate to see you beat yourself up. You're not being punished, your ass is being saved. It's not your fault that you're sitting on the border, the blame for that is squarely on some else's shoulders and we have a little kid out there that may be nothing but a shield for Ignacio. I'm afraid if we don't find him he's going to be dead or worse. As if that isn't enough, I wonder what he is being used to cover up."

"I have a question too. If this kid Jorge is part of whatever this is, why doesn't he have a younger boy with him? Did his shield die or did he not need one?" Brock asked as he reached over and pushed numbers on this hands free.

"McAllen," said the phone.

"Brock here, we have two buses coming to you. What is their status?"

"One moment, I'll check. Sorry sir we only have one bus scheduled to arrive from your location and it should be here in about ten minutes."

"What?" Brock almost screamed, "We had two leave our location. Where is the other one going?"

Again the voice replied, "One moment. Sir, your location confirms two buses left, but only one is coming here. No one seems to know where the second bus is going or who authorized it."

"Okay, find out where that other bus is and how many people are on it and who the driver is. Any or all of that information would be appreciated ASAP. We may have a situation starting, also find out which bus Agent Addison is on, that I need now. Call back on this number. Thanks."

Brock started hammering the steering wheel. "Shit, shit, shit! How the hell did this happen?"

Phillips looked out his side window and said, "Next question is how many times in the last few months has it happened?"

Brock's phone rang, "Yeah, go."

"Sir, this is McAllen and we can't locate any agent with the first or last name of Addison."

"I figured as much," Brock replied. "When that bus shows up I want everyone on it isolated, I need to see them. That means the driver too. I have Dr. Phillips with me our ETA is about fifteen minutes."

Phillips stretched out in the seat as much as his long legs would allow and said, "They are taking advantage of all the confusion the overwhelming numbers is causing. All agents are too busy to take care of what they were hired to do. If a new agent shows up, they welcome the help, not question who sent him. We have no photo of this guy Addison and the only person we know who has seen him face to face is Agent Sanchez." He sat up and took out his phone and dialed.

"Julie, Dr. Phillips here. Do me a favor and see if you can locate the whereabouts of Agent Sanchez. Yeah, the cute one if you say so. I want him kept around the facility for a few days. Call his immediate boss and give him some kind of excuse to keep Sanchez inside, I'll explain later. Yeah, I am quite sure you can keep him busy," Phillips laughed, hung up and started to stretch out again.

Brock looked over at him, "Now don't get comfortable and take a nap, we're almost there and we're going to be busy. I want to talk to the driver and I need you to see if our questionable kids are in this group, I doubt it but we need to be sure."

Phillips smiled, "You got it, but I think I will divide them up, ask a few questions, see if I get any physical reactions and move on from there." Phillips stared to chuckle, "Must be the lawyer part of me peeking out. Don't worry I won't Mirandize them."

9

When they arrived at the facility Phillips was amazed at what he saw. A clean, well-lit intake area with computers everywhere, all the personnel had computers and at the end of each long table was a printer. The walls were a pale institutional yellow, large tiles of light brown and the same yellow made up the flooring. Some of the tiles were chipped in places, but they were clean and unstained. This was a big difference from the facility where he worked. He wasn't really sure what he had expected, but it wasn't this. After taking a few steps inside they were met by a border patrol agent who led them toward a hallway.

Without ceremony the agent said to Brock, "I put the driver in one of our interview rooms and explained that he wasn't in any kind of trouble, just that you needed to talk to him." Then looking at Phillips he said, "I got you a translator and she will help you with the group from the bus, you will also have another agent who will take them back to processing when you have finished with them. Is there something going on here I need to be aware of?"

Brock shrugged, "Let me talk to this driver and while Phillips is doing his end I'll apprise you of the situation, if we have one."

"Okay, I can go along with that," the agent said as he opened the interview room door.

Phillips then followed the agent to the end of the hall and into another large room of the same yellows and browns with long tables and benches. A lovely woman walked up to them and said, "I'm Amelia your translator, I understand you want to speak to the people from the bus. I have taken the liberty of dividing them into small groups and putting them in separate rooms. If for some reason they all decide to speak at once, having to listen to only five or ten is a bit easier."

Phillips looked to the right side of the room where he had noticed smaller, multi windowed rooms that looked into the main room. Each room held from five to ten people, some with children playing on the floor at their feet. He looked at Amelia and said, "Thank you for taking the initiative, it'll save us some time. I don't have many questions and Mr. Brock may be joining us later. If I might ask, how long have you been assigned here?"

Amelia rested her hip on the edge of a table, sighed and said, "Three months, sometimes it feels a lot longer."

"Not many English speakers coming across or if they do they hide it," said Phillips. "I've been at the Medical Center south of here, they just keep coming. They are in better shape than I would have thought, I guess they are being fed a bit better, but some of them need more medical attention than I can give them at the facility."

Amelia looked at the windowed rooms, "I heard they had a new doctor coming, they need more people, not rotating hours down there. Sometimes I feel that this will never end, so many children without parents." She stopped abruptly and looked back at Phillips.

"Have you had any problems here, anything that seems a bit strange or not quite right? I know that is an odd question, but with this missing bus I have to ask. If you don't want to say anything to me, you can talk to Mr. Brock if it makes you feel more comfortable."

She sat further up on the table. "The only problem I have had is with the dialects. I'm not new to this and I thought I knew them all, but once in a while I wonder if I am really hearing Spanish, I know it isn't Portuguese. I don't know what it is. They understand what I am saying, but I have problems understanding them. There is just something off, maybe I'm losing part of my hearing or mind."

"Have you mentioned this to anyone else?" Phillips asked.

"No, I don't want to lose my job or find myself talking to a shrink."

The wheels in Phillips head started moving. "Are you sure no one else has noticed this? I mean it might not be you, maybe some of these people have started using odd language to keep themselves safe from prying ears, so to speak. This new dialect may have come about as a protective device because of the violence with the cartels. It's something to think about. Out of curiosity have you noticed any of the boys acting oddly, especially younger boys with older siblings?"

"It's difficult to determine odd behavior among these boys. They start off standoffish, shy or just plain scared, then within a few minutes they are regular kids." she replied.

Phillips put his hands in his pockets, "Just thought I'd ask, but if you get a chance to talk with any of the other translators ask them about the dialect thing. Tell them I was asking, that way you'll be covered. Now, let's go talk to these people and get them on their way."

The first group Phillips talked to did not know anything about the boys, but many of them were concerned about the second bus stopping on the side of the road. It was the same story with every group from the bus, the bus had pulled over, their bus stopped behind it and the drivers spoke for a few minutes then their bus left and they arrived here. None of them knew if the second bus or its passengers had arrived nor did they know anyone on the second bus. One woman with two children did ask if her sister was going to arrive soon. She told Phillips that she had lost track of her sister, Jazmin, when they were getting ready to board the bus and she was worried. Philips assured her he would see what he could find out.

Phillips was just finishing up with the last group when Brock came through the door. "We need to go now!" Brock said.

"Wait," Phillips walked over to Amelia, "Thank you again for your help. Here is my cell number as well as Mr. Brocks, please give me a call after you have spoken to the other translators."

As they walked away Brock asked, "What did you get?"

"You first," said Phillips.

"Well, right now we are going to talk to their transportation people. It appears, according to the driver that the other bus pulled off the road and has not shown up anywhere."

"That's the same story I got from all the people I talk to," agreed Phillips.

The agent in the transportation office confirmed everything they had learned and informed them that two agents had been sent out to back track and locate the bus. So far nothing had come back from the agents.

Brock shook his head, "Raise them on the radio, see where they are and get a report."

The agent looked at him wide eyed, "You think something is up? Are they in any kind of danger?"

"I don't want to jump ahead of myself, but yeah they could be," Brock answered. "We're going for coffee come get me when you have something."

They walked out the door and Brock said, "Nothing we can do and no place to go until we hear from these guys. I need a notebook and a cup of something stronger than coffee, but coffee with have to do for now."

They stopped at one of the desks in the hall and procured two notebooks and went into the cafeteria area. Seated at one of the tables they began writing and filling each other in on the interviews.

Brock recounted what the driver had told him, "He said that he noticed the other bus had pulled off the road behind him, so he turned around to check on them. He talked to the other driver and the guy told him one of the kids got sick. They were standing between the two buses, but he could hear what sounded like someone throwing up. The driver of the second bus told him to go on, that they would be behind him as soon as the kid felt better. This driver insisted on staying in case he needed to take on more passengers, the other guy waved him off and said there was no problem just a little car sickness. So our driver left, he never saw who was on the stopped bus. What bothers me is, why this kid didn't get sick on the drive from the border pickup."

Phillips filled Brock in on what he had learned from the group on the first bus as well as what the translator had told him. "I really don't understand the dialect thing," Phillips said. "I hope Amelia calls back with some feedback, for some reason it really bothers me. Also, one of the women told me her sister was not on the bus, that during the confusion of boarding they got separated."

Both of their cells rang at the same time. Brock got up from the table then started pacing, running his hand through his hair. It was one of the transportation agents.

"Okay," the agent said, "Here's what we got and I don't like it. The agents we sent out couldn't find the bus, but did find where it pulled over. Sorry it took so long for them to get back to us, but they wanted to find the spot and check it out before they called. They found tire tracks that could belong to a small bus, no signs of vomit just foot prints. By the way, that chopper that you requested earlier got temporarily diverted, but it's now back up and is actively looking for the missing bus. When I hear anything else you'll be the first to know."

Brock hung up and looked over at Phillips, who was on his phone.

"Dr. Phillips, this is Julie and I wanted to let you know that Sanchez is in the facility. I called his boss and told him that Sanchez may have been exposed by one of the kids and we needed to keep him under observation for a day or two. He never even asked what he might have been exposed to." She laughed. "I also asked Sanchez to write up his interaction with Addison and give us his description. He told me that he doesn't really know Addison, had never worked with him before although he has seen him around from time to time. Sanchez asked me what was going on, I didn't think I should say too much, but I did fill him in on Addison not being found in the system." Julie was trying to catch her breath when she asked, "Have you found Rogelio or the bus?"

Phillips answered, "Not yet, we're working on it. Did you just give me all that info in one breath?"

"Pretty much," she replied still out of breath.

"Thanks for getting all of that you've done for us, good work on the report from Sanchez. One more favor, my car is in the security lot and I'd like you to check on it once in a while. I don't think it is going anywhere, but I'd feel better if someone was keeping an eye on it for me."

"I can do that. Any idea when you will be back here?" she asked. "Right now it is pretty slow around here so we have it covered, but tomorrow morning could change things."

"I don't know when I will be back and I hope it stays slow for you. I'll give you a call back when I know how much longer I'll be and thank you again for everything you're doing."

"No problem. I'll keep an eye for any more kids like Rogelio. You guys be careful."

Phillips walked back to over to the table, started to sit down, then grabbed his phone again and hit redial. "Julie, I lied about the one more favor thing. Another one just came to mind." He explained about the dialect thing and asked her to check around and see if anyone had noticed it at her facility and find out if anyone else knew or had worked with Addison.

He looked across the table at Brock then lowered his head to the table and sighed.

10

Five minutes later Brock and Phillips were still sitting at the table, not a word had been spoken. Brock finally broke the silence, "I would say we were wasting our time, but we've got nowhere to go."

Phillips shifted his shoulders as if to loosen them up, "Hell, where I'm from this isn't called wasting time, we call it thinking."

"Well," asked Brock, "Think of anything?"

"Yep"

"You want to tell me or should I just pretend you didn't answer in the affirmative?"

"I thought," replied Phillips as he stood up, "That a steak would taste good right about now and the rest is irrelevant."

Brock laughed, "At least it's a good thought and I know just the place. I need to make a couple more phone calls and we will be out of here."

"You're going to call state and local in on this. Good idea, we need all the help we can get."

As Brock dialed his phone he looked at Phillips, "A thinker and a mind reader, great."

After Brock called state and local he notified transportation of who he had called in and asked them to notify El Paso. El Paso is the hub of all things immigration and since they had a problem, El Paso had to be brought up to date.

Driving to the restaurant Brock said, "I really hated calling the bureaucracy up there. I thought we could clear this up today, but this looks like it has become something bigger and statewide. Of course calling in the posse makes it statewide, on paper, that is."

"Well at least the FBI isn't involved, no crime yet." Phillips stated.

"Oh man, don't say yet," Brock whined.

He pulled into a parking lot next to a rustic wooden building with a faded red roof. When they walked around front there were Christmas lights lining the front window and an open sign that gave the hours of business. Phillips turned and looked at Brock, "Here for steak?"

Brock opened the door, "Don't let it fool you, they serve a great slab of steak and do not make fun of the menu." He stepped inside and as Phillips started to follow him a car honked. He turned to look in the direction of the honk and caught the sign on a taxi that was advertising the Valley Veterinary Clinic.

As they walked to a booth in the back Phillips took in the room, modest sized and busy. Along the back and down the left side were booths, all in rustic wood. Down the right side was a counter with stools for those people in a hurry or eating alone. A waitress was running back and forth behind the counter tending to customers and dodging other waitresses picking up orders. A set of double swinging doors to the left of the counter gave access to the second exit and the kitchen for large orders to be picked up. There were six tables in the center of the room all with four place settings. "Evidentially they do a very brisk business here." said Phillips.

"In a few minutes you will find out why they do," replied Brock.

Phillips found himself looking at a simple menu with advertisements running down the side of each of the two pages. He decided on his steak and as he closed the menu he noticed another ad for the animal clinic. Brock didn't even bother to look at the menu, he knew what he wanted and he wanted it charred rare.

Phillips eyed Brock, "I want to get a room for the night. I want to go over those files and the lists we made and I don't want to do it at the facility. I want to take a shower, have a beer and be relaxed while I do it. You can drop me at a motel or we can share a room."

Brock, playing with his fork, cocked his head and said, "We'll get two queens, ground floor and I have never been hit on so subtly".

"Subtly, schmudlty I just need a place to think."

The platters, not plates, were served and the steaks were so big that the baked potato required its own plate. Phillips had to admit to himself that not only was it a slab of steak it was probably the best he'd ever had. Now he knew why they were so busy.

With no room for dessert they checked into one of the suites at The Inn and fought the urge to sleep off their huge meal. Phillips had put his black bag in the trunk with Brock's go bag and as he pulled it out he said, "Good thing I keep an extra set of scrubs in here otherwise you'd have to marry me."

"Okay honeybun, go take your shower and I'll go pick up supplies." replied Brock.

By the time Brock returned to the room, Phillips had showered and had the files and notes out on the large desk. The desk was already large enough, but Phillips had removed the phone, magazines and hospitality book to make more room. He had pulled another chair over, placed the floor and desk lamps strategically for the best lighting.

"Honey, I'm home," called Brock as he came through the door. He looked around, "I love what you've done with the place."

"I do what I can. What's in the bags?"

"Beer, snacks, coffee, toothpaste, toothbrushes and two pairs of white cotton socks."

"I can understand everything but the socks." Phillips said.

"I'm wearing running shoes tomorrow, if we get a break on this thing I want to be ready to run."

Phillips smiled, "Oh, the shoes will look great with your suit."

"Screw the suit, its jeans tomorrow," Brock yelled through the bathroom door.

Twenty minutes later, showers finished, beers and notebooks open they proceeded to go through the files. Phillips asked, "How did we get all these files? Last time I saw them they were in your office."

"They were, but they needed them here with the arrivals so they sent a car up. Remember, we also had the files from the previous group. While you were interviewing those people they made copies for us, so now we've got about one hundred and forty six files."

"I'm glad we have them, it'll give us a better overall picture. We only looked at the boys files for the scar and I think we should look at everyone. We have the contact info, but we don't know about the scars." Philips stated.

"You think the women have them?" asked Brock.

"No, not really, but I still think we should look. I thought I would read the file info to you while you take the notes. Your handwriting is clearer than mine. Then you can go over the files again to be sure I didn't miss anything and I'll go over the notes. I don't know how much good it will do, but at least we are doing something."

"I know what you mean, I feel like we should have heard something on that bus."

11

Halfway through the files they took a break and made coffee. Phillips asked, "Why'd you buy coffee?"

"I figured we would need more than what the motel supplies and I don't like motel coffee."

"I don't like it either. I know a gal that hates it so much that she travels with a coffee suitcase."

"No kidding?" Brock laughed.

"No joke. She uses one of the carry-on sized suitcases. Not just coffee either, she has a coffee pot, cups and anything you might need. A regular kitchen actually. She doesn't trust the cleanliness of hotel cups or the pot, not even those pod things."

"Well, I can understand that. Now if she could figure out what to do about shower pressure and the beds, I'd marry her," quipped Brock. "Is she a doctor too?"

"No, a veterinarian," Phillips answered, then said it again. "A vet, a vet! Where's my phone?"

"What happened" asked Brock.

"Something just clicked in my head. Did you ask the transportation people if they have a low-jack or some kind of tracking system on all the buses?" Phillips asked as he dialed his phone.

Brock picked up his phone.

When they had finished their calls, Brock asked, "What gives?"

Phillips explained about the sign on the taxi and the ad on the menu, "For some reason it was rattling around in my head, now I know why. The gal I was telling you about is not just a vet, she worked or works with ID chips, tracking devices for animals. They wanted to develop something long range to track pricy animals. Anyway, and this is a long shot, but what if those scars really are from implanted tracking devices? That's why I called her. I wanted to know if it could be done. She said theoretically it could, but the side effects to the human nervous system could be a problem especially if it was continuous tracking. The tracking device for an animal is only turned on when the animal goes missing."

"You think the cartel is tracking them?" Brock asked.

Phillips paused then said, "I don't know, that's your job. What did transportation say?"

Brock sat on the sofa, "They had already checked and apologized for not contacting me. All their buses are accounted for, it's not theirs,"

"What do you mean not theirs, are all the buses accounted for in the entire system?"

"Yes," Brock answered. "We need to know if anyone else is missing besides the three boys. The night crew is on now, so we probably won't get an answer until tomorrow, but I'm going to call anyway."

When Brock closed his phone Phillips said, "Got another call for you to make. When I was talking to my friend she said that the implanted tracking devices give off a ping and it can cause a static effect. You need to find out if anyone has reported any odd problems with their computer. The ones who would most likely notice would be your computer geeks because of the high tech systems and gadgets they use. I don't know who to contact, but figured that would be up your alley. Something else, can we get a security tape?"

Brock started dialing again, "Let me guess. You want the meeting between Ignacio and Jorge, I also want to see the tape from their dinner together. They keep them for seventy-two hours before they get taped over."

Brock got off the phone and they went back to the files. Phillips put another stack on the floor, "Okay, that takes care of all but the lone females. We have about twenty of them, so this should go quickly. Good thing too, because I could use some sleep."

"Me too, but I thought you doctors never slept."

"Sometimes it feels like it, thirteen to eighteen hours a day most of the time. Like they say, sleep when you can."

Phillips got to the fifth file, "This girl has an uncle in Atlanta, what are the odds. She's sixteen from Guatemala and someone took her picture. Very few of these have photos."

"Nah, the only time they take a photo is when something doesn't seem right," Brock said reaching for the photo, "Or looking at her, they're hot. Looks like she fell down a few times. What's her name?"

"Yolanda," Phillips took the photo from Brock. "Cut and bruising near left eye and temple, cut to left cheek also with bruising. Same type of cut to the area just left of center on her chin. Yep, she fell down a lot and on somebody's ring." Phillips handed the photo to Brock again, "Look at her arm."

Brock took the photo, looked at it then back to Phillips, "Shit! So we've got six males, eight including Ignacio and Jorge and 1 female so far. We have five males from the prior group and we have no idea where they are, so forget them. Be interesting to see who's on the missing bus." Brock picked up his phone and looked at it, "Wish we could get some answers before morning."

Phillips started going through the last of the files, they found one more with a photo and a scar on her arm. He sat there looking at the girl in her torn clothes, but no sad or troubled eyes. Not happy either, a kind of excitement in them. "I'm starting to read things into the photos that aren't there," he said as he flipped the photo onto the file. It landed face down and on the back he saw the name 'Sanchez'. He pulled over the files they had set aside, pulled out the photos of the other kids and flipped them all over. Every photo had Sanchez written on the back.

He picked up his phone, "Hey Julie, it's me. Did I wake you? Good. Is Sanchez nearby? I have a question for him. Thanks." Phillips shuffled the photos as he waited. Then, "Sorry to bother you, but we noticed that you took some photos of the illegals and signed the back. Why do you do that?"

Brock listen to the one sided conversation as he took notes from the last of the files. He heard Phillips say, "Okay, hold on a sec," as he flipped all the photos facedown, "Got it, thanks. I will and enjoy your late dinner."

Phillips closed his phone and handed the photos to Brock, "Sanchez needs a new pay grade. When I noticed that he had signed the back of these photos I wondered why. It's so if anyone has any questions they know who to contact, the kicker is why he takes them and he has a code. Take the photo of Ignacio," he told Brock, "turn it over and look in the lower right corner. See that B, it means behavior, the L next to it is language, same for Jorge. Yolanda is L and I for injury. The other girl is L only. Now look at Rogelio, nothing. His picture was taken only because they are brothers. Sanchez said he doesn't write anything on the initial contact sheet because there is no place to put it, plus they don't have the time. He said he started doing this because he was noticing odd things going on with the kids. He added the L later because he was hearing a different dialect. Before you ask, he did notify El Paso. Thus all the hand held cameras on the border."

Brock shook his head, "I bet El Paso isn't keeping a database on this. Hell, DHS is even sending them to other states without quarantine. Forget asking them for any information, looks like we are on our own."

"Won't be the first time," Phillips grunted.

"What?" Brock asked.

"Nothing. Do we have all the notes we need?"

"Yeah, I looked at the last of them while you were on with Sanchez. So, we now have eight males and two females, no idea what the scars mean, what the dialect thing is, where they are or what happened to the bus."

Phillips yawned, "We still have more questions than answers. I'm calling it a night."

Brock stifled a yawn, "Maybe we will have some answers in the morning. I want to return the files to them, no sense in carrying them around with us. Maybe they'll have the security tapes by the time we get there."

Phillips, already changed and in bed, asked, "Can we keep the photos for a while? We might need them."

"Sure, don't see why not." With that Brock flopped face down on the bed.

Phillips stared at the ceiling then whispered, "Are you asleep?"

"No."

"Can we fax Ignacio's photo to CTC?"

Phillips was referring to the Counter Terrorist Center which was established in 1986 and kept a database of known terrorists around the world.

Brock yawned, "We can do that, but I don't think they have cartel people in that database. How do you know about the CTC?"

"Hey, I read a lot" said Phillips.

12

Phillips eyes snapped open, he rolled over and reached for the bedside clock. The numbers read 4:15am, "Crap," he uttered as he fell back on his pillow, "No getting around it, I'm up." He started the coffee and jumped into the shower.

By the time he got out of the shower, Brock had the coffee poured. "I tried not wake you, no sense in both of us being up," Philips said.

"No problem, I'm not really sure I slept. I had a flashback last night of the all-nighters we pulled at Harvard. Stacks of books and paper sticking out everywhere, food wrappers and empty NoDoz boxes. I'm as determined as I was back then, just older and more tired."

"Well," said Phillips smiling broadly, "If we can get something going today you may find out that you are not as old and tired as you think. Ed, like you said before, you just haven't used it."

"I hope you're right. I'm going to dive through the shower, here's my phone, just in case."

While Brock showered Phillips packed the car and checked the items in his black bag. He was double checking the room when Brock walked out of the bathroom and said, "You know if you weren't a doctor I would swear you worked for the agency. Let's get some breakfast then head over to the facility."

When they arrived inside the facility it was early enough for it to still be quiet. The shift was changing, they could only hope that the people they dealt with were fresh and clear headed. They dropped off the files, faxed the photo and request to CTC and asked if the security tape they requested had arrived. They were told no, but that it should be arriving soon and someone was working of the list they wanted.

"Again we wait. Let's get some coffee," Brock said.

When they walked back into the office, coffee in hand, they found a smiling border patrol agent wearing a windbreaker. "Good morning," said the agent, "Are you Brock and Phillips?"

Brock stuck out his hand and introduced himself and Phillips, "What can we do for you?"

"I'm Agent Jim Sanchez and I brought the tapes for you."

Phillips shook the agent's hand, "Sanchez, really good to meet you, sorry but we couldn't see your name bar."

"Oh, when I'm traveling in a civilian vehicle I wear the windbreaker to cover the shirt. Cuts down on being a shooting victim."

Sanchez took off the windbreaker and his muscular back and arms could be seen through the fit of his shirt. Standing six feet even, with dark hair, dark eyes and huge smile showing perfect teeth stood that out against his tanned skin.

"Okay," Brock said, "let's take a look at these tapes."

They walked toward one of the empty back offices and Sanchez explained, "Julie wanted me to drive these down. She thought maybe I could translate part of it for you. There is no sound on the tapes, but in some cases I can read their lips. Julie and I haven't seen the tapes, so we may have to run through them more than once."

Brock slipped in the first tape and it showed the holding area. "We have a camera for each section," Sanchez said, "And they are equipped with night vision optics. You never know what will happen in the dark." Phillips brighten at this news.

Sanchez noticed the expression on Phillips face, "Julie thought you would like that."

The tape was rolling though at a snail's pace so Brock hit fast forward. When they saw Rogelio enter a frame they stopped the tape and backed it up. They watched the boys' line up for dinner and Phillips said, "Back it up to where Jorge makes contact with Ignacio." Brock back it up until it showed Ignacio walking into the enclosure. They continued to watch as Jorge made eye contact with Ignacio and then walked across the room.

"There!" said Phillips. "See how Jorge pushes both of his t-shirt sleeves up? Bet he is showing his scar."

Sanchez jumped in, "Jorge says something about it being warm."

"So, off comes Ignacio's t-shirt to show his scar. Sneaky," Phillips said. His brain hiccup the previous day was justified, these two guys were part of whatever this was. The showing of the scars was the password.

Brock added, "Rogelio never moved and was not introduced."

They watched as Jorge walked back over to his bed and the call for dinner was made. They watched as Ignacio said something to Rogelio as they got in line. Brock and Phillips both looked at Sanchez.

"All Ignacio said was that they were going to eat, to stay with him and they would be out of here soon. He called him 'my little man', not brother. That seems kind of odd to me."

Phillips suggested that they watch the tape from the eating area and he would watch the overnight section from the first tape afterward.

With the second tape running they watched the boys' line up outside the door and walk inside the eating area. They sat at the same table, Jorge sitting across from Ignacio, they watched as Phillips and the translator spoke to Jorge and leave. As soon as they had left Ignacio says something to Jorge. They backed it up and Sanchez said, "He is saying something like 'how many', run it again." They ran it three more times.

"It looks like he said 'how many are there of us', that is as close as I can get. Jorge answers him, but I need you to run that again." They ran it again.

"Looks like," Sanchez rubbed his forehead, "I'm not sure, do it again."

They watched Sanchez as he tried to figure it out. "Jorge put his hand to his face so I'm not sure if I missed anything, but what I get is him saying 'hundreds maybe thousands', which makes sense if he is talking about illegal kids. I can't be positive under these circumstances, lip reading Spanish is a bit difficult for me."

Brock and Phillips looked at each other.

They kept watching the tape to see how Rogelio got the mustard. At one point Rogelio starts to get up when Ignacio reaches out for this arm to stop him. Rogelio turns his head toward the wall and points, but they cannot see what he says or what Ignacio says as he is looking in the direction Rogelio is pointing. Ignacio lets go of his arm, Rogelio walks over to a table and picks something up. Rogelio looks over his shoulder, Ignacio is not looking at him so he picks up more and puts his hand in his pocket. When he gets back to the table he has two packets of ketchup in his hand and places other packets in front of Ignacio.

"Smart kid," said Sanchez.

Brock took Sanchez with him to the front of the offices while Phillips stayed to watch the end of the first tape. He hit fast forward until he sees Rogelio start moving, is was the dream. While he watched Rogelio he took out his cell phone and made a call.

Shortly after the bad dream Rogelio slowly got up off the bed and started peeling back the bedding. He reached in his pocket, then started writing his note. He even waited for it to dry a bit before he replaced the thin mattress and crawled under the blanket.

Phillips watched it again and talking to himself said, "You are a smart kid and you moved like a cat. Nobody ever knew you were awake."

Phillips rewound the tape, popped it out, took it to the main office and thanked the personnel for their help. As he reached the door one of the office girls stopped him, handed him a piece of paper and told him it was the list of those who were unaccounted for. He took a quick look at it, thanked her and went to look for Brock.

He found Brock in an intersecting hallway putting his phone away.

"I just cleared it for Sanchez to go with us, I figured we could put him to good use. He has his civilian clothes in the car, so he's changing now."

Phillips handed him the list, "Looks like six of our boys and the two girls are on that bus plus one more girl. Who is Jazmin Espinoza?"

"We'll have to check the notes, it doesn't ring a bell."

"I got it," said Phillips, "Jazmin is the name of that woman's sister, the one who got lost when they were boarding the buses. We need to double check it."

They saw Sanchez coming down the hall as Brock's phone rang. He flipped it open, "Brock. Where?" he listened to the person on the other end then said, "We're on our way." He looked at Phillips, "They found a bus."

"Where?" asked Phillips, "Did they find the kids?"

"The bus is in Falfurrias. With a tail wind and that nasty siren we should be there in forty-five minutes or less. They have a deputy meeting us at What-a-Burger, we'll follow him from there."

Phillips looked at Sanchez, "Are you sure you want to do this?"

"Yes sir. This is a lot better than sitting around the facility pretending to possibly have a disease and lying to your boss about it. Plus, Julie can really come up with busy work. I bet her 'honey-do list' is a nightmare."

"You don't have to call me sir, Phillips is good enough. Hop in and buckle up, I have a job for you."

Grill lights flashing, siren screaming, they sped out of the parking lot and headed for highway 281.

13

Falfurrias, Texas population approximately 4,981, located in Brooks County, ninety miles east of Laredo, seventy-eight miles from Corpus Christi and 163 miles from San Antonio. Founded by Edward Cunningham Lasater and named after his ranch La Mota De Falfurrias which in 1893 was one of the largest ranches in Texas at 350,000 acres. There is one County Sheriff with an organization of non-paid police officers who volunteer their time as deputy sheriffs and are known as the Border Brotherhood of Texas. They staff three patrol units and provide a variety of services throughout their fourteen hour shifts. "Shit," said Phillips coming out of his thoughts.

"What?" said Brock, "Did you forget something?"

"No I was just wrapped up in my thoughts." He picked up the notebooks and gave one of them to Sanchez.

"These are the notes we took on everyone at the facility. We need to look for a Jazmin Espinoza, she's on the missing list and she doesn't fit the profile."

After twenty minutes Phillips found her, "She's on the women with children list and it appears she was with another woman and listed as the aunt, sister of the mother. So now we have confirmation that the woman in McAllen is her sister. Wonder why she is on the missing bus, was it confusion or on purpose."

Sanchez added, "That must be her because there is no one on these lists by that name."

Next Phillips took a blank piece of paper out of a notebook and wrote Rogelio's message on it and handed it over the seat to Sanchez.

"This is our next puzzle. We're fairly certain that the first part is saying Ignacio is not Ignacio and that they are not going to Atlanta. It's the last part we can't figure out. At first I thought it was Tampa, but I can't figure out why they would go to Florida. Take a look at it and see if you get any ideas."

Sanchez took the paper, sat back and thought a minute then leaned forward again and said, "How about Tamaulipas?"

Brock said, "That's the Mexican state that Matamoros is in, what about it?"

"Not just a place," replied Sanchez "It's a cartel and possibly the oldest cartel in Mexico. Old man Guerra started it way back in the 1930's, he started running alcohol to the U.S. during Prohibition then as times changed he got into drugs, prostitution and some extortion. Through the years as it got passed down they got into assassination, human trafficking, you name it and they are into it. The Cali Cartel sends drugs through Tampico to them. These guys are really bad and they are international, I'm talking Europe, Asia, West Africa and South America I mean everywhere."

Sanchez continued, "At one point they decided they needed another wing, an enforcement wing, so they got more bad guys and started the Zeta, but in 2010 there were some problems and they had a falling out, split apart and now they're enemies. They are always shooting at each other. The Sinaloa Cartel doesn't like Zeta either so they financially back the Gulf Cartel, which, by the way, is what the Tamaulipas Cartel now calls itself. Remember in 1980 and then again in the 1990's they were finding all those bodies all over Matamoros? Well, that was these guys and remember these guys are right across the border from Brownsville."

Brock shook his head, "I hadn't thought of the Gulf Cartel and to be honest about it I did not associate them with Tamaulipas. So the 'tam' in this message could be these guys. I knew there was another reason we needed you."

"But," inserted Phillips, "If these boys are part of the cartel why are they here? Bringing one kid across the border is not actually human trafficking, unless he got away from them and they picked him up again. Except I think they would have killed him on the spot, they wouldn't bother with bringing him across. I think there's more to it."

Brock looked at Phillips. "The kid could be a hostage, being used for cover or even blackmail. If Ignacio is not his brother and they are traveling together, then Rogelio must be important to somebody. Something to think about." He pulled off the highway and into an area full of gas stations attached to quick shops and fast food chains. "I'm going to fill the tank, why don't you guys go inside and get drinks, snacks and water I think we are going to need them."

When they came back out Phillips and Sanchez threw their purchases in the trunk and Sanchez got back in the car. While they were waiting for Phillips, Brock looked in the back seat at Sanchez, "I need you to think about the dialect thing you noticed. One of the translators in McAllen noticed the same thing and it's something we need to pin down. It may be nothing, but we need to know one way or another."

"A couple of the other guys noticed it too. Let me think on it then I'll make a few calls to get their take on it," Sanchez replied.

Phillips got back in the car and handed out surgical gloves, "I thought we should wear these when we get to the scene, we may be able to get some prints on these guys. God I hope this is our bus."

Brock headed back to the highway for the five minute drive to meet the deputy.

14

They followed the deputy out highway 285, a two lane that ran through a landscape of sand, sage and mesquite with the occasional dirt road or driveway. No lights, no sirens, no traffic. They pulled up behind two other units parked on the shoulder, got out and watched as the deputy took a U-turn to head back into town. They saw the gaping hole in the barbed wire fence that ran along the opposite side of a shallow ditch, two stands of good sized Mesquite trees stood fifteen feet from the fence with tire tracks running through the gap between them. Being sure not to step on the tire tracks, they followed them as they curved through the trees and saw the bus twenty yards ahead in another grove of mesquite trees. The surrounding area was soft sandy soil, mesquite trees, sagebrush and spindly grass that looked more like weeds.

They crossed the small sandy clearing and walked over to two men standing to the right of the bus. Both were dressed in khaki pants and shirts, the obligatory boots and hats, wide belt and weapon. The sheriff, the older of the two, looked to be in his late sixties, six feet tall and overweight. The other man stood five-seven, 150 pounds and in his late thirties.

The sheriff stuck out his hand, "Sheriff Abrams, you guys must be Brock, Phillips and Sanchez. Want to tell you guys this is a strange one."

Brock shook his hand and reached for his ID, "I'm Ed Brock this is Dr. Jake Phillips and that is Agent Jim Sanchez. What ya got?"

"No need for ID." Abrams continued, "Well, we have a bus with two right side flat tires that apparently skidded off the road and ran through the fence. Only there are no skid marks on the road. Come look at this."

They followed Abrams to the ditch that ran along the road. Abrams pointed to the road, "See no skid marks," he moved his hand in the direction of the tracks, "And when it went through the ditch it was controlled. There's no scuff marks when the vehicle hit the other side of the ditch, which means that it was eased over the ditch. Then there's the fence." Abrams took a deep breath, "When a vehicle runs through a wire fence the wire breaks at different points because of stress and the fence posts nearest the break get loose. These all broke at the same point, probably cut, not stress, the posts are nice and tight. So the bus was driven in here on purpose."

Abrams turned and walked in the direction of the bus, "If that isn't enough, here you have tread marks in the sand, but none of them are from flat tires and," Abrams pointed a few feet ahead, "The rear end of the bus got stuck right here in the soft sand and they spun the wheels trying to get out, but it didn't help."

Brock knelt down and looked at the two holes from the tires and the spray of sand. He stood up and pointed toward the bus, "How did they get the bus over there? They didn't push it out, to heavy and no shoes prints."

Abrams took off his hat, ran a handkerchief around the band, put it back on and said, "First I need to let you know we have not been inside the bus, only looked in the windows to be sure no one was injured. We have not combed the area for evidence. The BOLO you put out on the vehicle made us think it was more than a stolen bus, considering where it originated. This is in our county and we should have jurisdiction, but we don't have the man power. We will help in any way we can, but we are handing it over to you guys."

Abrams started walking again and before Brock could say anything he continued, "We have a big problem up here. Not just Brooks County, but Duval, Premont and more. The illegals think a walk through here is a piece of cake, but the sand is soft and walking a long distance is slow and saps your strength. We average four hundred dead illegals in six months. I can't say they died in those months, but that's how many we find. On top of that we have 'coyotes' using the back roads to bring them through. Hell, we've even had a few gun battles out here." Abrams stopped when he got to his deputy, "This is Deputy Hanson. I wouldn't let him touch anything because I wanted you to see it first. We did take pictures of the road, ditch, tracks, fence, bus and the overall scene. When you decide to go in the bus he will take photos for you, just let him know what you need. Now, back to this bus."

Abrams walked a bit further and pointed to the ground, "It looks like someone brought a vehicle through those trees, backed it up to the bus and pulled it out."

Brock and Phillips walked over to the trees Abrams had pointed out. On the other side of the trees were the tire tracks from a second vehicle. Brock followed them with his hand, "He's right. The other vehicle came through here, pulled up into the brush to make his turn and backed right up to the front of the bus."

They followed the tracks back to the bus and Phillips said, "Looks like only the driver got out, no prints on the other side of the tracks. If you look right here," he pointed to the area where the bus had been stuck, "from this angle you can see the mark from the tow rope or chain in the sand." He turned to Abrams, "I'd like to go hunting with you sometime you've got a good eye."

Abrams laughed, "Yeah it's from hunting those damned hogs."

Brock said, "We need to start combing the area and see what else we can pick up. Let's start with the bus."

They opened the bus door, had the deputy take an overall photo, then they started looking seat by seat. Every time they found anything, Brock made a note in the notebook on a hastily drawn sketch of the interior and a photo was taken. Halfway through their search they had found only candy and gum wrappers. At the next set of seats Brock called the deputy over for a photo, then picked up a balled up piece of paper. He called over his shoulder, "Take a look at this, it looks like a receipt for computer time."

Phillips looked at it, "Is there one of those mail drop computer places in McAllen or nearby? There's no address on this."

Brock put the paper in his pocket, "We're going to find out when we finish here. I've got a list going." He moved to the next seat when the flash from the camera went off behind him. He turned to see Phillips sliding across the seat and he took a step back.

Phillips turned to him, "I think we have a finger print in mustard. It looks like an intentional thumb print. Do we have the print guys coming or are we taking the bus to them?"

"I have them on standby. After we search the perimeter I'll have a better idea of what I'm going to do."

Phillips looked back at the print then slid out of the seat and walked behind it. He leaned over the back of the seat and looked at the wall then asked the deputy if he could get a shot of the crevice where the seat and wall came together. He then moved out into the aisle so the deputy could get to the area and see the crevice.

When the deputy finished, Phillips slid across the seat again and pulled the corner of a piece of paper from the crevice. Very slowly, with gloved hands, he teased the rest of the paper out of the crevice.

The paper was folded, not crumpled and appeared to be torn from a road map. Phillips carefully unfolded it, a smile spread across his face then quickly turned to a frown. He said nothing, just handed it to Brock.

15

The paper was from a map of Texas and was torn so it showed the Gulf Coast portion. Brock saw three brownish yellow fingerprints, one on Corpus Christi, one on Houston and the last on Port Arthur. The print placed on Houston had a circle around it.

Brock asked the deputy to finish checking the bus, then turned to Phillips, "Let's go outside."

As they stepped off the bus Brock said, "Another puzzle, but this one might be a bit easier. There were eight maybe ten kids and possibly two adults on the bus, I don't know whether to count Jazmin as adult or child. Anyway, this could be where they are taking the kids. Some of them go to Corpus, some to Houston and the rest to Port Arthur and because of the circle I think Rogelio is going to Houston."

"That works," said Phillips, "but why mark all three cities? Why not just mark the one where you are going, why show Port Arthur?"

"Maybe he wants us to know the entire route," replied Brock. "Plus now we have this other vehicle showing up. Was whoever helped pull this bus out of the sand a passerby or part of this and their next mode of transportation? There is definitely something going on here."

Phillips turned to look at the road, "Bigger problem, how are we going to find them?"

"I think I might be able to help with that." They turned to see Abrams. "The man that owns this ranch is the one who spotted the bus, I should say his son spotted it. They should be here shortly, I asked them not to come over here until after you had time to go over the scene. I just called them."

As he finished speaking they could hear a large pick-up truck stop on the road. They walked to the road and saw two men get out of the truck and head in their direction. Abrams introduced them only as Russell and his son R.J. and that they lived about a half mile down the road. Russell was a barrel chested man about sixty years old, stood six feet tall and wore a ten gallon hat. His son was a duplication of his father only about thirty-five years younger. Smiles and 'howdys' were exchanged with a slap on the back for Abrams.

Abrams cleared his throat, "Russell, why don't you tell them how you found the bus."

Russell pushed his hat back a bit, "Well, we have a pretty big ranch, lots of acreage and lots of problems. One of the big problems is the illegals coming through here. They tear up the fences and the livestock get out. A number of the people crossing the property get lost and die. We have lots of watering places for the cattle and we keep a cup chained to the pipes so that these folks can help themselves to water, but they never have anything to put water in so they just drink their fill." He sighed and went on, "They die of thirst later. We eventually find them and call the sheriff. Anyway, R.J. is into all the high tech stuff, so he got the idea of using drones."

Sanchez interrupted, "What about the Aerostats? They use downward looking radar."

"Well son," said Russell, "When they are up and working they help as far as knowing that people are out there, be we need to know more." He looked at R.J., "Why don't you explain it."

"Sure. Without giving you the history," he said rolling his eyes in the direction of his father, "here's how it works. I have several drones with night vision capabilities, streaming video feeds and other stuff. I send out the first drone to start sweeping the fences around 11:00pm and every hour after that I put another one in the air. This is done continuously until about 7:00am, these are the prime hours for foot traffic since its cooler." R.J shifted his weight and went on, "What I'm looking for is broken fence line and of course people. When I find where they are coming through the fence I drop a paint ball filled with iridescent paint, sometimes I will drop two, and it marks the spot for us. I also get the GPS co-ordinates, then we can go out and do the repairs before we lose livestock."

Phillips asked, "How can you keep the drones up for so long and why iridescent paint?"

R.J. smiled, "I used that paint so I can closely check the spot again for the next few nights. I could use the GPS, but it is easier to spot the paint since I will be flying over that area anyway. Keeping them up is the easy part. When they finish their circuit of the ranch I slip in a fresh battery pack and send it out again. I built all them myself to the specs that we needed and I control all of them with the computer. Also, each one sends its live feed to separate screens in my little computer hub. So I just sit and watch until I see something, then I can send it back for another pass. If I need to I can send the drone a command and it drops a small paint ball."

"So, one of your drones spotted the bus?" asked Brock.

"Yes about 1:00am this morning. When I went back for a second pass I saw people standing outside the bus, so I just hovered until the next drone got there. I had them up at about 200 feet and used my zoom to get a better look. When the third drone showed up I brought the first drone home and just kept rotating them for about an hour and a half. That's when the SUV showed up."

"Wait!" Brock said. "You saw the SUV that stopped to help them?"

"Not exactly" replied R.J. "The SUV pulled up near the bus, a guy got out and talked to one of the guys from the bus, no hand shaking or anything, it was like they knew each other. Then the guy got back in the SUV, backed up, went around through the trees and backed up to the bus. They hooked the bus up to the SUV and towed it further into the mesquite. The SUV circled back to the people and three of them stood around talking for a while. This is when I got to thinking something was up, so I brought the drones down for a closer look and when I saw kids being brought to the SUV, I made my move. One at a time I brought the drones in and dropped the paint on the roof of the SUV. Before you ask, they never knew it happened. The SUV is high enough they can't see the paint and no one even flinched when they hit. You send a chopper up and it can spot that thing in a rain storm. Oh, the paint colors are bright pink and a yellowish green. I also have the feeds on tape if you need them. There's static on them, but you can still see what is going on in that little clearing."

"That's pretty amazing," Brock said. "How big are these drones?"

R.J. held out his hands and replied, "About eighteen inch diameter, black, eight spokes come out from the center with propellers on top of each spoke and rows of little legs underneath to hold the paint."

"Did you say there was static on the feeds?" asked Phillips

"Yeah, more than usual. Some days I have no static, some days a light scatter, but this morning it was really bad."

Brock pulled out his phone, "I need to make some calls."

"Wait," R.J. put his hand up, "There's something else you should know. When they were taking the kids to the SUV, one of the guys took a kid by the arm and led him or her into the mesquite and only one came back."

"Why didn't you tell me about that earlier!" anger from Abrams.

"Well, I figured the living needed the attention first," replied R.J.

"Crap!" Brock walked away then circled back. "Okay, I'm getting on the phone. Everyone else spread out and see what you can find." With that said he stomped off to the car.

Sanchez looked at Phillips, "When I was checking the perimeter, I did the two quadrants between the bus and the road and there was nothing. If you could step over step here," Sanchez motion for Phillips to follow him. "I don't think we need civilians doing this type of search."

"I agree." Phillips looked at R.J. "Which direction did this guy take the kid?" asked Phillips.

R.J. pushed his hat back, "He walked toward the side of the bus and it looked like he shot out the tires, all I could see was two quick pin points of light. Then he and the kid walked to the front of the bus and disappeared into the trees.

"So," Sanchez said, "it could be anywhere except back this way. I guess it could be worse."

Phillips looked at Russell, "You and R.J. stay here and when Brock comes back tell him what you told us and what we are doing. Abrams, you and Hanson pick a direction, Sanchez and I will start near the front of the bus. We need to sweep the area forward, right and left of the bus. I don't need to tell you what to look for."

16

Sanchez went into the trees and brush directly in front of the bus. He moved slowly pushing the tree branches, brush and grass away with his hands, looking right and left as he went. He found some broken twigs hanging from the low growing sage, then picked up foot prints going into and coming out of the area. He walked a bit further and found where the grass had been trampled as if someone was walking in a circle. "Maybe the kid was giving him some trouble, maybe trying to get away", thought Sanchez. He picked his way around the edge of the circle and found signs pointing in the direction they had taken. He picked up prints again in the soft sand that led him to the left into heavier grass and small rocks. He had lost the trail.

He yelled, "Phillips. Hey Phillips, I need you."

Phillips called back, "I went left of the bus. Where are you?"

"Okay," replied Sanchez, "I'm slightly left of a direct line from the bus."

"Got ya," said Phillips ten feet away from him, "What do you need?"

Sanchez told him about the signs and foot prints then showed him where he had lost the trail. They walked straight ahead on the grassy, rocky area until they came to soft sand, but no tracks.

Sanchez pointed to the ground along the edge of the grassy area, "It looks like this is a natural run off when it rains. See how the edge is broken off and the sand starts?" Sweeping with his arm, "The water comes through here, causes a small gulley and the small rocks pile up along the edge when the sand washes out from beneath them. This little berm is about forty feet long. Let's walk along the edge and look for prints, you go one way I'll go the other. When we get to the end, turn around and walk down the center and we will meet in the middle."

They walked the edge, found nothing and started on their way back. Both men looked right and left as they walked. Sanchez stopping to look at the tree and sage line before continuing. He stopped for the fourth time, looked at the tree line and started sprinting toward it. At a low growing mesquite, he dropped to his knees and began throwing loose brush and sand off to the side.

"Here, over here," Sanchez yelled.

Phillips had already started running toward him. He stopped, dropped down next to Sanchez and said, "Screw any evidence."

Luckily there was not much cover to remove and the face was the first thing they saw. It was a female with her arm thrown across the lower half of her face. Sanchez reach down and carefully tried to move her arm. As soon as he got it away from her mouth her eyes open then closed again.

In unison they said, "She's alive."

"It's Jazmin," said Phillips, "she's the only one we don't have a picture of. Let's get her out of here and check her out."

They moved her to the shade of a larger tree and started checking for a bullet wound. Phillips found a through and through under her right rib close to her side. Sand had matted the wounds as well as around her eyes and mouth. Sanchez reach down to the lower pocket in his cargo pants and pulled out a bottle of water.

"It's only a half-bottle, but it should be enough. See if you can lift her head a little for me, I want to wash her lips off before I try to get water into her."

Phillips raised her head. The wetness on her lips startled her, then she realized what it was and reached for the bottle. Sanchez held it out of reach.

"Just drink a little", he told her in Spanish, "or you will be sick." He held the bottle to her mouth, "We are going to move you to our car. We are the police, you're going to be alright." She smiled and passed out again.

Phillips lifted her from under the tree, "Jim you go first, pick the quickest way back and try not to whack us with tree limbs."

When they got close to the clearing Sanchez yelled, "Brock, she's alive. Brock, Abrams come on back."

Phillips said, "Let's get her in the car, open the back door for me. See if you can raise Brock on his cell."

Before Sanchez could make the call Brock came jogging toward the car from the direction of the bus with Abrams trailing behind. Sanchez filled them in and Abrams made the call for an ambulance. Brock walked up to the car and stuck his head inside.

"How's she doing?"

"She's going to be okay. She needs to get to a hospital, the wound is packed with sand, it helped stem the bleeding, but it needs to be cleaned out before infection sets in. I got some water down her and she keeps trying to tell me something, but my Spanish is not that good. Let's get Sanchez in here."

Phillips and Sanchez traded places and Phillips leaned back in the car, "Talk to her and see what you can get. Don't bother translating, she's weak and is in and out of consciousness, just talk. You can translate later."

Sanchez took her hand and she opened her eyes. He sat hunched over in the back seat while Brock and Phillips stood outside the door. By the time Sanchez got out of the car they could hear the ambulance siren in the distance.

Sanchez uncapped a bottle of water and drank half of it, "She is very weak and she is scared, not for herself, but for the kids. She says the men are very bad and up to no good, her words exactly. Sometimes they speak in English, other times they speak a language she doesn't know. When they talk to Rogelio and Yolanda they speak Spanish. The other girl, Maria, she says is very mean and speaks funny sounding Spanish. After that she was speaking in broken sentences, but from what I could put together they went to a coffee place, used a computer and spent the night in a hotel. Mixed up in all of this she was asking about her sister, was worried about what was going to happen to her and cried off and on. I can't tell you what all it all means, but at least we know why it took them so long to get here."

Brock ran his hand through his hair, "Them not being in a hurry bothers me, but at least it gives us time to find them." He turned to Abrams, "How many abandoned vehicles to you find in your county in a six month period?"

"Oh, I don't know, it depends on the time of year, but I would say we average about six to eight. Most of those are stolen vehicles from the border towns, San Antonio or Corpus Christi. We haven't had any buses in a long time."

"For the next few months whenever you find an abandoned vehicle, I need you to notify the people at this number." Brock handed him a card with a phone number written on the back. "I'm having the bus towed to one of our yards, probably Corpus. They will be here in a couple of hours, when they get here they will cover the bus and seal it. Until they get here I want this area sealed, when they finish they will release it. I want that bus torn apart, even the seats. Back in the 1980's the cartels were using immigration buses to smuggle drugs across the border. I want to be sure they didn't do that here."

Abrams said, "If they start that again we will have to begin looking for corruption along the border as well as at officials statewide." He turned to Hanson, "It's a nasty business and everyone has to be looked at in every county. And you son, you will get to be part of losing friends and gaining enemies."

The ambulance arrived and Phillips talked to the EMTs while Brock and Sanchez assured Jazmin that she was going to get the best of care and her family would be notified and brought to her. Phillips finished filling in the EMT's about Jazmin and started toward the car as Brock took his turn with the EMTs.

Phillips took out his phone, dialed and leaned against the hood of the car. Unnoticed by Phillips, Sanchez had been walking behind him and walked to the rear door. Sanchez could only hear one side of the conversation and he really didn't care, he was too tired.

"Did you get anything?" Phillips said into the phone and then listened. "Great. Shoot that over to Lena and she will see that it gets where it needs to be. Anything on the others?" He listened again, "You don't say, well that is interesting and different. Find Chad, fill him in and have him fly into Corpus Christi and call me when he lands. Also, tell the others to be on standby." He paused to listen, "Not yet, I'm going to wait until the news is delivered. Thanks." He closed his phone and turned to see the back half of Sanchez sticking out the back door of the car.

"Jim, what are you doing?"

"Oh hey. I'm just cleaning off the seat. If I have to sit back here I don't need half of west Texas sitting here with me," he said as he threw some weeds out the door. He picked up grass off the floor, "I got some of the sand out, but it needs more than a hand sweep to get it all out. At least now most of it is off the seat and on the floor."

Brock walked up, "Let's get out of here. I've got eyes in the air heading toward Corpus, they will check the highway, gas and rest stops as well as motels. Hell, I told them to check everything. I hope they use more than one bird."

Sanchez spoke up, "Since these guys don't appear to be in a hurry, there are about six ways they can get to Corpus. I would say that the 359 route is out, the other three roads are usually not that busy and they might stand out, although 285 and 44 south would take you straight to highway 77. Sorry to say it, but I think they are in Corpus as we speak."

"Okay," said Brock, "lights and sirens all the way."

17

Brock shut down the siren as they drove into the Robstown area. No one had spoken on their drive from Falfurrias, all eyes had been looking for any sign of an SUV with three adults and a load of kids.

Phillips broke the silence, "That Abrams is a piece of work. He could have saved us time if he had brought Russell and R.J to the site sooner. He had talked to them and knew everything that had happened, yet he wanted us to think he figured it out. There was no way he could have known which direction the SUV was moving, hell it could have backed into the trees and pulled that bus with a front mounted wench. He also missed the tracks in the sand, the people on that bus moved around the clearing for at least an hour and I'll bet they even relieved themselves. I noticed the smaller foot prints that I'm thinking belonged to Rogelio, he didn't walk around as much as the others did. If those tracks I found where the SUV hooked up to the bus were on the passenger side instead of the drivers, then we are maybe looking at one more adult that did not show himself at the site. I thought when I gave Abrams the compliment he would come clean. I guess he doesn't get to show any expertise out there, the State probably takes over when bodies start showing up."

"He also didn't mention that the SUV came across the ditch further down the road," Sanchez added, "I noticed tires tracks when I was searching the area near the road and followed them until I found where they'd cut the fence. I wonder why they didn't come in behind the bus." He was cut off by his cell phone.

"Sanchez here." He listened then said, "Great, thanks I'll pass on the info."

"That was one of the guys I put on checking out the dialect reports. He said other guys had noticed it, but let it go. One guy did have something for us, he said a couple of weeks ago he heard two of the boys whispering to each other, so he moved up closer to them and they weren't speaking Spanish. The guy said it sounded like something from the Middle East, but he wasn't sure. Don't laugh at me, I'm just the messenger."

"I'm not laughing"' said Phillips, "It might actually make sense."

Brocks' phone chimed, "Brock here. Yeah I sent a photo." He listened as he pulled off the road, shock showed on his face. "You're sure about this? Let me get somewhere and I'll call you back," he said as he hung up.

He turned to look at Phillips and Sanchez, "That was the ID on the photo of Ignacio that we sent out. We need to find a motel where I can receive a fax." Sanchez looked at Phillips but said nothing.

They found a motel and Brock got two adjoining rooms. "We are going to need a temporary base of operations, might as well be here," Brock said as he opened the door to the room. "The ID we got on Ignacio is not good news."

As they walked into the room Brock dialed his phone and gave the person on the other end the fax number of the motel. He hung up and continued, "This guy is not really a kid, he is twenty-six and he has jumped from one terrorist group to another. He is Lebanese/Egyptian and one angry young man. Since we have so many questions on these missing people and since one of them is a known terrorist, they have heightened the terror alert on airports. They are not making it known to the public as they want to catch this guy and they don't want to scare him off. I hope they don't Mirandize him, I hope they send him to the basement."

"Freelance terrorist or mercenary terrorists," muttered Phillips.

"What?" Sanchez asked.

"Just a term we have for them. We call them freelance or mercenary terrorists because they choose the mission they want to do and then hire out to the highest bidder. They do not give their lives on a mission, they find someone else to give theirs only the other person doesn't know they are going to die. They use kids, women, the handicapped, either mentally or physically, they don't care. They are on a religious jihad and the only thing that counts is the outcome and the amount of money they can collect. It would be nice if we could find out who he is working for."

"I thought these guys wanted to die. You know the whole virgin thing," Sanchez commented.

"Not these guys," replied Phillips, they don't want to die, they want the money. They say they hate us and our way of life, but they love the almighty coin of the realm. There are not many of them, ten that we know of and have on film. Now we have to add a twist, we have to add a female to the group."

Brock who had been sitting at the table totally confused said, "What the hell are you talking about? Where did you get this information?"

"My question is, who are you?" Sanchez said.

"I'm Dr. Jake Phillips, the same guy I was yesterday and the same guy I have always been. Who I am has not changed, but part of the job has. My information is solid and by now has been passed on to the CIA, the people who sent it to me are the ones I work for or in most cases work with and they are reliable. They got a hit on one other person from our list, I expect to get all the information within a few hours, maybe less.

Brock scooted down and stretched out in his chair, folded his arms across his chest and a little angrily said, "Okay old pal, are you going to tell us what is going on and do I need a drink?"

Phillips stood, "Yeah, I think all of us need one. I'll go buy a bottle, Sanchez you get ice. Brock you need to see if your fax has come in yet."

"I think you are buying time," said Brock as he walked out the door.

Fifteen minutes later Phillips walked in the room with a bottle of bourbon, a six pack of beer and his black bag.

Brock was holding the fax in his hand. "Did you know who this guy was?" Brock asked in an accusing tone.

"No, I didn't. Not until this afternoon," Phillips replied.

"If you had an idea that this Wafcue was a killer why didn't you say something?" shouted Brock.

Phillips said, "His name is pronounced Wafeek spelled Wafiq and you know it. Again, I did not know who he was or is. I asked you to send his photo in on a hunch, nothing else. It's just my people got it figured out before your people did."

Brock shouted again, "Your people, your people! What the hell is this? What kind of game are you playing?"

Phillips poured a splash of bourbon over ice, "Cut the attitude Ed. I don't give a shit who got the ID first as long as we have one."

Sanchez popped open a beer, "If you guys want to have a pissing contest over this be my guest. I'll go in the other room and the winner can come and get me when the explanation part starts."

Brock walked over and poured a drink, "You're right. I'm sorry. I just don't like things being kept from me when I'm on a possible case. So, go on, explain."

Phillips settled himself in the desk chair so that he could look directly at Brock and Sanchez as they sat at the table. He ran a hand through his hair, leaned forward placing his elbows on his thighs.

"I will try and make this short, but what I tell both of you can go no further than this room. Ed, you cannot go back to the shop and start trying to investigate or even ask if anyone knows anything about what I am going to tell you. Even if they do know they won't say anything they can't. It is as matter of security and safety."

18

Phillips walked across the room and put fresh ice in his glass, but no bourbon, as he walked back to his chair he started speaking.

"When it was requested that I go to Iraq to help with the wounded and the children, they sent me through modified Seal training at their facility. While they bruised and battered me, they also sent me through the intelligence section, the thought being I might overhear things between the civilians or notice something they could use. An incident happened, which I can't discuss, but I was glad I had all that training because it gave me a heads up when things started to go bad."

"Almost a year later when I got home I was offered a job with the CIA, I declined. I wanted to go home and sleep for a week, eat steak at every meal and be a normal doctor. Not long after, I received a visit from two men who also offered me a job, maybe I should say they offered me an opportunity. I didn't want anything to do with these guys or whoever they worked for, but the more they talked the more intrigued I became. These guys were no thugs, they were just average looking guys who could probably kill you with one hand. What they said interested me so much that when they asked if I would go see the headman, I said yes."

"I won't go into the details of the meeting but suffice to say I joined them. Brock, remember those two weeks we spent fishing? Well, that was my gift to myself for making to through their four month training session. I trained at the Special Ops. Center, not only the physical courses, but the more rigorous mental courses. I thought my head would explode. I never paid attention to the small things going on around me, after the pre Iraq sessions and Special Ops. Sessions, not much gets past me."

"I'm still a doctor, that's my job, but it's also my cover. The organization I work for is both clandestine and covert. We operate outside restrictions and answer to no one. Brock, you've got your different levels of classifieds that I would never be privy to. My position is much the same. What I can tell you is our intelligence is unsurpassed. *Unsurpassed.*" Brock broke in "Say no more. I've heard of such outfits, but I never thought I'd run into one of you."

"You probably have, but didn't know it. For every upward position in the military there are darker more specialized outfits where I reside."

"You guys are Middle Earth types, aren't you?" Brock said with a smile.

Grinning back Phillips said "We're deeper than that. It's pretty hot where we are."

"So, what's your intel say?" asked Brock.

"Intel found Wafiq, aka Ignacio, and now on our last girl, Maria. By the way, my fault for not paying more attention when we got her name from the files, I was too interested in the injuries on Yolanda. I sent her photo in later. Oh, I also need to tell you I'm expecting someone to fly into Corpus today."

The room was silent except for the sound of the air conditioner, Brock and Sanchez were both staring at the floor. Phillips stood up, stretched and started to walk across the room when Brock cleared his throat.

Brock got serious and said, "When I said at the hotel about being on our own, you made the remark that it wouldn't be the first time. I guess you really meant it, it must have been a bad situation."

Phillips sighed, "Yes, it was."

Brock was just about to ask if anyone was hungry when Phillips phone rang. He looked at the ID, "This is the friend I was expecting."

He answered the call, "Chippendales, can I help you?"

The person on the other end said something, he laughed and opened the door, "I'll be right over." He stopped in his tracks and closed his phone.

Brock and Sanchez gave each other questioning looks as Phillips stepped back into the room followed by a man dressed in black jeans, a grey t-shirt and black leather jacket. He stood six-two, was 220 pounds of muscle and had military short dark hair and piercing gray eyes.

Chad Allen was an ex-Navy SEAL and was known for his expertise as a sniper and his close work. Anyone who was unlucky enough to take him on face to face did not live to tell about it, his face wasn't associated with his work and he took pains to keep it that way. He never spoke to the people he was hunting, his job was to help hunt them down and either help bring them in or eliminate them. By the time he was put on a job the talking was over, he felt they had had their chance and blew it. He worked hard at keeping his work separate from his everyday life, who he was on the job was an alter ego who was paid to kill in order to protect other lives.

Phillips said, "This is the friend I was expecting. This is Chad Allen, Chad this is Agent Ed Brock and Border Agent Jim Sanchez. Chad is here at my request, if we need him, he's the best at what he does." He looked at Chad, "Thought you were going to call me from the airport, I was going to pick you up."

"Thanks, but you know I need to have my own car, I called ahead so one would be at the airport. So, have you guys heard anything about whereabouts?"

Brock answered, "Not yet. I would do some pushing but it doesn't do anything but piss people off. We were thinking about getting something to eat. You want to join us?"

"Thanks, that sounds great, but before we go I need to borrow Jake for a few minutes. We'll be in my room, I'm down at the other end."

Phillips picked up his black bag and opened the door. He looked back at Brock, "This shouldn't take very long and with luck we'll get some news." After the door had closed behind them Sanchez waited for a beat and looking at Brock said, "Any idea what that was about or who that guy might be? I know he more than likely works for the same outfit Jake does, so I'm guessing Intel or fire power."

Brock replied, "I think fire power and I'm thinking sniper."

"Why do you say that?"

"Did you see his hands? He has slender hands like Jakes'. Most of the good snipers I know have hands like that."

"Yeah, and he needs his own vehicle so he is probably armored up. I guess Jake will fill us in when gets back.

"Don't count on too much filling in." Brock said. "Outfits, like the one Jakes with make the NSA look like blabbermouths. One thing I can say is that I trust Jake with my life."

"Can I ask you something?" Sanchez asked without waiting "What was that Middle Earth type you were talking about?"

Brock smiled "We both went to the same college at a very young age and as you can guess it was rough. Not academically, but socially. A group of jock type students constantly gave us a hard time so we started playing shadow games with them. We changed our routines, spread subtle misinformation and followed them around when they were looking for us, stuff like that. We called them Middle Earth types because they were just standard students. When one of us said something stupid, the other one would say jokingly "Are you one of those Middle Earth types?" The other would reply, "No I'm deeper than that and it's hot where I am." It got us through college and looking back on it now, that's probably where our training started for our present occupations."

Standing up and stretching Brock said, "Right now I'm going to take this opportunity to get flat, that bed is calling my name."

19

Phillips and Chad had gotten to the other room and as they walked in Chad said, "I've got three rooms down and the one right above us, so we are clear to talk. I brought the equipment I thought we might need and have sent guys to Port Arthur and some are here, they're scouting the refineries. The office thinks these guys, since Wafiq is involved, are going to blow up or damage as much as they can in a coordinated effort. They also think that Corpus and Port Arthur will be refinery hits."

"That's what I was thinking. The only thing I'm worried about," replied Phillips, "is Houston. The refineries are spread out, so I was thinking the shipping channel might be on their list. If they decided to hit the Hartman Bridge they could block the channel, I just don't think they could bring it down. They would have to have something as big as what was used in Oklahoma City. They could set off a charge and use it as a short diversion, then when everyone is looking at that they set off coordinated preplaced charges at refineries and tank farms. It's a lot to think about, I guess we'll just have to follow them."

Chad picked up a folder, "Here is the info we got on those photos. I think you should take a look at what we got on one called Maria."

Phillips took the folder, "I'm going to go over this with Brock and Sanchez and I want you there."

"I take that to mean that you told them about your other job? How did they, mainly Brock, take it?"

"Brock was surprisingly fine with it. Sanchez might be a little confused but he'll be ok."

Phillips turned toward a row of black cases against the wall, "What else do you have for me?"

Chad opened a large hard case and took out a smaller case, "I've brought several things for us to go through. In this small case I have any medical supplies you might need, keep the whole case. The rest of the case has ammo, fire arms, a few flash bangs, vests and miscellaneous items." He took out another small case, "This is a new Glock 19 which I have pre-fired and cleaned, my gift to you. Under that I have some multi compartment custom packs for the odd items, which we'll go through." He picked up another hard case off the floor and put it on the bed, "Last but not least," he opened the case, "a Cornershot M16. All the gear for it is in here, mount camera, flashlight, scopes, etc. If you're not going to use it, I will. I hate those hard to reach places."

"I have my H&K .45, the M11 and the Micro Uzi," he pick up the Glock, "and now a new Glock, thank you." Phillips mind wandered back to his last Glock.

On the last mission he and Chad had worked together they found themselves in a situation where it was just the two of them against four very nasty gang types. If these guys caught them they would be tortured, maimed and their body parts would more than likely never have been found. Chad decided it was do or die and being out of ammo for his hand gun, he borrowed the Glock from Phillips. Before he made his move he told Jake, "I will probably die when I charge them, but don't stop firing at them until we're both dead." They were backed up against the edge of a cliff that rose over one hundred feet above crashing waves and rocks. Chad belly crawled around the large rock that was giving them cover and made his way behind some low growing bushes. Then turned and gave Jake the signal that he was ready. Jake picked up a large rock and in true movie fashion, threw in the direction of and to the right of the rocks the bad guy were behind. It hit the top of the rocks and started bouncing down the right side toward the cliff. The gunman on the far left made the mistake of standing up to see what it was and Chad nailed him with one shot to the head. The three that were left started firing in Chad's direction which pulled the guy on the far right from behind cover, Jake got him. At Chads' signal they both charged the two that were left, going left and right they moved around the rocks. When the smoke had cleared the last two bad guys were dead, Jake had a knot on his head from cracking it on the boulder and Chad was on the ground with a bullet hole in his arm. The Glock, unfortunately, was at the bottom of the cliff somewhere having been knock out of Chads' hand when he was hit. Chad called over to Phillips, "I'm okay, but your gun isn't. Looks like I will be getting you a new one." Phillips had told him not to worry about it since his plan, as hokey as it was, had worked.

"How many rounds in your M11? Hello, Phillips, M11, how many rounds?"

"Sorry, I was just thinking about my old Glock. The M11 is a thirteen round 9mm and before you ask, yes I would like an extra full clip, that way I'll have three. We need to find out from Brock what his ammo situation is and I don't know what Sanchez uses since border patrol isn't allowed to fire their weapons anymore. We'll have to ask and you keep the M16, it makes me feel safer."

"Okay, here's your extra clip, it's a twenty and it's full. Now to the packs, I suggest you take at least one and body cameras, vests and night vision for all three of you. The rest is up to you."

Phillips began picking things out if the case and putting them in his black bag, digital camera and recorder, flashlights, batteries, extra latex gloves and 3 night optics. He covered it all with the pack and zipped it up.

"We need to get back to Brock. Getting them geared up and read in on what you brought may take a while and I don't think time is on our side."

They grabbed what they needed and walked back to the other room. They opened the door as Brock was getting off the phone.

"They've located the SUV! Brock rubbed his hands together, "It's at a small motel that's on the edge of a residential area. Luckily it's one story so the paint on top of the SUV won't be noticed. Can we get someone over there to keep an eye on them?"

"I'm on it. Give me the address." Chad said.

Brock handed him a note pad as he walked out the door dialing his cell.

Brock looked at Phillips, "Sanchez and I have been thinking about that map and we think these guys are going for refineries and maybe the air base here in Corpus. I don't know if I would have gone in that direction, but with this terrorist around it's a possibility. I just called to let the powers that be know our thinking and they agree. What we can't agree on is Houston, unless they are actually going for Texas City." Brock pointed to the cases and vests that Phillips and Chad were carrying, "What is all that?"

Chad came back into the room, picked up his cases and placed them and the vests on the bed then walked over and turned on the television. "We've brought you some toys."

Phillips put his bag and cases on the bed and looked at Brock, "How much ammunition do you have?"

"Two clips one in the chamber."

"Worse case, do you need more?"

Brock shrugged, "Worse case, yeah I do. At least one more."

Phillips looked at Sanchez, "When was the last time you qualified?"

"About six months ago, not that they let us fire on the job."

"Have you ever used an H&K .45?" Phillips asked.

"I've used just about all of them including an AK-47. I belong to a group that goes out in the desert just to blow things up. We even have a cannon," Sanchez replied.

"Well, in that case I guess we'll give you a gun," Phillips handed him the H&K.

Sanchez took the gun, "Thank you, but what should I do with this?" Sanchez reached in his shirt and pulled out a .357.

"Holy Crap!" said Brock, "I didn't know you were carrying."

"It's a custom made holster that fits under my arm and close to the body, a friend made it for me. I carry it when I'm off duty, I have a concealed permit. Since you're offering I will take the H&K, two is always better than one."

Chad opened one of the cases and handed out clips and ammo, "You guys should be in good shape, but take an extra box for each weapon. We don't know what we're headed into or exactly how many are involved. This little group may have others joining them."

Phillips reached into his bag, took out the custom pack and explained each item as he placed them in the compartments. He refreshed them on the use of the night optics and handed out the vests, "Chad, are these ceramic?"

"Yeah, they will stop just about anything, just be sure the sides are tight. You don't want anything going in that way."

Phillips got down to the medical supplies in his bag, took them out and the divider they were in, then remove a piece of black felt. From the bottom of the bag he got his M11 and placed it on the felt then reached in and brought out the Micro-Uzi.

"You mean we've been driving around with that in the trunk?" asked Brock.

"Well, yeah. I didn't think it was a good thing to leave it in my car."

"Do you always have that with you?"

"Pretty much. This is my go bag and since I never know where I'll be if a call comes, it seemed the best option. Are we all squared away with equipment? If so, I would suggest that two of us go get some burgers, we should eat here. We've got a lot to cover and we don't know how much time we have."

"Sounds good to me," Chad reached for the door, "Jim you go with me, we'll take my car."

Phillips finished packing his bag, this time with the medical supplies on the bottom, zipped it up and put it between the wall and the bed. He placed the pack and the vests on top and the other medical bag beside it. He sat on the bed, leaned back on the pillows and headboard, sighed, closed his eyes for a minute, and then sat up on the edge of the bed again.

"Hey, Brock," he leaned forward and placed his elbows on his knees, "I need to talk to you."

Brock looked at him, "I'm listening."

"This is your case, I want to make that clear. I called in my end because I wanted Chad here, we can put resources in place faster and as you can tell, we have immediate access to equipment. Chad has information for us and needs to fill us in on what action he has taken so far. He's not being pushy, it is just the way we work. If you disagree with anything he has done or any suggestions he makes, feel free to voice your opinion, it's your case."

"I think I hear a 'but' on its way again."

"Yeah, I was going to say, but think it through before you veto anything. I have found that he is right ninety-nine percent of the time."

Brock flopped down on the bed, "I am finding the way you guys work interesting. I don't think my guys will be here until tomorrow afternoon and we will probably be on the road when they touchdown, if they touch down. The guys in Houston are supposedly already on it, but who knows what they are doing, probably waiting to hear from us. Anyway there is not much they can do, American soil you know. I'm pretty sure the FBI has been informed, but they usually don't do anything except watch until a crime is committed. DHS knows, but how else will they react other than what they have already done with the airports." He sighed, "I guess I really understand why your organization exists. If we would communicate with other agencies and work together or at least get out of each other's way, we might be able to accomplish things faster."

Phillips put his head back on the pillow, "Do you think Sanchez is going to be alright?"

"I think he'll be just fine. I think he's itching to see some action."

"I just don't want him to get so gung-ho that he makes a mistake," Phillips said. "Chad took him so he could get a read on him. Psychology major, he's great at reading facial expressions and body language. He can spot a lie even if it's on video."

Brock sat up, "All your guys are specialized aren't they, I mean top of their field."

"Not just guys, we've got women too. Every time I'm going to be working with someone I don't know, the office sends me their background. They do that so you know what the person's expertise is and any quirks they might have. Nobody talks about themselves in this organization, egos don't go very far in this business and egos can get you killed."

"Your friend the vet?"

"Yeah, she's an electronics expert and a hell of a shot."

20

Chad and Sanchez came in carrying bags of burgers, fries, onion rings and large bottles of soda. Sanchez was grinning from ear to ear.

"I gather from the look on Jims' face that he was impressed with your ride." Phillips reached for the bags of fries.

Sanchez tried to control himself, "He has everything in that car. Some stuff I didn't know existed yet."

Chad laughed, "He figured out it wasn't a rental."

They brought in the table from the adjoining room and piled all the food on one of the tables. While Phillips went to get ice, Sanchez got the extra glasses from the other room and checked to be sure the refrigerators were cold, he looked up to see Chad staring at him. "Just being sure we can keep leftovers cold if are any. What can I say, I like late night snacks."

Chad shook his head, "I was just wondering if that would keep ice cream cold."

When Phillips walked back into the room he saw Chad and Sanchez laughing, "What did I miss?"

"Nothing," replied Chad, "Jim and I just found out we have something in common."

Brock grabbed burger, "Do we start the briefing now or after we eat?"

"Don't know why we don't start now, our new friends out there aren't going to sit around forever." Chad reached for a burger and took a bite, "First I need to take care of this."

As he chewed he reached in his jacket pocket, "Jake, here's your new phone. Can't be traced or hacked, it's a new type of satellite phone. Brock do you have an encrypted or SAT phone?"

"I don't have one for the border work, it's not a designated case. If you think I really need one, I'll make a call and get one."

"Don't call, I'll get one for you, I always have extras. I would like to say we don't need them, but I can't. You never know who is listening and if these guys are rigged with personal tracking, who knows what else they have. Jim, I'll also get you one in case you have to make a call for one of us. You really don't need one to call home, but in case of emergency you'll have one."

Sanchez said, "No reason to call home and the boss knows I'm with Brock. I'll turn my personal cell off and just use yours if I need to call any of the guys for more information."

As Chad started to speak again, Sanchez took out his cell and turned it off. Phillips happened to look over at him and notice that he was also removing the sim card.

"I may be going out on a limb here," Chad was saying, "but at this point I don't trust anyone I don't know. Someone authorized those buses and the transfer, we don't know if it came from CBP, DHS or both. Somebody wanted those people moved quickly and I don't think they counted on one kid calling attention to them. From what we've been able to put together, a call came in to make the transfer as McAllen had room for them. The first bus was not full, yet the smaller bus showed anyway and loaded our targets and for some reason Jazmin. Transportation knew two buses were leaving their facility and assumed McAllen was aware, but McAllen transportation was only expecting one bus per a phone call they received. So, who made those calls?"

Chad went on, "We have our people and CIA trying to track the signals from the personal trackers, we hope to get a better idea of the frequency now that they are stationery. We also have Rogelio's photo being circulated to find out who he really is and where he is from."

"Central American countries are not very cooperative, so we have people on the ground. Since he speaks English he either has at least one English speaking parent, he attends a good school or he is tutored. This information really narrows down the areas that have to be canvassed. Cost Rica is more cooperative and they try to keep track of missing children, so that will make it easier on our people there. Of course everyone on the ground needs to be mindful of gangs and smugglers."

Chad picked up one of the files on the table, "This is Wafiq, aka Ignacio. He is only known by that name, we have been watching him for some time and have lots of info, but can't find a last name, we are still looking. He is not a nice guy! He is a murderer, a torturer and he doesn't care about age, gender or religious beliefs. If you are his target or in his way he will kill you and not quickly. He will kill anyone in the way of his payday, I can't stress this enough. The file will give you any background you need, plus there are several photos. Any questions so far?" Chad looked at them, "Good."

"Next we have Ali, aka Jorge," Chad picked up the second file. "Jorge is actually Ali bin Souk, a name he gave himself. He is believed to be Lebanese and a bit of a psychotic. He is their demolitions guy. He is known for precise placement of explosives for maximum effect. Nothing much is known about his background before he became a terrorist, including why he named himself after a market place."

"Excuse me," Sanchez said. "What do you mean by a 'name he took'?"

"Good question. Some of these terrorist have been involved since they were very young, some of them since age six. They could have been orphaned, the older ones could have been disown by their family, runaways or recruits. Whatever the reason, they have been divorced from their family for a long time. Many of them will choose a new name, either the name of a region, town, or even an animal. Sometimes this name will give us an idea of where they came from if we can't actually trace them, there are many aspects of tracing these people, which I will not go into. Many we can't trace, only guess, but we have been known to get lucky."

"This is the file on Yolanda, who is actually Yolanda Alverez. She is a Latina from Tampico, is known to run with the cartel boys and minor gang members. A couple of years ago she fell off the map and was missing for about six months, then just as suddenly she showed up again. Our informant told us she wouldn't tell anyone where she had been, but she had obviously come into a lot of money. She had some face reconstruction done, but the informant told us she still has her birth mark. In case you miss it in the file, it is on her left hip. At this point we are not sure why she is with these people."

Sanchez stood up, slipped his cell in his pocket and excused himself. Phillips noticed the look on his face and how pale he had become. He looked over to see if Brock or Chad had noticed it, then realized that Sanchez was facing away from them.

They took a short break until Sanchez could return from the other room and Chad took the opportunity to go to his room and get the extra phones. Phillips stepped outside and Brock followed him.

"What's up?"

"Nothing," replied Phillips, "Just needed some fresh air and move around a bit."

"That's not exactly the truth," said Brock, "but I can wait until you want to talk. I know that look on your face, something is rattling around up there. Just don't wait too long." Brock turned and walked back into the room at the same time as Sanchez.

"Sorry," said Sanchez, "I think I either ate to fast or something disagreed with me."

"Well, I hope it wasn't the food, this is not the time," replied Brock.

Chad walked through the door, "Hey, you okay? Don't get sick on us now, it'll have to wait." He turned and looked out the door, "Where did Phillips go?"

"I'm here, just enjoying the view of the highway."

Chad closed the door and picked up the last file. "This is Arel Shoukri, aka Maria for this operation. She is well known to us. There are photos of her in the file taken in various places in various disguises. Claims are that she is Egyptian, but we have our doubts. She shares facial ID markers with the children and grandchildren of a terrorist of high rank, sorry, I can't disclose who that is, but we feel that is why she is tolerated by the men and treated as an equal. I might also add that most of the men fear her and keep their distance. She is sly, ruthless and as dangerous as Wafiq. She speaks English, French, German and Italian as well as her native tongue. She is ingenious with disguises, as you will see from the photos, and has a brilliant and quick mind. You will also see in her file that she carry's two knives, one on her thigh and one on her forearm. They are stilettos, very thin and very sharp and she is very quick with them. Be cautious around her, I mean that in every sense. She has also been known to wear a hat pin, this can be a lethal weapon if used correctly. By the way, a hat pin doesn't necessarily go on a hat. In the 1920's through the early 1940's, women traveled by train a lot and if accosted by a male would simply pull out the hat pin and stick their assailant. Believe it or not it was quite a deterrent."

"Be sure and look at all the photos, they can be helpful. I know I don't have to say that, but it is just a reminder. Now, to go over what has been done. As I told Phillips, there are guys monitoring the motel counting heads and taking pictures for identification. They have their orders to watch for Rogelio and keep tabs on him. There are people scouting the refineries in Port Arthur, here in Corpus and we have Brocks' guys and FBI checking the Houston area refineries. A few of our guys are checking the Hartman Bridge and Texas City. Once we get a frequency on the tracking devices we will try to track them individually and put our own devices on the vehicles they are using."

"Brock, the last time I heard CIA has picked up no chatter on any threats or operations here. Would you mind putting in a call and getting an update? Here's the new phone."

"I've tried to cover everything, so if you have any questions or new insight, now's the time."

Sanchez cleared his throat, "So I guess the odd dialect thing we were picking up was Arabic sneaking through their Spanish. What you need to understand is that we noticed this months ago, not just with these people. Remember, I started that code because we were picking up odd behavior and the language thing. If what Jorge said about hundreds being here, he might have been correct in his estimate. To me that means more targets either now or later and we don't have access to those border photos of kids with scars. Also I wouldn't rule out some of them crossing the border in Arizona or New Mexico as mules."

Phillips stood up, "I haven't heard from that translator in McAllen. I'll call her and see what she has found out and put her mind at ease by letting her know that others have noticed the same thing. I'll also find out how long ago she noticed. I think that once we get a frequency on the devices we might be able to find the others, unless there actually are hundreds of them. Someone is watching their movements, but for how long is another question."

"It's a shame that guy with the drones doesn't have a million of them," Brock said. "If he did we could comb the country looking for static." He stood up and started pacing, "Static! Do you know how much static is out there? If this threat is viable, I don't see a way of finding all these people. We need to stay with what we have, follow these guys, bring them down and proceed from there. I'll call Langley get the info Chad requested, fill them in on what we've come up with and let them handle it. What a mess and all because of idiot politicians."

"It could be worse." All eyes turned to Sanchez. "I'm just thinking out loud."

"What do you mean 'could be worse'?" asked Brock.

"Well, if these guys had decided to enter the U.S. using the human trafficking routes, we'd never know about it."

"Wait, if you know about these routes then most of them must be under surveillance," said Brock.

"It's not that easy," Sanchez hung his head. "When they discover a route and start cracking down, these guys just find another one. Sometimes it's just a few guys bringing them across on foot through the desert to a pick up point, then you also have the water route." He ran his hand through his hair, "It's like the Ho Chi Minh Trail, no matter how many times you hit it, it just moves. It gives me a headache thinking about it. Since these guys were obviously in a hurry to get across and do it undetected, I don't think we need to worry about the trafficking route. They know the border routine and they had the transportation taken care of in advance. Trafficking is a slower process with longer routes. This was easier for them because they could control the situation better, the other route depends on too many people and conditions."

"I think the key words here are 'control the situation'," sighed Brock. "Whoever put this together has enough pull and control to authorize and cover up personnel and vehicles.

21

Brock took his phone into the other room to call Langley, Chad had given Sanchez his secure phone and was going over usage and emergency keys. They were all tired and frustrated.

Phillips decided this was a good time to call Amelia, then call Julie and maybe when Chad was finished he would get a chance to talk to him alone.

Amelia picked up on the second ring.

"Hello, this is Dr. Phillips. Do you remember me?"

"Yes, I do. I'm glad you called," she replied.

As soon as he heard her voice he remembered how statuesque and lovely she was. The cascade of dark hair, those deep brown eyes and a smile to melt even the hardest heart.

"I hate to bother you, but did you have a chance to talk to anyone else about what we discussed?"

"Yes, I finally put my worries behind me and did some investigating and it turns out that almost everyone had noticed and, like me, they thought they were losing it."

"One of the reasons I'm calling is to let you know that several of the border patrol agents had noticed it too. Do you or any of the others remember when it was first noticed?"

"I remember that I first noticed it when I arrived here, almost right away actually. One of the others noticed it about three months ago and a lady who has worked this part of the border for a few years, said she noticed it about six months ago. She thought her hearing was going because she only heard it once in a while, then about four months ago she was hearing it more often. She was going to have her hearing checked when she overheard two young men talking and realized they were speaking Arabic."

"Is she sure it was Arabic, that it couldn't have been something else?"

"Yes she is positive. She worked in the Middle East for a few years translating for the oil companies."

"Did she report it?"

"Yes, she wrote it up and kept a copy of the report. She said she always writes up the reports instead of doing it verbally, that way she has proof she did it. She never heard back from anyone except for a written acknowledgement."

"One more thing. Would you keep a list of anyone who comes through there with a questionable dialect? Nothing formal, just the name and any visible scars or discolorations."

"Dr. Phillips, you have me intrigued. Is there anything I should be worried about as far as my health?"

"No, nothing like that, just spy verses spy," he laughed.

"Maybe that should be spies verses spy since there are so many of them and only one of you," she laughed softly. "Tell you what, I'll even have the others keep a list, it will break the monotony."

"You only need to do it for a few days. It will give me an idea of how many OTM's we're getting. I worry about their immune systems not adapting. I really appreciate this and when I get back there I'll take you to dinner."

"You've got a deal. Sounds like they put you on rotation, trust me that's better for you. The people coming across can really get to you."

"Thanks again and I'll talk to you soon."

He ended the call and whispered to himself, 'crap'. Then he called Julie.

Talk about your opposites, Phillips thought, where Amelia was tall and stately Julie was average height with what he thought of as a cute figure, rather athletic looking. She had dark brown hair, but in the sun or bright light it looked more auburn and she wore it shoulder length. Her eyes were a blue-green and changed from one color to the other depending on what she was wearing. He remembered the first few times he saw her it kind of threw him, he knew he had seen blue eyes, but the next day they looked more green than blue. When he finally mentioned it to her she had said it was her inexpensive way of accessorizing. He mentally slapped himself as he dialed the phone, this was not time to get involved.

Julies' phone went to voice mail so he left a message saying that it looked like he would be gone for a few weeks. He would try and have someone come by to pick up his car and they might want to look for a replacement. He left the number of his other phone for her to call if necessary. When he hung up he felt a little disappointed.

Brock came back into the room and saw Phillips staring at his phone.

"What's up? You look as frustrated as I feel."

"The translator, Amelia, has confirmed what Sanchez told us. They noticed the dialect thing as far back as six months ago, one of the other translators recognized it as Arabic. Anyway, I have her making a list of any new people who come through that have the dialect or any scars, she said she would ask the others to do the same. I told her it was a health issue only for those coming across, strictly a doctor thing and nothing to worry about."

Brock sat on the other bed, "I told Langley what we heard about that and filled them in on everything. They said they would handle it and inform the Feds, I hope they do what they say because it doesn't sound like a good situation."

"They still haven't heard any chatter and I don't think they will. There's no reason for it, this operation, if you can call it that, is compartmentalized. It's as if everything was set up before it started. Like the mind games we played at school, we decided what we were going to do and never discussed the plan again, we just did it."

"Yeah, I've been thinking along the same lines," Phillips said. "These guys are taking their time, I think they are waiting for everything to be in place. All the players have to be ready if, and that's a big if, they are using more people than what we have here. They also need their equipment to be delivered or dropped off at a pick up point. You're right about the chatter, if someone is tracking them there is no reason to make contact with anyone and whoever is doing the tracking doesn't need to report to anyone else unless something goes wrong. I do know one thing, we need to get some sleep while we can, even if it's just for a few hours."

Brock looked at Chad and Sanchez on the other side of the room.

"Yeah once we start moving sleep will be a nap on the road in the back seat of the car. Maybe."

Phillips watched Brock stare across the room. "Something's bothering you."

"Nah, I'll talk to you about it later, I need to sort through some things. No information in one area too much in another," Brock walked over to Chad.

"What do you think about getting some sleep?"

Chad stood and stretched, "I'm in completed agreement. I'm going back to the room and call my guys and see how they're doing, if they have any news of consequence I'll let you guys know. See you in a few hours."

Brock locked the door behind Chad and opened his bag, "I need a shower and clean clothes. I'm going to hang my stuff on the shower rod, maybe it will freshen things up a bit. You have anything you want to hang in there?"

Sanchez looked over at him. "At least you have a change of clothes, this is all I have. After I shower I'll try your method, if that doesn't work maybe we can grab a can of air freshener from the housekeeping room and spray each other down."

"Hold on," Phillips stood up. "Before we do this let's go over and see the motel where these guys are staying." He already had his phone to his ear.

"Chad, are you still dressed? I want to take a ride over to that motel, I need to see it. Okay, we'll be outside."

"Chad will be down in a minute, we'll take his car." Phillips picked up his jacket and gun and turned up the sound on the TV.

"What are you thinking?" Brock asked.

"I'll explain in the car, Sanchez be sure your door is still locked and turn up your TV."

As they drove over to meet the surveillance team Phillips explained that he needed to see the SUV and the layout of the motel.

"I'm not planning a rescue mission, I just need to see what kind of taste these guys have. By that I mean are they high profile or low and telling me doesn't let me actually lay eyes on it. I get a better sense if I see it myself, plus I might get an idea on which room they have the kid in, unless you already know."

"I don't think anyone who is watching knows," replied Chad. "The team has only seen two of the occupants and that is when they go out to pick up food. Three rooms and just two faces for anyone to identify, pretty good planning in my book. I bet those two guys are also the ones who got the rooms."

They pulled up behind a beat up Taurus as the passenger side door opened. The team member walked over to Chads side as he powered the window down.

"Who's coming with me? If it's all of you, keep the noise down." Chad did not introduce him or anyone in his car.

They all walked into a small apartment building and up to the second floor. The apartment was small, clean, well decorated and on the back side of the building. The two windows in the back looked directly at the motel room doors with an unobstructed view. The motel itself was well taken care of and looked to be in a mid-level price range. The parking lot was not full, but it had enough cars in it to show the motel was probably half full with one vehicle being a white panel van, another a small rental truck, the rest were cars and SUV's.

The other team member was watching from one of the windows and did not turn around or speak to them. The one who had brought them upstairs handed Chad a pair of binoculars.

"The rooms we are watching are the third from the right, the second door from that one and third one is second door from that one. We checked with the motel and the doors in between are adjoining the occupied rooms. So these guys are spread out, probably because of their extra passengers. The bathroom windows are too small for anyone to crawl through, except maybe the seven year old. We have not seen any weapons go in or out, but that doesn't mean they don't have them. They could have taken weapons in before we got eyes on them. No one has gone near those rooms except for the two guys I told you about. When they go out for a food run they always take the same vehicle, the SUV in front of the room on the far right. If they communicate with the other rooms it must be by phone because the only time they go to the other rooms is to deliver the food, but they never go inside."

"The panel van and rental truck showed up separately about 2 hours ago and they are in the rooms on the left end. If they are associated with these guys, we have no confirmation. We have photos of the two gophers, but no ID on them as yet. We could not get photos of the people from the van or truck as their backs were to us, but we did a check on the plates that went nowhere, everything is a rental. When they come out again we'll get them on film. The other SUV showed up a while ago and the driver went into one of the suspect rooms. No facial on him, we only saw his back. He's about five feet ten, dark hair."

"The guys watching from the back side of the motel have seen nothing but lights in the bathroom and the windows are slightly opened."

"Do you think there is any way to get a device on the SUV's and have they noticed the paint on top of the one SUV?" Phillips asked.

"If you get us the devices, we can get them attached in about three seconds. So, yeah, it can be done. They haven't given any indication that they noticed the paint, at least not since we've been here. I know the rental car people will not be happy about it."

Phillips ran his hand through his hair, "I wish there was some way I could let the kid know that we're here, that we got his message."

"You know you can't do that," Brock said. "If the kid knows, then he loses the fear factor and these guys will pick up on it."

"I know, I know. It would just be for my own peace of mind." Phillips turned to the team, "When these guys make their move to leave, we'll be following them. What I need you guys to do, after they leave, is get into those rooms and see if the kid left another message. It could be anything and hidden in the easiest place for him to get to and it could be written in mustard. Don't skip any nook, cranny or trash can."

"Roger that, think like a kid."

When they got back inside their car Brock said, "They must feel confident, otherwise they wouldn't be that deep in the motel with no rear exit."

"That," added Sanchez, "or they know we're watching and feel confident that we won't hit them."

22

Phillips rolled over, moaned and opened his eyes, he looked at the bedside clock that said 6:15am. He rolled over in the other direction and saw Brock looking at him with one eye open.

"How long have you been awake and did you start the coffee?" Phillips asked.

"I've had one eye open for about ten minutes, the other one is still asleep. I fixed the coffee pot last night, but have yet to plug it in, feel free to do the honors."

Phillips plugged in the coffee, went into the bathroom and when he came out fell across the bed, "I'm just going to be here long enough for coffee to get ready, then I'll get dressed. I think I got too much sleep last night, things started running around in my head, I didn't think I'd sleep and the next thing I know it's morning. Guess I was wrong. Is your other eye awake yet?"

"It doesn't want to wake up. Anyway I don't need it, I can crack this case with one eye. Ahh.., there it goes. Jeez, I haven't done that since Harvard, it must be the company. I'll get the coffee on my way back, just stay where you are I need to talk to you."

Phillips fluffed his pillows, sat up against the headboard and used the remote to click on the TV. He mentally reran the events of the previous day and knew what Brock wanted to talk about, but he would wait for him to bring it up. He thought back to the all night study session he and Brock used to have. After their second year Brock would wake up and one eye would refused to open, it didn't happen all the time only about once a week. It cracked them up every time it happened and they would roll around laughing until their sides hurt.

As Brock came out of the bathroom Phillips said, "You know, if we had been older when your eye got a mind of its own, we would have worried about it. Probably would have been at the infirmary every couple of weeks."

Brock poured the coffee, "I know, when I finally told my mom about it all the color drained from her face and then she broke down laughing. So much for overprotection, not in my house." He did a visual check of the connecting door and put their coffee on the nightstand as he sat on the bed.

"I've got two things on my mind and while no one else is around here's the first one, I need to ask you about Sanchez. Last night when we were going over the files I saw Sanchez freeze when Chad mentioned the birthmark on Yolanda, he appeared to be holding his breath. I don't know what it means, but I hope he tells us about whatever it is on his own."

"I noticed it, but I didn't think you or Chad did. He was white as a sheet when he went into the other room and he took his phone with him. I was going to talk to Chad yesterday about it, but didn't have the opportunity. I'll talk to him after I get dressed and have him run a deep check. What's the other thing?"

Brock took another sip of coffee and reached for this pants, "Have you given any thought to our players? We have some nasty people here who are obviously terrorists, I don't think they are looking for sanctuary," he said sarcastically. "Then you have a female Mexican National, who doesn't fit unless she is representing a cartel and a young boy who has got to be a hostage. If there are more of them who have crossed the border, I don't think they are of the same caliber and I'm betting they are here to cause diversions. I know, I have nothing to back it up so don't remind me. Maybe all this sitting around and contemplating is causing my mind to work overtime."

"I understand what you're saying," replied Phillips, "and I've given it some thought, but I think they are here to screw up the infrastructure. It won't take much to do that, the government is pretty much doing it on their own. Hell, if the bad guys would wait another three years they can walk in here and take over without a shot fired. If a small fire at a major airport can shut down thousands of flights, you can imagine what a few well-placed explosives could do. If they could pull it off undetected and disappear into the population, we would have a hell of a time finding them. Then they would be free to do it again. Only problem for them this time is we know who they are and they don't know it. If we confront them and can't stop them, they will have to leave the country, if we can stop them then they're dead. I only hope we can save Rogelio."

Phillips started getting dressed and grabbed his phone, "I'm going to call Chad and meet with him in his room. I want him to start that deep check."

Phillips brushed his teeth and washed up while Brock poured another cup of coffee and knocked on the connecting door. As Phillips walked passed him he gave him a thumbs up.

Phillips knocked on Chads door, found him talking on the phone and was given the one minute sign. After Chad hung up a smile spread across his face and he motioned Phillips to sit.

"I haven't seen you smile like that in a long time," Phillips said.

"A lot to smile about. I got more sleep than I thought and we have our tracking devices. The guys should have them within the hour, I just hope we get them in time. I hoped we would get them during dark hours, it makes it easier to place them. These guys are good at diversions, so they'll get them placed, no problem as long as they have a vehicle to put them on. Once our guys have the devices in place, we'll go over there and get the receivers. What's up with you?"

"Last night when we were going over the files, Brock and I noticed that Sanchez had an odd reaction to the info on Yolanda. I wanted to ask you to do a deep check on him in case there is something we need to know about. I was going to talk to you last night, but didn't have an opening."

"Yeah, I noticed it, I didn't realize you had seen it, should have known better. My first thought was old girlfriend, but she's on the wrong side of the border and the law."

Chad walked over and turned on the TV before continuing. "I already started the check on him, I made the call last night when I got back. For what it's worth I don't think Sanchez is one of the bad guys, I think he's on our side. I'm worried about who he reports to and if that person is on our side."

"I know," Phillips walked over and turned up the sound on the TV. "If he has blind trust in his superiors it could be a problem. These border guys don't blame their superiors for them being handcuffed in their job, they blame Washington."

The breaking news alert on the television caught their attention. There had been a seventeen car pile-up on the highway outside Phoenix, four dead and several injured. A reporter at the site was interviewing a witness who was holding a towel to his head. As the man spoke the camera panned to a white panel van and an SUV that had rolled, one was upside down the other on its side. The cameraman was trying to focus on some of the victims and caught two young men looking at the SUV. He zoomed in just as one of them turned toward the camera. Phillips and Chad didn't need to lean toward the screen to see it, there on the guys' arm was the scar.

Phillips already had his phone to his ear as he charged out the door and ran toward his room colliding with Brock as he rounded a corner.

"You saw it"

"Yeah, we saw it. Where's Sanchez?" asked Phillips.

"Holding down the fort. I had gone into his room to check out the news with him when the report came on. Boy, you had to be blind not to see the scar."

"I need to make a call, hold on."

Phillips finished his call and turned to Brock, "Sorry, I needed to get guys on site in Phoenix. Chad is also making a call and he'll be down when he's finished." They continued walking to the room. "Chad noticed the reaction from Sanchez and made a call last night, so we'll know soon if there is a problem."

"That was a short call you made, very short," Brock said. "I have to ask, how do you get guys anything done with a ten second phone call? I made my call and got transferred twice."

"That one I can answer. I give only the necessary info and a code for what I need, the center takes care of the rest. I couldn't make too many calls before we got here, especially since Sanchez may have overheard one of them. Chad took care of setting things up here until we arrived."

They got back to the room and found Sanchez where Brock had left him, in front of the news. The media was still at the crash site and Sanchez wasn't just watching the coverage he was taking notes. He looked up when they came in, "Did you and Chad see this?"

Phillips nodded, "I called for guys on the ground to cover it, if they aren't already there. What's with the notes?"

"Oh, these. I'm watching the background and taking notes on vehicles, debris, people and plate numbers when I can get them. I don't have a lot, I figured maybe the guy with the scar wasn't alone and I might see who else was with him. I was really interested in the panel van and what was inside. It's a long shot to look at all of this, but you never know. Like the van that flipped, I know there are no people inside, but every time the camera pans over there our scar guy and one other guy are pacing near it and I saw scar guy go over to the SUV twice." Sanchez never took his eyes off the screen while he was explaining his surveillance. "I started doing this about two years ago as an observation game."

Brocks' phone rang as Chad entered the room. He hung up from the short call, "Okay, my guys say the van and SUV are going to be impounded along with two other vehicles. They didn't mention the drivers, any passengers or the reason for impounding. The local cops are cooperating with the Feds and the Feds will be going over the vehicles. That's it. So right now we still know nothing." He turn to Phillips, "I take it your guys had something to do with the impounding."

"I thought it would help the agencies involved if they had a look at the interiors."

Sanchez stood up and stretched, "The traffic is probably backed up all the way to LA by now since this thing blocked both sides of I-10 and where it's located there is no way around it."

Suddenly there was excitement on the screen and the reporter was yelling, "Get back! Get back!" Then to the camera he said, "The white van has suddenly caught fire and the officials here are trying to move people away from the area so the fire truck can get through. The driver of the van has not been located and first responders say there was no one in the van when they arrived. We, here on the ground, thought that everyone was accounted for and had been spoken to by the Highway Patrol and checked out by paramedics. We are now fearful that the driver might have gone back into the van after personal items." While the reporter spoke the cameraman was holding the zoomed in picture of the van as they walked further away. The SUV had just entered the frame when the van exploded in a huge ball of flame and black smoke laced with white tendrils.

The blast threw the cameraman to the ground, but the camera frame remained sideways on the van. The reporter was coughing and trying to get his voice under control as he asked if the cameraman was okay. The reporter could be heard saying, "Stay on the van, stay on the van."

"As you can tell," the reporter coughed, "There has been a huge explosion and fiery debris has been thrown everywhere. We are moving further away as the smoke is very thick and acrid." At that point another explosion rocked the van.

"Are you still on the van?" the reporter asked. "This is horrific! Two people have been hit by some of the debris and the paramedics are attempting to get them to the ambulance."

The camera turned to show the reporter. He was covered in dirt, his clothes were torn and he was standing with one shoulder lower than the other. His face was scratched, a gash on the side of his head was oozing blood, the sleeve of his shirt was torn and blood was visible below the tear. He turned to point at the SUV and the picture caught the back of his shirt, which was also torn and bloodied.

"The SUV that was near the van is now ablaze as well as the surrounding brush and grass. The falling hot debris has more than likely caused the smaller fires. If gas was leaking from the other vehicle if may also have been ignited by debris.

I don't know what was in that van, but if it was that volatile it should not have been in a van rolling down our highways at seventy miles per hour."

As the four men watched the TV screen, Phillips dialed his phone again. At the same moment he spoke, the SUVs' gas tanks exploded. Phillips walked out of the room.

"Well that was convenient," said Brock. "A bit too convenient to my way of thinking. Do these guys think we can't figure out what's going on or what they used to blow it up? I hope they can bring these guys in for a chat, it could prove interesting, but I have a feeling that they've fled the scene."

He walked to the connecting door, "I think we should pack up and as soon as we get word that the receivers are here, we need to go over to the surveillance site. I don't know if this will speed up their timetable, but I want to be closer. We need to see which SUV Rogelio gets into, I know it will make Phillips feel better and we know Wafiq is going to be with the kid. Sanchez, stay on the news report and your notes in case something else happens."

Brock and Chad had finished stacking the cases near the door when Phillips walked back into the room and motioned for them to follow him into the other room.

"Here's what we've got," Phillips said as he sat at the table. "Some asshole in a Vette caused the accident, he's deceased and his car is in a million pieces spread across I-10. Our guys in Phoenix were already on site when I called, they assessed the situation and called in the Feds and mixed in with them, so the info I have is the same as what the Feds have up to this point."

"I won't go into the particulars of the accident, but it's bad. One of the fatalities happens to have the scar we've been seeing. The ME has been asked to excise the area of the scar and turn over whatever he finds to the Fed who is accompanying the body. One of our people who is an expert on such devices will work with the Federal expert so that we will have firsthand knowledge. Photos will be taken during the process of recovering the device. At least we'll know what type of device we're dealing with, but it may take a while to get the results. I doubt they will have anything for us to use on this operation, so we will just go ahead with how we are handling it"

"Sanchez, did you keep those notes you were taking?"

Sanchez reached in the pocket of his windbreaker and took them out. "Yes, they're all here. I also wrote down the time the report started, the time of the first explosion and the time the SUV went up. It seemed to me that it took a long time after the rollover for that van to catch fire."

"Good, we may need to go over them again. All three agencies will be getting a video copy of that report from the TV station and they are checking to see if the other stations had people out there and if the helicopters were filming. I'm saying three agencies as the CIA is being called in because of the possibility of foreign operatives. It seems that one of our scar guys was heard by several people to be stomping around the SUV and yelling in what sounded like Arabic. One of those who heard him is a veteran who served in the Middle East and he said the guy was blaming the white infidels for the accident and using a string of expletives that would make his father blush. So Ed, it looks like you're the lead for the CIA. If we can get buttoned up and out of here, we might be able to avoid the Feds joining us."

"They've got the boys in the white jumpsuit bagging what's left of the van and SUV and all of it will be transported to the lab in Phoenix. They are also keeping the local PD and Highway Patrol involved since they come in contact with more people. My understanding is that once they get what they can off the vehicles, reports will be sent out to law enforcement nationwide. As you know it takes days for them to get anything done, so we may have this wrapped up by then. We can only hope."

"The people from the SUV and van cannot be located. So now I'm wondering if all the pacing Sanchez noted was them waiting for ride out of there. Now for your joke of the day, the Feds want to keep this out of the news."

"Oh brother," laughed Sanchez. "Everyone who thinks of themselves as an expert, every G-man wannabe and conspiracy theorist is going to jump all over this if they saw the broadcast. The film is probably already on the internet."

"By the way, the reporter and cameraman are at the hospital," Phillips added. The reporter, as you saw, has a big gash on his head, he also had a chunk of metal in his arm from the blast, the blood on his back was from another gash, but no metal in it. The cameraman has a deep gash on his head, facial lacerations and a separated shoulder. I hope that station gives them a raise, they evidently look like they were in a combat zone. They did one hell of a job."

Brock picked up some of the cases and started for the door. "Let's get this stuff loaded up and get out of here. Don't know about you guys, but I have no desire to have a Fed join us, too much red tape."

Chad said, "I'm already loaded up and I called the team to tell them we were coming over. I'm keeping my rooms here, if we don't use them the surveillance team will. I'll go get my car and we'll head over to the apartment. When we get there we'll have to stagger our entry so we don't arouse any suspicion. Sanchez and I will go in first, wait ten minutes and the follow us in."

Sanchez and Brock looked at Phillips. Sanchez asked, "Rooms?"

Phillips chuckled, "Yeah, rooms. Chad likes his space."

23

By the time Brock and Phillips got to the second floor apartment, Chad and Sanchez had made themselves comfortable about two feet from one of the windows. Chad got up and walked over to them.

"They're getting ready to place the devices," Chad said. "Since they have to do this in broad daylight they came up with a plan and it only takes one of them, which leaves the other one to look for any trouble. They hired a woman and her son, actually it's one of the landlords' daughters and her son. This should be interesting if he doesn't get himself shot. We're waiting for them to show up in the parking lot, so find a spot not to close to the windows."

As they watched a woman and a man carrying a child with a baseball glove, walked into the motel parking lot. The couple walked to the end of the parking lot close to where the SUVs were parked and the man put the boy down, took the glove, walked away then turned to face the little boy and his mother. He rolled the ball to the boy and he would chase it down and roll it back. Once the boy was stopping the ball before it rolled away, the man started throwing the ball underhand so it would bounce before it reached the boy and his mother. A few times the mother had to catch the ball before it got too far away. A few of these throws ,a lot of squealing and laughter, and the boy tried to throw it back, it took several tries before he was finally getting the ball to his target. Now each time the man threw the ball he would move a little further away from the boy.

As the man stood from picking up the ball, he saw the curtain in one of the rooms move, he now knew they were being watched so he moved one step closer to the boy. This time when he boy threw the ball it went way right and the man had to chase it down. As the game of catch proceeded, the boy would sometimes throw to the right, other times to the left, one time the man had to crawl under a dumpster. As the man chased down the ball again he noticed the curtain in the room drop back down, they had lost interest. Before he threw the ball this time he gave the woman and the boy a nod and when the boy threw the ball back it went under one of the SUVs, the man got down on the ground and went under it to retrieve the ball. The game continued and the man had to crawl under the SUVs several times after the ball.

Soon the little boy grew tired and they left the parking lot with the man again carrying the child.

Sanchez turned from the window, "That was brilliant. Do you think it worked?"

"If they come out and check under their vehicles, then no," Chad laughed.

The other team member came in and tossed his baseball glove over by his briefcase. "That was fun, but my clothes are ruined."

Phillips patted the man on the shoulder, "That was great. How did you guys come up with that?"

"I don't know, it just popped into my head. I did get everything in place where they won't find it, but we have a problem."

"Let me guess, now you have to take her out to dinner," Chad said.

"No, worse. There are tracking devices already on the vehicles, all three of them."

Phillips turned around so fast he almost lost his balance, "They're already being tracked?"

"Yep, I saw the first one, then when I went under the other vehicles I checked and they had them too. They're not ours, so no problem there. I got pictures of them, that's why I went under them so many times. I transmitted them on my way back here, maybe our people can identify them."

"Can I take a look at them?" Brock asked as he held out his hand. He looked at the pictures, "They don't look like anything we use. Thanks," he said handing the camera back, "I just wanted to rule out our agency, you never know."

"It was a good thing you found a kid that wanted to play catch," said Sanchez, "but throwing under those cars was lucky."

"Not really, the kid already plays ball, he's older than he looks and before we went out we worked out a code for everything. The step forward and the nods were all planned, I asked him to act like a little kid who had never played ball. He did a really good job of imitating his little cousin, who by the way, he has been teaching to play."

Phillips walked over to the window, "Any movement?"

"No, nothing yet, but they may wait if they suspect anything. I would if I thought I was being watched. Your receivers are on the table, one for each vehicle. The logistics are terrible since we don't know which of the other two cars are going out of town. The receivers are marked 1, 2 and 3, 1 being your vehicle with the paint on it, the other two receivers will be monitored and the one headed out of town will be given to your two guys headed for Port Arthur. The Port Arthur guys and the Corpus Christi guys are staying together right down the street, so we can hand off the receivers at the same time with very little time lost. We didn't bother with the van or the rental truck because if they are connected to this they will be staying close to the other vehicles. We checked the receivers to be sure they were working, but now that the devices are attached, you might want to check them again."

"How many times have you guys had people under surveillance that once they got together, take this much time to move?" asked Brock. "A rough estimate will work."

"If it's a male and female team," the agent replied, "sometimes a week, no need to tell you why. Male teams will meet several times, but when they finally get in one place they usually move in two days or less. Here you're dealing with a whole different ball game, excuse the reference, I don't think these guys are in a hurry, I get the impression they're waiting for someone to give them the go ahead. This is not an independent operation, they're secretive, keeping a low profile as it were. If you served in Afghanistan or Iraq you'll know what I'm talking about when I say they think they have all the time in the world, Inshallah, it will be done."

Brock shoved his hands in his pockets, "So you think these guys are Middle Eastern?"

"From the photos I've seen, except for the two Mexicans, I think so. As for the drivers I can't say until they come out and we can get photos. The two guys who go and get the food I would say are American or European."

"Hey," the team member at the window said, "We have movement, turn on the receivers. One guy coming out of the door, I'm getting his picture now."

Chad headed for the door as Phillips monitored the receivers.

"It's not going to be our car, so let me see where he's going, can't be too far," said Chad.

"I'll go with you," said the other surveillance agent.

"This one shows movement," Phillips said as he tossed the receiver to Chad. "I'll call you if anyone else starts to move."

When they were out the door Phillips moved toward the window, "Can I take a look at the photo?"

The agent handed him the digital camera. "I got several so there should be at least one good one. He doesn't look American to me."

Phillips went through the photos as Brock looked over his shoulder, "I don't recognize him and don't know why I thought I would. Wishful thinking I guess. How about you Ed?"

"He looks vaguely familiar in the sense of somebody you walk past more than once, but I don't know who he is."

From across the room Sanchez asked, "May I see them?"

"Sure," Phillips said walking over and handing him the camera.

Sanchez started looking at the pictures then went through them again slowly, scrutinizing each picture.

"It's Addison," he said looking at Phillips. "At least it's the man calling himself Addison."

"Well, we knew he was with them at one point and now we know he's still around. Maybe we can get his real name."

Sanchez continued to study the pictures, "I've seen this guy somewhere, I mean before I saw him at the facility. I didn't notice before because we were walking over to do the interviews and we were side by side. I had enough for a sketch, but not enough for a good ID. Wish I could figure out where I've seen him, that day at the facility was only the second time I had seen him there."

Phillips took the camera back over to the agent at the window, "I hope we can get photos of the other guys, I'd like to know who else we're dealing with."

The door to a room near the other end of the motel opened. A man carrying a suitcase and a woman with a baby came out of the room. He opened the car door for her and put the suitcase in the trunk as she put the baby in the backseat. He walked back into the room and came out with a small crib and another small case. She got into the car on the driver's side and he walked over and got in the rental truck.

Phillips said, "I don't think they are connected to this, but did you get pictures?"

"Yep, and you never can tell. People do strange things for money."

Brock sat near the window again, "This is a nice apartment. How did you talk the occupants into letting you use it? Our guys and the Feds are known for muscling their way in."

"We got lucky, to be honest. When we got over here and saw how perfect the building was placed for our needs, we talked to the landlord and asked him if he had an apartment with windows that looked at the motel parking lot. He had his place, but it was ground floor so not a good angle. There are two on the third floor, but we figured they would be up to high, so we asked to look at the ones on the second floor. This one was perfect because it gives us a slight angle, even if they pull up closer to the door to shield who is getting in the SUV, we can still see them. Not as well as we'd like, but we can count heads and get our photos. One of the doors would be blocked from view, it's to the adjoining room, so we're rolling the dice on that one. Anyway, the person who lives here is the landlords other daughter, so we figured she either doesn't pay rent or its less than anyone else would pay. We offered her a thousand cash and told her we would probably need it for a week. By the look on her face I knew she wasn't going to quibble over the price. Usually people try and hold out for more money, kinda makes me mad when they do that. I mean, it's free money, we keep the place clean and bring our own food. Hell, we even wash the linens before we leave. Sorry, politics and surveillance are two things you don't want to get me started on."

"What about religion?" Brock asked.

"Don't care if you have one or not. It's like ex-wives, none of my business."

Phillips asked, "Do you guys want a night off? We've got motel rooms you can use and two of us will stand in for you."

"Thanks for the offer, but once you start something like this, you settle into it and if you leave for very long it feels like you have to start all over when you get back."

"Amen!" Brock and Sanchez said in unison.

A few minutes later Chad and the other agent returned.

"It might have been worth the trip," Chad said. "The guy went to a pay phone, at a liquor store and stopped and got an arm load of fast food. I got the number of the phone and called it in, they'll try and find out who this guy called. It might lead to something. Let's go back to the motel, the Feds won't look for you in my rooms, they don't know I'm here. We'll leave the big stuff in my SUV. Now, let's go eat."

They returned to Chads' motel rooms after a lite lunch and dropping food off for the guys doing surveillance. Phillips had insisted on picking up food for the two men and putting it on this expense account, he felt he owed them something after the job they had done that morning. They put Sanchez in the room

118

adjoining Chad, Phillips and Brock took the room on the other side of Chad. The three man had calls to make, Sanchez wanted to go over his notes on the accident and write up an outline of his interactions with Rogelio and Addison to see if he was missing anything. Sanchez didn't say anything to the others, but he had a lot of thinking to do.

24

Jim Sanchez was in turmoil over what to do, what was the right thing to do. The text message wasn't what he had expected. Lately nothing had been as he expected.

At the briefing, when Chad was talking about the girl Yolanda and the facial reconstruction he thought of her as just another suspect. When Chad mentioned the birthmark he knew who it was, he almost became physically ill and couldn't get out of the room fast enough. All he could think to do was to make the call and wait for a message, those were his orders. Well, now he had his answer, but not the one he wanted.

He knew Phillips had noticed his reaction, they probably all had and that meant they would dig deeper, which is the one thing the people at the top didn't want. He was not supposed to question the higher ups or their decisions, but in this case he did. He couldn't understand the secrecy, this concerned the safety of the border and the people it was supposed to protect. The average person should know what to watch for when there was a threat and how to protect themselves from it. If he withheld what he knew and how he knew Yolanda he might be hurting the case and therefore the people he tried to protect. At this thought he made up his mind, he would tell them. The message read 'Not necessary', but as far has he was concerned it was very necessary.

A little over two years ago a pair of border agents were tracking down a small group of illegals north of Laredo, they thought they were probably mules. The agents had left their vehicle and were following a dry stream bed, one walking in the depression the other along the edge. As they came up to a stand of mesquite trees three men with guns stepped out in front of them, they wore desert camo with camo ski masks and carried AK-47s as well as side arms and knives. The man in the center of the group stepped forward and spoke to them with only a slight accent. He told them they could go no further, that they had to go back, that they had seen nothing and the next time they would disappear. He told them to nod if they understood their new orders. The two agents nodded and started walking backwards the way they had come. When they had walk about fifty yards the men stepped back behind the trees.

The incident was reported, but two weeks later two agents south of Laredo were pistol whipped as another warning. Both incidents were spread by word of mouth, it took another month before a bulletin was sent out. Agents had to devise new ways of tracking and sometimes setting traps for illegals, from standing on the tops of their vehicles with binoculars to waiting at both ends of known trails in order to get the job done. No one knew what was coming across the border that needed that kind of security and it was making all of them nervous.

Word came down that a special unit was being put together, an undercover unit that would cross the border and attempt to find out what was being smuggled, why the high security and who was behind it. It would be put together with border patrol volunteers who had the right skills and if the Mexican Government found out they were there, the U.S. Border Patrol would disavow any knowledge of their actions. If they were killed or captured there was nothing that could be done, they were on their own. The men that were chosen were of Hispanic heritage or Hispanic looking and were fluent in Spanish. They were ready to move in one week and the only briefing they had lasted less than an hour. Their objective was confirmed, they were told not to engage in violence of any kind and they were to keep a low profile as men looking for work and a way across the border. They were given official, yet rudimentary, documents showing they were citizens of Mexico and given enough money to last thirty days. There was no pep talk, their supervisor only shook the hand of each man and told them to be safe. Jim Sanchez was one of these men.

The four men, two from his unit, Sanchez and Bob Frank and two from Brownsville/Matamoros, were slipped across the border north of Zapata, Texas and began to make their way up to Nuevo Laredo. They met up at a predetermined point with two border agents from El Paso, there were no agents from Laredo as they might be recognized. They found a dormitory type room in a seedy building that the locals called a hotel, it was crowded for the six men, but they were men without much money seeking a job. The inside of the room had six cot style beds, two small three drawer dressers, two straight back wooden chairs and as much dirt and dust as the streets outside, but everywhere they would go for the next few weeks would be the same.

The first two days the six men familiarize themselves with the area, being sure that they spoke to the shopkeepers and bartenders. They moved around the area as a group of friends, making it known that they were all looking for work, any kind of work. They made small talk, asked general questions, laughed and joked with the people they met. The evening of the second day they split up into teams of two and went in three different directions, Sanchez and Bob Frank wandered through the market. While looking at the fruits and vegetables they again inquired about jobs, twice they asked about possible ways to get across the border and worked their way to one of the popular cantinas. They started up conversations, found the men easy to talk to and got advice from many of them on finding a job, but none of them spoke of smuggling or border crossing. On the third day Sanchez went to the market alone and was approached by a beautiful young girl who looked to be fifteen years old, she was trying to sell him some freshly cut flowers. He told her no thank you, but she continued to pester him. He rounded a corner and went into a cantina thinking she would stay outside and eventually find someone else to bother. He sat down at a small table and ordered a beer, suddenly she sat down across from him. He again told her he did not want flowers, she told him that she wasn't there to sell him flowers.

She smiled and said, "My name is Yolanda and I am here to offer you and your friends a job and a way across the border."

She was there to recruit him and his friends. She explained that her friends could get them across the border for free, all they had to do was take a package with them, if they decided to come back, then they would be paid for the job. Sanchez told her he needed to talk to his friends first, he could not make the decision on his own. She understood and told him she would find him again in a few days, then she left the cantina. He caught site of her the next day when he and Bob were in the crowded market, they began following her.

She met up with three men at the edge of the market. The men had a lethal look about them, large for Mexicans, well-muscled and Sanchez could tell they were armed. The way the men stood reminded him of body guards or secret service agents, legs slightly spread, eyes always watching and they wore crisp, clean, light weight clothing. Yolanda and the men stood and talked for a few minutes then they walked down a nearby alley together. Sanchez and Bob continued to follow, but kept their distance and acted as casual as possible without looking like they were acting. They came out of the alley and saw their targets hurrying across the street. Before Sanchez and his partner could make it onto the street, shots were fired. They dropped, looked for cover and watched as Yolanda and the three men with her exchanged gun fire with five other men. Yolanda did not have a weapon, but one of the men she was with shoved a gun at her and she began to fire. From what Sanchez could see she looked like she had never fired a gun. When it was over the five men were down as was Yolanda and one of her friends. They watched as Yolanda started to move, she had been shot in the shoulder, her friend had been shot in the leg. One of the men picked her up as the other man was also helped up and they quickly moved out of the area. Sanchez did not follow and they did not see Yolanda again for two weeks.

During those two weeks the two agents from El Paso had uncovered the whereabouts of four of the weapons from the Fast and Furious operation, but didn't think they could get their hands on them and even if they did, they had no idea what they would do with them. The pair of agents from Matamoros had been having a beer and had overheard a conversation between some men at the next table. The men were talking about a small city in the desert where men had target practice with large guns. Sanchez figured it might a training camp, three agents agreed and they all decided to pay more attention to bar talk, if they could pick up a lead it would help. The two from El Paso did not agree and laughed it off as rumor. Sanchez let it go, anyway there was no way to find it and even if they found someone to follow they couldn't since they didn't have a car, so he stayed silent. The agents discussed it and decided to put it in the report and let the boss handle getting aerial pictures and confirmation. They were here to look for the smugglers, as the agent from El Paso put it, let someone else take care of it.

When Sanchez saw Yolanda again he was having something to eat at a tortilleria and he asked if she would like to join him. He ordered her some food as she sat and moved her chair very close to him. This is where he found out her name was Yolanda Barajas, she was eighteen years old and as they ate and talked she would continuously reach over and touch his arm, at one point she placed her hand on his thigh. Their conversation had been about her family, how she had to help support them by sending money home and how she had to find a better job. Sanchez revealed nothing about himself and before she left the table, Sanchez told her that his friends were still thinking about the job offer, she leaned over kissed him on the cheek and thanked him for the food. He watched her walk away and smiled, he knew she was manipulating him by coming on to him, he also knew that one of her jobs was probably as a prostitute and a beautiful one.

The six agents continued working the streets, bars and local hangouts, but could not get a solid lead on anything. Sanchez was afraid he would have to take Yolanda up on the offer to cross the border and that would complicate things, especially if he backed out at the last minute. He had been keeping in touch with her, buying her lunch once in a while, sometimes talking to her at the market, but he was always watching her and Bob Frank was always watching them.

One of the agents from El Paso finally got a job as a taxi driver, he had no license, but most of the drivers didn't. Now they would have a car available, it was beat up and dented, but it ran. The other agents continued mining for information, Sanchez and his partner tried to stay on Yolanda. After another week of surveillance they had heard more about the city in the desert, but no exact location. Sanchez and Bob had found where Yolanda was living, it was a large rundown house that rented rooms as long as you didn't conduct your business in them. Sanchez had spoken to the owner about renting a room for his cousin and the man told him, "I don't rent to whores, gamblers or people who do drugs." Sanchez didn't believe him, how could you rent in this neighborhood and get anything else. Sanchez left him with the idea that he would speak with his cousin about the room.

Sanchez and his partner found out after watching her for three days that if she had any visitors they were either laborers or other women and lived in the same building. When she met with her large gunmen friends it was in the market or cantina, never at her room. Then she disappeared, no sign of her anywhere, they continued to watch the house for signs of her. After two days a car being driven by one of the gunmen pulled up in front of the building and she got out, her clothes were dirty, her hair was matted and she appeared to be sunburned. Once she walked inside and the car was gone, they went back to their room. On the walk back, Sanchez told his partner he wanted to talk to her alone and he would try and find her at the market the next day.

He casually ran into her at the market and mentioned that he hadn't seen her around lately. She explained that her mother had become ill and she had to make a trip home and she would be returning home next week for a few days to help take care of her. She told him she hated taking the bus because she got so dirty, but it couldn't be helped since she didn't have a car. Sanchez showed the required amount of sympathy and told her if he had a car he would take her. She said it was okay and asked him to walk with her. She looked even lovelier today than usual, her long black hair flowed down her back and she wore a pale yellow dress decorated with small green leaves splashed across it and thin straps over her shoulders. She took his hand as they walked down an alley, turned through an arched portal and into a small garden that was well manicured with hedges and bright red and yellow flowers that surrounded a small working fountain. She pulled him toward the fountain, then released the grip on his hand and walked ahead of him a few paces and turned to face him. She was speaking of how much she loved the garden and came here often to get away from the noise and the people. As she continued to speak she turned her back to him, she slowly picked up the hem of her dress and with the same slow ease, pulled it over her head. She wore nothing underneath. He stood there in awe at her beautiful body, brown, toned, tight ass and a small birthmark. She slowly turned toward him and again he found himself unable to take his take his eyes off of her, the firm breast, the slope of her smooth hips, not an ounce of unwanted flesh. She stepped forward, took his hand placed it on her breast, kissed him, turned slightly and pulled him toward the back of the garden. She was speaking, but he didn't hear her, his own thoughts running through his head, *this is wrong, no I can't do this,* but God how he wanted her. She turned her face to him, put her hands on the sides of his face and kissed him deeply and passionately. His hands moved down both sides of her body, over her hips and back up again, her skin was so smooth, so soft and he could feel the heat of her. He ran his hand down her back, over her buttocks and pulled her even closer to him. He felt himself swell with desire as he ran his hands over her shoulders and down to her breast, he wanted to experience every inch of her skin, he bent to kiss her breast, then stopped. She looked at him with half closed eyes and asked if he knew of a better place to make love than this beautiful garden, then kissed him again. This time her hands went to his waist, then her hand slid down and over the bulge that pushed against the fabric of his jeans. She push her body tighter against his, gently moved her hips from side to side against him. She whispered for him to come with her as she took his hand and led him further behind the fountain. He stopped dead in his tracks, she turned to him and he shook his head. "No I can't do this, not now, after you have visited your mother we'll come back here, but not now." Before she could say anything he turned and walked away, out of the garden and into the alley.

He kept walking, almost running, until he felt he had put enough distance between them and slowed his pace. He didn't know how far he had walked or exactly where his was, nothing looked familiar to him, everything looked cleaner and not as rundown. The saw a beer sign in the window of a place that back home would the neighborhood bar, he went inside, ordered a beer and sat in a dark corner. He put his head in his hands and berated himself, what was he thinking, that was to close, he could have compromised everything, his integrity would have been questioned, worse he would have hated himself. As he drank his beer he slowly regained control and began to think clearly now that his blood flow was back to normal. She had lied about riding the bus when there was no need to even bring it up, he wondered if everything about her was a lie. He had to keep her under surveillance, he could no longer speak to her or meet with her, but they needed to follow her on her trip next week.

This is exactly what he purposed to the other agents that night. He told them what he and Bob had observed when she returned home, the gunman friend driving the car, about the lie and what she had told him about leaving again, but he didn't tell them about the garden. They all agreed it would be worth their time, they also agreed if things gave the slightest hint they were going wrong they would abort. The two from El Paso hesitated, but finally agreed. Two agents would be left behind to cover for them and report what they were doing if they never returned. They all felt the need to find something to justify the operation, a few guns and a rumor were not enough. They had been hitting a wall when it came to the activity on the border, maybe this was connected or maybe it was nothing.

Sanchez and Bob continued to watch her, waiting for a sign that she was leaving town, the only thing they noticed was she looked tired, didn't smile or laugh much with her friends anymore. He would like to think it was because of him, but he knew better. Maybe her real lover had dumped her or the upcoming trip could be worrying her. Whatever it was he had to put it aside, the only thing he was concerned about was the trip and where it would lead. It was early evening when they saw her come out of her building carrying a box, she walked across the street and walked up to an older woman standing in her yard. They exchanged a few words and Yolanda opened the box to show the woman the contents, it was canned and boxed food, flour and sugar, some of which had been opened. She was cleaning house, this was it, she was preparing to leave and not just for a few days. They hurried back to their room and the other agents.

Early the next morning they parked the taxi were it wouldn't be seen, but they could watch the house. She came out at 6am and sat on the steps, no suitcase, no bags, just a purse. Fifteen minutes later the car pulled up with the three men inside. The back door opened, she turned to look at the house, then climbed in the car.

They were on Highway 2 twenty minutes later headed north with the agents car following at a distance. As they got further into the desert they dropped back, the highway was not that busy and you could see vehicles from miles away through the shimmering desert air as it heated up. The highway was a two lane with the low mesquite and scrub brush as far as the eye could see. Sanchez sat in the passenger seat with binoculars to watch the car ahead, Bob and one of the men from Matamoros sat in the back one with a map the other taking notes. When they got near Piedras Negras they turned south on Highway 57, which was a four lane highway that would eventually run parallel to the Sierra Madre Oriental Mountains. They were approaching parallel to the heart of the mountains when the car turned right off the highway onto a hard packed dirt road. They drove past the road, pulled off and then backed up to make the turn, the car was just a speck in the distance with a plume of dust following it. They were going to have to follow slower than they wanted, but they didn't want the dust to give them away. The shoulders of the road were very close with more vegetation than Sanchez expected, tall cactus, mesquite, more scrub brush and as they got to the higher elevation, what looked like small Madrone trees. The soil was sandy, rocky and grayish brown, probably volcanic, and the dust was cloying. They would have to find somewhere to wash the car before they got back to town, if they got back, no need in advertising were you've been.

After a few more miles the plume in front of them dissipated, the car had stopped, from here on they would have to watch out for possible security. They stopped their car and waited to see if anything was coming back their way. Sanchez had his binoculars up, but there was nothing to see and it was silent. As he started to say something a sound reached them, they froze, one of the men in the back seat thought it sounded like a tank. Sanchez thought they were all going to die in a fiery explosion until he realized the sound was moving away from them. They eased the car forward so Sanchez could find the source of the noise with the binoculars, he suddenly motioned the driver to stop the car. He got out of the car and walked up the road until he got near the crest of the hill, then went into the brush to get a look at what was on the other side. When he saw what was going on he motioned the others to follow him on foot, they didn't need anything to help them see the personnel carrier on large tires. It was opposite them across a small valley climbing up to the ridge, the large tires throwing the loose soil behind it. The car they had been following had parked at the bottom of the hill off the road with two other cars, the carrier had picked them up. They discussed driving down the hill, parking with the other cars and following on foot, but the likelihood of four men being seen crossing the valley was high and the terrain would be difficult to walk. Sanchez decided he and one other would cut across a gulley and get up on the ridge, then follow it until he could see something with the glasses. When he did he would have the other guy verify the sighting, therefore he wanted the agent from the Matamoros office with him. The El Paso agent driving the car would drive down to the parked cars, turn around, come back to this point and wait for them. They would move as fast as they could and if they saw any security teams they would turn back.

The two men took off at a trot using the bushes as cover and made it to the gulley. As they started running for the ridge they could hear gunfire start in the distance, it was ahead and off to their right. It was further to the ridge than Sanchez had first thought and when they got there they had to stop long enough to catch their breath and wish they had brought water. They stayed low and made their way along the ridge with Sanchez stopping to check the sightline, using only the sound of gunfire as a reference. They saw a huge plume of dust and moved toward it, as they got opposite they found an outcrop of large rocks and used it for cover.

Below them and partially hidden from view in a large ravine were men with weapons, an obstacle course and heavy vehicles. They could see the tops of buildings, but could not make out what or how many there were. These mountains were a heavy tourist area, but tourists were not going down there, even if they wanted to they would have to have special vehicles to get down into the valley. The two men took in everything they could and turned to start back. Sanchez took out a cell phone and took two quick pictures and prayed they would be good enough to verify what they had seen. As they made it over the ridge in the direction they had come, the heavy automatic gunfire started, mixed with what sounded like grenades. They stayed low and ran faster on the return trip, neither one caring now whether they were seen or not. When they got to within fifty yards of the car they heard the engine turn over, within ten feet and the doors flew open. Before the doors were closed they were moving down the road, trying to catch their breath and drink water at the same time. By the time they reach the highway both men were able to talk again and Sanchez related the scene at the bottom of the valley. The agents looked at one another and smiled, they had gotten what they came for.

On the way back to town they stopped, rinsed off the car and drove the rest of the way in silence.

In their room that night they related the story to the two agents who had stayed behind and decided to stay a few more days. Sanchez, Bob and the two from Matamoros wanted to stay longer and see what else they could get, but the El Paso guys kept saying they had gotten as much as they could and saw no reason to stay. The El Paso agents would leave in two days and the rest leaving in four.

In the days that followed Sanchez watched the market for Yolanda, but did not go back to the house. He asked around again about any jobs going across the border and was told that suddenly nothing was moving across, it had just stopped and no one knew why. The day before he left he went through the same routine asking about the jobs and got the same story from different people. The people who recruited and paid the smugglers had gone, left with no word on if or when they would return. He was alone having his last beer when the man he had just spoken to came over and sat with him. He told Sanchez he had done four trips to the river, that the money was good and he would miss it, he then added that he had never seen so much security, that it must have been important people that wanted to cross. He never saw the faces of the people he took across because they always kept their faces covered and they never opened the boxes they carried. Sanchez told the man he had been in town for several weeks and wondered why they had not met before. The man laughed and told him that this was his favorite place to drink and they would have met if he hadn't been out of town. He had made a lot of money and needed to take it to his wife in Chihuahua and maybe make another baby, he had returned only yesterday. He sighed and wondered aloud if he would ever make that much money again. Sanchez bought him another beer and told him he was going south to find his money, they both laughed, wished each other well and parted company.

Sanchez and the other men made their way back to Zapata and called in to be picked up. When he got back to the office he filed his report, which would be compared with the other reports. He then called the El Paso agent and told him about his conversation with the smuggler, he felt since the other agents knew about it, the El Paso agents should be made aware. He knew the real reason he had called was to rub in the fact that he had been right, there was more to find.

Several days later Sanchez and Bob Frank were called into a private room and told to forget everything they had learned and seen in Mexico, they were to forget it even happened. The station chief had received a phone call, he would not say who had called, but the caller told him the operation should never have happened, that the person who had authorized it had overstepped. He told them that all the agents involved had been given the same orders. He gave them a phone number to use if they ever heard anyone talking about the operation or if anyone from Mexico they had dealt with showed up on this side of the border.

The two agents left the private room and when they felt safe enough to talk, they discussed the meeting. Both men had a gut feeling something was wrong, that this was a cover-up, they both had questions about what they had learned, but it was a dead end now and they both resolved to put it behind them as ordered.

The one thing Jim Sanchez had a difficult time forgetting was the lovely Yolanda. He wondered if she ever made it back, he never saw her or the three men again after they drove off into the desert.

The only time he saw her now was when he called to mind the garden and the sight of her standing near the fountain.

25

Sanchez finished his paperwork and surfed the TV networks for news broadcasts and finally settled on a twenty-four hour channel. He sat at the table because the bed would probably put him to sleep and he needed to stay focused on the task at hand. He figured they would send him back to his job and he would never hear the truth, if anything, about the outcome of the operation. On the bright side, maybe they would look at what had happened in Mexico and see a connection to what was happening now. A stretch maybe, but a possibility. He heard Brock and Phillips enter Chads room and went to join them.

Phillips sat and was the first to speak, "Anybody get any new info?"

Brock shrugged, "No chatter, as we expected, but the overseas units are looking for anything, any kind of thread or Intel about the personal tracking devices. My gut tells me we will not find a connection to them in the Middle East. They're also focusing on any recent Intel on Wafiq and Arel, they're checking in three different countries. The office got the photos that your people sent them and are going over them. That's it."

"All I did was report in with a status update," Chad said. "They did tell me they should have that call traced in a few hours. They sent one of the guys from the Port Arthur team over to try and get prints off the phone, but there were several of them so they will have to check all of them. If everyone didn't have cell phones there would have been a lot more. I talked to the two teams and reiterated our concerns about coordinated events and explained that these guys may be checking in with each other. If one of them misses a check in it could alert the others, so to hold off on taking any of them down unless it looks like they are making a move on their own."

Phillips sighed, "Everything is the same, but moving along, if that makes any sense. All names of personnel on the southern and Canadian border have been checked and there is only one named Addison and she doesn't fit the description. They're close to tracking down the devices that were found on the vehicles, one of the techs told me they look familiar to him. They retrieved the device from the arm of our dead guy and it is on its' way to the lab, also they are trying to identify him. Naturally the ID he carried was fake, the name on it was Marion Wayne from Williston, North Dakota and unless he has risen from the grave and got a great tan, it's not him. The search for information on Rogelio is progressing slowly, but they're doing their best considering where they have to search. On a different note, I did find it interesting that the surveillance agent had the same suspicions we had on these guys and their operation. It's not a confirmation, but it makes me feel better. So here we sit again."

Sanchez clear his throat and spoke, "I have something we need to discuss. First, I wrote these up," he handed Phillips two sets of papers. "One is a copy of the notes I took on the news report, the other is an outline on my interactions with Rogelio and Addison. I don't know if anything in there is significant, but I thought rewriting it might bring something else out that I had forgotten. I wrote a report for Julie, but thought you should have one."

Sanchez shifted in his seat, "I'm pretty sure you all saw my reaction when Chad was briefing us on Yolanda and it was as much of a surprise to me as it was to you. Yolanda is a fairly common name in Mexico, but when the birthmark was mentioned, that is what sent me into a tailspin. This happened a couple of years ago and I thought it was over and forgotten, guess I was wrong."

They sat in silence as Sanchez told them of the threats to the agents on the border, the operation in Mexico, even about the episode in the garden. He left nothing out of his story including the abrupt end and subsequent cover-up of the operation and the text message he received. They could all see how difficult it was for him to talk about, especially when it came to the episode in the garden.

He paced, sat, paced again and ran his fingers through his hair. They all knew he was going against direct orders from someone in CBP or DHS and if he was exposed for releasing the information it could cost him his job or depending on why it was covered up, his life.

When he finished he sat down and held up his hand palm forward asking them not to speak, he had something to add.

"I know you asked us not to make any calls, but you have to understand the position I was in concerning Yolanda and the link to the operation. I look at it now and realize I should have let it go, just told you about it and never have made that call. For all I know that call may have compromised your operation. I didn't say where I was, I only left a message saying that Yolanda had come across the border and asking if I should tell you about her. I have been thinking hard about this, running through options to try and undo what I've done or at least put a patch on it. I came up with two options. I can call in and say I'm coming back, that the whole thing was a dead end and to put me back on the roster. The other is the same story, but ask for a week of vacation to get some sleep. I'll tell them I'm going to my sisters, but instead stay here and see this thing through. If you want to send me back, I understand. It will piss me off, but I'll be pissed at myself. If you do send me back I have one request, when this is over call me and let me know the outcome. Not the whole story, just the bottom line. For what it's worth, I don't think Yolanda is the problem, I think it's what we found."

Sanchez stood up, "With that said, I need a drink. I'm going to buy some beer. Don't get up. I don't need a ride, I need to walk."

Brock stood and moved to the door, "No, you need to stay here. If you need to walk do some more pacing. I'll go get the beer."

"I get it, you guys don't trust me. Guess that's understandable."

"That ain't it. We just don't want to lose the momentum," Brock said as he left.

Phillips had his pen and notepad on the table, he didn't say anything, didn't look at Sanchez, only stared at the wall pulling on his lower lip.

Sanchez couldn't tell if Phillips was angry or just disgusted, Brock didn't sound happy when he left and Chad just sat there staring at him with no expression. Sanchez figured he was about to have his ass handed to him and then he would be injected with a mind altering drug. He could imagine himself waking up in the desert or a foreign country with no memory, he might become one of those guys you see walking around talking to imaginary people.

Phillips slowly turned his head and looked at Sanchez.

"I'm going to ask you some questions. This is not an interrogation, consider it a debriefing. I will start with the simple stuff as I need Brock to hear everything first hand. I need you to give me the phone number you called."

Sanchez took out his personal cell and gave him the number.

"I need the number the text message was sent from and the exact message."

Sanchez handed him the phone with the text message on the screen. Phillips wrote down the message and noted the number. It was the same.

"When you call this number what does the outgoing message say?"

"Nothing, except to leave a message. There is no number confirmation and it is one of those computer generated voices."

"Whose number is it?"

"I have no idea. The number was given to all of us to use if anything came up."

"You've never heard a voice connected to this number?"

"No, I haven't."

"How many times have you called this number and when was the first time?"

"I've only called once and that was the last night."

Brock walked back into the room with two bags and walked straight to the sink area by the bathroom. He opened the bags, put a six pack of beer in the refrigerator, took the other six pack to Chad and put two bags of chips on the desk. He took a seat and asked, "What did I miss?"

Phillips didn't say anything, but handed him the notepad. Brock read it, handed it back and sat on the bed. "Continue," he said as he took out his notepad.

"Who authorized the Mexico incursion?" Phillips asked.

"I was never told," Sanchez replied.

"Were the men handpicked or were they volunteers? Before you answer, I know you may have covered some of these question, but they have to be asked and answered."

"I understand about the questions. There were a lot of border agents that volunteered as the threats were against all of us. Then I guess the list was narrowed down to a manageable number, but I don't know all of the criteria. Those names left on the list were narrowed down further to those who looked Hispanic and spoke fluent Spanish. I don't know if there was anything else involved with the final choices."

"Did you know everyone on the team?"

"I knew two of them."

"Did you know or had you ever met the two border agents from El Paso?"

"No, I didn't even recognize their names."

"Were you with the agents who found the questionable guns and did you ever see the guns?"

"No on both questions. The El Paso guys told the rest of us about it."

"What happened to the guns?"

"I don't know."

"Whose decision was it to come back across the border?"

"It was a group decision."

"Who brought it up first?"

Sanchez thought for a moment, "I'm trying to remember the exact conversation. I know I remarked there was nothing we could do about what we saw in the desert, it would take aerial observation to determine what was going on out there. I wanted to stay and see who else went out there, even if we just tailed them to the road it would be enough. Four of us really wanted to stay on it, so I guess you could say the El Paso guys were pushing to leave."

"Could the four of you had stayed?"

"No, we went in as a team, we left as a team."

"I want you to think before you answer this. At any time did you feel you were being led or manipulated by the El Paso agents?"

Sanchez sat back like someone had punched him, the look on his face was shock. "Are you telling me that the whole operation could have been a sham that we were meant to fail?"

"No, I'm asking you," Phillips stated.

"I...I never looked at it like that," stuttered Sanchez. "I would have to go back and look at things again. They didn't know we were watching Yolanda, Bob and I never said anything about it to anyone until we suggested following her and the three men. They knew about the shootout, but that was all over town."

"So the trip to the desert was sprung on them. At any time after you suggested the tail did they argue or try to dissuade you?"

"Not that I recall. I remember they hesitated a bit initially, but I really don't remember them saying anything."

"Do you remember the names of the border agents from El Paso?"

"I remember one was Dearing. I'm not sure of the other one, I would have to look it up. I don't remember it because he didn't make much of an impression on me. He never said much, he let Dearing do all the talking."

"What do you mean you would have to look it up?"

"I kept a copy of the report."

"Where is it?"

"The hard copy is at home, but I typed it up on a new computer my sister had gotten, so it should be there too."

"Does anyone know where you typed the report?"

"No, I usually do it at home, but my sister was after me to try out her new system."

Phillips turned to Chad, "Pull up that picture of Gus for me."

Chad handed his phone to Phillips. As Phillips handed the phone to Sanchez he asked, "Does this man look familiar to you?"

Sanchez look at the photo on the screen and they could see the question form on his face.

"Yes, this is the guy from the cantina, the one I met right before we left. He's the one who told me about the smuggling. How did you get a picture of him?"

Phillips took the phone from him, "I can't tell you that. If we get shots of the border agents from El Paso, do you think you could pick out the men?"

"It was time ago, but unless they grew beards I could," replied Sanchez.

Phillips turned to Chad again, "See if we can get photo rosters starting two years ago, if we can then we will set up your lap top."

"I have some questions, if you don't mind," said Brock

Phillips nodded to him.

"During the day when you started watching Yolanda, you said it was you and Bob Frank. Where were the agents from El Paso?"

"I don't know. Eventually the guy named Dearing got the taxi job, but the only time they ever mentioned what they were doing is when they told us about finding the guns. I guess later Dearing was driving the taxi around, but I have no idea where or what his partner was doing. I do know that the two from Matamoros were mining the cantinas, cafes and streets for a lead. We ran into them a few times and before you ask, they were nowhere near where we had been."

"So these guys from El Paso never told anyone where they were going or what they were working on?" Brock asked.

"To my knowledge, no."

"Other than keeping the surveillance on Yolanda quiet, did you tell the others what area you would be in or what you were working on?"

"Yes and when we were tailing Yolanda we told the others we were trying to nail down a lead on a group of smugglers."

"One last question," Brock said. "At any time did you think you were being followed and did you or Bob watch for a tail?"

"Since we had asked so many questions, Bob and I felt we needed to put distance between us. If he was asking questions or following a person of interest, I would watch for a tail on him and backtrack on myself to be sure I didn't have one. When I was tailing Yolanda or talking to her he did the same, we were especially worried about her three armed friends, but he did watch for anyone. If he had seen anyone from our team around, he would have mentioned it. We had all agreed to take different areas and then later switch if we felt we could get more information."

"Thanks," Brock said.

Phillips looked at Chad, "Do you have any questions?"

"Not right now, but I might come up with some later."

Phillips got the cold six pack and opened another beer, handed the rest to Chad to pass around and walked back to his chair.

"Jim, we understand loyalty, trust and faith in your fellow agents and the people above you. If you put the word 'blind' in front them you lose your integrity because you no longer question anything. We also understand obeying orders, but sometimes you find yourself questioning those orders. What I'm asking you to do for the next few minutes is to forget those three words."

Phillips shifted in his chair, "We know about the Mexico operation, but there was a lot we didn't know until you told us. We didn't vet you in the beginning because you had been cleared for your employment and honestly we didn't think this Rogelio thing would become what it has. When it started developing into something bigger a call to Julie told us of your exemplary record, but your reaction to Yolanda required a deeper check. The Mexico operation was hidden, it had only been given a passing reference, obviously deemed unimportant, but then one of our people found two small incidents that seemed odd for something not worth mentioning. She spread out her search and if not for that we would never have known about the operation."

"One of the agents you evidently worked with in Mexico had been talking about the operation. He'd get drunk and start telling anyone who would listen about what a big deal he was running the operation and so on. He had been running his mouth for about two weeks when he was killed in a car accident that didn't match the scene or his injuries. Very sloppy. Also, Agent Dearing was promoted to a desk job six months after you guys came back."

"These two incidents taken separately would mean nothing, but when put together with a possible cover-up, it doesn't look good and you have to question it. Also, you have to question why it was covered up in the first place since it ostensibly didn't confirm anything. I'm looking at this and I don't see where the El Paso guys were of any help, except driving to the desert. I think the whole operation was set up to make it look like something was being done about the threat. Whoever set this up put agents with you to monitor what was being found, what everyone of you were doing and if necessary, steer you in a different direction. I think you caught them flatfooted when it came to tailing Yolanda out of town, they had no excuse not to do it and they probably thought you wouldn't find anything, They didn't expect you to walk that ridge."

Brock spoke up, "Did you tell them about the cell phone picture?"

"No, once I looked at it and saw how blurry it was I decided it was of no use to us."

"What happened to it?"

"I still have it on my phone. I couldn't bring myself to delete it." Sanchez called up the pictures on his phone and handed it to Brock.

Brock looked at the pictures and handed the phone to Phillips. "Do you think we can clean these up enough to use them? I think most of this is dust, I just want it clear enough to tell what's down there."

"I don't know," replied Phillips, "Let's send them to both offices and see what they can do."

He nodded at Chad to send them, then leaned back in his chair and looked back at Sanchez.

"Now, back to you. You are staying with us, you can't go back. Since you left that message, if you go back now it might look like we know something. Anyway, we may need you to make another call to the mystery machine."

26

"Thanks, all of you," Sanchez said as he looked around. "I'll try not to screw up again."

"Actually," said Brock, "I don't think you screwed up at all. I think you put somebody on notice. I don't know who, but he's thinking about it, but you better watch your back, you may be wearing a target. Don't worry we'll help protect you if necessary, at least he, or they, don't know where you are, yet."

"Jake, can we get someone over to get the computer Jim used to write that report and check on his place to be sure it is still in one piece?" Brock asked.

"Don't know why not," replied Phillips. "Sanchez, call your sister and let her know she'll be getting a new computer. Also tell her to leave the empty boxes where they can be seen from the street. They'll need to sit there for a few days. Oh, and tell her that the old hard drive will be copied for her, minus your report, she won't lose anything.

"Do you want me to send one of our people from the hospital to check on Jims place?" Chad asked. "The hospital is closer to his place than anyone else is and one person can watch Jazmin for an hour."

"Yeah and while you're talking to them find out why we haven't gotten an update on Jazmin."

Phillips turned to Sanchez, "You need to tell Chad where your copy of the report is and we'll get it out of there for safe keeping, if it's still there."

"You really think someone wants that report?" asked Sanchez.

"If whoever this is thinks you kept a copy, they'll want it. I don't think they'll go to your sisters' place, but I don't want to take any chances. If they can't find it on your computer, they'll check everyplace they can think of until they do find it. Where did you put your copy?"

"It's a federal document, so it went into my safe. I don't think anyone would find the safe, even if they burned the place down everything inside it would still be intact."

"They'd find it Sanchez, it would be the only thing left in one piece."

"Okay, I'll tell you where the safe is and then you let me know if they'll find it." Sanchez paused and smiled, "I have a tankless hot water heater in the attic, but I left the old heater in the utility room. I vented the top of it in case of fire, then reinforced the bottom, cut a door in it, put in a trigger that unlatches the door, and placed the safe inside. The door slides up and then comes completely off, you spin the heater around to get to the door. I made sure you couldn't see the door unless you were really looking for it."

Phillips laughed, "I think you might be on to something with that. It won't explode and most hot water heaters are still around after a fire, charred, but intact. If they've been to your place, we'll find out how smart you are."

Sanchez told Chad about the safe, gave him the combination and called his sister. Chad called the hospital, sent two of his guys to get the report and Phillips called in for a new computer. Brock didn't make any calls, he had an incoming call. He went outside and paced the walkway as he listened. He asked a few questions, closed his phone, then leaned against his car, arms crossed over his chest and thought.

When Brock went back into the room he saw that everyone had finished their calls. He stood there and looked at Phillips as all eyes turned to him. The look on his face matched that of the one on Phillips.

"What's going on?" asked Sanchez.

Phillips motioned for Brock to take it.

Brock sat down heavily on the bed. "We just got word that a border agent from Brownsville/ Matamoros was killed."

Sanchez stared at him in silence.

"Brownsville Emergency personnel responded this morning to a fire a block off Boca Chica. A small house was engulfed in flames, it was all they could do to keep the fire from spreading. They pulled one body out a few hours ago and they are fairly sure it's Agent Ramirez. They'll get a positive ID at autopsy, but they already know cause of death." Brock looked over at Sanchez. "He was shot in the head. I believe he was killed because of the Mexico Op and I think it would be a good idea if you called Bob Frank, he needs to disappear. No credit cards and tell him to stay away from relatives. Use your secure phone and don't identify yourself to anyone but him."

Sanchez started dialing and walked away.

"I guess you were right about that call Sanchez made. Whoever got put on notice isn't wasting anytime cleaning up," Phillips said. "I don't think Dearing and the other guy are on the hit list, I think they were paid, but you never know how far this will go. This is much bigger than we thought and I thought it was big when we found those guys at the accident in Arizona."

"Has your organization had expanding operations like this before?" asked Brock. "No details, this is just curiosity."

Phillips looked over at Chad and shrugged. "We've had a couple, but only one that had this many turns in it."

"Yeah, that one was messy," added Chad.

Sanchez came back from his room, "I got him at home, told him not to ask any question, told him what he needed to do and not to waste any time. I also told him I would call him back in two hours on his cell and explain. When I call him I'll get a landline number and use that to explain this to him. Jeez, I hope he gets out."

He started to walk back to his room, then turned and gave Brock a funny look.

"I never gave you his name." Sanchez said suspiciously, "Before, when you asked me if I knew any of the guys that went to Mexico. You only asked me the names of the El Paso guys, not the two guys I knew. How did you know it was Ramirez and how do you know it was these guys?"

"His name came up when we looked into the Mexico operation. Plus this was sloppy work." Brock replied. "The first guy was sloppy, cause of death didn't match the evidence. If whoever killed Ramirez started the fire, he wasn't very smart or it wasn't started on purpose. You don't shoot them in the head, you drug them. Injection or ingestion, not a bullet, knife or strangulation. The only physical evidence you want is smoke inhalation. I think the sloppy job was on purpose."

Sanchez spoke up, "You're right it wasn't cartel, not the right kind of crime scene, plus Ramirez was a good guy, he was clean."

"I'll take your word on that," said Brock. "But you're right on the crime scene, it wasn't cartel."

Chad stood up and started to pace. "I wish we had more to go on, it's driving me nuts not shooting at someone, I should at least be chasing them down."

Incredulously Sanchez asked, "You enjoy shooting people?"

"That's my job and yes I enjoy blowing up the bad guy. There is a little bit of psycho in every sniper, it's a sneaky job and it's tough. You're putting a bullet in the head of someone you've never met, who knows their life is in danger every day, but they don't know today is the day and they don't see it coming. So I guess you could say I'm a sanctioned psycho. Now don't start analyzing me, I know right from wrong and I know it's a job not my life."

"Since I have everyone's attention," Chad continued, "I have some news. Jazmin is doing fine, her sister is with her most of the time. The reason we haven't had an update is because she wouldn't speak to anyone in law enforcement. She will only speak to the man who saved her life and spoke to her in Spanish, she doesn't trust anyone but him. Why they didn't report this to us earlier, I don't know."

Phillips grabbed his phone as he walked to the door, "Idiots, they should have called."

Phillips walked back in still seething from his conversation. "Okay, this is where we stand. They didn't call because they felt they had nothing to report, so I set them straight on that issue. Jazmin will only talk to Jim and she told them she had to talk to him. If that isn't something to report, I don't know what is. They are going to call back." He handed Sanchez a notepad and pen, "You know what to do and before you hang up, if she's given you any new information, be sure and tell her you may call back with more questions. Take the call in the other room so we won't distract you."

Sanchez walked into the adjoining room, but did not close the door. Phillips watched him walk away and ran both hands through his hair, "Don't know about you guys, but I think I'm going to explode. How can they hire people who can't discern what's important?"

Phillips chewed on his lip and paced a bit. He stopped in front of Brock, "We've got to start putting this thing together. We're getting bits and pieces from all over the place. I'm to a point where I can't tell what is relevant to those guys out there holding Rogelio and what is just chafe from other bad guys. I feel that it's all connected, but shit is coming at us from all directions and we're getting no answers. In the mean time we sit and wait for those asshole to make a move."

Phillips headed for the door.

"Where are you going?" Brock asked.

"I'm getting that big notebook from the car."

"Well, you'll need these." Brock tossed him the keys. "While you're at it get mine too."

"What notebooks?" Chad asked.

"We used bigger notebooks when we were putting together the names of illegals that had those scars and those who were possibly on the missing bus. We were writing like crazy, but that seems like a long time ago," Brock said. "I was jazzed about getting back in the chase, I guess I conveniently forgot how nerve racking it can be. He's right, we need to start writing this stuff down and draw some lines. There's so many little things that are getting lost in the process."

Phillips walked back in and put the notebooks on the table. "I'm glad motels still put pens in the rooms, we may run out of ink. Chad, we'll include your info and anything Sanchez gets in both notebooks.

Chads' phone rang, he answered then almost immediately hung up. "They got the photo roster from El Paso and sent it to us. I'm going to fire up the lap top, it may take a while to download. This may not make sense, but I have a feeling this will give us information that doesn't lead anywhere."

Brock and Phillips exchanged looks. "I think we're all on the same page, but we have to get Sanchez to confirm what we are already thinking."

Sanchez walk into the room, "Confirm what?"

"Chad got the El Paso roster, so now you can confirm the guys who were in Mexico," Phillips said. "How did it go with Jazmin?"

"Really good and she did have info for us. Ahh, you got your notebooks," Sanchez said. "I was wondering when you were going to get them out, we need them. Okay, Jazmin says to thank all of you for saving her life and she insisted on telling me the whole story. So if you guys are ready I'll start at the beginning, unless you have another idea."

"I'd like to hear it from the beginning, I need to know how she got on the wrong bus," replied Brock. Phillips agreed.

"Jazmin said they had been gathered together and were walking to the buses, as they got close to the door someone behind her fell and knocked her down. When she got up she had lost track of her sister and found herself behind some boys getting on the bus. As she entered the bus she realized it was not the bus her sister was on, there were very few people on it. There was a boy and girl behind her, she figured they were all going to the same place so she took a seat in the back. She said there were two men on the bus, the driver and a border agent, but she doesn't know the names. When the bus stopped and the other bus went on without them, she got worried. I asked her why the bus stopped and she told me she didn't know, but the driver got off and when the other bus came back he told it to go on without them. She became very frightened and started to cry. I little boy came and sat with her and told her it would be okay and held her hand. At this point I will not go into all her fears as that is not what we're interested in. The bus drove into a town she didn't know the name of and one of the men got off and went into a place that sold coffee, sent packages and had computers. The man was gone for a long time and when he came back he had something for them to drink. When they left the store they went to a motel and the same man went in and got a place for them to sleep, her words. They all had to sleep in one room while the two men, the little boy and his brother slept in the other room. She said it seemed strange to her that the men took the two boys to their room."

Sanchez paused, "Any questions so far?"

Phillips handed him a bottle of water and told him to go on.

"I won't go into the drive to Falfurrias as there isn't much there except she said it was a slow drive with many bathroom stops and they stopped to get food. Rogelio attached himself to her and she said it made his brother angry, but the man told him something and he left them alone. Rogelio slept with his head in her lap or on her shoulder most of the drive. She confirmed what we thought about how the bus got off the road and into the trees. The men made them stay on the bus, but some of the others were allowed to get off and wander around. It was when most of them were off the bus that Rogelio found the map. She said he was very busy with it and when he had finished she asked him what he was doing and he told her it was better if she didn't know. She said he was such a brave little boy so it surprised her a bit later when tears started rolling down his cheeks. She held him and he started telling her a strange story. He told her he was from Costa Rica and his parents called him Roger, not Rogelio. He also told her he had to go with the men to save lives, but that it was too late for his brother."

"Wait, he's from Costa Rica?" asked Phillips. "I need to call and get our people in Costa Rica."

"Hang on, there isn't much more. She said Rogelio told her that his friend the doctor would save him. She and Rogelio were finally allowed to get off the bus and walk around, but were told to stay close where they could be seen. Rogelio walked over to some trees and she joined him. He stood guard so she could relieve herself and she did the same for him. Rogelio would walk around in a tight circle and would not let her walk to far from the trees. Jazmin said she found that strange until she realized he was either going to make a run for it or was going to hide and use the trees as cover. When they saw headlights coming through the trees, the two men made them get back on the bus. She said that when the other car got to the bus she couldn't understand them, because they spoke in a language she had never heard before. It sounded like they were trying to get something out of their throats. She confirmed that they shot out the tires on the bus and she thinks the reason they tried to kill her was because they thought the boy had told her something. She also said to tell you that the dark girl on the bus is very mean and bad, she slaps the other girl all the time. She said, and I quote, "These people are very curious, they pray a lot, they talk funny and most of them were not very nice."

"Holy crap!" said Brock. "No need to update us my ass!"

27

After recovering from the initial shock of Jazmin's conversation with Sanchez, Brock and Phillips began making calls.

Phillips called his office and gave them the information on Rogelio and told them a full report would follow within a few hours. He was told that they would contact the team in Costa Rica and as soon as they heard anything they would call.

Brock called Langley and reported the same to his people and asked if they had heard anything from overseas.

Chad sat Sanchez in front of the computer to start looking at the photo roster.

"Why is there paper across the bottom of the screen?" Sanchez asked.

"The photos have the names under them and I need you to ID these guys by face not name. We don't want this to be questioned, so like the police would show you, you are given faces and no names. When you find either of these guys let me know."

Chad went over to the table where Phillips was working, "When Sanchez is finished, use the lap top and get your report off to the office. There's a direct link on there."

Brock had walked over to Sanchez, "Before you get too far into that, I need to ask you a question. Do you mind?"

Sanchez leaned back and looked at him, "No, I don't mind. Just don't make it a hard question."

Brock laughed, "No it's not hard and you don't have to answer it right now. It's a question I need you to think about for a while. I know you have to concentrate on these photos, so save thinking about this for later. When you were in Mexico, did you hear anyone using the strange dialect? It could have been on the street, in a bar, anywhere at all. It may have been something you thought you heard wrong, but in fact you heard it right. It would have been a fleeting thought, so it might be hard to remember. I just want to see if this language thing was going on two years ago, if you can't remember anything don't worry about it."

"No problem. It will take some thinking to pull something like that out of my head two years after the fact, but I'll give a try."

Brock walked toward Phillips and saw Chad spread out on the bed with issues of Guns and Ammo, First Freedom magazine and a gun catalog. He continued to the table to start putting entries in his notebook. As he sat Phillips phone rang.

Phillips answered his phone and walked into the adjoining room. When he came back he said, "They think they know where the devices on the SUVs came from. That was my tech and he said that these devices were replaced by newer ones about a year ago. This type was never used by us nor are they what the CIA has ever used. You're going to love this, they were originally used by the FBI, DHS and the DOJ."

"To quote Brock, 'Holy Crap!'" said Chad. "That means the ATF, DEA and CBP has or had access to them as well. Now that really narrows it down."

"Take the CBP out of it," Sanchez said from across the room. "We wouldn't use them. I wouldn't rule out somebody higher up sneaking around and using them, but those of us on the ground don't have the time to mess with them. How's that for throwing loyalty and trust out the window. You should find out if the bus or those vehicles in Arizona have them and keep in mind that the FBI is working on those vehicles. Be sure your guys are paying attention, don't want anything to disappear." He had never taken his eyes off the computer screen.

"Well, if CBP is out, that at least takes twenty-three thousand people off the list," laughed Chad. "All we need now is to find out how to get another hundred and fifty thousand off of it to make our job easier."

Phillips, who had been staring at Sanchez, pick up his phone again, "I'm calling the tech back and see how many devices we're talking about and see if there is any way to find out who has them now. Chad, give them a call on the Arizona vehicles and see what they've gotten so far and remind them to keep their eyes open."

Before Phillips could dial his phone Brock said, "I'm going to pick up some food. I'll surprise you."

Sanchez continued going through the roster, but was having trouble concentrating. He didn't like the direction things were moving, one co-worker was dead and another was hiding out and for all he knew his life was in danger. Now it looked like people in government positions might be implicated. He wasn't naive, he had been around for the Fast and Furious mess and they had lost some good people because of those guns. The implications had gone as high as possible during that investigation and no one was held responsible. It looked as if this might be headed the same way and this time he was going to be sure someone was not only held accountable, but paid for their actions.

Meanwhile, Brock had pulled into a parking lot two blocks from the motel and called Langley. He called John Bracken, who was the man you called when something covert was going on inside the U.S. Border. He and John had known each other since he was in grade school in California and he knew that of all the people in the CIA, he could trust John with anything. He called John on his direct line.

"Hello and how the hell did you get this number?" John said.

"You gave it to me and I'm on a secure phone."

"Ed, what the hell. I haven't heard from you in two months. What's with the new number?"

"It's a long story and I need to ask a favor. I don't have much time, so I'll give you the short version."

Brock gave him a quick briefing, then asked if he could do some checking to narrow down who might have used the devices in question.

"If our people have photos of the devices I'll see what I can do," John said.

"The photos were sent over there, but if they can't find them let me know and I'll send you copies."

"Tell you what Ed, send me a set directly. The fewer people that know I'm looking into this the better. This is investigating on U.S soil on U.S. personnel and you know what that means, caution."

"I know, now you understand why I'm calling you. I'm down here with Phillips and he doesn't know about this call, there is also a CBP agent with us named Sanchez. He's one of the guys that went into Mexico, the guy killed in Brownsville is one of the guys that was there with him. If this leads us to someone higher up, it will really shake him up, not to mention the public at large. If you come up with anything then I'll tell them I went behind their backs and I'll take the flack, until then this is private. You know I wouldn't ask you to do this, but I don't trust many people right now."

Bracken leaned forward and moved the phone to his other ear, "You realize that if I do find something I will have to turn it over to the FBI and that wouldn't be a good idea."

This was Johns' way of saying 'convince me'. Brock thought the story itself would have been enough, evidently John wanted assurances. He had nothing to trade, John would have to take him at his word.

"Don't do it. No one knows about any of this and no one has to know until we can nail it down and even then we don't have to do anything. All I want is information, a lead we can follow, then if we get a name, or names, we'll call the Feds in, I promise. Phillips is on this too and he won't do anything to jeopardize you, the information or the case. John, you're the best 'sneaky Pete' I know, they'll never suspect a thing."

"That's all I wanted to hear, but it may take some time. How do you like the border?"

"Thanks and I hate it. It was boring up until now. You know I don't like sitting on my ass," Brock laughed.

"I think when this is over you should come in from the cold."

"I'd love to, if you think enough time has passed," Brock sighed.

"I think something can be arranged, just don't burn yourself on this one. Get me those pictures." John hung up.

Brock called up the pictures Chad had sent him and got them off to John.

John Bracken had eluded to the reason Brock was on the border. It was an Afghanistan op and Brock thought he was under deep cover, but the local he was working with was under deeper cover and was working both sides. Brock got what he was looking for, but it cost him. He got burned, his identity had been sent out and he had to be smuggled out of Afghanistan in a large weapons crate. It could have been worse, it could have been his coffin.

When he got back stateside he was debriefed and given a desk job for a few months, then they put him in the 'cold' watching the border. He had been told it was only temporary, but six months later he was still watching a border that leaked like a sieve and waiting to go back to real work.

28

Brock unlocked the door to their motel room to find no one there.

"Hello, anybody here?"

"We're in here," a voice called from the adjoining room.

Brock headed for the other room, "What are you...," he stopped in mid-question. His mouth dropped open and he almost laughed.

Sanchez stood on one of the beds, Chad on the other. Phillips stood on the floor between the two with papers in one hand and a roll of duct tape in the other. On the wall above the beds they had taped pieces of notebook paper.

"An evidence/suspect grid, you guys must have gotten bored while I was gone."

"I got to thinking," Phillips said. "It would be a hassle for all of us to try and look at a notebook at the same time. I asked the guys about it and Sanchez suggested this. I used the notebook paper and Chad had a marker in his car, we figured an ink pen wouldn't show up as much. I think it will work and we can take it down when we are through with it. After we get it up we can discuss it, I'll take notes then photos. The photos will act as a portable board, I'll take them down to the lobby and print them out. What do you think?"

"It's not bad."

"Of course it's not bad, after all," Phillips said hitching up his pants, "we're professionals."

Brock laughed at his friend, "It may be a funny way of doing things, but I think it'll work." He continued to look at the progression of paper.

"I get the AZ, but what is DSG?" asked Brock

"That," said Sanchez," is Dead Scar Guy."

"RSGx2," said Chad, "are the Runaway Scar Guys. We were going to do MSG for 'missing', but decided it might be confusing. I know we aren't sure if the second guy had a scar, we are presuming that he did."

"So," said Brock, "if we didn't know Wafiqs' name he would have been OSG, Original Scar Guy."

Phillips laughed, "It does sound funny, but we had to come up with something to designate who we were talking about. Everything is almost up, we started with the facility and progressed with each action or individual up until now. You'll notice we have put nothing up about the Mexico operation. That was my decision. It may become relevant later, but right now I want this to be about getting these guys. If this leans in that direction, then we will add the Mexico information. I mean the only thing we have that ties the two is Yolanda and right now I don't think that's enough."

"I put Corpus, Houston and Port Arthur behind a large blank space, for fill in purposes. I also put paper with just a question mark on it to show we're waiting for answers in those areas."

"What's the reason for the big question mark behind the cities?" asked Brock.

"That's because we don't know if it ends there." answered Chad.

Brock nodded. "You guys finish this up and I'll bring in the food. If I do it alone we should finish up at about the same time."

Brock had just finished setting out the food and plates when they walked in from the other room.

"Who are you feeding?" asked Phillips

"Hey, I decided we needed some good Tex-Mex and a lot of it."

"You have enough enchiladas here to feed a platoon not to mention everything else," Chad said with his arms spread wide.

"My, my, tamales. Brock you are heaven sent." said Sanchez rubbing his hands together.

"But wait there's more," Brock said opening the refrigerator and pulling out cold Coronas.

"I hate to say this, but I don't think either of our offices would approve of this," Phillips said picking up a plate.

"Screw 'em," said Brock. "This is on me and when this op is over we'll celebrate again. We needed something to lift our spirits and this was the only thing I could think of since we aren't in Colombia," Brock joked. "Plus," he held up a small brown paper bag, "I got candies for Rogelio."

Since the order was so big the restaurant owner threw in plates and silverware. He told Brock to just leave everything at the front desk and they would pick it up later. The owners' wife told him dessert was on her and packed a nice dessert for them. It had taken longer for the food than he had expected, because he had ordered so much that the kitchen had to make extra. He didn't care how long it took or how much it cost, he was feeling better since this thing had started. He was out from behind a desk and there was a possibility he would be transferred back to D.C. He was actually using his brain, it was a bit rusty, but it still worked.

They dug in and ate without saying much except how good everything tasted and laughing about having to waddle after bad guys instead of chasing them down.

As they finished cleaning up Phillips said, "I really don't want to get back to business, but I think we should all shower and suit up. These guys have been sitting for too long and when they move it may be fast and we don't know when we will have access to showers again. We have three rooms so three showers, we could use the fourth room, but someone needs to monitor the phones. You guys shower and I'll photograph the wall and watch the phones. When we are ready then we can go over what we have."

He turned to Sanchez, "The clothes you put on are the ones you will sleep in, I don't care if you take your shirt off, but nothing comes off that will slow down our departure."

Sanchez looked at him, "Do you know how long I have been in these clothes? I don't know how you guys can stand to be around me. I'm covered in Falfurrias debris, sweat and I have blood spots from Jazmin. Even I can smell my clothes."

Chad looked at Phillips, "You know his clothes are pretty rank. You and Brock take showers, I'll take the phones and take Jim to get new clothes. There's a place down the road, it won't take us long."

"Okay," Phillips said. "No prom shopping, just grab what you need and get back here. Take Brocks' car, we don't need a vehicle loaded with weapons getting stolen or broken into."

Brock handed them his keys and said, "Pick up a box of black trash bags while you're out. I'll use one to put this stuff in for the restaurant and we can use another one for those smelly clothes. Unless you want them just sitting in your car for the next few days."

Chad and Sanchez walked out the door and as they got into Brocks car Sanchez asked, "What did he mean by 'prom shopping'?"

"That is a reference to how long it takes to shop for your Senior Prom."

"It took me an hour and that including the fitting and putting down the rental fee for the tux," Sanchez said.

"Yeah, but you aren't female." Chad laughed.

29

"Now I feel good," Sanchez proclaimed as he came out of the adjoining room. "Taking a shower and then putting on the same dirty clothes just doesn't seem right. At least now I feel more like a human being."

"New clothes will do that for you," Phillips chuckled.

"Not just new clothes, but clean ones." Sanchez replied.

Chad walked out of the bathroom in his TDU trousers, Under Armour T-shirt and headed for the desk chair. He picked up his black T-shirt, slid it over his head, then sat down and started to put on his Desert Boots. Lined up on the desk was his Glock, H&K .45, Benchmark knife and phone.

Sanchez looked from Chad to Phillips then back at Chad, "You guys are identical." Then to Brock, "Must be standard office attire."

Brock laughed, "Don't look now, but you appear to be dressed the same."

"No I'm not," Sanchez turned to look in the mirror. "Crap, I've lost my individuality." His shoulders slumped and he looked across the room. "Nope, here ya go," he said as he walked over and put on his baseball cap, "Now I'm different."

Chad looked down shook his head and smiled.

"Let's go," Phillips broke in as he stood. "We need to go over this stuff and clean up the wall."

They all gathered in the adjoining room and started going over the wall they had created. Starting with the initial intake of Ignacio and Rogelio and going through everything that had happened since. They added notes on some of the papers, questions on the others and a lot of arrows referring to other pages. All of this was cataloged in the notebook Phillips carried. They still had no answers, those were in the hands of Lab Techs and people in Costa Rica. They all knew that following the SUV's would at least be forward movement on the case and might net them some answers. They all agreed that stopping these people and rescuing Rogelio were still the priorities. In the end they all knew the whole thing might be taken out of their hands.

Phillips stood looking at the wall as Chad and Sanchez finished taking down the papers and stacking them in order. "I'm taking the camera down to the front office and use their computer to get the pictures printed, I'll take the bag of restaurant stuff me. While I'm there I'll let them know we need to keep the room for an undetermined amount of time, I'm sure the surveillance guys can use some down time."

"Hold on," Chad said, "I'll walk out with you." He turned to Sanchez and Brock, "I'm going out for a while. I'll be back shortly."

After Phillips and Chad left Brock asked Sanchez, "So you identified Dearing, but not the other guy?"

"His photo wasn't in there and I went through it three times. I'm thinking he may have been outside help, like you said before, he was paid help. Maybe he was there to keep an eye on all of us, including Dearing. If that's the case then this thing goes higher up than El Paso, especially when you consider no one is mentioned as authorizing the trip and then the eventual cover-up. It takes someone besides a supervisor to do all that and I don't think the head honcho in El Paso can do it either."

"So what are you thinking, DHS or DOJ?"

"Why not both?" replied Sanchez. "The number I called is a D.C. area code, but I doubt it will lead us to a name. I bet it was a burner phone."

"A burner phone for two years? That's a stretch, but I guess if you've got the power anything is possible." Brock said.

Sanchez leaned back in the chair, "I know we can't prove anything from two years ago, even if there was a trail it would be really cold by now. If we can pin the death of Ramirez on them we might be able to trace the reason he was killed back to the Mexico operation. I know, it's next to impossible."

"No, wait a minute, let's break this down," Brock was getting excited. "If Ramirez was killed because of the Mexico op, then something you guys found was important. If they waited this long to start covering their ass, then what you found must be connected to this. See where I'm going?"

"Yeah, but we don't know if Ramirez was killed for some other reason. We're going to have to wait and see what the cops find out," Sanchez sighed.

"What if the cops are paid off?" Brock asked. "I think we need to find someone to snoop around and see if there was another reason."

"I have someone I could ask. Crap, I forgot to call Bob back!"

Sanchez grabbed his phone and ran into the other room as Phillips came back from the front office.

"What's wrong with him?" Phillips asked.

"Sanchez and I were just brainstorming and he remembered he had to call Bob Frank. He has a pretty good head on the shoulders, he's good at analytics. Hope he's good under fire. How did the pictures turn out?"

"Not bad, they're workable. Where's Chad?" Phillips asked.

"Not back yet. Didn't he tell you where he was going?"

"His tank is here, so he's close by." Phillips answered.

"Calling it a tank is pretty accurate considering how armored up he is." Brock laughed. "Hey, you seem distracted.

"Sorry, yeah, I am. Do you think having Jazmin work with a sketch artist would get us anywhere with an identity on the bus and SUV drivers?"

"I don't know, it might. Why don't we have Sanchez call her and see if she's willing to do it," Brock replied.

Both of their phones rang so they knew it was from their respective offices. The conversations were concise and neither man looked happy.

"So?" asked Phillips.

"Same as yours more than likely. DSG?"

"Yep." Phillips replied, "Let's wait until everyone is here."

Chad walked back into the room, "Where's Sanchez?"

Phillips looked up, "He's in the other room on the phone with Bob Frank." He walk over and turned on the television, "We received some info about five minutes ago that we need to go over, but I want to wait for Sanchez. What were you up to?"

"Oh, I was loosening up my boots, I like to do that when I haven't worn them for a while."

Sanchez walked out of the adjoining room and found everyone staring at him.

"What? Why are you looking at me like that?"

"Nothing," answered Phillips, "We were just waiting to hear if your friend is okay."

"That's not what your faces said," Sanchez replied.

"We just got a call and were waiting to discuss it," Brock said.

"Go ahead, this can wait," Sanchez put his notepad on the table.

Brock motioned for Phillips to proceed.

Phillips sat on a corner of the bed, "They got an ID on our DSG. He's an illegal who has been living in Phoenix for the last three years in an encampment. The only way we got his name was because the local PD has picked him up twice, once for drunk in public and once for petty theft. No jail time, he was on their catch and release program, if you get my meaning. Evidently his buddies got worried about him a few months ago because he was missing for three weeks and they filed a missing person report. When he finally turned up again they went back to the PD and told them he was back and okay. When the report was first filed his buddies were questioned further and they said he had been disappearing off and on for about four months. He would usually turn up after a day or two with a piece of new clothing, food for everyone or money in his pocket. Sometimes the guy would be gone for as long as two weeks, but when he hadn't been back for three weeks they got worried. When he finally showed up on the street again he told them he had gotten a part time job and would be driving a van for some guys and it was going to be good money. They did see him a couple of times with two other guys who were well dressed, not suits, and figured these were the guys he was working for. He was picked up by the white van two days before he was killed in the accident."

"So, whoever these people are they are recruiting off the streets," offered Sanchez. "I wonder how many more like him they recruited and if they had him running back and forth across the border down by Nogales. I guess the bigger question would be, on which side of the border he got the scar."

"I think a good bet would be either side," interjected Brock. "If they are recruiting these guys it would make sense to do it on the side of the border they were recruited from, maybe people wanting to come across the border have been recruited by these guys. They're probably using them for unimportant tasks anyway. These recruits are expendable assets."

Phillips had been writing everything down in the notebook and looked over at Sanchez. "Do you think Jazmin saw the bus and SUV drivers well enough to get a sketch done of them?"

"I'm not sure about the SUV driver, but she was on that bus a long time. I'll call and ask her."

"Before you call over there, tell us about Bob Frank," Brock requested.

Sanchez sat back down, "Bob got out fast, made sure he wasn't being followed and headed over to his storage unit. He took what he had packed in his duffle put it on the back of his Harley, put his car in the storage unit and used the Harley to get out of town. He used the Harley in case anyone was looking for his car, anyway he's in Port Mansfield. I have a land line number for him as he dismantled his cell phone. No one knows about the storage unit as it isn't in his name and neither is the bike."

"How is he registered at the motel?" Brock asked.

"He's not. There aren't really any motels down there, they only have these lodge places for folks who are going to be down there for a while fishing or RV parks. He's staying with some biker buddies down there." Sanchez started to laugh, "He says he's going to grow a beard, dye his hair and spend time fishing and drinking beer."

"That's not a bad idea," Phillips said. "Might as well make the best of it."

"Well, I kind of changed his plans for him," Sanchez said. "Ed and I had some questions about Ramirez and I asked him to do some checking around. He said to give him time to grow some hair on his face and he'd look into it. I should probably have cleared it with you first but since I had him on the phone, I went ahead with it. Hope that's alright."

"What questions did you guys have?" Phillips asked.

Brock filled him in on the conversation and added that he thought it was a good idea as long as Bob was careful and it might tie up a loose end.

While Brock was filling Phillips and Chad in, Sanchez called Jazmin. When he got off the phone he told Philips, "She says she'll do what she can, whatever we need she'll help. She says she wants these bad guys stopped and Rogelio and the young girl saved. By young girl I think she means Yolanda because the other girl hits her all the time."

Before Sanchez could finish, Chad was on his phone making arrangements for a sketch artist. As he closed his phone it rang, the conversation was short.

"That was the guys I sent to get the report Sanchez wrote. They found it and everything there appears to be in one piece and they're on their way back to the hospital. I let them know about a sketch artist coming over and they said to tell Sanchez and I quote, "Great job with the safe, they would never have seen it." So it looks like the hot water heater idea works because my guys are good, very good."

Phillips finished his notes, sighed and stood up. "I'm going to go through that custom pack again and I want both of you to go through it with me. If I can't get to the case and we need something, you guys will have to handle it. We need to familiarize ourselves as to where everything is, so when you put your hand in there you're not fumbling around. A female with our organization once told me that women don't have a fumbling problem because they have eyes on their fingertips."

Chad laughed, "That must be Pepa."

"Paper, you work with someone named Paper?" Brock asked.

"Not 'Paper', its Paypa. The southern way of saying paper, but spelled P-E-P-A," Chad replied. "Don't let the name fool you, she may sound like a sweet southern belle, in reality she's smart, sanctioned and one of the best I've worked with."

Phillips smiled, "You might add that she does look innocent."

"Wow, a sanctioned female," Sanchez groaned, "Now that could make a date with her dangerous."

They went through the custom pack twice and once they were satisfied with it, they settled down to watch the news, sleep and wait.

At 2am two phones rang. They were both answered on the second ring.

30

Rogelio spent his time curled up in a corner of the motel room with two pillows and a blanket. He ate and slept in his little corner, he spoke to no one and hadn't spoken since they had left Falfurrias. He didn't cry or whine, he never nodded or shook his head in response to questions. When food came he ate, took his shower when told to and went to the bathroom when necessary. He had cocooned himself within his own skin, he would not give these people the satisfaction of acknowledging anything they said or did. This was his way of fighting back, fighting back in the only way he knew how, silence.

The bus driver and the girl named Yolanda seemed to be the only ones who worried about him now. Ignacio had bought him some comic books to read when they had stopped for gas and sometimes he would sit down and tell him everything would be alright. Rogelio knew things were not alright, they would never be alright. They had killed Jazmin and he knew they would kill him too, it was just a matter of time.

He had pleaded with them, promised them he had not told her anything, he even promised to stay away from her, but they killed her anyway. The man in the border patrol uniform had led her away, Rogelio was yelling promises as he tried to follow, but Ignacio held him back. He heard the man shoot the tires on the bus and then caught a glimpse of Jazmin as they went through the trees. He heard her arguing with the man and Rogelio thought maybe she was trying to get away. Ignacio took him to the opposite side of the SUV and told him to stay there or there would be consequences, so he stayed. He heard the shot and felt his stomach lurch then he felt something like an empty spot in his heart. He felt strange, weak, so he leaned against the side of the SUV. He wanted to cry, but knew he shouldn't, then he felt like he was going to be sick. He turned and leaned sideways against the car resting his face and head against the metal as he fought the sick feeling. Suddenly he felt and heard a small noise vibrate through the metal. He listened, not moving his head and heard it two more times. He slowly looked around and saw nothing, he looked up and saw a small object floating high above the SUV. He looked around to see if anyone was watching him and he heard the noise again. No one was paying any attention to him so he looked up again, but the object was gone.

When the man who had taken Jazmin came back, Ignacio came over to him and said it was time to go and put him in the SUV. As they drove away he realized no one had seen the object in the sky or heard anything. The mean girl was yelling at Yolanda again because she was crying and Ignacio told her to stop yelling. Then they all started talking to each other in the strange language and ignored him. As long as they ignored him it would give him time to think about what he had seen and what it meant. As he started to get drowsy it dawned on him, it must have been a drone, not the big ones you saw on television, but a smaller one. He didn't know what is was doing out there or what caused the small noise, he just wanted to believe that it saw him.

Now he sat in his corner, he was trying to find a place to leave a message and deciding what to say. He didn't know if they had found his other messages or if they knew what they meant. He didn't know if the doctor or anyone was following him, but he had to believe someone was because if not he would definitely die. That's why he had to keep leaving messages, it was the only hope he had. He still had some packets of mustard and he could always use the sauce from the piece of pizza he had hidden. He didn't have many places he could leave the message and still didn't know what to say. He realized he only had one choice, it had worked before, maybe, so he would use it again. Now what would he say.

When everyone was going to bed he pulled the blanket over his head and waited. He lay there a long time waiting for them to fall asleep, finally he heard the sounds of snoring. He was thankful he wasn't in the other room because there were too many people in there. He opened the mustard and carefully started writing his message in the dark, trying to keep the letters from overlapping. When he was finished he put a pillow over the message and prayed as he fell asleep.

A few hours later he was awakened by the sounds of movement in the room and sat up. He saw the others coming out of the adjoining room and even saw people he had not seen before. They were all talking in the strange language and walking out the door. Ignacio came over to him and told him they were leaving. Rogelio sat on his blanket refusing to move. Ignacio walked over to him and yelled, "Get up, we have to go! Get up now!" Rogelio still sat refusing to move. Ignacio yanked him to his feet then picked him up and started to reach toward the blanket and pillows. Rogelio knew he had to do something or Ignacio would see the message. He began screaming, hitting and kicking Ignacio trying to distract him, to stop him from moving the bedding. One of the men told Ignacio something the Rogelio didn't understand, but Ignacio turned away from the corner and headed for the door. Ignacio cursed at him and carried him out to the SUV closing the motel door behind them.

Rogelio hit his head as Ignacio threw him into the back seat and was still cursing as he got into the front seat. Rogelio saw Yolanda, she grabbed his hand and squeezed it.

They sat outside the motel room for another five minutes, long minutes for Rogelio. He thought one of the men would surely go back into the room. As they finally drove away it was all he could do not to breathe a sigh of relief.

31

Phillips hung up his phone and immediately hit a series of numbers then hit send. The numbers alerted all members of his team that they were on the move. By the time he and Brock opened their door, Chad and Sanchez were opening theirs. They each carried two black bags of varying sizes, but the expressions on their faces were the same, serious and down to business.

Brock left the motel parking lot right behind Chad, Phillips called the surveillance team to get an update and remind them to look for a message from Rogelio.

"They are loading up the second SUV," he said as he hung up, "the first one that left had a driver and one other male in it. They haven't seen Rogelio yet."

They parked near the motel and watched as the second SUV pulled onto the street, Phillips looked at the receiver to be sure the SUV's hadn't been switched, it was not theirs. He looked up in time to see their other mobile surveillance car take up its position behind the second SUV.

Sanchez picked up the binoculars off the back seat, "At least we won't have to sit on their asses to follow them."

"Yeah, but we need to keep a visual on them because of Rogelio. We don't want these guys to decide to off someone on the road and not be able to stop them."

"These binoculars are really powerful, wish I had something like this on the job," Sanchez said.

"There's another pair in the glove box, but they are night vision and smaller. Don't use them at night in oncoming traffic, you'll go blind for a while." Brock informed them. "What is taking that third SUV so long?"

As Brock finished his question Phillips phone rang. It was a short conversation.

"That was an update," said Phillips. "Our SUV is just sitting there, but we have two large males, two other males, two females and Rogelio in it. They said he raised quite a ruckus going to the car and was basically thrown into the back seat. Our guys are getting ready to go in as soon as it's clear. I'm thinking there should have been three large males in that car, I guess one of them is in another car."

The vehicle they had been waiting for pulled to the head of the motel driveway and turned onto the street, the light on the receiver went to steady green. They waited until the vehicle was well away from them before following, again with Chad in the lead. They turned south on I-37 then east over the bay bridge and connected to Highway 35. With no traffic and dawn hours way they kept their distance.

A double click came over the walkie-talkie on the front seat, Phillips pick it up. "Go."

"In about five minutes I'm going to turn off," Chads voice came over the air. "You take the lead and I'll be back on the road three minutes later. This is going to be tough with no traffic. Let's keep switching off for a while, then I think Sanchez needs to ride with me. Over."

"Roger that," Phillips answered, "after that I'll try and make myself smaller. Out."

"What's with making yourself smaller?" asked Sanchez.

"It's a visual. We change the number of people in the car or the size of the people, it makes it appear like the car has changed. If you saw three people following you for three hundred miles at 2am you might get a bit suspicious. If the number of people in the car changes you might think it was a different car. Of course these guys won't see us for a while."

"What about a helicopter?" Brock asked.

"I've got one on standby for later, if we need it." Phillips answered. "We should hit the Houston area around rush hour and I want eyes on that SUV no matter which direction they go, except south toward Galveston."

Chad double clicked the walkie-talkie signaling he was pulling off, Phillips replied with a single click.

The green light stayed steady and they had switched car positions twice on the drive east. As they neared the town of Tivoli, Phillips phone rang.

"This is Tim, from your surveillance team. Sorry for the delay in calling, but we had to call in the local PD, we have a body."

"What? Whose?"

"We're not positive on the identification. It's male, in his late forties and by the license he was carrying, it may be your bus driver. We took his prints to be sure the license wasn't a plant. They put him in the bathtub, maybe to keep him out of site until they left."

"What happened to him, how did he die?"

"He was stabbed and according to the on-sight prelim by the ME he was stabbed mid stomach with an upward thrust. We won't know the kind of weapon used until the autopsy, but the ME says it was thin bladed."

"Have him check wound size against a stiletto, it sounds like the work of our girl Arel. He either said something or touched her, she's funny that way."

"There's more," Tim sighed. "His throat was cut and his face was cut up pretty bad, that's another reason for the prints. All of those cut were done post-mortem, someone was very angry. I need to tell you that these two rooms were a mess, food and the containers all over the place, the towels used multiple times and it smells and not just of decomp. They must not have let the maids in and the owner of this place is not going to be happy, but the print guys are. Want to bet they don't get any hits on them? The boy, Rogelio, made himself a little nest of pillows and a blanket in a corner of the room. It had to have been him because the space was too small for anyone else and no one else would have written the message."

"Great, and nice lead in by the way. What does it say?"

"I hope you know what this means because none of us do. It was written on the wall behind one of the pillows and looks like it was written in mustard and some of it is faint. It is printed as four separate words,

Sec tio mat DC

All of that is in lowercase except the "S" and the "DC". The first letter may have been a mistake that he couldn't correct. Good luck with it, the kids' pretty imaginative."

"Do me a favor and send me a picture of it, get it as clear as you can and take a second shot using a digital camera. I really appreciate what you guys have done. When you finish up there go over to our motel, I kept the rooms for you guys and the front desk has the key. Let me know if you find anything else."

Phillips hung up his phone, "Sanchez, grab your note book and write this down." He gave Sanchez the message Rogelio had left and filled them in on what had been found in the motel room.

"Well, part of this is easy," Sanchez said. The last part is Uncle Mat and DC must mean Washington,"

"I figured that part out, it's the first word I don't know," replied Phillips.

Brock held out his hand "Let me see it.

Brock held the notebook under the dash light then handed it back. "Huh," he said, "could be second Uncle, seconds as reference to time or the Security and Exchange Commission. Whatever it is, his uncle is evidently in Washington D.C., be nice if we had a last name."

"If we can find his parents we'll get one," replied Phillips.

The SUV turned into the Buckee Station in Port Lavaca, Brock continued down Highway 35 while Chad pulled up to a gas pump two down from the SUV. He topped off his tank and carefully took in the occupants. They took turns going inside the store, some coming out with snacks and drinks. Rogelio and Wafiq, Chad could not think of him as Ignacio, walked toward the store. Rogelio shuffling his feet, chewing on his fingers and looking at the ground. When he came back out he had what looked like a comic book in his hands.

Chad finished cleaning his windshield as slowly as possible and got back into the car. The SUV was still not ready to leave so he pulled to the side of the parking lot, took out a map and pretended to study it. The SUV finally pulled away from the pump, but instead of getting back on the highway it stayed on Main Street and headed downtown.

Brock had taken the opportunity to put gas in his car at a station a few blocks away and Sanchez ran inside to pick up coffee and water. He had been back in the car and finish a bottle of water when they finally heard Chad on the radio.

"They are on Main. Do you still have a signal?"

The reply was a single click.

Chad looked in his rearview mirror and saw Brock turn the corner behind him, he reached over, double clicked the radio, turned down the next street and made a U-turn.

Port Lavaca was never a very big town and most of the downtown businesses never recovered after an economic decline a number of years ago. It had three main business streets, one being Main Street, which is also Highway 87, and the other being Commerce Street, which runs along the water's edge. After a bypass was put in on the edge of town, most of the downtown businesses that had survived moved in that direction. It quickly built up between the Causeway and Main Street with, banks, motels, a Walmart, restaurants and anything else a traveler might need, but it remained a shrimp and oyster town. Having the Gulf of Mexico on one side and a bay on the other it is a good place for boating, as well as fishing for the casual fisherman. On the east end of the Causeway sits Point Comfort, a bedroom community on the bay. There are no amenities only homes, a school and the two local industries, Alcoa and Formosa Plastics. At night the horizon east of Port Lavaca is ablaze with the orange and yellow lights from the two large plants that border Highway 35.

Brock looked at the houses and businesses as they drove down Main to the old downtown area.

"Not a happy looking place is it?"

"A lot of these families have been here for decades," Philips answered. "There are a number of jobs here compared to what it was twenty-five years ago. I don't know how some of these families held it together, the only thing I can come up with is that there has always been a lot of traffic on Highway 35. It must have been enough to sustain these folks until they could get the State to come in and widen the highway. I have heard there's a great barbeque place here and it's been here for a long time, wish we had time to try it out."

They saw the SUV make a left at the end of Main. Brock was far enough behind that when he got to the end of Main he eased to a stop slower than necessary. Suddenly Chad came over the radio, "Make a right! Make a right!" Brock looked in the mirror and saw that Chad had pulled over a block behind him, so he made the right on Commerce St.

"Make another right at the next street and come up behind me. Sorry for the panic, but I was afraid you guys would go straight."

Phillips asked, "Why not go straight?"

"Didn't you look down that hill? That's the marina and dock for the shrimp and oyster boats," Chad said as Brock pulled up behind him.

Chad got out of the car and walked back to Brock and Phillips as he did his best 'good ol' boy' walk. Sanchez got out of the car and joined Chad on the sidewalk.

"Why didn't you want us to go down there?" Brock asked.

"For one thing it would take you a while to turn around and for another, I was trying to figure out why these guys were coming down here. Then it dawned on me, the docks, they came down here because of the docks. A small insignificant port with fishing docks and poor security."

As if on cue, a rental truck came up the driveway from the docks and turned right.

"Crap, I forgot," Phillips groaned. "A number of years ago when the town was starting to come out of its decline, there were stories about a Chiquita Banana truck, actually it was a truck painted to look like a Chiquita Banana truck, being used to pick up drug deliveries from the boats at the dock. The dock at that time was fairly small and you could watch them unload from the restaurant that used to sit on that vacant lot on the corner. No one ever did anything about it, the State cops put it down to rumor. It was a big joke that it was never looked into more closely, a banana truck picking up fish is pretty strange. Maybe the State guys didn't want to mess with it or maybe they figured the town needed the help. When I saw that truck come up the ramp it triggered the memory, hell I didn't know the docks were down there."

Brock was laughing, "A banana truck on a fishing dock had to be picking something up besides fish, unless they were getting their bananas shipped direct. These guys were outrageously stupid to think no one would notice, the only thing that makes it worse is that they got away with it. I can just see the traffic stop..." he was laughing so hard he couldn't finish the sentence.

Chad shook his head, "Maybe the banana guy was making a few dollars on the side dealing in hands." Chad broke down laughing and sat on the sidewalk.

Sanchez looked at them questioningly, then his eyes brightened, "I got it, hands of bananas and," he paused. "You guys have got to get a grip."

Chad looked up from the sidewalk, "Okay, I'm okay. Give me a hand up will you," and he started laughing again.

Sanchez nudged him with his foot and Chad got up still trying to control himself.

"I'm taking Sanchez with me now," said Chad. "Go, get behind those guys."

Chad and Sanchez got into the car and watched Brock as he eased down the parking lanes until they could see through the large display windows of the corner store. They caught sight of the back of the truck as it pulled away from the curb and started moving down Commerce. Brock followed at more than the required distance and saw both vehicles turn on a street that ran past a swimming pool and toward the bay. He looked in the mirror and saw Chad behind him so he drove past the street and turned left at the next corner. Chad made the turn at the pool and slowly followed as the SUV parked near a small beach area with the truck close behind, Chad pulled into a small RV park and called Philips.

"Where are you?"

"About a block behind where you turned, we can see you. What are they doing?" Phillips asked.

"Nothing right now. Get closer if you can, there's a park thing across from where we are now and it has picnic tables. It will be on your left, meet us there."

Chad drove over to the little park and pulled up to one of the covered picnic tables. He turned to Sanchez and filled him in on what his job was for the next ten or fifteen minutes, grabbed the baseball cap and told him not to leave the vehicle. He then got out, walked over to the table and sat down.

A few minutes later Brock pulled up. As Brock and Phillips got out of the car Chad walked over and shook Brocks hand.

"What are you doing?" Brock asked.

"Just play acting in case we are being watched, follow my lead. Jake put this hat on and let's walk over to the table."

They all sat at the table and Chad handed Phillips a small pair of binoculars.

"Brock and I are going to walk over there and do some more acting, I need you to take a good look at the truck driver and the occupants of the SUV."

"Where's Sanchez?" Phillips asked.

"He's got his own job to do, but he's in the front seat," answered Chad. "I don't want us here to long, so let's do this."

He and Brock walked a few feet from the table and looking in the opposite direction Chad held up his arm and pointed here and there with a sweeping motion.

Brock chuckled, "This should catch the attention of those guys and maybe put them at ease. If they are looking at us they aren't seeing Phillips, very good idea. By the way, I think that is our rental truck from the motel."

"How can you tell?"

"The front passenger side fender and bumper are dented. I noticed it when we were watching them leave the motel. When we turn around you can see the bumper is buckled and slightly twisted."

Chad laughed, "You are observant, I didn't even think of looking at the truck that closely. I have Sanchez using the other binoculars to see if he can pick anything up with his lip reading. I have him so low in the front seat his back may never be the same. Fill Phillips in for me, now let's get out of here."

They walked back over to the table, Phillips stood up and they started back to their cars. When they got close they shook hands, Phillips passed the cap and binoculars back to Chad.

Chad smiled, "Nice doing business with you."

"Yeah, the checks in the mail," Brock laughed.

"I'm going over to the other side of the causeway, I'll catch you over there," Chad informed Phillips.

Chad turned onto the highway and started across the bridge. The water of Lavaca Bay was calm, a clear blue, with the sea birds and sail boats finishing off the picture.

"You know," Sanchez said, "it's really pretty here. It's a shame those two industrial plants loom over all of it."

"At least the Alcoa Plant is far enough out on the point, but Formosa is an eyesore," Chad offered. "Any luck lip reading?"

"No, I couldn't get one word. They just stood and talked, the woman with them went down to the beach. I had a good view, I just didn't recognize the language."

Chad shrugged, "I'll lay odds it was Arabic."

32

The remainder of the drive to the Houston area was uneventful and as they got near the town of Alvin, Phillips took a deep breath.

"We're getting into close quarters now," Phillips sighed. "I'll let the helicopter pilots know our location, it'll put them on their toes."

He looked over at Brock as he ended the call, "You've been very quiet. What's rattling around up there?"

"I'm not sure exactly," Brock answered. "This doesn't track right for me. These guys sit in a motel doing nothing, when they leave they meet a truck, that was with them previously at the motel, at a dock on the Gulf. Not forgetting the truck left a day ahead of them. This tells me that what they were waiting for came by boat and had to come in at a place that lacked security. Question one is what is it that had to be brought in that way? Which leads me to another question. What were those other guys waiting for? If we are right about Corpus Christi and Port Arthur why were those guys at the motel in Corpus for so long? It would make more sense to be at your destination instead of everyone in one place, especially if it's a coordinated effort. I understand the guys in our SUV, they are probably heading up this project, but the Port Arthur guys should have already been at their target. They don't need what's in the truck, otherwise they would be here too, same with the Corpus guys. Why did they stay in Corpus Christi when they were waiting for a boat to dock in Port Lavaca? There are plenty of motels there. Either these guys aren't as smart as we thought or this is misdirection. Why don't you have Chad check with his guys in Corpus and see what's going on there and call the guys following the other SUV and see where they are."

Phillips found that the Port Arthur team was on I-10 still headed east and nothing of any consequence had happened. Chad called back and told Phillips that the Corpus suspects had gone home. After leaving the motel the driver had dropped off the other guy at a house, he went to another house, locked his car and went inside. The surveillance team had called in the locals so they could have surveillance on both houses.

"Well, that makes sense. No hurry in getting to your target, if nobody else is at theirs," Brock grunted.

The truck and SUV turned onto Highway 6 and into a motel. Brock drove passed it, turned around and parked so they could see the front of the motel. Chad had slowed at the motel and turned into a dirt parking lot next to the motel.

"Heads up," came over the radio, "You have another rental truck and a white panel van headed your way."

Brock check his mirror, "Here it comes."

The two vehicles pulled into the same parking lot Chad had chosen. Brock moved his car off the street and into a parking lot facing the motel as two more panel vans parked near Chad. The occupants of the four vehicles, eight men, got out and walked to the motel. They were all wearing painters' pants and T-shirts.

Chad got on the radio, "I'm going in."

Phillips came back, "You can't do that."

"Why not? They don't know who I am and Sanchez is staying here. I'm walking in. I want to find out if these guys are staying here."

Phillips didn't reply as he watched Chad moving toward the motel.

Brock smiled, "I guess that's one way to find out what's going on."

Chad walked into the motel office and inquired about vacancies and restaurants.

The guy behind the desk stood, "We got lots of empty rooms and plenty of eating places down the road."

"I saw all those men walking in here and I didn't think you'd have any rooms left," Chad smiled at the man.

"Them?" the desk clerk jerked his thumb in the direction of the room. "They're not staying here. A guy rented two rooms over the phone, said he needed one for him and one for his sister and her husband. He said he would be expecting some friends to drop by, I guess that was them."

"They look like the Mexican house painters I hired a while back," Chad offered.

"Those ain't Mexicans, I don't know what they are, but not Mexicans," the clerk said shaking his head. "If they aren't out of here by dark, I'll have to go move them along or get some more money."

Chad knew better than to press the guy for a name, so he inquired about rates and said he'd be back. As he reached for the door a black sedan with tinted windows pulled into the motel and up to the occupied rooms. He walked down the drive to the street and looked over his shoulder to try and see who got out of the car. He only got a profile wearing sunglasses.

Chad climbed back in the car, picked up the radio and filled everyone in on what he had found out and asked if they had a read on the sedan.

Brock came over the radio, "We didn't get a plate number. I thought it looked odd going in there, so I checked for plates, but the rear plate had mud on it. We'll check the front plate when it comes out, but I think that nice clean car also has a muddy front plate."

"It's too early to find rooms close by, so I suggest we just sit and wait. We can take turns trying to get some sleep, but hell it's time for coffee. Who wants to make the run?"

Chad and Sanchez went to get coffee while Brock and Philips kept watch. Brock turned to Phillips, "We haven't heard anything from anybody on all the stuff the labs are working on and that bothers me."

"I was thinking the same thing. I think I'll give them a call and see what the problem is," Phillips said picking up his cell.

Brock picked up the notebook and began looking through it, when he got to the printed photos he paged through them three times and couldn't find what he was looking for.

Phillips got off the phone and did not look happy. "The device that we found on the dead guy in Arizona was active and it's linked up with the other devices. They didn't call us because they can't pinpoint the signal. They said it's bouncing around between three, sometimes four different places. There are several signals going to these places and they aren't really sure where ours is ending up. They haven't gotten a signature on the maker or where it could have been made, but they're still working on it."

"Screw where it was made, I want to know why it's here," Brock said in frustration. "Did they give you any of the locations where these things are pinging?

"Yeah, vague locations. Central America probably Nicaragua, the east coast Virginia/DC area and Cyprus," Phillips informed him.

"Did you get the photo of Addison from the surveillance guy? It's not in the book."

"That should be on my phone along with the picture of the message Rogelio left us. I'll send it to you." Phillips got busy searching his phone.

Brock was sitting and staring out the window when his cell rang, he looked at the ID, it was Bracken. He opened his door and answered the phone as he walked to the back of the car.

"Good morning and you're up early," he said.

"Once I started looking into things I found it hard to put it aside. Those tracking devices you found on the vehicles, that model was phased out and replaced by newer ones, so your information was correct. My guy tells me the older ones were destroyed, but one hundred of them were held out to be used in training. You want to guess who requested them?" Bracken asked.

"I have a few ideas, but I'm going with the DOJ," Brock answered.

"Bingo! I did more sniffing around to see where they went and no one knows what I'm talking about. I then pulled the paper on the request and it was signed by the AG himself."

"You're telling me that Rick Olden signed for them? Since when does he sign for anything, he won't even pick up a lunch check." Brock said.

"Well, this is his signature, maybe he thought it would get lost," Bracken replied.

"So from there they could have gone anywhere. Rats!"

"I didn't stop there. I have guys on the inside of everything, so I made some calls. I wanted to do this above board, but since I couldn't get a straight answer I went underground. Don't worry these guys are paid to keep their eyes open and mouths shut. This all happened about a year and a half ago, but they remembered it because it struck them as strange that real devices would be used in training. The short end is that some of the devices went to ATF the rest to DHS."

Brock sighed, "Thanks, I think. I owe you again, I always seem to be in your debt."

Bracken laughed, "Let's keep it that way, but don't sound so down. I think you might be on to something here. There is no real reason for the DOJ to have these old devices, they had the new ones issued two weeks after this request. If they are being used on these vehicles then they are being tracked by someone and my guys say they can't find any evidence of that. Which says they are being tracked on the outside. These agencies wouldn't do that because they'd need whatever they got for prosecutorial purposes and that requires everything being done in house and by the book."

Brock ran his hand through his hair, "I had a feeling when they found those things that something wasn't right. I knew no one else was watching these guys, otherwise when we called it in we would have been told to back off. Everything we have leads us to believe someone on the inside had a hand in this."

Bracken cleared his throat, "If you don't mind, I'd like to put in my two cents. You can think about it, then take whatever action you decide."

Before Brock could answer Chad pulled in from the coffee run. Sanchez walked over to him with a large coffee and seeing the serious look on his face, simply handed it to him and walked away.

Chad looked over a Phillips, "Who is Brock talking to?"

"No idea, but he's doing more listening than talking."

"If you could see the look on his face, you'd know it was serious," Sanchez put in.

Brock got off the phone, walked over to them, grabbed a donut and filled them in on the information he had gotten on the devices.

"I took the liberty of telling my guy about the message from Rogelio, I didn't think you would mind." He paused, "We all know who the head of DHS is, but does anyone know the name of the number two guy?"

No one answered at first, then Chad said, "I think the last name is Hayes."

"Close," replied Brock. "Number two is Mr. Matt Haynes. So I'm thinking the message, 'Sec tio mat DC', roughly translates to 'Security Uncle Matt Haynes DC'. Any thoughts?"

33

Phillips stood and stared blankly at Brock, then appeared to come to his senses. "You're sure about this because this is not something to joke about."

"Now you've got to be kidding. Do you actually think I would joke about something this serious? Go online and look it up for yourself," Brock turned and got back in the car.

Phillips punched numbers into his phone, but it wasn't to go online. When he hung up he turned to Chad, "I called for some extra teams. They told me you had two in Houston, so get them over here." With that he walked around to the other side of the car and got in.

Chad shrugged his shoulders and looked at Sanchez, "Looks like the twins need a nap. Let's go."

Chad drove back over to his parking lot and parked close enough to the vans to maybe overhear a conversation, but not so close to cause a problem. He called the other teams and then leaned his head back on the headrest and started mumbling to himself. Sanchez sat in silence.

Finally Chad said, "I've never seen Jake like this before, he's always right on the mark and never gets pissy. He's one of the most focused guys I've ever worked with. It must be the kid, he's making this a personal thing, maybe trying to right a wrong."

"Sorry," Sanchez said, "I'm not following."

Chad sighed, "I probably shouldn't say anything, but you need to know where all this might be coming from, but you never heard this from anyone. The incident he mention that happened in the Middle East happened at the hospital. The doctors were checking out a bunch of kids when an attack came. They fought like hell and finally got enough help to drive the attackers back. When the smoke cleared they had lost two doctors, a couple of nurses, twelve adults and ten children the oldest was four years old. The doctors and security had killed a large number of their attackers and saved a lot of people, including kids, but the ones that died," his voice trailed off almost to a whisper. He cleared his throat, "When kids get killed it breaks your heart, I don't care how much of a man you are or you think you are, it does something inside that you can't put away. I think Jake feels he could have done more or seen it coming, but you can't because you're doing your job and his job was not to watch for the bad guys. So, maybe saving this kid is what he needs. That's it, that's all I'm going to say about it and you will say nothing about it." Chad's mood changed, "When my guys get here you and I are going to go someplace and shoot a few rounds." He picked up his phone and started looking for shooting ranges, then picked up the radio.

"You guys still there and breathing?" he radioed.

"Very funny. Did you call your teams?" Phillips asked.

"They're on their way. One was in Dickenson and should be here any time now and the other one is probably an hour out. Just a heads up, Sanchez and I are going to the range when they get here. I need to square away my toys and I want to check out Sanchez, he might need the practice. The range is about thirty minutes, at most from here and we have the radio so it shouldn't be a problem."

"I'd rather you didn't, but I understand the reasoning," Phillips said and click off.

"You want to talk now?" Brock asked.

"Nothing to talk about."

"Sure there is. If Haynes is the uncle, we'll have to approach the parents without letting the bad guys know. Then we have to get Rogelio and Haynes at the same time. I can have a couple of our guys watch Haynes and when we have Rogelio they can grab Haynes, discreetly of course."

"We need to see how deep Haynes is in this thing," Phillips added. "You know you could have found a better way of giving me the information."

"How was I supposed to tell you? I couldn't just tell you and not Chad and Sanchez, they needed to know too. I was given a possible link and delivered the name over donuts and coffee. We aren't at the office in a conference room sharing the latest evidence."

Phillips phone rang, he answered, grabbed the notebook and started writing.

He hung up and immediately picked up the radio, "You there?"

"Yeah, go."

"I just got an update on things and wanted to fill everyone in at the same time. They traced the call from the pay phone in Corpus Christi. It went to DC to a burner phone, so that trail is cold and all the fingerprints were a dead end. One of the prints is not on any database, including military, so that is probably our guy. The van in Arizona was carrying explosives, they found all kinds of residue, but not the big stuff I was expecting. It's weird, they found dynamite, blasting caps and C-4. Sounds like a delivery to more than one place. The van and SUV did have the tracking devices on them that match our photos, they were mangled, but identifiable." Phillips paused and asked, "Any questions or suggestions so far?"

"Yeah." Chad answered. "If they did fingerprints on that bus then this guy, Addison, should have left some prints behind. I think we should get facial pictures to go with the prints and that would give us a positive ID. That print on the phone may not have been his, it could belong to anyone and I think the prints from the bus would be a good double check, same with the motel prints."

"Good idea, I'll get on that when we're finished. Next, they got a lot of prints from the motel and are going through them in Corpus Christi and now the FBI has entered the picture big time. The body in the bath tub was confirmed as the bus driver and because he was employed by the Border Patrol, a government agency, the FBI wants to take it over. Corpus PD is fighting them so that will give us more time, not a lot maybe a few hours. The ME says the autopsy should be complete later today, minus the blood work."

"Lucky for us they don't know where we are?" interjected Sanchez.

"Got that right," Brock said.

"Have them check that end room where that couple with the truck was staying." Chad said. "The guy touched the door knob with his bare hands, so there may be prints there. We have reason to need them now. Something else just hit me, we should probably have that boat in Port Lavaca checked out and the sooner the better. The crew might have something for us, if nothing else they can tell us where they picked up the cargo. Hell, they may not even be legal."

"Better to know than not know," said Phillips. "I'll get these calls made now. I don't know if we can get anyone to Lavaca as fast as we need them, but I'll see what I can do. If you think of anything else let me know. I'm over and out."

Phillips set the radio down and noticed Brock staring at him, "What now."

"Nothing, I like the way you guys keep everything compartmentalize." Brock said. "You rattle off the information quickly and precisely section by section and when you ask for input, your guys don't cross over to a different area. You cover each area separately, any other group doing this would be all over the place."

"That's how they train us to do it." Phillips said. "The big boys upstairs don't like a confused briefing, you only ask questions or make suggestions on topic, no crossover, no wasted time."

"What happens if you are in a room with other law enforcement, how do you keep them in line?"

"They're informed ahead of time how it works. We also tell them that if they want to they can wait until the end of the meeting to ask questions. It works out okay. We do have a slight problem with the FBI, sometimes they get a bit pushy and that is why we try to keep all the agencies in the loop from the beginning, when necessary. We don't want to have to play catch-up with those guys."

"Our briefings are fairly smooth and orderly, but nothing like yours." Brock said.

Phillips phone rang again, after he answered he bolted upright almost jumping out of his seat. He asked a few questions, hung up and sat staring out the windshield.

He finally turned to Brock and clicked the radio so they could hear him in Chads vehicle. "They've located where Rogelio's parents live."

34

Brock looked at Phillips, "Confirmed?"

"Not exactly," Phillips replied. "Chad you guys still there?"

"Yes, still here, go ahead."

"I guess I should have said they found the link between Haynes and Rogelio. Once I gave them the reference to Haynes, they started running a check on his family and he has a sister who lives in Costa Rica. She's married to a doctor, they have, or had two sons, the oldest was reported as possibly deceased about five months ago, but they never recovered a body. The other son is Roger, seven years old."

"What do they mean 'possibly deceased'?" Brock asked.

"Two hikers found a body, checked it for identification and found a student card with his name on it. They went to the police, gave them the card and directions to the site, but when the cops arrived there was no body or any sign that one had been there. The cops went to the address the hikers had given them as their place of residence, but they weren't there. So the official report listed cause of death as 'unknown, suspicious, with no positive ID'."

"Seems a bit odd to me," Brock said.

"No shit. I think the cops feel the same way," Phillips replied. "Why would people search a dead body for ID, why not just report it? Most folks don't want to touch a body much less search it, unless they were looking for valuables. I bet whoever lives at that address knew nothing about the hikers."

"It could be that the student card was turned in as a threat to the parents. Maybe the older son is being held hostage down there, which makes this situation even worse." Brock added. "Where do the parents live?"

"No confirmation, but the information we have says they live on the Gulf of Mexico side near Limon. If the brother is being held hostage, he could have been transported by boat to anywhere on the globe. Damn it!" Phillips hit the door with the side of his fist. "So now they take the second son to apply more pressure."

"Relax, for all we know the older brother is already dead. These people used the student card to get to the parents and take Rogelio, or Roger, as their hostage. They wouldn't need two hostages, the older son would have been enough. They take the other son and say they will do the same to him. Which tells me that Haynes and his sister are close and they are using the kid to keep Haynes in line. If I had a sister I know I wouldn't want to be the reason she lost her remaining son."

"We need to get confirmation on this," Chad came over the radio. "It sounds like we've got the right information, but let's get confirmation. Someone needs to get Haynes under wraps, he should take a business trip and soon. Be sure his immediate family is protected, maybe they should go with him."

Phillips came back, "I'll give the office a call and see what they can come up with for us."

"Okay, but wait a minute my guys are here," Chad said. "I'm leaving the radio open so you can hear."

An SUV pulled into the parking lot and parked near one of the panel vans, two guys got out and walked over to Chad and leaned in the windows. Chad introduced them as Ralphie and Lou and filled them in on the set up.

"Do you guys have any tracking devices with you?"

"Never leave home without them," Lou answered.

"Good," Chad replied. "Put one on that truck," Chad pointed to the truck from the motel. "You and Phillips can decide where you want to put the other one. We also need you to check and see if there are already devices on the vehicles, the other vehicles we tagged have them. We just don't know who put them on there. Then you need to decide who follows what. The other guys should be here soon. Also, give your cell number to Phillips."

Chad pulled a map out of the glove box, got out of the car, walked to the front and spread the map on the hood. He motioned for the two men to join him. As he looked at the map he said, "One of you go ahead and put a device on that truck, we'll look busy and cover for you. If you find that other device, use your cell and get a picture."

Sanchez put on his baseball cap, got out of the car and pretended to check the tires. After Lou had placed the device and walked back over to them, Sanchez joined the three men just as Lou was saying that there was another device and he had a picture.

"Not only that," Lou was saying, "but there is a good size hole in the bottom of that truck. Whoever they rented it from doesn't do inspections."

"How big is the hole?" asked Sanchez.

"About the size of your foot, big enough to get wet inside during a big rain storm," Lou answered.

"I'll be right back," Sanchez said as he started across the street.

Sanchez ran up to Phillips, "I need your digital camera. There's a hole in the bottom of the truck and I think we might be able to get a picture of what's inside."

"That's a long shot," Phillips said "but right now I'll try just about anything."

Phillips handed him the camera, he stuck it under his shirt and took off across the street again. When he rejoined Chad he said to Lou, "I would like you to see if you can get some pictures through that hole. Just stick the camera through the hole and snap a few at different angles, I'd do it but you know where the hole is and it will be quicker."

"You got it," Lou said and took off at a fast walk and disappeared under the truck.

As they waited Sanchez kept looking over his shoulder praying that the driver of the truck wouldn't show up. He finally looked over and saw Lou coming back from the direction of their car instead of the truck.

Lou was chuckling, "I decided to use my own misdirection. No sense in looking suspicious, I maneuvered around two vehicles so I could come back from ours. Here's your camera, I got about five shots and I have no idea if they are any good. It would be nice if I could make that hole bigger and get my head through it, even better would be to get inside."

Sanchez thanked him, pretended to take pictures of the map and the men, then took the camera back to Phillips. "Okay, he got five shots of the interior, but we haven't looked at them. Hope some of them show us something, but they may have to be enhanced. Crap, the computer is in Chads car. I'll go get it while you check out what he got."

Phillips began reviewing the photos, then handed the camera to Brock, "Looks like he got a couple of good ones. Those look like armament and ammo crates, big ones, unfortunately we can't see the stencil. I have an idea what they may be, but before I say anything I want to hear from you."

"Well," Brock said, "they are big."

"Very funny."

"If I had to guess, I would say some of those crates look like they may hold missiles, the shoulder mounted type. Too blurry to be positive and you can just make out part of a stencil on one of them. Get them to your guys and see what they can do." Brock watched Sanchez come back from across the street, "Wish I still smoked."

Sanchez gave the lap top to Phillips, then looked over at Brock, "I want to thank you guys again for keeping me with you, I'm learning a lot and I get to use my brain for a change."

Brock replied, "You used your brain a lot in Mexico and are proving to be an asset here."

"That's his way of saying you're welcome, think nothing of it and glad to have you aboard," Phillips said. "You'll have to excuse him, he's lamenting that he quit smoking." They heard Brock grunt and Phillips added, "Tell Lou he did get some good pictures and as soon as I get a confirmation I'll fill everyone in on what we have or may have."

Phillips opened the lap top and looked back at Sanchez, "You guys getting ready to take off?"

"Yes, I think so. You know Chad better than I do, but I think he needs to blow off some excess energy and frustration. His toys appear to be his conduit, anyway I want to pick his brain on firearms and get some pointers."

"Don't let him stay to long, time gets way from him when he's on the range," Phillips said.

"I figure we probably have an hour or two. I think those guys are in there resting up for what's to come, wish we could do the same." Sanchez patted the window frame and walked back across the street.

35

Chad and Sanchez pulled onto Highway 35, made a right on FM 1462 then drove toward the shooting range with Sanchez leafing through his notebook and mumbling to himself. He stopped, looked out the window then started writing himself notes in the margins. Finally Chad couldn't stand it anymore.

"What are you doing?"

"I'm going through my notes and asking myself questions," he looked over at Chad, "you know, for clarification purposes. I write the answers next to the area they pertain to and the notes in the margins are questions I can't answer,"

"Is there anything I can clarify for you?" Chad asked.

"Probably, but I didn't want to bother you, in case they sounded like idiotic questions."

"In this particular case, I don't think anything would sound idiotic. Try me."

"Great," Sanchez said, paging toward the front of the notebook. "Did anyone follow the guys at the motel who went out and got the food?"

"I know they were followed for the first two days, but after that I'm not sure. Since every time they went out it was straight to a restaurant and then back again, probably not. Once they set the pattern, the guys probably thought it wasn't necessary."

Sanchez finished writing and asked, "Was there always someone watching the suspected targets or just the suspects?"

"There was always someone on the suspects and we had cars cruising the targets."

"So, someone could conceivably time the cars routes, slip in and plant an explosive device. One trip to a restaurant to pick up a late dinner and a device could have been planted." Sanchez pondered.

"I guess you're right, maybe I should have the guys do another ground check." Chad said.

Sanchez looked at him, "Sorry, I was thinking out loud. I wasn't second guessing your guys."

"No, no, you're right. The targets are so big that patrols seemed like the thing to do, but one trip to watch the timing and the next trip to plant the device. Let me call these guys."

They arrived at the shooting range as Chad finished his call to Corpus Christi. "There are two cars patrolling about ten minutes apart. They've now decided to tighten it up and are going to ask for another car. Thanks for that. Guess I'm not thinking and I won't make any more excuses. Now let's go kill some targets."

Chad opened up the back of the SUV, "We're going to take the hand guns first, when we get loosened up we'll come out and get the big toys. I usually prefer to go to outdoor ranges, but sometimes it's good to shoot indoors so you know how it feels. What I'm trying to say and not doing very well, is most CQ firing is in an indoor setting, CQ being Close Quarters. For us it would more than likely be a fairly large building, with local PD it is usually homes, apartments and that sort of thing. Also, at a range you have ear protection, but as you are aware you don't wear that in the real world. We have earwigs for communication in one ear, which helps and a lot of the guys will put a piece of cotton in the other ear. I don't cover my other ear because I want to hear everything going on around me, I won't hold it against you if you want to cover your other ear if we get in a fire fight."

They grabbed their gear and headed inside. They started with their preferred weapon at max distance and worked their way to near. Chad handed Sanchez the Glock, "You're very good, but I want you to try this one."

Sanchez took the gun, worked the action, put up a fresh target and ran it to full distance. His first three shots were a bit wide, but the rest were center body mass and clustered. As he ran the target back in he said, "This has a good feel to it, this must be the newest one."

Chad nodded, set new targets and they continued for another fifteen minutes. Chad said, "Now we go for the big guys."

They packed up the guns, stopped to tell to the range master they were going for their rifles and asked if anyone else was shooting in that area. They were told it was clear, Chad asked if they could have to themselves for about half an hour and showed him his credentials.

"Do you always have people recognize your credentials?" Sanchez asked as they walked to the car.

"Most of the time we don't have a problem. They have no idea who we are, but it looks official so they don't ask questions."

The two men carried in the cases containing the weapons and spent another forty-five minutes firing.

Sanchez finally said, "I promised Phillips we wouldn't be gone more than an hour and we're passed that."

"Yeah, he gets knotted up when I leave to go to a range. Sometimes I think it's because he can't go with me, he likes doing this as much as I do. Give him a call on the radio and let him know we're headed back, he'll feel better after he hears from us."

"How did you know this place was here?" Sanchez asked.

"The first thing I do when I get into a town is find the shooting range. I think it says a lot about a place if they have one, it's just the way I think. Some people have to have a shopping mall, a lake or a golf course, me, I need a range. Now go call Phillips."

Phillips was relieved to hear from them, "On your way back, find a place to pick up some food and clean the residue off your hands. Chad, if you're listening, I need to fill you in on some things, so after food comes a briefing."

"Got it," Chad replied then added, "By the way, Sanchez here is a good shot. Can't say what he's like under pressure, but he can definitely handle a weapon."

"Glad to hear that," Brock put in, "Hey, get me two of everything I'm starving."

As they drove away from the shooting range Sanchez said, "I enjoyed that, thanks for letting me tag along, at least now you know I can handle a weapon. Why didn't you take the M16 or the .338 Lapua inside?"

"I don't like to advertise and even with no one else firing, the range guy would have seen it. Sometimes even seasoned shooters get a bit nervous if a .338 comes through the door. How did you know I had a .338, I never mentioned it?"

"I saw the case and just made an educated guess," Sanchez smiled back at him.

He stared out the side window for a moment then turned back to Chad. "If this mess does go up the chain to someone in DC, I'll be more disappointed than I was with Fast and Furious. I was ticked off about that, but this is worse since its taking place within our borders. I'm glad my grandfather isn't alive to see all of this shit, he was a self-made patriot."

"What do you mean?" Chad asked.

"I don't know if self-made is the correct term, but it fits. He came to the United States from Mexico legally, applied for citizenship, took the test, was sworn in and proudly displayed his papers in a frame on the living room wall. It was his dream to become as he put it, 'a citizen of the greatest country of the whole world that God created. Where peoples could be what he wants to be and the family would be free to not starve.' His English wasn't very good, but we all knew what he meant and he would preach to us all the time about using our freedom to make ourselves better. He would not have understood why, when things were good, someone would turn against his country and do things like this."

As they pulled up next to Brocks' car, Chad said, "I would sympathize with your grandfather, I don't understand it either."

36

Phillips and Chad left it up to Brock and Sanchez to change the position of the cars and started to walk down the street. Phillips had explained to Sanchez that this was office talk and therefore couldn't be discussed openly. The two men walked casually for a while then Phillips checked the radio to be sure they couldn't be overheard.

"How did it go?" Phillips asked.

"He's a very good shot, handles weapons with respect and confidence. I thought maybe he was bullshitting about being able to shoot anything, but he wasn't. Don't get me wrong, he's good, but not as good as we are. He may react differently in a hot situation, we won't know that until we see him under pressure. I think with more training he just might be a decent sniper, but he definitely needs to get his breathing under control."

"I don't want to use him as a sniper. I'd like to have you and I paired on this one, but that's not going to happen, I feel responsible for Brock. If this goes bad I don't want any of this on his shoulders, he's here because the CIA wants him here, but I wouldn't put it passed them to throw him to the wolves. You can pair up with Sanchez or we can trade him off for one of your other guys, it's up to you."

"I'll keep him. It won't be babysitting, but it will be close. You're talking like we're going to move on these guys. Are we ready for that?"

"As soon as I get word on Haynes and what they find in those photos, we will. Those crates were big and I don't want to wait for them to set things up before we move. By that time it may be too late. I'd like to be more isolated than this in case..," Philips paused, "Well, just in case. By the way, good call on getting those photos."

"That wasn't my idea, Sanchez came up with that. I didn't know what he was doing until he got back with the camera." Chad said.

"Then I'll thank him. Oh, that sedan left the motel and Brock was correct, the front plate was muddy."

They turned around and started back to the cars when Phillips said, "You better talk to Sanchez and get him ready. I'd do it, but he's working with you and needs to know your quirks."

"Quirks, I don't have any quirks."

Phillips started laughing, "Yeah you do and you know what I'm talking about."

When they got closer to the motel they split up, Phillips crossed the street and spotted Brock's car parked where Chads used to be. Chad spotted Sanchez parked at an angle in the lot across from the motel.

As he climbed in the front seat he asked, "Can you get a good look at those guys when they come out?"

"Yeah, I tried a few different angles and this was the best one and it's better than being so close to the vans. Over here I can see more than one person at a time and if they speak English or Spanish I'll be able to read them, but my expectations are low."

"If you can pick something up from them it would be a plus, otherwise we'll handle it the way we usually do. I hope you realize this could turn messy, I don't think these guys are going to lay down their arms and surrender. How do you feel about putting your life on the line?" Chad asked.

Sanchez leaned his head against the headrest, looked out the windshield and thought for a moment. When he spoke his voice was quiet and reverent, "Every day when I go to work I carry a weapon I'm not allowed to discharge, I hunt drug and human traffickers as well as the illegals. The illegals are fairly docile, thirsty, hungry and scared, the traffickers are hostile and carry weapons. From the minute I step out of my truck I have a target on me and I'll never see it coming. It could come from anywhere, from across the river or through the trees. I have a buddy who was tracking some illegals and had his knee shot out when he rounded the corner of some bushes and ran into drug runners. He was lucky, they could have killed him. So, in answer to your question, I have no problem putting my life on the line. At least this time it won't be a surprise."

"I know that sounded like a stupid question, but it had to be asked. Phillips is teaming us up on this and we had to be sure where you stood. We will probably not be in close, but watching for strikes from outside their perimeter. We will still carry side arms in case we get into trouble, otherwise we use our long range toys."

"We will all wear earwigs for communications and carry flash bangs and until we get a timeline we don't know what else we need. I do need to fill you in on how I work so that we work more like a team rather than individuals. We use clock positions, as I'm sure you do, I do not like anyone at my six. I get itchy when anyone is behind me, plus you can see my six if you are at three or nine and I can see yours. Don't talk unless it's important, I don't like chatter. Once I get on the job that is my entire focus and you are going to have Phillips and Brock listening to you. Phillips and Brock will be number one and two respectively, I am number three and you are four. When speaking to one of us use our number, as an example you might say 'one at your three', translated that's 'Phillips watch your three position'. We will carry these numbers for the duration of this case, even if you and I go in first."

"Phillips is waiting to hear if they have moved on Haynes and what they found on your pictures. Once he gets his questions answered then we'll look for the right time and place to take these guys. This is basically a heads up and tutorial for you, if you decide you want out just say the word and don't worry, not one of us will hold it against you. If you have any questions between now and the time we move, all you have to do is ask. Oh, any injuries will be paid for by our people as well as any pay you might lose."

"Yeah, like I'm worried about hospital bills," Sanchez said.

"Don't worry, they'll pay the funeral bill too," Chad laughed.

37

Rogelio lay curled up in a corner of the motel room, same corner different motel and this time Yolanda lay there with him. He had held her hand until she had cried herself to sleep, he then pulled the blanket up over her shoulders and curled under his own blanket.

All the men and the mean girl were in the other room and he could hear them arguing. He didn't understand what they were saying and most of the time when they talked they sounded angry. He had decided it must be the strange language that made them sound that way, because sometimes they would laugh. He heard someone drive up and come into the other room, it sounded like one person and when he spoke their language is was softer sounding, not like he was trying to clear his throat. He knew that this time they really were arguing because something was thrown against the wall. He was afraid they had killed someone. He didn't want to see that again, he could only hope that when they killed him they would use a gun. He squeezed his eyes closed, but the vision of what had happened played behind his eye lids and he couldn't make it stop.

The mean girl was standing in their room at the other motel talking to Ignacio and looking at Yolanda. The bus driver had walked in and whispered something in her ear, she turned to him, smiling at him, then pushed her hand toward him. He had suddenly stepped back, grabbed his chest and stomach. Blood was coming through his fingers and shirt, staining his pants, the driver stumbled and fell against the wall. Then the mean girl started yelling at him, but the man couldn't hear her, he was dead or very close to it. His eyes and mouth were open, but his eyes looked strange and he made no sound. Ignacio yelled at Yolanda and him to get up and help, they made them carry the drivers feet as they took him into the bathroom. Before they could get out of the bathroom the mean girl started saying things in a low voice and started cutting the bus drivers face, then she cut his throat. He knew the man had to be dead because the cuts only had a little bit of blood, so why she was cutting him was a mystery.

His eyes popped open, he heard Ignacio, Jorge and the mean girl talking as they came into the room. Ignacio walked to the end of the bed and looked in the corner at Rogelio, "We are going to sleep because we will be leaving again soon. You stay where you are, you can't get out of the room and there is no place for you to go. Do you understand?"

Rogelio nodded and pulled the blanket closer to his face. He heard Ignacio lay down on the bed, say a few words to the girl and Jorge, then all was quiet.

Rogelio felt like screaming at Ignacio, tell him he spoke Spanish like a baby and tell him that he didn't want to leave because he would look like the bus driver if he did. He reached up and touched the bump on his head it hurt a little, but being thrown in the back seat of the SUV was a small price to pay to keep them from seeing the message he had left on the wall.

He had slept for the first part of the drive with his head on Yolanda's shoulder and her head leaning on the window. He awakened when they stopped at the gas station, he wanted something to eat, but he would not tell them anything. They took turns going inside, when it was his turn Ignacio walked him across the driveway to the store. He noticed an SUV that looked familiar, but he could be wrong, he couldn't figure out when he would have seen it.

When they stopped at the little beach it was much lighter outside, the men got out to talk to the driver of the truck and he saw the SUV again. He got up on his knees, faced the back and sat on his feet with his head resting on the back of the seat. He pretended to have his eyes closed, but they were only small slits as he watched the other SUV. He saw another car pull up near the SUV and he watched two men get out. He almost jumped when he saw one of the men, he looked like the doctor. He couldn't be sure, maybe he was just wishing it was. He turned around again and faced front.

They left the little town and he was about to go back to sleep when he noticed he could see the images in the outside rear view mirror. Sadly all he could see was the top of the truck following them, he was too short to see the full image. He looked around for something to sit on, but there was nothing he could use without calling attention to himself. He told himself he probably wouldn't be able to see if the other SUV was following them because the truck behind them would block his view and anyway he was only imagining things.

Now he felt it was up to him to help himself. He had no more messages to leave or anything to write them with, except maybe blood. That thought made him smile a little because it would not be his blood he left on the wall. He looked down at his hands and realized he was twisting the blanket so hard that his knuckles where turning white. He released the blanket and tried to smooth the wrinkles out of it. He stopped, looked at the sleeping Yolanda and found that he was no longer afraid, but angry. He thought she was one of them, but it turned out that they were using her the way they were using him. He didn't think they had stolen her from her family, he thought they had talked her into joining them. She had been treated like part of their group until a few days ago, then for some reason they had turned against her. They had killed Jazmin, someone he cared about, he would not let them kill Yolanda.

He settled under his blanket and tried to decide what his next step should be, whatever it was he had to be careful. He needed a weapon, something he could hide and be able to use quickly. These people would notice if a gun or knife was missing, so he would have to make his own weapon. He thought about everything in the motel room that he could make into a weapon. At home they had two old beds in the garden shed and they had springs in the bottom, but these beds were new, probably didn't use springs and the bottoms were closed off. He could unscrew one side of a drawer handle, but screws were short and probably wouldn't kill anyone.

He slowly sat up, trying not to wake Yolanda and crawled on the floor toward to foot of the bed. He looked at the chair by the desk and the two chairs at the table, he had to get to them. He kept as close to the beds as he could without touching them, he didn't want to take a chance on the movement of the bed waking someone up. He made it to the swivel chair at the desk and looked under it, there was a large spring, but if he took it off the chair might fall over if someone sat in it. He crawled over to one of the chairs by the table, there was nothing under the seat or under the table top that he could use. He crawled back to the foot of the closest bed and stared at the swivel chair. No one had sat in it yet because they always met in the other room, maybe they would think it was already broken. He moved over to the chair and looked at the spring again, it was thick and if he got it off he probably would not be able to straighten it out enough. The more he looked at it the more he realized he would not be able to remove it without making a lot of noise. He started crawling back to his corner and got as far as the second bed when the bed moved. He stopped, lay flat and held his breath, that's when he saw it.

Under the cabinet that held the television, he saw something shiny. The bed didn't move again, so someone must only have rolled over, he felt safe to move again. He belly crawled to the cabinet and carefully stuck his hand under it, it was narrow and if he had not been flat on the floor he never would have seen it. It felt like metal, he slowly pulled it forward until he could see it clearly, then grabbed it and moved quickly back to the corner. He pulled the blanket over himself and tried to get his breathing under control, his heart was beating so fast he was afraid it would never slow down. He didn't realize how scared he had been.

He moved the blanket down far enough so he could see exactly what treasure he had found, he knew it was a knife, but what kind. He looked down and saw a shiny steak knife, well part of it was shiny. The sharp part of the blade had dirt and rug fibers stuck to it, but it was a knife. He started cleaning it off with part of the blanket, the dirt was old maybe some old steak remains, and was coming off easily. He stuck the knife in his sock so that the blade went all the way to the bottom of his shoe. He straightened his leg out, bent it, then straightened it again, flexed his foot, it felt okay. He would have it remember to be careful when he stood up.

He put his head on the pillow and thought he felt different, he didn't feel like a little kid, he felt older somehow. As he closed his eyes a smile spread across his face and he almost laughed.

38

Phillips sat slumped in the front seat of the car, "Whatever happened to that girl Diane?"

"You mean twin peaks Diane?"

Phillips chuckled, "Yeah, that one."

"Ahh, the history of Diane. She's still at Langley, was transferred to one of the offices in the big building, takes care of written debriefs and final reports. I really don't know what she does, I'm surprised she still has a job," Brock said.

"Are you referring to the screw up?"

"All she had to do was track and trace, be sure we had the correct and latest info on people. At least it wasn't my case she ruined."

"Ruined is not exactly the term I would use. She almost got a guy killed, as it is he had to be in rehab for three months," Phillips replied.

"Yeah, ruined doesn't cut it, but if it had been my case I would've taken it personally. The incident happened a few weeks after I broke it off."

"Maybe she thought it was your case, which means she screwed up twice," Phillips smiled broadly at Brock.

"I'd tell you where to put that comment, but I already thought of that. Why she would pick on me out of all the guys she's dated, I couldn't tell you. Maybe she was after the other guy, she could've been seeing him at the same time she was seeing me or at least near the end. Maybe he dumped her right after I did and she couldn't handle it."

"Did you mention it to him?"

"Nope, don't see any reason to do that, if he's worried about it he can ask Internal Affairs to look into it. Funny, asking that division to look into an actual affair. Anyway, the incident was looked into and she was demoted, but I doubt they looked too deeply into her extracurricular activities. They classified it as a 'simple error'. Simple my ass, a guy almost died." Brock grumbled. "On a brighter note, have you heard anything lately from Daisy Duke?"

"Jeez, I knew that was coming and the answer is no."

"Come on now Jake, she's a beautiful girl and looks just like the real Daisy from head to toe. I still don't understand why you broke that off, she is something else."

"She's something else alright. I'll give you her number, but be prepared and forewarned." Phillips said.

"Prepared for what exactly?" Brock asked.

"If you don't know anything about women's shoes, start reading up on the subject. While you're at it, you might as well get to know different types of manicures, polish colors and what causes fingernails to split or get flakey. Don't forget hair products, know your hair products."

Brock laughed, "That's not what I wanted to hear."

Phillips looked over at him, "Why can't women be interested in guns, hunting, ammunition, sports and things like that? I always seem to get hooked up with superficial, head in the cloud types. Don't get me wrong, I want a feminine woman, but I want one that doesn't have a heart attack when you bring up camping. Someone like Pepa, but less lethal."

"Pepa?" asked Brock, "How well do you know her?"

"Well enough to know not to mispronounce her name," Phillips chuckled. "I've worked with her and Chad a couple of times, the woman knows her stuff. You can ask, but let me just say she's the kind of woman that considers cleaning her weapons and checking the perimeter security a romantic evening. Whatever you do don't drop by unannounced thinking you might get lucky, the only luck you'd get is just being Tased. Like I said, less lethal."

"So, she's not into shoes and nail polish?" Brock asked.

"Far from it, unless you consider Desert Boots fashionable. Again, don't get me wrong, she can be and is, as feminine as they come when she wants to be, but her idea of shopping is going to a gun broker in Israel. A successful shopping trip would be getting a good price on an M16 or Corner Shot and ammo, she loves to debate ammo. A woman like her is rare."

"They're out there, I've met some, but they're all married to coworkers. What about that one at the facility? She seemed nice and the down to earth type."

"Which facility?" Phillips asked.

"The one where we were working, her name is Julie," Brock answered.

"I thought you might be talking about Amanda," Phillips said.

"Who's Amanda? Never mind, she's the one from the other facility right?"

"Yeah, I owe her a dinner and told her when I got back I'd call her," Phillips sighed. "I'll take Julie to dinner too, see what happens."

"My God man, you're not picking out a new car. Get to know them on the job, see if you have anything in common. Go ahead and take Amanda to dinner since you've already mentioned it to her, but don't get involved yet."

"Like that worked for you." Phillips shot back.

"Hey, Diane and I were just fine until she got weird. We'd been seeing each other for four months then she started getting weird. I thought it was something I'd done, but I hadn't change anything or said anything that wasn't normal for me. I was out of town so much I thought maybe she was interested in somebody else and then the more I thought about it I figured maybe she wanted to get married. I even asked her one time if she ever thought about having kids and her answer was 'God no, who wants to be married', so I had my answer to that question. Never could figure out what was going on with her, that's why I broke it off. I couldn't deal with my job and her at the same time."

"You should probably have mentioned that to the people investigating her screw up. Maybe she's into something she shouldn't be." Phillips suggested.

"I did, I told them she had seemed a bit off lately and was acting strangely. I didn't tell them we had been seeing each other and they never mentioned it. I don't think they paid any attention."

Phillips yawned, "Sounds like a half assed investigation. Is she related to someone so important that they overlook things?"

"Not that I know of, but you have a point." Brock stretched, "Change of topic, I think when this case is over we should take a fishing trip. It's been a long time since the last one and I could use a few days on a lake with a bar nearby."

"Sounds good to me. Think about where we should go, but let's definitely do lake or stream. We could do Costa Rica and then I could check up on Rogelio while we're there. By the way before we leave the subject Pepa has a sister, Leigh."

"Is she less lethal?" Brock asked.

"I think so, she isn't in the business. Although I hear she's handy with gardening tools."

"We haven't heard anything on the status of Rogelio's parents and we should have by now," Phillips continued. "I think I'll call and bug them, see what they have."

"You just gave them the information, they've gotten the town pinpointed, so they may need more time."

"Okay, then I'll light a fire under them." Phillips picked up his cell and made the call.

Brock got out of the car, did a couple of stretches, walked around the parking lot, squatted down and started drawing in the dirt that covered the lot. He drew a squiggly upside down T, midway through the single leg he drew another line bisecting it, above that line on the upper right the put a large circle. On both sides of the leg between the parallel lines he drew various circles and toward the bottom of the leg on the lower left a larger circle. He was studying it when Phillips walked up.

"What are you doing, revisiting your childhood?"

"I was trying to remember were the big refineries and tank farms were," Brock replied. "This bottom line is the coast line, the center line is the shipping channel and this top line is I-10. I put that big circle at the top because that is where the big Chevron refinery is, the lower big circle is Texas City and the smaller circles are the tank farms, etc. There are other refineries around there, but I'm not sure of the exact placement. It would help if we could get Chad to pull up an aerial view on his computer. I just want to get an idea of the place, get a feel for it."

"I'll call him and we can take a look at it," Phillips said, "but I want to take these guys before they get close enough to those places to cause trouble."

"I know, but we're already close to these places on the west side of the channel. We aren't going to have a lot of room, that's why I want to see what we have to work with out there. On top of that, we don't know what they're carrying."

Phillips called Chad on the radio, asked for the aerial photos and told him to call back when he had them. As he put the radio down his phone it rang, he looked at the caller ID and answered.

"You got something for me?" and then Phillips just listened. He finally asked, "Do have an educated guess? I won't hold you to it," Phillips waited, "Thanks, I'll let you know."

He looked at Brock, "We may know what they picked up in Port Lavaca. We need to see what Chad has for us."

39

Phillips had Brock drive across the street to Chads vehicle saying they all needed to see the views of the shipping channel and surrounding area. He wouldn't say anything about the call he'd received, he wanted to brief everyone at the same time. They parked next to Chads SUV and got into the back seat.

"Thought I was supposed to call you," Chad said.

"I got a call that changed my mind. This is not a positive identification, but the best guess is that those crates probably are shoulder fired weapons. Mathis in the photo lab said he got them cleared up as best he could and the crates are the right size and the symbol that is partially visible matches. The only thing that would throw it off is if they reused the crates for something else and I don't want to take that chance."

"That news tells me we have to move on these guys, but not here," Chad said. "Is that why you wanted aerial views?"

"No, actually while I was on the phone Brock was drawing what he could remember of the area in the dirt over there and wanted to see them."

Chad turned the lap top so they could all see the screen, then zoomed in so the buildings could be seen clearly. He slowly scrolled up to get an idea of the density, then moved to the east side of the channel and scrolled down again.

"Pretty much the way I remember it," said Brock, "Just more of it."

Sanchez shook his head, "There are a lot of targets there, a lot to cover."

"Took the words right out of my mouth," Chad voiced. "Let me back this picture out a bit and show you something. I don't have our position on the frame, but look at this," he tapped the lower left corner of the screen. "This is Texas City, as you can see it's a big facility and close to us." He tapped the upper right corner of the

214

screen, "This is the big Chevron facility and it's right on the north side of I-10 and in between the two on the east side of the channel you have the huge Exxon facility. If these guys have shoulder fired missiles, Chevron could be hit from the service road on the east bound side of I-10. Exxon could be hit if they fire from the west side of the channel or if they have a boat they could get even closer using one of these little islands, but I wouldn't hit Exxon. A closer target and one you could get away from fast, would be the Shell Refinery. It's right here at Beltway 8 and Highway 225 and there are two or three points where it looks like you would have an easy shot. Last but not least Texas City could be hit from any direction."

"Why wouldn't you hit Exxon?" Brock asked.

"It looks like it has a lot of older tanks there and they're probably not in use. If I had a few extra shots and the time I might finish off with it, but it wouldn't be one of my primary targets. If you were going to hit it from the west side of the channel, you would almost drive right by the Shell Refinery to get within range, so why bother."

"How do you know all this?" Brock asked, "Are you a savant or something?"

Chad laughed, "No, Sanchez and I already looked it up. We were curious." Chad looked at Phillips, "I would like to get a look at the Texas City Refinery in person. Sanchez and I need to get a feel for the actual place so we know what we have to work with and maybe try and read these guys minds."

"How far away would you say we were?" inquired Brock.

"We are about thirty minutes from Texas City and 45 minutes from the Shell Refinery, but the other guys will take care of Shell and Chevron. Unless you're rethinking this and want to let the other guys have Texas City," Chad replied.

Phillips sat back, "No, this one sounds more difficult, so we should take it."

"I agree," said Brock, "lets' go take a look. I don't think these guys are going anywhere for a while. They'll probably wait until dusk or early morning for easy cover."

Chad picked up his phone, "Lou, need you guys to come over here and take our position. We're going on a field trip and I need you to keep an eye on things. We should be back in about an hour and a half and then we'll fill you in on what we think is going to go down. Also, do me a favor and find out where the hell the other car is. We're leaving now, I'll give you a call before we get back."

Chad closed his phone, started the car and said, "Let's get some drinks and see how fast we can get there and back."

They stopped got drinks, topped of the tank and turned south on Highway 6.

Two blocks down the road Brock said, "At least we don't have to worry about them taking the ferry over to the peninsula, they have security that checks every truck and spot checks cars waiting to get on."

"How competent are they?" Chad asked.

"Can't answer that, but I hope they would notice weapons."

"I wouldn't count on that," put in Sanchez. "Almost all the people they hire are local, they take classes, but unless they learn how to identify weapons crates and the symbols on them, they won't know what to look for. I went through there a few months ago, all they do is check the manifest on the big rigs, have them open up the back and just give it a quick look. No real search and manifests can be forged. On top of that rental trucks are not required to have a manifest. Once in a while they'll have a real gun toting DHS Officer, but not often. I do know they're building a new security check point on both landings and I heard that all vehicles will be screened, but again it all depends on who is doing the screening."

"Nothing like giving the citizens a false sense of security. Here you have a huge amount of potentially explosive materials and no real security to speak of," Brock added.

"DHS does have guidelines," Sanchez said. "Vessels that carry up to 150 passengers are screened, 150 to 500 passenger vessels undergo a more thorough search and places like Seattle, which carry over 500 passengers, undergo an extensive inspection. Almost all ferries are considered highways and fall under the watch of the state's Department of Transportation, which eventually answers to DHS. The ferry landings all have security cameras and they not only look at the vehicles, but they're also supposed to keep an eye on the personnel to be sure their doing their jobs. It's pretty obvious to me that no one is monitoring the cameras or a lot of people would lose their jobs."

"Well, it does fall under that first category of less than 150, of course if I was a bad guy that's what I would look for, easy security," Brock said. "At least no one can commandeer the ferry, you can bet there is more than one weapon on board, especially on the bridge."

"Ferry security might not know a crate of weapons from a crate of china, but I will give them credit for one thing. They won't let you on the ferry if you have a gas can," Phillips laughed.

"Holy Crap!" Chad exclaimed as they got their first look at the area. "It sure is a lot bigger than it looks on the aerial views."

"Wait until you get closer, we're still about six miles out, it will give you a creepy feeling in the bottom of your belly, but I won't say anymore I want you to be surprised," Phillips sighed. "Make a right on Highway 146, I want you to see it all."

"Geez, no high points, I was really looking for a high point," Chad mumbled.

"This ain't California son, Texas slopes gently into the water. The only high point you'll find is an overpass," Phillips teased Chad.

They made the right turn onto Highway 146 and headed south again passing homes and businesses. Then suddenly Dow Chemical was visible on their left.

"There's no buffer zone between Dow and homes, these people must really have no fear," Chad said in disbelief.

As they drove down the highway chemical plants covered the entire left side for as far as they could see. White smoke billowing from multiple unseen places, tall metallic tubes jutting into the air, sections of pipes and braces everywhere and everything packed closely together.

"Just stay on 146 until you get to 197, take a left and then just follow it," Phillip said. "I want you to get the full impact

Chad turned onto 197, drove over two sets of train tracks, looked to his right and saw a nature preserve, he smiled and almost laughed. A few seconds later his smile was gone. Both sides of the four lane were bordered by refinery, nothing but metal everywhere he looked, including up. They were driving through a canyon of pipes that were twisted and bent into huge box type structures at least fifty feet high. Interspersed among the structures were cooling units that looked like giant radiators, metal tubes a hundred feet high and higher, long pipes that stuck into the sky with flares emerging from them. There was no skyline or horizon, only the sky above. Driveways in the areas were manned by security check points, but no security on the thirty mile per hour highway.

"Holy Mother of God!" Chad gulped. "I've been in a lot of bad places, but nothing made me feel like this. I don't know if I can put it words, but my skin's crawling and you're right about the feeling in your belly. I guess claustrophobic would be close, but that's not quite right either. We are driving through an open tunnel of potential death and there would be nothing you could do to protect yourself." He said over his shoulder to Sanchez, "Have you ever been here?"

"No, never and I can tell you I don't like the feeling either. What about you Brock?"

"I've been to refineries before, but nothing like this, it makes you want to hold your breath," Brock replied.

Phillips pointed through the front window, "You've got Valero on your right and Marathon Oil on your left, these two plus Dow Chemical are the biggest ones here. There are a few small companies tucked in here including trucking and pipeline companies. There are pockets of places just like this all the way up the channel to Baytown. There's a pipeline that starts out in the Gulf where some of the ships offload and then it is piped across the peninsula, the bay and into this area. When we get back take a look at your aerial views again and think back to your drive through here. It's sobering."

"What is it, about a mile, mile and a half drive through here?" Brock asked.

"I'm not sure, guess we could have checked the mileage. We can drive through again if you want to." Phillips replied.

"No thanks, not unless we have to." Brock chuckled.

Three blocks from the refinery area sat the town of Texas City, small and quiet. They made a left at a stop light and headed back to highway 146.

"I still can't get it into my head that people can live this close to all of that," Chad said. "Now we need to look at the highways and potential places for these guys to take aim. Actually they don't have to aim, just point and shoot and they'll hit something, two well-placed shots and this place will come to a halt."

They cruised the highways four more times, picked out spots that were far enough away not to get the shooters blown up and allowed an easy escape. No one in the car liked the options.

"This is going to take some planning on our part, we're probably going to have to come after these guys almost head-on. Highway 3 has that over pass we can use if they set up below it, but following them and then getting up there will take some time. Highway 146 had two possibilities, but again our set up time would be longer than theirs. Jake, you need to get hold of everyone and let them know what kind of weapons we may be looking at so they can get some kind of plan together. Be sure and stress how serious this is getting. Also call the office and fill them in, they'll need to know where to pick up the bodies." Chad said.

"Won't the cops take care of those?" Sanchez asked.
"I'm talking about ours." Chad replied.

40

On the drive back to Alvin, Sanchez had taken out his ever present notebook and started sketching the areas around the refineries that they had picked out. Phillips started writing up an outline for a plan of action for each specific area, he would have to work in the rescue of Rogelio as things progressed. He knew that everything could change no matter what they planned, but they always started with an outline of scenarios. They would have to pull up the aerials of the Shell Refinery on 225 so that the team that took it would know what they were getting into and could do some planning of their own. With luck the weapons going to Shell could be stopped before they got there.

Phillips looked at Chad then over at Brock, "What's wrong nobody's talking, somebody say something."

"I'm too busy to talk," Sanchez said without looking up.

"Come on Chad you're too quiet, you too Ed." Phillips said.

Brock looked at him, "I need to make a call and so do you guys. One of you needs to call your guys that went to Port Arthur, see where they are and get some kind of report from them, same with the guys in Corpus Christi. I bet not one of the guys being watched is doing anything, just another day in the life."

"You're right," agreed Chad, "something's off."

"Did you guys have an epiphany while I was making notes?" Phillips asked.

"Yeah," Brock and Chad said in unison.

Phillips turned with his back to the door and looked in the direction of both men. "Now you guys are reading each other's minds. What gives?"

"You tell him Ed."

"Okay, think about it Jake. Why so many trucks and vans? If they are all full of weapons and explosives, like the ones we got pictures of, they can't use all of them here. What are they going to do with them? They might get off three or four shots at Texas City, if they all fire at the same time. They will be on the run after that, so I guess they just hide the rest of the munitions. I don't think so."

This statement got the attention of Sanchez and he looked in back at Brock, then over at Chad. He started to say something then thought better of it.

As Brock finished, Chad took over, "The second thing is, Rogelio gave us directions from what he overheard before the bus driver was killed. The bus driver spoke in Spanish or English so Rogelio understood what was going on when he overheard them giving directions, but now with the driver dead he has no idea what these guys are talking about or what is going on. Rogelio gave us a route, or what he thought was a route, Corpus Christi to Houston to Port Arthur. He knew he wasn't going to Port Arthur that's why he circled Houston, but that's all he knew." Chad said.

Brock continued, "Then add in the fact that there was a van with various explosives inside, that crashed in Arizona. We have one dead guy with a scar and two missing guys, one with a scar, that are connected to that crash. The van and SUV involved had tracking devices on them, just like our vehicles here. I don't remember if the van was on the west bound lanes, Sanchez check your notes, please."

Sanchez pulled out the folded pages and went through them. "Nothing definitive here. The crash happened on the west bound lanes, but tied up traffic on both east and west because vehicles tore through the median and hit east bound vehicles. We would need to get the official report to see the whole picture, but I think if I'm following your train of thought correctly, it really wouldn't make that much difference. If you're thinking what I think you're thinking, I need to call Bob and tell him to back off, now."

"Yeah, do it now." Chad said.

Sanchez grabbed his phone and started punching in numbers.

"Fuck me!" groaned Phillips, then hit the door with the side of his fist, "Damn it to hell!"

Chad swung into the parking lot and pulled up next to Lou's car and noticed the other team sitting in the back seat. Chad got out and walked around to the driver side window, "Glad you're all here," he looked in the back seat. "Took you guys long enough, Ray."

"Yeah well, big accident. What can I say," Ray replied.

"Never one with words are you Ray. You guys sit tight, we have a bunch of calls to make and then we'll brief you. Anything happen across the street?"

"Nope, quiet as a cemetery," Lou said.

Chad looked off in the distance and patted the top of the car, "I'll be back in a few."

He walked over to Phillips, "I'll call Port Arthur and see what's going on with them."

"Okay, I'll get the guys in Corpus," Phillips grumbled. "Why didn't I see it, where the hell is my brain?"

"Since there doesn't seem to be a female involved, I'd say it's the kid. Don't let it bother you, we caught it and that's what counts. Let's get on with the business at hand, save the kid and the world while we're at it."

Brock had called Bracken, left a message and was waiting for a callback. Chad and Phillips walked over to where his was pacing.

"You were right, the guys being watched in Corpus are doing normal things, one is playing catch with his kid and the other one took his wife to work. The local PD questioned them about the murder at the motel, told the one guy his car was seen there. He told them he had been there, but didn't know anything about a murder. They questioned him further and he produced a copy of a bill and a receipt for payment of the job he and his buddy were hired for about three weeks ago. They work for an outfit that finds odds jobs for people out of work, this job was to run errands for some people staying at the motel. He told them the errands were all for food or trips to the grocery store and they were required to stay at the motel. He also told them is was the strangest job he had ever had, the people were very impolite and he only talked with two of them, but he knew more people were inside because of all the food orders. I told our guys to stay on him anyway." Phillips looked over a Chad, "What about your call?"

"If you liked your conversation, you're going to love this. The team followed them to Port Arthur and right into a subdivision. The car they followed took them to a house, where the guys spent an hour inside, another vehicle showed up and then both vehicles left together. They were followed to a motel in Beaumont where they are now sitting and nothing is moving but traffic on the freeway," Chad shrugged as he finished. "Well, at least we know where they aren't."

Phillips said, "Okay I'll bite. Where aren't they?"

"On the road blowing things up. Here comes Sanchez, hope he talked to his friend."

"Got him," Sanchez said as he walked up, "I made him a happy man, he said he would rather be fishing with a beer in his hand anyway."

"What did you tell him?" Brock asked.

"Just that we didn't need the information anymore, he didn't ask any questions he knows better. Even in our line of work it's sometimes better not to know. He hadn't left yet he was going to leave tomorrow, now instead of gassing up the bike he's going fishing. I did tell him to continue watching his back and if anything looked strange he should take appropriate measures. What about you guys and your calls?"

"Brock is waiting for a call now, so let's go over to the car and we'll brief all of you with what we have," Phillips said.

Brock leaned on his car door, watched the three men as they walked away and tried to decide what he was going to tell Bracken. He had just decided that the truth was still the best when his phone played the theme song from Get Smart.

"Hope I didn't interrupt anything," Brock said.

"No, I just wanted to talk in private as I have a feeling this isn't good news," Bracken answered.

"That depends on what you consider good news verses bad, but that aside I do have a lot to tell you." Brock began bringing Bracken up to speed as briefly as possible. He left very little out, he even included the vulnerability of the refineries.

"That's it for now. The four of us will come up with something to bring these guys down, but not in the middle of town," Brock finished.

Bracken let out a large breath, "I should alert the authorities, the FBI and all the state guys, but I don't want to tell them everything. I'll need to think about this, but not long."

"I really need you to hold off until we are sure these guys are moving on down the road and see how they split up."

"If they have the kind of weapons you described, we need to get the situation under control. The guys have to be stupid to transport this kind of stuff in a rental truck or van," Bracken responded.

"Remember the pictures were blurry, it's just an educated guess and the authorities don't need or use probable cause to stop vehicles. Hell, look at that poor tournament poker player who all that money on him. The locals in Iowa stopped him saw all that money he had and confiscated it. The guy goes to court the charges were thrown out, thousands in attorney fees trying to get it back and he still hasn't gotten back yet. So, the authorities could stop them and conduct a search, but we have the kid to worry about. If they stop the guys we are following it could turn out to be a hostage crisis and these guys will kill themselves and the kid without hesitation. Not only that, but they could shoot the cops as they got out of their car. I wouldn't put anything passed these guys, they're on a mission. Anyway, Phillips wants to wait until the Haynes family and the kids' family are secure before we make a move. If the authorities move in too soon then they could kill all or some family members."

"What are they doing about the two families?" Bracken asked.

"I haven't heard anything about the Haynes plan, but they are putting people with the family in Costa Rica," Brock replied.

"See what you can find out and let me know. Tell them Langley needs to know, don't mention me by name. This is a mess," Bracken said.

Brock could picture his old friend/boss rubbing his hand back and forth across his short cropped hair.

"It's going to be difficult to take care of all the aspects," Bracken added. "Phillips is smart and he works with some of the best, I just hope they realize how far reaching this is going to get and I include D.C. in that. The only way to make the family in Costa Rica safe is to move them or kill anyone who knows the family is involved, so let's say fifty people low end. Another way is to make it look like these guys you're following screwed up and that will maybe keep the family safe from reprisals. I have some assets down there, I think I'll give them a call, if you don't mind my hand in this."

"No, not at all," Brock replied. "I take it that your assets down there are not CIA."

"Not exactly and if you play your cards right, someday I'll introduce you to them," Bracken responded. "By the way, you never heard me say anything."

"I thought we were talking about bone fishing," Brock said.

Bracken laughed, "Tell you what. Let me tell the Feebies that my people heard about possible large caliber weapons being moved around in the US and see if I can get them to keep an eye on some of their suspects, camps and mosques. I'll point them to the accident in Arizona and the contents of the van, but as soon as you have the kid, call and I will give them something more solid."

"I think, in a roundabout way, you may have given me an idea. I'll run it by Jake and see if he wants to run with it," Brock said.

"Tell me," Bracken insisted.

Brock proceeded to tell him what he had in mind. When he was finished he could hear Bracken drumming his pen on the desk.

"That would definitely put the screw up on them. Let me know if Phillips goes for it and for God's sake be careful. I don't want to have to explain to your mother how you got killed on American soil," Bracken snorted.

"I'll be as careful as I can and thanks again," Brock replied.

"Actually bone fishing sounds like a good idea. We need to make time for it," Bracken said and was gone.

41

Brock made another call, this time to his office, then leaned against the car looking down at the phone and thinking about Bracken.

He had known John Bracken his whole life and had lovingly called him Uncle John. He had never known what John did for a living, all he knew was that John was his parents' best friend. He was there for every birthday and Christmas, if he wasn't there it was because he was traveling. It wasn't until he was seventeen that he learned Uncle John worked for the government, he didn't learn it was the CIA until he had been at Langley for a week. He had been assured that John had nothing to do with him being recruited, but he knew that if someone on the inside put your name in the hat you pretty much had the job. The only thing that could keep you out would be a bad security check or if you screwed up. John had laughed off the idea he had pulled strings and told him, "We need someone with some brains working here and you're it."

John had been his friend, mentor and at one time his boss, now he was at the top and everyone's boss. He remembered when John told him, "Don't expect any special treatment, if you screw up it's on you and if they want to fire your ass don't expect me to step in." He knew John was a bit younger than his parents and he still didn't know what the special bond was between them, but he was grateful for it.

He came out of his reverie, pushed off from the car and walked over to Phillips and the other men. They were all dressed in jeans, T-shirts and boots or running shoes.

"Good thing we aren't all wearing suits, we'd look like a spook convention," Brock smiled at them.

"We just briefed everyone and were discussing options," Phillips said.

"Yeah, that's what I was doing, have to keep the boss up to date. He said the Feds needed to be notified, but I talked him into holding off for a bit longer because of the possible hostage and the families. He mentioned that this could hurt a lot more people than just the families if one of these vehicles explodes. He also made an off the cuff statement that if these guys screwed it would take the blame off the family when we make our move," Brock said. "He also said that we might be able to help them screw up."

"That might work, at least they wouldn't be able to blame anyone but themselves," Phillips concurred.

"If we wait for everyone to be out of harm's way it could take another day or two and I don't want to wait that long," Brock said and looked over at the motel in time to see a car pull up.

The car parked on the street and sat there idling. A few minutes later a woman came down the motel driveway and got in the front seat.

Chad snapped his fingers and pointed at Lou. Lou and Ralphie jumped in the car, waited a safe amount of time and pulled onto the street to tail the woman.

Chad looked at Phillips, "That was our girl Arel in disguise. She must feel safe because she didn't even look in our direction," he looked at Brock, "You were saying."

Brock looked at Chad then Phillips, "Aren't you concerned about that?"

"Nope," replied Chad, "They can handle it."

"Okay then, here's what I was thinking. We need to find a way to draw attention to the rental trucks, but I'm not proficient enough to build what I need." Brock proceeded to explain what he had in mind.

"My hope is that it would give the authorities a really good reason to look in the back of that truck without pointing the finger at the families involved and from there your guess is as good as mine." Brock looked at each of them looking for a reaction, Phillips

P.A. Stockton

and Chad were looking at the ground thinking, but Ray had a huge smile on his face.

Phillips finally looked up, "It might work, but we have to put it together."

"My friend here," Chad patted Ray on the shoulder, "is just the one to do it."

"Oh, goodie," Ray said bouncing on the balls of his feet, "a scavenger hunt." He elbowed his partner, "Let's go."

Brock chuckled as the two men got into their car, "He was almost giddy over this."

"Yeah, he gets that way sometimes. He's naturally quiet, very intense, but when it comes down to getting the job done his enthusiasm is over the top." Chad grinned, "He's our five foot seven McGiver. Give him a room full of junk and he'll build you just about anything you want."

"How quickly can he get this done?" Brock asked.

"We never push him," Phillips said, "He knows the time line and we want it done right."

"Maybe you should put him on a drone project," Brock smiled.

"We already have people on that, but in the field he'll find a way to alter it to fit his needs," Phillips smiled back. "What we need to do now is get a plan together and look at contingencies, we may stop the truck, but that SUV could keep going."

"I don't know about you, but I don't want to be around that truck after it stops," Chad said.

"I think you're right. Things could go wrong, and according to Murphy they will, so I don't want to be anywhere close if it blows," Brock said.

"What about the responders?" Sanchez asked.

"When they pull up to the truck and see the occupants standing well away from it, I think they will get the idea. Hell, they might even run away like the guys in Arizona," Phillips answered. "If it makes you feel better, when we call it in I'll find a way to warn them."

230

"I've been meaning to ask you about that," Sanchez said. "What happened to those guys in Arizona, how did they disappear so fast, did they run into the desert?"

"I think during the explosions they took off, either into the desert or maybe there was another car stuck in traffic. If they had another car they run to it, make a U-turn across the median and they're gone. Remember we saw one of those guys on a cell phone. They may have been told to blow the vehicles and take off. Our office captured still images of them off the tape, so they may turn up."

"I doubt they could give us anything to go on, they were probably just drivers, but they could tell us where they were going," Brock added.

Sanchez reached into his pocket to pull out his chirping cell phone, looked at the ID, answered and walked a short distance from the group. He spoke for almost ten minutes and walked back over to Phillips.

"That was Bob, he just heard something interesting and thought he would pass it on to us. Some of his riding buddies were on their way from Abilene to spend a few days fishing and they called to let him know they were going to be delayed. They left early this morning and stopped at one of those roadside parks near Menard on Highway 83. There was a white van parked there with its' hood up, so they went looking for the driver to see if they could help, but they couldn't find him. They couldn't find anyone, not even a note on the windshield. They wondered if he was asleep in the back of the van and didn't hear them calling for him. Anyway, they knocked on the doors and the side of the van and didn't get a response, so they tried the doors. The passenger side was unlocked so they opened it to take a look and maybe get a name off the registration, but when they looked between the seats and into the back they figured they needed to call the cops."

"Let me guess," said Philips, "they found weapons."

"Not just weapons, a lot of ammo. The two guys gave statements to the cops, but since they were the ones to find this stuff, they have to hang around and talk to the FBI and anyone else who shows up."

"Looks like these guys are screwing up without our help," said Brock. "How much did you tell Bob that he thought you should know about this?"

"I told him it looked like weapons were coming in from who knows where and to keep an ear to the ground," Sanchez replied. "I also told him to keep it quiet since we didn't have anything solid."

"I need to make a phone call," Phillips sighed.

"Me too," Brock nodded.

When they got off their respective calls Chad said, "We have been unprepared for this job. I know, I know, we didn't know what we were getting into, but I want to be more prepared next time. I'm going to added fiber optics, parabolic, and computer tracking to my travel items. I'm not going to leave home without them, we sure as hell could have used them on this case. I might even add heat sensors." Looking at Sanchez he said, "Let's go get food, we all need it. I know, Brock, two of everything.

As they pulled out of the parking lot Chad looked over at Sanchez. "What else did Bob say?"

"What makes you think he said anything else?" Sanchez asked.

"You were on longer than the transfer of information would take and the look on your face."

"I'm that easy to read?"

"Yeah, you are. It might be a good idea if you worked on the ability not to react to things you overhear, are told or questions that are asked. Like when we were coming back from Texas City and talking about that we might have misread these guys. You almost said something, but changed your mind. If it seems important enough to give you pause, then you should voice it. If you have second thoughts because you think it might sound like a stupid question, you'll never know if it was actually relevant because you didn't speak up. You'll find out later if it was relevant, but sometimes you need to know sooner, it might save a life. Now, tell me about Bob."

"He's pissed off. I guess you could say he doesn't like the idea of vehicles full of weapons driving around the country and he wants to do something about it. I didn't say anything about the stuff in Arizona, his buddies did. They saw it on television. I told him to stand down, that he was supposed to be hiding out, staying safe until we knew what was going on with the Mexico operation. He assured me he would wait until his friends got down there and then he'd give it more thought. I was afraid he would say something to the guys and asked him not to say anything. He informed me that they knew first hand so what difference did it make, but he would keep quiet."

Sanchez paused then sighed, "I'm afraid he and his buddies might do something stupid. There are several in his band of merry men who are Vets and they just might take what they saw as a serious threat."

"We'll come up with something you can tell him to calm him down. He can't go around stopping every white panel van he sees, he'll get himself arrested. In the mean time you have done all you can and he won't see his buddies for a few more hours. Now let's feed Brock before he starts growling."

42

When they finished lunch Chad reached over and opened his door, "We need to try and get some sleep. I'd like us to get at least two hours, but that's not going to happen, so just get what you can. Brock, you and Sanchez stay here, you've got more room in your car if one of you moves to the backseat. Phillips and I will use mine and I'll take first watch, if some of my guys get back I'll turn it over to them. I suggest a power nap."

"So, what do you think?" Chad asked as they settled in his front seat.

"I think," said Phillips, "this thing is too big. I think our guys in the SUV are still the ones we need to concentrate on for now. I think the vans are outliers and I've got our people chasing around looking for more possible van incidents or anything that looks related to the vehicle found with the weapons. I have them filling in the Feds, especially now that they are on that van in Menard, I emphasized that we need to stay on these guys. I'm sure Brock told his guys, so now we have to hope that nobody interferes with us."

"When the guys get back I'm going to have them get the VIN and plate numbers off all those vehicles, you can call them in and maybe we can get a lead on where they came from or who handed out the keys," Chad said. "Try and get some sleep, there's nothing we can do until the two crews get back. If I think of anything I'll let you know."

Phillips closed his eyes and within a few minutes his breathing had slowed and deepened. Chad watched the motel and began running things through his head and making a mental list.

He needed to finish prepping Sanchez and get his guys on the VIN numbers. With the death and mutilation of the bus driver, he was not seeing this chase ending in a clean and easy way. He knew the chances of Rogelio getting shot or killed were high, too many people watching him for him to get away without an injury, but he was also worried about Sanchez getting his ass shot. He decided that no matter what, he had to keep Sanchez with him in a sniper capacity since he still didn't know how Sanchez was under fire.

Chad thought back on the drive through the refineries. He still wanted someone watching them just in case one or two of these guys peeled off and went over to take a few shots. If people were picketing during the strike that was supposed to start today, there would be enough confusion that it could be an advantage for a shooter. Maybe Brock or Phillips could alert the local PD and have them watch the highway. It just seemed like too good a target for someone to pass up.

His thoughts had just shifted to what Jazmin had said about Yolanda being slapped around when his guys following Arel pulled into the lot. He motioned them to stay put and slowly got out of the car easing the door closed.

"Tell me," he said leaning on the window.

"We followed her to Hobby Airport. Ralphie followed her inside and she took a Southwest flight to Oklahoma City," Lou said. "She only had a carry-on, which she did not bring out of the motel when she left. I called the office and gave them the information we got so they could see if she took another flight from there. We flashed our credentials at the desk and they gave us the name she flew under, it was Maria Galvez and she had a photo ID. Oh, we told the office that they might need to access video tape."

"Good work and thanks for calling it in," Chad said. "You made it back quick."

"Well yea, we didn't want to miss anything," Ralphie chuckled. "Where is everybody?"

"I suggested they try and get some sleep and now that you're here, I intend to try and do the same. Keep an eye on things," Chad said as he walked away.

Chad quietly eased himself back into the front seat, closed his eyes and drifted off. His sleep was interrupted by the sound of 'Uptown Girl' coming from his phone. He looked at the time and was shocked to see he had been asleep for half an hour, he shook his head to clear it and eased out of the car.

"Pepa, to what do I owe the honor?" Chad said

"Oh, gallant Knight I fear there is a dragon among us and he has really bad breath," came the reply.

"You got that right, something really stinks here," Chad said. "How are you and what can I do for you?"

"I'm fine and I'm just calling to give you a heads up. They picked up Haynes, his wife and kids about twenty minutes ago and they are bringing them down here. The family will stay with me and Haynes will be taken elsewhere, for obvious reasons. I will put them in the guest house and that way I won't have to lock up my toys. They'll be safe here, they can't get out without a code and I don't care how smart the kids are they can't get over the walls," Pepa replied.

Pepa DeWitt was a valuable asset and had built, with the help of her employers, a compound in Florida which is almost impossible to get into or out of without the proper codes. The security system was the best available, was monitored at the office and an off-site security facility, if one office was breached, they had back-up. The compound had two coded gates, one visible, the other undetectable and all codes were changed on a monthly basis. There was a tunnel that ran from a bedroom closet, under the property, the street and came out behind another gated home. The tunnel was double walled, sound and waterproof. At the farther end on the tunnel was a coded door that led to a small room which held, weapons, an extra go bag, cell phone and car keys. Behind the shelving was a small key pad which activated a ceiling panel that dropped down a set of stairs that led to the garage above. The garage door was actually a sliding wall that opened onto a large expanse of grass and a back gate. Pepa believed in the idiom, prepare for the worst hope for the best.

"Can't think of a better place. Are you okay with it?" Chad asked.

"Sure, they're sending a minder to stay with them, so I'm available if necessary."

"I'd invite you to join us, but by the time you got here we'd be who knows where."

"Sounds like another mess to me and I'd rather be in the Bahamas," Pepa laughed.

"It is and it isn't funny. Things are coming together slowly, we just need to get the other people secured and then we'll make our move. Is anyone watching Older?"

"Yeah, but it's touchy considering who he is. We have a couple of Secret Service guys on the Presidents detail alerted just to be on the safe side."

"Good idea, plus you know if Older is involved he can make calls from the White House. I wouldn't put it past him."

"You sound tired. How much sleep are you getting?" Pepa asked.

"Not enough. Two hours last night and about thirty minutes today."

"You've survived on less."

"Don't remind me."

"How about the others."

"Can't say for sure, but probably thirty or forty-five minutes more than what I've gotten. We will probably be running on adrenalin later."

"Take care of yourself, I don't want to break in someone new and Leigh would have to find someone else to bother."

"How is Leigh?" Chad asked.

"Fighting the fight against anything that comes her way," laughed Pepa.

Leigh DeWitt was Pepas' younger sister who swore the creeper vines on her fence were out to get her. The sisters had the same connection most twins had, but were a few years apart, they also shared the same twisted sense of humor. Leigh was divorced from a husband that both women referred to as Walter Mitty. She was always asking Chad or Pepa to take her on one of their 'adventures', as she called them, and she had a crush on Chad. Pepa knew about the crush, Chad was unaware and Leigh would never admit it.

Chad looked over his shoulder and saw Phillips standing next to the car stretching. "Looks like Jake is up and moving, I'm going to have you fill him in, he may have some questions. Keep your eyes open and keep me informed."

"Will do and you watch your back," Pepa said.

Chad got off the phone and walked over to Phillips, "Okay progress, you should be getting a call. I hope Haynes gives us something to work with, if he knows anything at all. He may not know anything to help us here, but he could give us something to nail the person at the top. Let's go talk to Brock and Sanchez."

Phillips phone chimed as they walked over to Brocks' car. He paced as he talked, expressions on his face changing several times, but no hand or arm movements. Chad took it all in and processed it as an information call with nothing to discuss, but important.

Phillips put the phone in his pocket and headed for Brock and Sanchez. Chad caught up with him, "What's up? Good news I hope."

"Interesting news," was all Phillips said as they reached Brock.

"You guys feel reenergized?" Phillips asked.

"Let me put it this way," Brock said, "I feel less tired."

"We've gotten some news," Phillips said. "They have Haynes and family in the air and headed to a secure location and I just got a call from our Techies. They started tracking those personal tracking devices and found a large number of them. Since they were having problems pinpointing where the signals are coming from, they started tracking back to the individuals. They sent a list to Chads' laptop, but a sampling is D.C, New York City and clusters in California, Texas and Arizona. He said the list is extensive that's why he sent it, so let's go look at it."

As they walked to Chads' SUV Phillips said, "Our little cluster here also shows up as well as a few in Beaumont. At least we know that the tracking is picking everything up, so the list should be interesting."

Chad opened the back of the SUV so they could all see the computer screen. As they stood around waiting for the list to generate Chad noticed that a folder containing maps had also been sent.

"Looks like they sent maps, they will probably tell us more than the list, but let's go ahead and look at the list first since it will give us numbers."

They slowly scrolled through the list and Sanchez took notes on the cities with the highest number of confirmed devices. He could hardly control himself as he waited for Chad to pull up the maps.

The first map was an overall look from coast to coast and they were amazed at the array of red dots that covered the map. The other maps were in sections made up of one to three States so the larger cities could be discerned. Almost every State had at least one cluster of dots, some States had multiple cities.

"California is almost a constant line of red down the coast, they must be covering the ports, look at Sacramento and the Delta area," Brock said. "It looks like they have both ends of the Golden Gate covered. We need to have your guys send us a zoomed map of that area as well as Los Angeles and San Diego."

"I'm making a list," put in Sanchez. "Anything we think we need a better look at I'm writing down. I'm interested in the High Desert area, north and south of Edwards Air Force Base. There are a few dots in the area, but you can't tell exactly where. Also I wonder if they have an interactive map that shows changes or movement from one area to another."

"Good question," Brock said. "Let's go to the next one."

"Holy crap, look at Montana. Why so many in Montana?" Sanchez asked.

"Easy to hide out and build a compound. Lots of room in Montana and if you look at Idaho there's not one dot there. I would attribute that to the states reputation." Brock said. "Let's take a look at Michigan and New York City, we know Michigan is going to have them, but how bad should be informative."

One section of Michigan looked like a blooming rose, New York City, D.C., Boston and other major cities had clusters sprinkled throughout, but nothing like Michigan. Nevada and Utah had small clusters in the middle of nowhere and surprisingly the Dallas, Houston and Miami areas had only small clusters.

After looking at all the maps Phillips called in the list Sanchez had written up, inquired about an interactive map and was informed that they were using one. He asked them who they had informed of the findings. They told him that the same list and maps had been sent to the FBI and CIA, but all agencies were holding the information out of reach of DHS for the time being. He was also told the CIA wanted them to see if they could find anything in Europe, Mexico and Canada. They had already looked at Mexico, before getting the request from the CIA and had sent the Mexico list and maps to all concerned. Chad went back to the screen and called up the Mexico information.

"Sanchez, here's that mountain range where you found the training camp," Chad called over his shoulder.

Sanchez looked at the screen, "Man, there are dots all over the place. Look, even over here near or on the border. Looks like that Jorge guy was right when he said it could be thousands. This is getting scary, I can only hope that most of the dots we've seen are dolts that they hired to help them move stuff and help set things up. If all these dots are bad guys then we're in deep shit, especially if they start removing the devices." He shook his head, "I think I'm getting a headache."

Phillips leaned over and whispered something in Chads' ear, Chad nodded and went to work on the key board. Florida popped up on the screen again and Chad used his finger to trace over an area. "I can't tell, you need to call in and have them send a more detailed map. Also, have them check the area where they're taking Haynes." Chad said to Philips.

Within five minutes the new map had been sent and Chad crossed his fingers as he opened it up. He called Phillips over and tapped one red dot, "Call them and tell them to watch this area for movement. If they find anything near the area where they're taking Haynes, they better watch for movement there as well. This dot is too coincidental and you know how I feel about that. I'll make the call and let her know."

While Phillips made his call, Chad called Pepa and explained about the maps they had been sent. "There are some of these dots near your location, it doesn't mean they are coming your way, it could be dots from the drivers or others that were hired, but there is one dot near you. I told the Techies monitoring the map to keep an eye out for movement and to check on wherever they are taking Haynes. Have your guests arrived?"

"No, they are on their way and should be here any minute. Why?" Pepa asked.

"I need you to go to the guest house when they arrive and check the upper arms of everyone that's there. If you see any scars, call me immediately."

"You don't have to explain, I figured it out. I'll call you back no matter what I find." Pepa ended the call.

Chad turned to fill Philips in when he saw Ray pull into the lot.

43

Chad walked passed Phillips on his way to talk to Ray, "Got Pepa, she'll call back." He turned to Ray, "Did you get it done?"

"Yeah and it's a piece of art, modern art. Come around to the back."

Ray opened the trunk and carefully removed a small tarp, "Okay, I made it narrow and sturdy. I figured that hole was maybe the width of my hand maybe a bit wider, but I didn't want to take the chance. It's just a common uncomplicated device which will be set off by a call from this burner phone, pun intended," Ray said as he looked at Phillips. Your power source is batteries, a bit of thin steel wool for a conductor and combustible material mixed with black powder." Ray pointed to the bottom of the device, "I set it up on strips of green wood woven together so that air can be sucked in when it ignites, everything on top of the wood will create a lot of smoke and when I say a lot I mean it. If there is anything in the back of that truck that is loose, like paper, it might cause a small fire, but nothing to worry about. Now, it's long because we need the smoke and I had to make up for the loss of width. I can slide this in the hole and if it slaps down on the floor it won't disturb anything, hell it could fall over and still work. Here's the phone and the number, when you're ready just dial, let it ring three times, make your call to the cops on this same phone, then do a break and toss. That's it, if it doesn't work I have a bazooka in the back seat." He slapped Sanchez on the back, "That's a joke son."

Phillips looked at Chad and Brock, both nodded, when he looked at Sanchez he saw a question. "Okay Sanchez, spit it out. What's bothering you?"

Sanchez hesitated, Chad looked at him and said, "Remember what I told you about questions."

"Okay, Ray, you said if there was paper in the back it might start a small fire. How big does the paper have to be and how big a fire?"

"When I put this in the truck and it lands on something, like a newspaper, it could conceivably catch the paper on fire. The spark from this thing is going to be a good size because we need the smoke, the wood is going to get very hot. Not hot enough to catch the crates on fire, but hot enough for paper, we want as much of this device to disappear as possible. Therefore, it has to generate enough heat to make that little cell phone unrecognizable."

Sanchez nodded as he looked at Phillips, then walked toward Chads' car.

"Let's do it," said Chad. "Lou, show him the hole then you and Ralph get the numbers off those vehicles and do it as quickly as possible," he turned and headed for Brocks' car with Brock and Phillips close behind.

"You do realize that he just fed Sanchez a load, right?" Brock said.

"Yeah, but we have to get this done and all we can do now is hope for the best outcome. In other words, we don't get blown up," Chad replied.

When they got to the car Chad filled them in on his conversation with Pepa. "I hope I'm wrong, but I'll bet you one of the family has a scar and it's probably Mrs. Haynes and whoever is doing this will want to keep track of the family. Jake will you make a call and have them contact whoever is traveling with Matt Haynes? They need to see if he has a scar and what are they going to do if they find them. I'd call but I want to keep the line open for Pepa."

Chad walked over to Sanchez, "You okay?"

"Sure, I'm okay. I just don't like this idea, there has to be a better way."

"Well, if you come up with a better plan let me know. In the meantime we have to stop that truck without pointing fingers at someone other than the folks driving it, this is what we have so we'll use it. Another thing to remember, you don't always have to agree with the decisions, you just have to understand the reasoning behind them and trust the people who make them. Jim, you're a smart guy not some dumb recruit. You've been fighting a war on the border, we fight a war on the move and sometimes you don't have a lot of choices on how you fight that war. Luckily we have never had any collateral damage and I don't expect to this time. Just hang in there, but if you want out at any time, just say the word and no judgment or hard feelings. For the record, you had doubts, you asked the question and that's a good thing."

"I just don't like how much that guy enjoys his work, it's like he enjoys blowing people up and that load of crap he gave me was just that, a load of crap." Sanchez said.

Chad chuckled, "You picked up on that, huh? That's another point in your favor. Ray doesn't like having to explain himself and he does enjoy blowing things up."

"Doesn't that bother you a little?" Sanchez asked.

"Nope, that's his job. Everyone that works for our outfit is handpicked for their expertise. Those guys in the cars watching suspects aren't low paid foot soldiers, they each have a talent. All of us, Philips and myself included, spend at least one month a year on surveillance. We all hate it, but we do it. Sometimes I get so itchy doing it that I go to the range to vent, Phillips reads medical journals and Pepa, well who knows what Pepa does. I can't give you any background on Ray, but I can tell you he's sane, an expert and loves his job."

"You can't or won't tell me?" asked Sanchez.

"Both." Chad replied and walked away.

"Problems?" asked Phillips as Chad sat in the back seat.

"I think he's worried about someone getting injured with that device and he had questions about Ray."

"We all have questions about Ray." Phillips chuckled.

"Anyway, I told him if he was uncomfortable and wanted out that we'd understand."

"Do you think you should just let him go with all he knows?" Brock asked.

"Better now than when it's over. We can have him sign a nondisclosure statement and send him home." Phillips said.

"I think he'll be alright, he's just having doubts. He wasn't in the military, so he isn't used to this kind of shit. If he trusts us, he'll stay. Did you get in touch with the Haynes team?"

"Yeah, they are going to call me back. Why they didn't check while they had me on the phone is another question." Phillips said. "Maybe we should start checking each other for scars, cue dastardly music as paranoia sets in on our heroes."

"I don't know if that's not such a bad idea." Brock said. "Not your guys, but anyone connected to DHS in any way and could get inside this operation should probably be checked. We don't have to worry about that here, I'm worried about elsewhere in the operation."

Phillips turned and looked at Brock, "You aren't kidding are you? You really think some of the Feds might have these things?"

"Hey, they're the FBI, I don't trust them. It's inherent to my organization."

Phillips and Chad both started laughing and noticed Sanchez walk up.

"Come on in and have a back seat. We were just laughing at Brocks distrust of the FBI," Chad said.

Brock started laughing, "It sounds like I'm losing it, but if Older is a bad guy he could have guys on the inside helping him out. His minions so to speak. He doesn't have a crystal ball, so he's going to need someone to keep an eye on things from the inside. Of course if he has people on the inside they may not have a scar, they wouldn't necessarily have to be tracked. Guess my mind is working overtime."

"Well, at least you're covering all the angles," Phillips said. He did a double take on Sanchez, "Sanchez, you look like someone just walked over your grave."

Sanchez swallowed, "I think I just figured out were I saw Addison before, but I'm not positive. I need to see some of the news photos of Mr. Older."

"We can do that," Chad said. "I'll go get the lap top."

Sanchez looked at Phillips, "When Brock was talking about an inside man, I was thinking that it wasn't such an off the wall thought. It would make perfect sense to have all your bases covered, if you have guards for your body, why not guards for your project. That's when it popped into my head, this guy standing behind Older in one of the news photos." Sanchez rubbed his hand across the top of his head.

Chad got back into the car and downloaded a file of photos, all of them were of Older from different news releases. "Our archives keep photos of all government big wigs, from the President on down and they each have their own file. This is the file on Older, go through the photos and see if you recognize anything."

By the third screen Sanchez had the photo and turned the computer around so everyone could see it. He had called it up so that it was the only photo on the screen, it showed a group of men coming out of a set of double doors. They all wore suits, were smiling and looked as if they didn't know they were being photographed.

Sanchez looked at Phillips, "The guy to the right of Older is one of his cronies or Secret Service, there's a guy standing in between and about a step or two behind them, see if he matches the photo you got in Corpus Christi. I'm sure it's him."

Phillips pulled out his cell phone and scrolled quickly through the photos, he stopped and went back. "Sorry scrolling to fast, I almost missed it. I think you're right, that photo is a little grainy, but it's him." He handed the phone to Brock who passed it Chad, "I do believe we have a match and now we just need to find out who he really is."

"I'll call and see if we can get his real name," Phillips said.

"I need to call this in as well, so when you get a name let me know who it is," Brock said as he got out of the car.

Chad continued to look at the screen, then went back into the file and paged forward.

"Is this the only time you've seen this guy with Older?" Chad asked.

"It's the only one I remembered, I haven't seen all his news photos so there might be another one," Sanchez replied.

"Hey, Phillips, have archives search this guy and see if they can find anymore photos of him," Chad yelled over his shoulder, he got a nod from Phillips. To Sanchez he said, "How did you know to go to this particular photo?"

Sanchez gave him a strange look then nodded, "This isn't a set up, I really did just remembered and the reason is weird. A bunch of us were sitting around drinking beer and venting over government meddling and the news was on, that's what started the conversation. The news actually ran footage of these guys coming out of a building in D.C. and then this still photo. One of the guys made a remark that it looked like a photo from 1930 or 1940, because of the way they were dressed. Another guy said they looked like part of The Mob and we picked up on it and started making jokes about Older and his cronies. It stuck in my mind because most of the jokes were about him being shot by one of the guns he sent over the border. The jokes probably would've put us behind bars."

"I had to ask, part of the job," Chad said as his phone played 'Witchy Woman'.

"About time, I was getting worried."

"And well you should my good man, we found a scar on Mrs. Haynes, upper arm." Pepa said. "They took her over to the hospital to have it removed, our Doc will meet them there, take it out and fly it back to Virginia. The word I got was they want it to look like the Mr. and Mrs. went on a quick trip out of town and are on a return flight. They don't want whoever is monitoring them to think they are running."

"Our guys with Mr. Haynes told me to fill you in on their situation. Haynes had one and so did one of the Feds with him, same hospital, same Doc, same story. The guys figured they should check everybody and when they asked this guy to remove his shirt he wouldn't comply. Long story short, the Fed is going to wake up with a sore jaw and he'll be flying back, with the devices, in Federal custody."

"How's Mrs. Haynes handling this?" Chad asked.

"She was crying with relief. She said she's been really worried and when they were flying down here she knew they would all be killed. She was shaking so badly when they got here, I thought she would come apart. Once we told her we were going to remove it she actually quit shaking, then started crying and thanking us. I told her she would be brought back here and no one could get to her or the children once those gates closed."

"Brock will be happy that his theory was correct, but Phillips won't be happy that Brock is one up on him," Chad said.

"Brock figured this would happen?"

"I guess you could put it that way," Chad replied and told her how Brock had been joking about being paranoid, mentioned his distrust of the FBI and that maybe some of them might be rigged with the devices. "I might also add that he also said they might not have them since they really didn't have to be tracked. Now that I think about it, if they weren't totally trusted they would have a device. I wonder if this guy you have down there will give up some information, he might not be that loyal to the cause. Whatever the 'cause' is."

"Joke or not, he was right. I've heard that those CIA guys can get paranoid, maybe it pays off. I'll call the guys back and pass on your thoughts on the matter. How bored are you?" Pepa asked.

"Very and if things don't start moving I'm going to have a breakdown. I don't mind a slow case, but I would like a bed to go with it. I know, we've been on slow cases before, but this is glacial."

"Well hon, after you are admitted to the institution I'll come and visit," Pepa said in sweet southern drawl. "Until then, ya'll take care."

Chad was smiling as he closed his phone.

44

The call Brock made to his office went as expected, all he was basically doing was checking in to let them know he was still alive. He checked to be sure they had been brought up to date by Phillips office and had received the data on the arm devices. He asked again about any chatter being received and there was nothing to indicate this operation was being discussed. The only thing that bothered him was the fact that regular chatter from known entities had dropped off, but chatter from ISIS had picked up. A lot of the chatter from the ISIS group was meant as propaganda and threats to those listening. He knew he should call Bracken and bring him up to date too, he just wished he had more to tell him.

Bracken picked up on the second ring, "I don't think I've gotten this many calls from you since you came back stateside."

"Just keeping you up to date in case things aren't going to the top," Brock said.

"Half the time they only tell me what they think I need to know, the other half is if they have a problem they can't solve. They take all the fun out of the job, so fill me in and I hope it's better than this paperwork."

Brock briefed him and when it came to the news about the mysterious Addison, he could hear Bracken stiffen and his mental wheels start to turn. He knew better than to say anything else, when Bracken was thinking you waited for him to speak. When he did speak he said nothing about Addison, he wanted the story on the FBI agent who had been assigned to Matt Haynes, Brock obliged.

"A compromised agent," Bracken said. "This puts a different light on things, it makes we wonder how many others there are. Let's hope they can keep him under wraps, we don't need him alerting anyone. You need to find out if this agent was aware this was a snatch and hide, find out if he spoke to anyone before or after they got on the plane. Also find out how long he's been with the agency. You have a name?"

"No name was mentioned," Brock replied.

"Now, about these maps our people requested. Do you think Phillips group can find these things overseas?"

"I don't know. All I know is our guys requested that they try. I don't think they'll find any over there, I believe this is strictly a U.S. operation. I can tell you the maps are impressive and unnerving. They found a large number in Mexico where Sanchez found what looked like a training camp and some scattered near the border" Brock replied.

"I'd like to see them. Is there any way you can get a photo to me? The coast to coast map is good enough, just something to give me the general idea."

"They sent everything over there already, but I understand the request and I'll see what I can get to you. It's a real shame we can't get in on this, at least deeper than what I'm doing."

Bracken laughed, "Yeah, no doubt we could do a better job of cleaning it up and I'm not referring to Phillips. I'd appreciate it if you would keep me up to date on this Addison character, a good picture of him would be nice. I'll call downstairs and see if they can send up some of the news stills we have, maybe I can pick him out from your description. This situation makes me real nervous, it would be nice if we, or you and Phillips, could nail Mr. Older. I don't like the guy, never have."

"Now that we have Addison pictured with Older, we have a better chance of finding him, I hope when we find him there are no firewalls between him and his boss. When I send the photo of the map I'll send one of Mexico and that photo of Addison, no reason for you to call downstairs. I'll also let you know what we find out from Haynes, it should be interesting. Just to be clear, when I make my check in call, I'm not involving anyone from our agency, I just check to be sure they received the stuff Phillips group sends them.

I'm letting Phillips and his group do all the work and deal with the FBI, we don't need the headache," Brock said.

Bracken heaved a sigh, "I wish I could be there when you set off your little toy in the back of that truck. Be even better if it blows," he chuckled. "It would serve them right. Say, be sure and find a way to alert the authorities that it might be a dangerous situation without getting yourselves involved. You can't have dead cops or firefighters, it would strengthen the case, but you don't want Americans injured or killed, that's what we're fighting against."

"Yeah, Sanchez brought that up earlier. We'll find a way, but we can't guarantee they'll heed the warning," Brock assured him.

"I know, collateral damage is a bitch."

"Phillips says they have never had any with any of their operations, so we can only hope that record holds," Brock said.

"Listen son, you watch your six, we have a fishing trip ahead of us," Bracken said as he broke the connection.

Brock started back toward the car and was met half way by Phillips.

"How's the old man?" Phillips asked.

"He sounds good and he's happy this isn't our mess." Brock replied and tucked his thumbs in his jeans pockets. "He sounded melancholy toward the end of the call, he wanted to be here when the truck goes. He even hinted that he wouldn't be unhappy if it blew. He said the same thing about warning the first responders."

"We will, but we can't control what they do. On another note, Chad sent the VIN and plate numbers, we should have information shortly."

"I need to send photos of the U.S and Mexico maps and the one of Addison to Bracken, he doesn't want to alert anyone downstairs that he's involved."

Chad waved them over to his vehicle, "We need to move the cars again. I have Sanchez checking the view from behind the construction dumpster and we can put your car behind the tractor trailer. The other guys will take care of themselves and Lou is getting a room in the motel so he can give us a heads up when they start to move. I told him if he takes a nap he better take one for all of us."

Sanchez came over to the group, "Okay, we should be alright over there and there are some rungs on the side of the dumpster we can use if we need them. I also checked the tractor trailer and it's been there for a while so I doubt anyone will be moving it."

"Let me send a couple of things off that I need to get from the lap top and then we can move," Brock said." Is there anything else we need to look at before we separate?"

"Not that I can think of right now," Phillips answered. "There are a few things we need to go over, but that can be done over the radio."

Chad and Sanchez pulled out of the lot to make the loop around the block and Brock had just finished sending his email, when Phillips phone chimed. He finished the call and picked up the radio to toggle Chad, "They've traced the some of those numbers."

"That was quick," said Chad, "They must all be from the same place."

"Close," Phillips replied. "The trucks are both rentals, one from Corpus Christi, the other from the Houston area. The one from Corpus was rented by a young couple, the one from Houston was rented by a small business moving office furniture. The ID's on both people were a dead end. The vans are all from a company based in Illinois, but is run by another company in Michigan that is owned by a dummy corporation that traces back to a shell company in California. Some of our people in California are going to check out the offices at the address we have. I wouldn't be surprised if they find them empty, but they could have a legitimate side."

"Especially if they have money to launder," put in Brock.

"They appear to have made one mistake," Phillips continued. "The CEO is listed as a Mr. Addison Roberts."

"So they have the first name as Addison, interesting. The chances of us having two guys with the name Addison is slim to none," Chad said.

"I'll make a quick call later and have the name combinations checked, but right now I want to know how you want to handle that truck."

"Sanchez has a good idea and I think it will work, I'll let him explain it," Chad said.

"I was thinking about the call to the cops and I think I should do it," Sanchez said. "I think the call should be made with a Mexican accent and when I warn them I'll say that I saw the people in the truck at a gas station, that they were not American and they looked nervous. That one stood at the back of the truck when they were pumping the gas and they kept looking around."

"I could say the same thing," Phillips replied.

"Yeah, but you're a white guy. I'm not being intentionally offensive, but if you call and tell them that, the cops will think you're paranoid or a racist. If I call they may take it more seriously, I doubt they will think a Mexican is paranoid of foreigners, especially if the accent is on the heavy side."

"I could use an accent, you just want to push the button," Phillips laughed.

"No, you can still make that call and push the button from your phone, if the other phone is destroyed they can't find your number. Hell, you can make the call to the cops, but if the dispatcher is fluent in Spanish and starts asking you questions in Spanish, it might be nice if you could answer."

"Very good," Phillips said, "Well thought out and you had all the right answers, I think you're close to graduation."

"I know, it all depends on how I handle the rest of this and how I am under fire. You do realize I'm not interviewing for a job, I have one."

"I'm only telling you, in a roundabout way, that you're doing a good job. Now, I suggest that we be the lead car and as we pass the truck I'll make the call. You guys stay far enough back so that if it blows you aren't caught in it, then when you see smoke make the call. I just hope these guys leave when it's light out so the smoke can be seen."

45

Chad sat slumped down in the front seat, eyes closed, "I'm glad Lou got that room at the motel, this way we don't have to sit in plain sight watching for something to happen. We could even catch a small nap. Now that we have a little time, you need to go through your notes and destroy them. You can keep the notes on the news broadcast, but the rest need to go. Phillips will be doing the same thing with his soon, everything we have has already been sent to our office. Even the files I used for the briefing have been handed off. We never keep any written information on our person or in the cars, if we get compromised we don't want any paper. Guns good, paper bad."

"Has anyone been in that position before?" Sanchez asked.

"Phillips and I haven't, but a few of the others have. Nobody got hurt, but they were questioned and with no proof of anything they were let go. All it takes is one small piece of paper with the wrong thing written on it and you're blown. Ask Brock, I bet everything he has put on his phone is gone and he has nothing written down, you'll find his notebook empty. He probably even has a clean SIM Card somewhere. Something else to remember is to always pick up your brass, they carry fingerprints and don't dispose of them close by. If you can, drop them in a body of water or down a sewer grate far, far away."

"I'll remember that, except where I work we have no brass, hell I don't even know why we are armed. The day will come when those people in D.C. will wish they had let us do our job to protect the borders and after looking at those trucks over there, that day may be closer than they think. I got to thinking about this going the other way. I mean, suppose Phillips hadn't been there to talk to Rogelio and these guys were able to get these weapons placed were it would really hurt us. We don't even know for sure what else is out there or how lethal. There are compounds in almost every State, we have aerial surveillance, but we have no idea what is really going on inside them. They could section off this country and unleash death and destruction that would make 9/11 look small in comparison. The only thing that makes me feel better is knowing that we have so many armed citizens. Now I sound paranoid," Sanchez chuckled.

"I hear ya," Chad said. "What bugs me is not just the middles east types crossing the border, it's that they're bringing in weapons through small unsecured ports. Shrimp or fishing boats can come in anywhere along the coast with their holds filled with weapons and no one knows the difference because they pull into private docks. We just have to hope that D.C. wakes up and in the mean time we keep our eyes open."

"There have been times when I feel useless and like my job is a waste of time. Then I'm out there and I find someone who..," Sanchez stopped mid-sentence. "Never mind, maybe I should talk to a shrink."

Chad almost broke in to tell him he was talking to a shrink, but decided it wasn't a good idea. Instead he nodded and told him that a lot of people in law enforcement, at some point, had doubts about the value of their jobs and then something would happen to renew their faith in what they were doing.

"Well, we're going put a kink in any plans these guys have and that makes the job worth every minute," Sanchez said.

"Now that we're talking about this stuff, I wonder if anybody got over to Port Lavaca to get information on the boat that the truck met. Let me sic Phillips on them," Chad said as he toggled the radio.

"Hey Phillips, have you heard anything on the boat in Port Lavaca?"

"No, nothing yet. I'll shake their tree in another half hour. Brock and I were just discussing how nice it is not staring at that motel and wondering if we could catch a catnap."

"Funny," Chad said, "Sanchez and I were just wondering the same thing. Let me know if you hear anything."

Chad turned the volume down on the radio as his cell phone played the tune to let him know Pepa was calling. "Everything alright down there?"

"Sure, I thought I'd let you know that we are stalling on sending the plane back, the thinking being it would be too quick of a turn around. Also, the devices have been removed and no one bled to death or blew up."

"That was fast," Chad said. "Where are they keeping the devices?"

"At the hospital," Pepa replied. "It makes a good cover, it looks like they are visiting someone. They gave me the honor of questioning Mrs. Haynes, they figured since she cried on my shoulder that is was a bonding moment and she might open up to me. So, while they worked on her husband I worked on her and it was a piece of cake. She would have opened up to anyone."

"Did you get anything solid?" Chad asked.

"Yes and no," Pepa sighed. "She knows Rogelio and the family, they call him Roger not Rogelio, but she didn't know he was involved. They were using her kids to threaten her, that's why she was shaking so badly when she arrived. Do you want the whole story or should I call Phillips?"

"If you'd like I can get him on the radio and you can brief all of us."

"Let's do that, it would be quicker. Between you and me, I called you because I don't feel that comfortable with Phillips. I always get the feeling he is interested in more than business, if you get my drift," Pepa said.

"He probably is, but that is a tough discussion to have right now. I think you should feel flattered and give it some serious thought."

"You can't talk and you know how I feel about relationships with co-workers, but back to the matter at hand. Get Phillips and let's do this, we'll talk later."

Chad put Pepa on speaker and toggled Phillips and Brock, "Wake up guys, I have Pepa on the phone and she has info for us."

"Pepa, thanks for calling. Tell me you have something good to tell us," Phillips said.

"I don't know how good it is, but Mrs. Haynes said her husband was under a lot of pressure. She said he was drinking more than usual, seemed depressed and when she'd ask him what was wrong he would just shake his head and wave her off. At one point he did mention that his job might be in jeopardy, it was shortly after this that some men came to their home and implanted the device in her arm."

"They were all at home and she had planned a drive to the lake house to try and get Mr. Haynes to relax. She thought a day on the lake with the kids would be good for him. They were getting ready to leave when some men came to the door, Haynes argued with them and they pushed their way inside. One of the men took the kids into another room while the other one took out a gun and told her and Haynes if they didn't do as they were told the kids would suffer. At this point another man came into the house carrying a bag and he implanted the device in her arm. He said it was only a tracking device, but if she was caught talking to anyone about it, she would lose her children. This guy then turned to Haynes, told him to remember the consequences he would face and then the men left."

"I told her it sounded like lines from an old movie. She said she would have laughed at them if she hadn't been so scared. Anyway, after the men left she broke down and when she had gotten control of herself she confronted her husband and asked him what the hell was going on. He told her she didn't need to know it would just make it more dangerous for her, she yelled back at him that it was already more dangerous because now the kids' lives were on the line."

"He finally told her that he had been approached in his office by some men, he wouldn't tell her who they were, and they threaten to kill her and the kids, if he didn't help them get some things across the border and into Texas. He told them he couldn't arrange that sort of thing and one of the guys punched him and said they knew better. They said it was simple, all he had to do was have a bus at a particular place and give the order for some of the illegals to be transferred. That was it, nothing more. He was then grabbed from behind, his suit coat and shirt were removed and they had implanted a thing in his arm. When they were finished they told him that they could now track him and as they walked out the door one of them said they would be in touch with instructions."

"At this point Mrs. Haynes said she always felt he was leaving something out because it took the men so long to get to her and the kids. She said he folded to fast and that wasn't like him, so they had to be holding something else over his head. She said and I quote, "Now that you've mentioned Roger it makes sense to me. He and his sister have always been very close, she's younger and when they lost their parents she was still in high school and all they had was each other. It really bothered him when she moved to Costa Rica, but he knew she was in love and she deserved a life and a family of her own. My guess is they not only threatened Roger, but his sister as well and that is why he folded. My poor Matt, I bet they already had Roger when they came to his office."

Pepa sighed, "I believe her. She was really torn up and still worried about what was going to happen to all of them. I mentioned a few names to her to see if they were involved and to get a reaction, but I got nothing. If you can think of anything else I need to ask her let me know, but I think I got it all. I'll be interested to hear what her husband has to say and see if it jibes with this. I have all of this being written up to send to the office, in case you need a copy later."

"I have a question," Brock said. "How long ago did all of this take place?"

"She's been living with it for about two weeks, but she doesn't know when they got to Mr. Haynes. I should also let you know that they are bringing Rogelio's parents here. The guest house is big so I can fit everyone in there for now. By the way Rogelio's last name is Vega, de la Vega to be exact. The grandparents moved to Cosa Rica from Spain about fifty years ago."

"So you're the official word on this."

"Yep. Since I had to call anyway they passed the job to me. I think Mrs. Haynes and Mrs. De la Vega can comfort each other, that's why I don't mind them staying together.'" Pepa said.

Phillips cleared his throat, "Okay, thanks for all this. We'll digest it and see if we can come up with any more questions. Haynes may have more answers for us." With that Phillips toggled down the radio.

"That's pretty rough on those families. Keep your eye on things there and watch yourself." Chad closed his phone and slumped down in his seat again.

Across the street at the motel Rogelio sat in the chair at the little table, staring at Ignacio as he slowly woke up. Ignacio sat on the edge of the bed and was startled to see Rogelio sitting there.

"Well little man, you are moving around. How do you feel, are you alright?" Ignacio asked him.

Rogelio continued to stare at him with flat eyes and said in a mixture of English and Spanish, "I want to go home. Tell me what I can do to get this over with, tell me what to do."

Ignacio smiled, "Ahh, little man. Yes, you can help." Ignacio walked over and put his hand on Rogelio's shoulder, "Yes I have the perfect job for you." He turned and walked out of the room.

Rogelio looked over at the bed, toward the corner where they slept and saw Yolanda raise her head so only her eyes were showing above the edge of the mattress. Their eyes met and he smiled.

46

Phillips and Brock had spent the last hour going over the notes Phillips had written trying to see if they had missed anything and committing the small details to memory. Phillips wanted to destroy the paper work and Brock had tried to talk him into holding on to it for a while longer. Phillips had won the argument on the grounds that the Office had everything so they no longer really needed the paper or anything tying them to the men or vehicles in case something went wrong.

"Where are your notes?" Phillips asked.

"I dumped them last night, I figured I didn't need them since you had it all," Brock answered. "My phone is clean too."

"So why were you trying to talk me out of destroying this stuff?"

"Just making you think it through, no real reason. I didn't want you coming back to me and saying that I should have stopped you," Brock smiled.

"Just because I made a few bad decisions in my life, that you could have stopped, doesn't mean I make bad decisions all the time. Now if you'll excuse me, I need to burn these," Phillips started to open his door, "There's a burn barrel over there that looks like it hasn't been used in a long time."

"Let me do it," Brock said. "You need to call about that boat." Brock took the papers and left the car as Phillips picked up his phone.

He stood over the barrel and watched the papers burn as he slowly fed the flames. "Amazing," he said to himself, "how fire puts people into a trance. No wonder there are so many arsonists out there." He stirred the ashes to be certain everything had burned and went back to the car.

Brock entered the car as Phillips closed his phone, "I'll get Chad and fill you all in on our never ending saga."

Phillips toggled the radio and yelled, "Wake up!"

"Holy crap," Chad replied, "You almost gave Sanchez a heart attack. What's up?"

"They sent a chopper and a couple of our guys to Port Lavaca and they just reported back. The guys they talked to at the dock said the rental truck met a large fishing boat and stuff was transferred to the truck. They couldn't tell what is was, but it looked like crates of frozen fish and since it was a charter boat they didn't think anything of it. Some of these larger boats have a 'quick-freeze' unit in the holds because they stay out for long periods of time. One guy they talked to said only one thing bothered him and that was the fact he had never seen the boat before. He has worked there for a long time and said he was familiar with the boats that come in, but this was a new one. He did get the name, Angelina, but no port of call was on it and it should have had one. He reported it to the Coast Guard as soon as he could, but didn't hear back from them. The chopper is taking our guys back to Corpus and if we want them to, they'll get their car and head our way."

"Not much to go on, but better than nothing. The Coast Guard won't find that boat, bet the name was changed and the port of call covered. I'll also bet that it went only a short distance down the coast and turned toward land," Chad said. "They'll want to get that boat out of open water, out of sight and clean up the name. It would be great if that dock had CCTV, then we could have a look for ourselves."

"I doubt if they have it, it's a pretty small place. There are probably only one or two in the whole town. I'll call the guys and see if they asked about cameras," Phillips said.

"When you call them, see if they got those fingerprints from that end room where the couple was staying," Chad added. "It's just a loose end we should tie up. By the way, I wonder what happened to the baby they were carrying around, maybe it was a decoy since they don't have the car she was driving."

"Ask them if they found any dirty diapers in the trash," Sanchez said. "I'm just saying, if the kid was real there would be dirty disposable diapers in the trash."

"I think your guys took photos of the car, so ask if they traced the plates, maybe she dropped the kid and the car off somewhere. That's all we need, a baby to worry about," Chad grumbled. "What the hell kind of case is this? All we need now is a clown car."

Chad and Sanchez could hear Brock laughing in the background, "It's not funny," Chad said.

Phillips started laughing, "Yes it is and if a clown car pulls up, it's going to be your fault."

"Maybe there's one in the rental truck," Brock was snorting with laughter. "Quick turn off the radio before we totally lose it, it isn't dignified, but neither is a clown car," Brock howled.

Chad turned down the radio, "What a team, good grief." He looked over at Sanchez who had his lips so tight together it looked as if he didn't have any and tears were rolling down his cheeks. As soon as he looked at Chad he burst out laughing. "Not you too," Chad said.

Sanchez nodded and tried to speak, "Sorry,' he said, "I can't help it." He got out of the car to try and gain control of himself and looked back at Chad, "I didn't give you trouble when you were on your ass laughing about a hand of bananas."

"Point taken," Chad sighed, shook his head, turned the radio volume up and toggled Phillips. "Sorry guys, guess I'm wound a bit tight right now."

"We were just wondering if you had kicked Sanchez out of the car," Phillips said.

"No, he got out on his own."

"If you need to, go ahead and take a walk. We'll still be here when you get back," Phillips said and turned the radio down.

"He doesn't like sitting around this long unless he has a weapon in his hand. He can sit for hours waiting in a nest and stay focused, but in a situation like this he gets antsy," Phillips said as he settled in the seat again.

"I don't blame him because my ass is pretty tried too. If I thought I could get away with it, I would walk across the street, kick in the door of that motel room and start shooting. Rogelio is probably curled up in a corner like he did in Corpus, so he would be safe. I could go in, put a bullet in the head of every living one of those bastards and smile as I walked out," Brock said.

Phillips looked at him, "That would be pretty cold, but I could go for that."

"Our profession is cold, you have to be cold to do what we're supposed to do. These assholes want jihad, they want to die on their terms and as long as they take some of us with them, they will get their virgins. There are people out there that say we are no better, but these assholes wage war to destroy as many people as they can, even their own. At least when we go to war it's to save people from those who want to do harm."

Brock sighed, "When we stepped in to help Afghanistan fight the Russians we opened up a can of worms or maybe a better term is we gave birth to a movement. My mentor and his family lived in Saudi Arabia for about six years, in the eastern provinces on the Persian Gulf, of course in Saudi they called it the Gulf of Arabia. They didn't live in a compound they lived in one of the towns and their home was two blocks from the Gulf. The only thing between them and the water was the palace of a Prince, one of the sons of King Faisal. The main streets were paved, but most of the side streets were packed sand, the sheep and cattle would be herded right between their house and the palace. It sounds rustic, but once you got downtown you had everything you could think of, the western influence, especially French, was everywhere. They even had American grocery stores and their children went to the American School. They traveled a lot to Beirut, Tehran, Karachi and Abu Dhabi without fear, well actually everyone had a problem traveling to

Tehran or anywhere in Iran because the security was so corrupt, but a hand full of bills did the trick."

"They lived there in the early to late seventies and life was a jet setters dream since you could travel anywhere in Europe or Asia and be treated like royalty. I remember the stories he'd tell about being in Beirut, they always stayed at the Phoenicia Hotel, it was elegant and the view looking out over the beautiful blue of the Mediterranean was something his wife said she would never forget. She also said that sounds of the shelling of the Palestinian Compound was something that was hard to forget. In 1975 the family had been staying at the Holiday Inn in Beirut for about a week, for business meetings and a few hours after they left a rocket hit the sixteenth floor of the hotel, the same floor as their room. The next month the Civil War got into full swing and they never went back, he said none of the tourist who visited Beirut in 1975 were aware that things were that bad. They had always been told to be aware of their surroundings and were told where not to go, but they never imagined it was that bad. No one ever told them that a conflict had started over the hotel district.

"His wife said the last time she saw Beirut, was when she and her kids were flying out of Saudi to meet her husband in London and they had to change planes in Beirut, it was December 1975. The airport was chaos and packed with hundreds of people, all of them pushing and shoving trying to get to attention of the security teams so they could get to an airline agent. When the security people saw her and realized she was American, they scooped her and the kids up and got them to the plane. She said as they flew over Beirut for the last time, she looked out the window and cried. Her beautiful Beirut, a place where people from all over the world came to visit, enjoy the sea, the night life and shop was in ruins with patches of smoke billowing up across the city."

"It was her first taste of war and hate and to this day she still says that the Arab people she met and live with were kinder to her than her neighbors in London. She finds it very hard to believe what the talking heads say about the Saudis being behind any of this."

Brock sat up, "Sorry, don't know why I went off on that tangent. I guess I was just comparing these assholes to the ones I always heard stories about."

"I guess mentioning Afghanistan brought it back to you," Phillips said. "I think your mentor was right in the middle of the beginning of everything. The Palestinian Black September attack was 1972 in Munich and a few years after that the PLO was expelled from Jordan into Lebanon and began to militarize the Palestinians in Lebanon, which in turn started the civil war in Beirut in 1975. The Afghan/Russia war was 1979 to 1989 and in November of 1979 was when the American Embassy in Tehran was taken over. Then there were small conflicts and bombings of American sites for years after that and no one had enough foresight to get intelligence going full bore. If they had, we may have had a different outcome."

"Come to think of it, bin Laden started al-Qaeda between 1988 and late '89, even before the war in Afghanistan ceased. Man, there's a lot of history there, we could talk about this for hours."

"I think the Cold War kept everyone looking at the sky in those days and Vietnam was coming to an end," Brock said. "Maybe if we had looked at the whole picture a lot of this terrorist shit could have been abated, but you know what they say 'hindsight is 20/20'."

"I reminded my mentor Beirut was under reconstruction," Brock continued, "That the Phoenicia Hotel is up and running again, that the shopping was almost back to normal and the city was alive again. Almost a miniature Paris. They told me that it wouldn't be the same if they went back, many of their friends had moved to other countries or had been collateral damage during the fighting and age would put a damper on the fun."

"Maybe on our fishing trip we can discuss the beginnings of ISIS," Phillips chuckled. "A lot of history there too."

Brock looked at him sternly, "No, on the trip we talk about women and fish."

The radio sent out a signal and Phillips picked it up. "It's Lou. We have movement at the two rooms, looks like they may be moving."

47

Rogelio was again sitting in the chair, he could hear the men talking in the next room. The door had been left ajar and he could see movement through the two inch crack in the door. He eased out of the chair and moved closer to the door to watch them. He had a small and narrow view, but he saw the man who called himself Jorge bending over a piece of clothing on the bed, he was laughing as he put a cell phone in the pocket and held it up to look at it. Rogelio stepped back from the door and walked over to the corner where Yolanda sat on their blankets.

He sat next to her and whispered, "I think they are making a suicide vest or coat and I think it's for me."

"How do you know that's what it is?" Yolanda asked him.

"I have seen them on the news and in movies. This clothing that he has is heavy looking, with lots of pockets that are closed. He was also stuffing wires into the lining."

Yolanda covered her face with her hands, "They are going to kill us and anyone who tries to help us. I thought and was told that I would be helping my country, I would be helping to change the fate of the people in Mexico. I spent weeks in the dirt and sun training to use guns in case I had to protect myself. These men aren't from Mexico, I don't know where they come from, but their Spanish is not very good. The man they call Addison told me that he was happy I had joined their cause and he was smiling when he said that the people of America were going to find out what it was like to have their own blood spilled on their soil. He told me I was only a woman, but was still useful. When I found out that they'd come here to kill and kill as many as they could, I told him I wanted no part of it and to send me back to Mexico, that is when they beat me. The woman told me it was too late and I would be a martyr in their cause and she always slapped me to remind me who was in charge. When she killed the bus driver I thought I was next and when I saw what she did to his face I thought, my mother will never know what happened to me. What have I done? Holy Mary forgive me, I'm so sorry."

"Don't cry," Rogelio told her. "I always knew they were going to kill me, there is no other way for them. At first I thought once they got across the border they would let me go, but the longer they kept me the more worried I got. When they killed Jasmine that was when I knew I would die too. I don't worry for me, I worry for my mother and for you. You did nothing to make them want to kill you, you don't deserve that."

He took her hand, "No matter what happens you can't let them see that we know what they are doing. I will pretend to be stupid, but I'll fool them because I'm not stupid and I will not die without putting up a fight. Do you understand what I am saying? We know nothing about the coat. Okay?"

Yolanda looked in his eyes and no longer saw a young boy, she wasn't sure what she saw. "Then I'm stupid too and if they make me wear one of those, we will fool them together. We will also kill them together."

They leaned back against the wall as Jorge came through the connecting door with a coat in his hand.

"Little man, come here I have a gift for you."

Rogelio walked over and looked at what Jorge held.

"It's a bullet proof jacket, I made it just for you. It will be heavy because I sewed pieces of metal in it to protect you. There are people who might come after us and I don't want you shot by mistake. Look there is a pocket for a cell phone, but I'll wait and give you the phone later. Try it on and let's see if it fits."

Rogelio slipped into the jacket, it was a little long and heavy, but he showed no reaction to the gift or its weight. Jorge looked him over, removed the jacket and turned toward the door to the other room.

"You don't need to wear it now, but we'll be leaving soon and then you'll need to wear it all the time," Jorge said.

Rogelio went over and sat with Yolanda again, "We need some sort of plan," she said. "The only thing I can think of is to get away and I know that isn't possible. We have no weapons, we don't know where we are or where we are going and we don't know how many people will be traveling with us. How can we plan anything when we know nothing?"

Rogelio calmly looked at her, "If you have an opportunity to get away, if you see some opening for yourself, you go and go as fast as you can. Do not look back and don't worry about me. If you can get away and find help, you must do it. They won't hurt me because you run away, I'm their protection, but if they catch you they'll not hesitate to kill you. I don't say this to be mean, but you mean nothing to them. I'm important to them, I'm their hostage. You, as they say in the movies, are excess baggage."

Yolanda looked at his eyes again, "Who are you? You're very smart for a young boy."

"My name is Roger, Rogelio, and my uncle works for the American government. They're using me against him, at least that's what I think. I don't know what they are planning, but from what you told me, it isn't good. The thing we must do is keep our eyes open, not talk to each other or show any reactions to what goes on around us. We will speak to each other with our eyes, using eye movement if it is something we want the other to see, if you get scared blink rapidly so I can maybe help. If you have to point do it so no one can see. The thing I want you to remember is I will not leave you behind, I promise."

"So," Yolanda said, "it will be like the game my sister and I used to play in the back seat of the car. My father would get mad if we made too much noise so we used a kind of sign language."

"Yes, think of it as that game. These men are in no hurry to get where they're going, so we may have time to get away or get help. Remember, continue to be scared and don't change the way you're behaving. We can't give them any reason to be suspicious of us."

Rogelio stood and went to sit in the chair, his face blank. He had told her all he dared, he couldn't tell her about the messages he had left or the SUV he had seen a few times with the same man driving. He couldn't tell her about the knife or the plan he was putting together in his head. He still was not sure he could trust her, they might have put her with him to trick him into thinking she was his friend.

Every time he had gone into the bathroom he had used the pipes under the toilet and sink to sharpen the knife. He had pretended to be sick so he could get into the bathroom more often and spend more time on his project. The knife wasn't as sharp as he wanted it to be, but it was as good as it was going to get. At least it was a weapon and he might be able to use it to get one of the guns.

He looked around the room, then down at his hands and thought of home, his father, his mother and the soul of his brother. He thought of the journey he had been on and where it was taking him. He thought of the seven year old boy he used to be and wondered if he would ever be that boy again, he doubted it. He wondered if Yolanda was really his friend and if he could save her, he was hoping he could. He had to remain calm and pick the right time. He almost smiled as he thought of the surprised look on the faces of these terrible men.

Jorge came back into the room with the jacket and hung it on the back of the other chair. The other girl came with him to get her things. He looked over at Yolanda, "You, come with me, we need your help. We want you to make the back of the car comfortable for you and my little friend." He turned to Rogelio, "I'm going to lock you in the room because we will be busy and cannot watch you. As soon as we are finished we'll be leaving."

The girl checked in her purse for something, grabbed her things and as she left something fell from her hand. Jorge took Yolanda, they all left the room and closed the door. Rogelio heard the lock turn and looked over at the jacket.

He got up from the chair, walked over and saw a stone on the floor near the edge of the bed. He picked it up and put it in his pocket, then he laid down across the end of the bed. He laced his fingers behind his head and stared at the ceiling. He looked over at the locked door and finally allowed a smile to spread across his face.

48

After the call from Lou, Phillips had Brock inform Chad while he contacted the chopper pilots to get them moving. Chad called his teams and put them on alert and called the team in Beaumont to see if they had any movement there. The team in Beaumont said no one at the motel had shown any activity, but would call when they did. Forty-five minutes later Lou made the second call.

"They're loading up now, they'd been messing around in the back of the SUV, taking blankets out to it, but looks like they are about ready. They just brought Rogelio out of the room and it looks like his wearing a suicide vest of some sort."

"Bastards!" Phillips said.

"My sentiments exactly," replied Lou. "I hate to bring this up, but you do realize we could have taken these guys out from where we're sitting. If I had driven out and picked two of you up, the four of us could've put them down before they knew we were here."

"First there are too many of them, second we want to get them with whatever is in those trucks and vans, and last, I don't want to spend the rest of this week trying to explain things to the local PD." Phillips said.

"I understand about getting them with the goods and the locals, I'm just saying we could have taken these guys down and let the drivers head for the trucks and then stop them. The main players are in the two adjoining rooms, you got five guys in there. The other drivers are in rooms directly across from here. With timed shots we could've knocked them all down at the same time and no one would be able to hit the switch on the vest. Okay, they're pulling out now, watch for your van drivers."

Brock pointed out the window, "There's the other drivers and the couple from the truck."

As soon as Phillips was sure they were headed toward Houston, he got the chopper in the air. They followed their quarry as they tried to go around Houston and avoid traffic, at times Phillips wasn't sure what they were trying to do. If it hadn't been for the chopper, the SUV and truck would have been lost in traffic, the white vans had gone in two different directions, none toward Houston. They now found themselves north of Houston on highway 59, moving in a north northwest direction with Lufkin as the next large city.

Chad toggled the radio, "Hey, I just got a call from the guys in Beaumont. They're on the road following their guys up highway 69, so they should be running parallel to us."

"Both those highway meet in Lufkin, be interesting to see where they go from there. I'm thinking I don't want to set that device off until after we see what happens in Lufkin. What do you think?" Philips asked.

Brock shook his head as Chad replied, "Yeah, if we set it off now it might spook them, but I don't think it will stop them. I'm curious as to where they are going, I just don't want to wait too long to set it off."

Phillips looked at Brock, "Why'd you shake your head?"

"It won't spook them, they'll have no idea what's wrong with the truck. All they're going to see is smoke, we hope. When the cops get there they'll be long gone and will meet up with the other van, either in Lufkin or further down the road. It'll just be a setback for them. You have to remember, these guys are not from here, they don't think the way we do, they don't get paranoid the way American bad guys do. I think the only American with them is the Addison guy and they aren't going to want to listen to him, now that they're on American soil, they just might shoot him," Brock said.

"I'm with Brock, set it off when we get the opening," Chad said.

"So okay, I hear what you're saying. I just wanted to push the envelope a bit. Let's wait until we get past Livingston and maybe the traffic will thin enough so no one else is endangered incase this this blows something besides smoke."

"That's only about thirty miles from here, so let's get our shit together," Chad said.

"I don't want you guys behind this thing when the cops arrive, only stay behind it long enough to be sure we have smoke and make the call. If the cops look in the back of that truck and find what we think is in there, then they may stop traffic until they clear up any danger," Phillips said. "Now, I'm pretty sure these guys are in communication with one another so we've got a few ways this thing can go. If the occupants of the truck know there is a problem, they'll contact the SUV then the SUV will either pick them up or abandon them, either way that SUV will be gone when the cops arrive. We will stay with the SUV, if they abandon the others and take off. You watch the truck from a safe distance and see what happens with the cops. If the SUV flips a U-turn then both of us will have to drive up the highway a bit, watch them to see what's going on and wait for them to come back by before we can continue the tail. Once you see smoke, get around that truck fast in case something goes wrong. I don't want to pick up any pieces. If we lose them we still have the tracking device and can find them again. Any questions?"

Brock spoke up, "What if the cops find your tracking device on that truck?"

"No problem," Chad answered. "Ray took it off while he was under there, we decided it wasn't a good thing to leave behind."

"I'm trying to keep this simple, simple is easy, but you know what they say about plans, they can get screwed," Phillips said. "Keep this radio open so we can monitor each other. Livingston is a big boating and fishing place, but I doubt we'll have any problems once we hit the other side of town. If they take the business route through town, it's still a straight shot."

"We're here and looks like they're staying on the main highway," Brock said.

"How far on the other side do you want to go before we hit the switch?" Chad asked.

"At least ten miles, further if we have traffic," Phillips responded.

"Sanchez, don't get nervous on us," Brock laughed, "Remember, tell the cops you're worried about the smoke."

"Hey, this was my idea and I'm a good actor, I had the lead in my senior play. Before you try being a smart ass, my graduating class was seven hundred."

"Yeah, but your acting class was three," Brock said, "and you were the only male."

"Nah, it was four if you include the teacher," Sanchez laughed, "and the play was 'Waiting for Godot'."

"Wow, an intellectual," Brock said.

"I hate to break up this laugh fest, but did you happen to check for cell phone reception out here?" Chad put in. "I know they'll have it in town, but ten miles out might be a different story."

"I have it, but I'll keep an eye on it." Phillips said.

"The transportation department is coming up on the left or at least that's what the sign says." Brock said.

"There should be a rehab place up here too. Once we get passed that we should have open highway," Phillips said.

"Here's your rehab, coming up on the left. We have some traffic moving south, glad this is four lane. Chad, how are we looking back there?" Brock asked.

"We've got traffic, but its way back there. I say after this next exit ramp we do it. Remember, let it ring a couple of times in case the connection is slow."

"I'm ready," Sanchez said. "I've got the emergency number punched in, just waiting to hit send. Let's do this."

"Okay," Phillips said "I'm calling."

"I'm passing," Brock came back.

"I'm on the third ring, now four. You got anything?" Phillips said.

"Give it a minute to filter out, but nothing yet," Chad said.

Sanchez was staring at the back of the truck wishing for smoke. He shifted his position, "I think I've got something. Yep, there it is. I'm making my call."

Sanchez told the emergency operator about the smoke as they started to pass the truck. Chad looked over at the SUV as they started to pass it and saw a small hand flat against the back window. He continued to look straight ahead as Sanchez still spoke with the operator.

"I'm only telling you what I am seeing," Sanchez told the operator. "There is more smoke coming out of the back now and I don't think the driver even knows about it. My wife, she is very scared. I am going to pass this truck, these men driving were acting strange at the gas place, they scared my wife and I don't want to be mixed up with them."

The operator was still talking as Sanchez looked behind them at the truck. Before he could turn back around he saw the back of the truck jump and rock as if it had hit something. Then the sound reached them, a muffled thump.

"You need to send help," he yelled into the phone. "Something exploded in the back of the truck, they are slowing down." He waited another few seconds before he hung up.

"It wasn't a big bang, I wonder what went off." Chad said. "Looks like the SUV slowed down too."

"What did the operator say?" Brock asked over the open radio.

"They have a unit nearby and he's sending it," Sanchez replied.

"Here he comes," Brock said. "He's southbound, I'm pulling off."

"Right behind you, the SUV stopped." Chad said. "Grab the glasses, I want to see what is going on back there."

Sanchez handed him the small binocs and jumped out of their SUV, "I'm going to pop the hood, hit the hood latch for me."

"Got it and good idea. Now let's see what's going on back there."

Phillips walked back to Chad as Brock headed for Sanchez. Brock and Sanchez used the hood of the vehicle as cover to watch the action behind them. Phillips and Chad watched through their binoculars.

"Looks like the SUV, picked up their people and got far enough in front to make it look like they were just curious," Chad said.

Brock and Sanchez walked over, "If they're stopped, they are probably discussing what happened and why," Brock said.

"The cop is driving up to them now," Phillips said.

They watched as the officer got out of this car and started speaking to the driver and pointing at the truck. The driver got out of the car and started pointing toward the field and gesturing with his arms. The officer waved them on their way and turned back toward his car as the SUV moved forward.

"They're coming this way, so act like we have car trouble," Chad said.

As the SUV passed them Phillips glanced up and saw Rogelio's face against the back window, "Crap, Rogelio saw us. Hope he doesn't blow it for us."

"I think he's smarter than that," Brock said. "I think he saw you when we passed them and he's just letting you know about it."

"Boy, there's a lot of smoke coming out of that truck, Ray may have out done himself," Chad said. "Looks like they have traffic stopped. Let's get out of here."

Sanchez closed the hood, got back in the car and they moved back onto the highway. They had gone about one hundred yards and Sanchez looked back at the smoking truck just as it blew.

"Holy shit! I think you can say Ray out did himself," Sanchez said. "I hope that cop is alright. He was still at his car, maybe he was far enough away to just get blown off his feet."

"Turn the radio on to the highway information station and let's see if they have anything to say," Chad said.

"We'll have to wait, sounds like nothing has been officially reported yet," Sanchez said.

Before Chad could comment his phone chirped. "Yeah, what's up?"

"Hey, it's Lou. I don't know what's going on, but the van we're tailing just flipped a turn through the median and is heading back."

"Sounds like our SUV is calling in his backup guns. Rays' device blew the truck, stay on them. I'll get back to you."

Chad closed his phone and as he put it on the seat it chirped again, "Now what?"

"It must have worked because our van just turned around," Ray said.

"It more than worked, it blew it," Chad said.

"So now this guy needs the shit he has in the vans. Guess he shouldn't have put so many eggs in one basket," Ray chuckled. "We're on them, so I guess we'll see you before too long."

"Did you get that Phillips?" Chad asked.

"Yeah, I got it. This means these guys will probably stop again and wait for the vans to catch up with them."

"I hope where ever they stop gives us cover," Brock said. "Hey, we have flashing lights headed our way on the southbound side."

"The Feds won't be far behind once the cops get an idea of what was in that truck." Phillips sighed. "We need more miles between us and the scene."

"Shall I dump the phone or do you want to wait a few more miles?" Sanchez asked.

"Give it a few more miles," replied Phillips. "Then tear it up and toss it."

"Roger that," said Sanchez. "Did you happen to see Rogelio? I got a view of a small hand on the window, so did Chad."

"You must have not heard me earlier with all the action going on, but I actually had eye contact with him. I hope he stays calm and doesn't blow it. Of course there is the chance he doesn't remember my face," Phillips said.

"You can bet he remembers both of our faces," Sanchez said. "We're the only two people, he thinks, who know about him. The other one he probably thinks is dead."

49

Rogelio and Yolanda had been told to sit in the cargo area of the SUV, Jorge had put the jacket on Rogelio and Ignacio had instructed them to not try and signal any of the cars as they drove through Houston. If they did it might cost the lives of innocent people as well as their own. Rogelio found it difficult to get comfortable with the heavy jacket on, but he found that sitting on his knees with a pillow beneath them was as good as it got. Keeping his balance was sometimes a problem, but putting his hand on one of the windows helped.

It seemed to Rogelio that it was taking a long time to drive through Houston. He was not interested in the tall buildings, he had been to D.C and other big cities and they all looked the same to him. He spent his time watching the traffic and Yolanda. She had no interest in the city and was curled up on a blanket with her eyes closed, he wasn't sure if she was scared or if she had no interest because she had seen it all before. If she had been to Houston or another city like it, she hadn't mentioned it to him and this bothered him.

He leaned forward and rested the top of his body on the edge of the backseat, this took some of the pressure off of his knees, but not much. He eased himself onto the side of his leg left leg and it felt better even if he was still off balance. He started to rub his ankles when he noticed they were driving into more open country, leaving Houston behind. The further they got from the border, the more his hopes for rescue diminished. He admonished himself for having these thoughts, if you gave up hope then you were giving up completely. He looked out the window as they passed another town and he wondered how long he had before time ran out.

The man called Addison was driving and Ignacio was on the phone with the people in the truck. Rogelio couldn't hear everything that was being said only a few words, but it didn't sound important and Ignacio was laughing. Rogelio got up on his knees again, turned to look at the truck behind them, started to lose his balance and placed his hand on the window again. A car had passed the truck and started to pass them, the man in the passenger seat was on his cell phone.

Rogelio blinked, then almost jumped as he recognized the doctor. He had to work hard not to show his elation at seeing his friend, he wished the doctor could see through the tinted window, but knew he couldn't. He continued to stare straight ahead instead of watching the car as it pulled ahead of them, thoughts were running through his head so fast that he couldn't settle on just one. Then another SUV started to pass them and before the man in the passenger seat turned away, Rogelio recognized him. It was the officer from the border. His heart soared, they were here to rescue him, but he had to remain calm. He told himself, "Don't do anything differently, be the same and don't change your plan, it might even help". He knew he couldn't tell Yolanda and he didn't dare let his guard down. If any of them became suspicious of him, then it was all over.

He suddenly realized that Ignacio was screaming into the phone, but he couldn't understand what was being said. Ignacio then said to Addison, "We have to go back, something is wrong with the truck. They tell me there is smoke coming out of the back."

Everything was happening at once, first he saw the doctor then he saw the border officer turn in his seat and as the other SUV pulled quickly ahead of them, a loud sound came from the truck behind them. Rogelio turned to look at the truck as it lurched to the side of the highway. Ignacio was yelling into the phone as Addison slowed down, stopped then started going in reverse. When they got close to the van the two people inside ran up to them and jumped into the SUV. They moved forward further down the edge of the highway putting distance between them and the truck and Addison had started asking the driver of the truck questions. He had again stopped the SUV and had turned to look at the people in back seat.

He wanted to know what had caused the smoke, maybe it was just the brakes or an exhaust leak. The driver of the truck assured him that it wasn't either of those things that this smoke had a different smell and neither of those things would cause the small explosion. Addison then suggested that it be towed and repaired, maybe it wasn't an explosion, made an axle or something had broken. Ignacio gave him an angry look and told him to leave, maybe someone would steal it and they couldn't be connected to the truck or its contents. Addison turned in the seat again and put the SUV in gear, but before he could move he saw a police officer pull up behind them and get out of his car. He walked up to the driver side window and motioned for the window to be rolled down.

"Are you with the truck?" the office asked.

"No, we saw smoke coming out of the truck and just stopped to see if we could help," answered Addison. "May I get out of the car?"

The Officer stepped back with his hand on his weapon, "Sure."

"We pulled up in time to see two people running away from the truck," Addison said. He pointed to a small field bordered by trees, "They ran in that direction, it looked like two men. That's all I know Officer. We're on our way to a reunion in Lufkin, looks like we might get there a bit late."

"When did you notice the smoke and how much was there?

"We were getting ready to pass the truck when we noticed smoke coming out of the rear door, not much, but enough for me to be concerned," Addison replied.

The Officer looked back at the truck then at the people in the SUV. "Okay, thanks for the information you people go ahead and be on your way. There is nothing you can do here," he said.

Rogelio had watched the officer quietly from the rear of the SUV and now watched out the back window as they pulled back onto the highway. He moved over by Yolanda on the passenger side and as they got close to the two cars parked on the side of the road, he pressed his face against the window. As they passed the cars Rogelio made eye contact with the doctor, then slowly leaned down and placed his head on a pillow. Addison and Ignacio were too busy talking with the other people to even notice him. He breathed a silent sigh of relief.

Suddenly there was a huge explosion. Rogelio and Yolanda jumped up and quickly looked out the back window at the large plume of smoke with streaks of fire running through it. Neither said a word, but turned to look at each other first with a surprised look on their faces, then as they looked back at the smoke billowing from the truck, they both broke into small smiles.

50

Ten minutes outside Lufkin Phillips got a call on his cell from Chad.

"We need to talk, just you and me. I don't want this to look like we don't trust anyone, it's just company business," Chad said without preamble.

"When?"

"As soon as we stop. These guys are going to change plates so they will probably pick a motel or someplace with a lot of cars. I guarantee you that cop got their plate number and they know it. I think they'll blow through Lufkin and head for Nacogdoches, it's a college town with more motels," Chad said.

"So, you think the cops alright, he was pretty close to that blast," Phillips said.

"He was close enough to get knocked down or shaken up, but his vehicle should've shielded him. The only thing on the radio highway broadcast is that they have closed down the area and are diverting traffic onto one of the oncoming lanes. Nothing about injuries and if a cop was injured the news media would be all over it and there has been nothing there either," Chad said.

"Roger that," Phillips said and closed his phone.

"Chad?" Brock asked.

"Yeah, he has some office business we have to discuss and he was giving me a heads ups," Phillips replied and then proceeded to fill Brock in on the rest of the conversation. In the SUV behind them, Sanchez cocked an eyebrow at Chad.

"What is this shit, you think you might hurt my feelings? Forget about it and I'm sure Brock would say the same thing. This job, all of our jobs, don't allow for feelings, we show compassion and empathy only when necessary. We each have people we have to answer to and I know there are things that I can't discuss with you. Do what you have to do," Sanchez said.

Chad looked over at him. "Not that I need to give you justification for what I said, but I'm going to give it to you anyway. I need to talk to Phillips and get something through his head. If Brock is around I'm afraid he might influence any decision Phillips makes. Don't get me wrong Brock is a good guy and a pro, but he and Phillips have a long history and friendship. I want Phillips to make this decision on his own because he'll have to live with it."

"He's going to have to live with it even if Brock does put his two cents in and you know it. But you're right, this is on him and I would hate to see him blame someone else's influence on the outcome," Sanchez said.

"I get the feeling you already know what this is about," Chad said.

"Yeah, I think I do. Let's talk about it after you talk to Phillips," Sanchez replied.

They followed the SUV carrying Rogelio to the 287/ Hwy 59 exit and skirted Lufkin passing the Hwy 69 ramp. All heads swiveled to look down the highway as if they could see the white van.

Chad's phone chimed, "Yeah." It was the Beaumont team.

"We're getting close to Lufkin and I have some info for you. The van stopped for gas, so we decided it was a good time for snacks. On the way passed the gas pumps we heard these guys talking about a house. They were chattering away, in English, all we could pick up was something about a house while they waited. I'll let you figure it out from there, my head hurts."

"We are on 59 above Lufkin and my guess is they're going to wait for the other vans to catch up with them. Interesting that they were speaking English, maybe your guys are homegrown," Chad said.

"When this thing started I figured them foreign influence, but after getting a better look at them and hearing them speak, I would say they are homegrown or have been here for quite some time. We'll follow these guys in and meet up with you shortly."

"Roger," Chad said and dialed Phillips to brief him on the call.

Sanchez took this time to call Bob Frank and see if anything new had developed.

"Yeah, I'm glad you called," Bob said. "I'm having a wonderful time. Nothing like spending all your time looking over your shoulder. The only time I feel relaxed is out on the boat, which by the way, I'm working on getting a job here and chucking the border."

"Why are you doing that? I thought you liked your job," Sanchez said.

"That, old friend is the news I have. It appears someone tossed my house, made a big mess. The neighbors called the cops when they saw the front door standing open. It was a good thing I called them, because they thought I had been abducted. To make a long story short I called one of your guys up near your place and had them check, your place had been tossed too. Probably a good thing we weren't home or we'd be in the morgue like," Bob paused. "Well, you know what I mean. Anyway, that is why I'm thinking of a job change, my old life is getting to hard to live. Right now I feel like my only job is staying alive and I don't like it."

"Don't give up yet. This thing is going to be cleaned up and life should get back to normal."

"If you get them all, there could be folks so deep down that you'll never know who they are. Plus you probably have people on the other side of the border who might want to finish the job. I may never feel completely safe again, but look at it this way, you'll always have a fishing boat available at low or no cost," Bob laughed.

Sanchez laughed along with his friend, "On my salary the cost is going to have to be low or no. Just keep your head down and eyes and ears open. I'll check back in a day or two and if anything comes up give me a call, who knows maybe we'll go into business together. We could call it 'Franchez Fishing Tours'. Take care."

Sanchez sighed after he broke the connection and looked at Chad. "They trashed Bob's place and mine, so they're still active back there and looking for us."

"I take it that Bob is ready to throw in the towel," Chad said.

"He may be right, these guys may look for us and those reports until we are no longer a threat. He wants to quit the border and disappear, can't say that I blame him." Sanchez let out a deep breath, "I can't think about that now, I'll let Bob think about it. We need to finish this and finish these guys, not just the ones in the SUV, but the ones at the top."

"What if we can't get the guys at the top? You said it yourself back there at the motel in Corpus, they got away with running guns. If what we think is correct, then these guys have the power to cover their asses and we can't touch them, at least not legally," Chad said.

"We'll have to wait to see how it goes, then look at the options," Sanchez said.

Chad smiled, "That's a felony."

Sanchez smiled back at him, "Yeah, but they have to catch you first."

"Looks like we are skirting town," Chad said as reached over and toggled the radio.

"Where do you think they are headed?"

"Not sure, but it looks like they wanted to avoid the traffic downtown. Up ahead are some large businesses and the fairgrounds, then an exit to a motel or Walmart. If they take the exit and go passed Walmart then they are headed into town, the traffic isn't as bad on this side of town," Phillips replied.

"You seem to know a lot about this place," Chad said.

"I had a cousin who went to school here, Stephen F. Austin College, and we used to visit, it's a pretty nice little town," Phillips said. "In case you're interested the fishing and hunting up here is pretty damn good."

"Not to be obvious, but there is only one thing we need to hunt now."

"Roger that, but again stating the obvious, gun shots are not unusual here. I doubt anyone would notice as long as they aren't heard in town," Phillips said.

"If they make the turn into town, you guys peel off and we'll follow them," Chad said.

"Will do, we'll be two or three cars behind you," Phillips replied.

Chad reached over and turned the volume down and looked at Sanchez. "That remark about gun shots seemed like a hint to me. Maybe it won't be that difficult to convince Phillips."

"Convince him of what? I don't know what you're talking about and I won't know until you talk to him," Sanchez said.

"Right I forgot. Okay, here we go, they are taking the exit so keep your eyes open."

After taking the exit they passed Walmart and headed to the downtown area, the closer they got to the college the more restaurants and motels they saw. Business Route 59 is a very narrow four lane with a center left turn lane and on weekends it feels like a two lane road. Most businesses and restaurants have ample parking lots, but during schools months parking or getting across the street is almost impossible. As Chad followed the SUV the traffic was bumper to bumper, restaurants were busy, parking lots were crowded and a lot of people were on the sidewalks. The SUV pulled into a crowded Italian restaurant and slowed as it cruised passed the parked cars. Chad toggled the radio.

"You guys find a place on this side of the street to park and watch, we'll go on down and turn around. It's a toss-up as to whether they will stay here or move on, but if they have a house they may want to meet the other van before moving to it."

"If they go to a motel around here we should just have one car go in to get a room. Brock and I will do it and use his credentials," Phillips said.

"Good idea. It should take these guys maybe fifteen minutes to change plates, but they may not be able to find a room in this area, it looks busy," Chad said.

"Yeah, the college entrance is just a few blocks from here," Phillips said. "A lot of the visiting families will rent a house because it's easier to get around rather than trying to get on the main drag."

Brock pulled into the lot next to a taco stand and Chad went down and used a gas station to turn around. Both vehicles waited for the SUV to exit the restaurant. Twenty minutes later the SUV pulled out of the restaurant and turned right, Brock pulled out two cars behind them.

Phillips toggled the radio, "They're coming your way, we're two cars back. Wait, they turned into a motel, we're pulling over again. We'll see if they get a room then go in and hope they have another vacancy. If they get a room we're going to have a problem. This is a small motel and Addison and Rogelio know our faces, but they don't know yours. We'll only get one room here, you and Sanchez get a room next door at the Days Inn, it backs up to this one. One of us will meet you over there."

"We're on our way," Chad replied.

Twenty minutes later Chad and Sanchez entered their room, first floor, last room on the end. It was a standard motel room, two beds, table in front of the window and a bath, but it had a small kitchen and was larger than expected. Chad stood and looked out the window across the parking lot and at the rooms facing them. To his right at the end of the rooms was a walkway, as he watched, Phillips emerged from it. He turned to Sanchez, "Phillips is here."

Sanchez rolled off his bed, "I'll go over and keep Brock company. Good thing it isn't broad daylight or I'd have to wear that ball cap again. For what it's worth I don't think you'll have any problems with Phillips seeing things your way, not that I know anything."

Chad smiled at him and opened the door, "Get outta here."

Phillips gave Sanchez the room number, watched as he jogged across the parking lot, then threw himself across the bed and sighed, "God, I'm tired."

He sat up again and looked around the room, "This is a good sized room, you should see ours, Phillips said. "It's a tight fit, we can't walk pass each other without walking across the bottom of the bed. So, what's up?"

"We need to discuss making a move on these guys," Chad said. The Feds are going to catch up with us and take it out of our hands. Hell, they're probably at the site where the truck blew up and once they find out was in it they'll be like ants at a picnic. This is your case, the decisions are up to you, but I felt like we needed to talk about it. Since we aren't riding together, I don't know what you're thinking."

"I've thought about all of that and once I saw where they were heading I knew we had to do something," Phillips said. "If they keep going north and get to Longview they'll hit I-20 and shortly after that they'll be out of state. I don't care where they were going anymore, I don't want them to leave Texas. Other States might frown on the way we handle this."

"On top of that, I got a text from the office and evidently a propaganda video has surfaced. The ISIS group is claiming they have cells in fifteen states and seventy-three American Jihadists, of course they aren't going to advertise how many they have sent across the border. We need to finish this, get what information we can from these guys and start tracking down their pals."

"Tracking down their pals is not really our job and we can't do anything unless we get the word from on high and you know it," Chad said.

"I know, but we might stumble upon another herd of them. Then we 'll have to get involved."

"Something else is bothering me," Chad said. "These guys must know we're following them, they can't be that unobservant. If they do know we're here, then we have to consider the house they're headed to might be a set up. I know we've been careful, but one of us has to be a pessimist."

"Okay when your guys get here we'll put them on surveillance in our room, grab some food and have a strategy meeting over here. I'm going up the office and get us a room here, your guys can have our room no one knows their faces." Phillips said.

Before Phillips reached the door his phone rang, he looked at the ID, "It's Sanchez. Yeah," he said into the phone. He walked over to the television and turned it on. "Okay, I got it. I'll call you back."

Phillips sat on the bed as his phone chimed again. "Phillips here. We're watching it now." He paused, looked down at the floor and started rubbing his forehead, "Okay, I'll call you back." He closed the phone and looked over at Chad, "That was Brock, he just got a call from Bracken," neither man smiled.

51

By the time Chad and Phillips turned their attention back to the news report the news anchor finished his report with a snide statement, "........a possible news blackout. As soon as more information or any information becomes available we'll get it to you."

"Well, that wasn't informative," Phillips said. "Did you catch any of it?"

"All I heard was something about a possible news blackout then something about Brock," Chad replied. "The part about Brock came from you."

"I'll call him back, wonder what the hell is going on now," Phillips said, but before he could make the call there was a knock at the door.

Chad pulled his gun, held it low on his thigh and opened the door. "I didn't know you were coming over."

"I wasn't, then I thought face to face was a better idea," Brock sighed.

"I've heard you sound happier," Phillips said as he walked over and turned the television off.

Brock looked at his watch, "As of fifteen minutes ago I'm technically on vacation."

Phillips quickly turned, "What, they pulled you from the case?"

"Not exactly. Let's sit and I'll fill you in on everything. Don't worry I have Sanchez keeping an eye on things and your guys should be showing up soon, so let's get this done."

Brock and Phillips sat in the hard backed chairs at the table, while Chad propped himself against the headboard of the bed, his gun, still out of its holster, lay on the bed at his side. Brock looked at it and nodded at him.

"Bracken called me about a white van that blew up near the North Carolina/Virginia state line, Virginia side, the one that was just on the news. It had been spotted by a deputy last night in a local park, but he thought it was someone who had pulled over to get some sleep, figured he'd check on it later and have them move on. He got side tracked with a traffic accident and didn't get back to it. Then today, one of their resident homeless guys got curious and evidently got inside the van and then somehow blew himself and the van into the next county. The local sheriff called in the State guys and they called in ATF, who in turn called our friends the FBI. Now the Feds are all over it because they feel it's connected to the truck down here and the van in Arizona. Bracken doesn't want our outfit connected to this now that the Feds are fully on it, but he doesn't want me off the case either. So, here I am on vacation. I'm unofficial, but Bracken will give me any info I need."

"I take it the van was abandoned," Phillips said.

"As far as anyone knows it was. It hadn't moved since the deputy spotted it and when they finish picking up the pieces they'll know if anyone else was inside, but if the homeless guy got inside I doubt there was anyone else around. Then the next questions would be, why did they abandon it and why did it blow?"

"So, it isn't really a news blackout it's because they know nothing and some local press put the story out," Phillips said.

"That's about it," Brock replied as he sat forward in his chair. "I did get a quick brief on the news we've missed the last two plus days. In case you didn't know, the truck that exploded near Livingston was carrying firearms and they're putting together what kind and how much munitions were on board. The ATF is moving around like ants on an anthill trying to figure out why it exploded, so far they have nothing. Tell Ray good job." Brock leaned back, "National news reports that we've got homegrown terrorists, a mix of teenagers and thirty somethings that are flooding social media trying to recruit and get donations for ISIS. Racial unrest is increasing, someone is hacking into government websites and the assholes in D.C. do nothing. Bracken said they are taking extra measures and beefing up security on our own computers. That's about it for now."

"That was quicker than watching the news and more enjoyable. Quick and concise is how it should be," Chad said. "Which is how we need to take these guys down."

"Nice segue," Phillips said. "I say the next time they stop we just shoot them all, they're kidnappers. Maybe we *should* have taken them at the motel."

"You know we couldn't have done that. We didn't have enough probable cause or evidence at that time," Brock said. "Now we have a definite kidnapping and a dead body."

Chad shifted on the bed and picked up his gun, "If they do have a place near here we can make a move on them there. Once we see the layout it won't take long to figure out how to do it. Jeez, I sound like a bad movie, maybe I need sleep."

Chad got up, holstered his gun and started pacing, Brock and Phillips looked at each other, then back at Chad. Neither spoke as he continued pacing, then walked to the door and opened it. He just stood in the open door with his hands on either side of the door, staring out at the semi dark parking lot. He started tapping his foot, shook his head as if he was carrying on an internal dialog. The vibration of his phone broke into his thoughts. It was the team from Port Arthur.

"Where are you?" Chad asked

"At the Executive. We followed the van here. Where are you?"

"Right next door. I'm going to hand you to Phillips and he'll give you their room number over there. When you get there tell Sanchez to get back over here and that you are going to take his watch for the next half hour. Give me five minutes before you knock on the door, I need to give him a heads up."

He handed the phone to Phillips, he gave them the room number, handed the phone back and Chad called Sanchez.

Phillips finally spoke, "When Sanchez gets here I think we should get food. I don't know about you guys, but I find it hard to think on an empty stomach. What's bothering you Chad?"

"I'm not sure yet." Chad ran his fingers through his hair and walked back to the door. "Something's not right, I can feel it, but I don't know what it is. We need to make a few calls and then maybe we can put it together or I can drop it."

"We need to see if these receivers have an auto alert on them, that way we can set them and hope they wake us if these guys hit the road. I'm sure they do, but we need to check anyway," Chad said. "We need food and sleep, at least four or five hours. One of you should get another room here and tell the guys in your room what we're doing. We need to toss a coin and see who is going to go find food."

"I'll go get another room and then get food. If you're not particular I'll just get what I can find," Brock said. "Your guys don't know me and I'd feel more comfortable with you or Phillips handling them."

Brock and Phillips walked to the door, as Brock walked out Phillips looked back at Chad. Chad shrugged and said, "Sorry, I know I'm giving you grief, but we need to get some questions answered." He dialed his phone, "I'll call the guys in your room, fill them in and see if they have any input."

"Lots of questions," Sanchez said as he walked up, "I have at least one question."

"If it's about food, you're going with Brock to find some," Phillips said.

"Good idea," Brock said, "I can use extra hands. I'm going to get food for the other guys too. We might need to get on their good side."

Phillips looked out over the parking lot then back to Brock, "While you're out there watch for other white vans that might be parked on the street near motels or in motel lots. I know we can't tell good vans from bad ones, but at least we'll be doing our due diligence."

Brock and Sanchez walked toward the motel office and Phillips stood staring at the ground. He was hungry and tired of following an SUV all over the state. He wanted to get Rogelio back to his parents without any of his guys getting hurt, he wanted to find the guy at the top and tear him a new one. Maybe, just maybe he could get some answers from this asshole, he sure as hell wasn't getting any now. He felt like he was being watched, he looked up and Chad was staring at him.

"So, not a bad little town from what I've seen," Chad said.

Phillips leaned against Chads' SUV, his arms folded across his chest, "They have good fishing around here and as I said earlier, the hunting is good. It has quite a history, the oldest town in Texas, is was designated a town in 1779. Lots of historical people spent time in this town and fell in love with it, celebrities too. The Marx Bros. decided to go into comedy while they were doing their singing act here in 1912 and Groucho was always mentioning it. They even named the country in their movie 'Duck Soup' after their experience here, Freedonia, because at one time the Fredonian Republic Flag flew over this town. You've heard of the Six Flags over Texas, well Nacogdoches has the honor of Nine Flags, which is more than any other place. John Wayne liked it here too, he came back to visit often and he even mentioned it in some his movies. You should look it up sometime, lots of history, all the way back 10,000 years ago when it was an Indian settlement."

Phillips shifted his position a bit, "I'll give you a piece of odd history. There was a guy, William Goins, there is a discussion whether it was spelled Goyens. Anyway, he was the son of a white mother and black father, he operated a trucking service, a local inn, a blacksmith works and had a plantation outside Nacogdoches on Goins Hill. He was married to a white woman and owned slaves. He was an agent for the Cherokee and very prominent in helping out the Texas Army during the Revolution. I guess you could say he was one of the first to cross the race barrier, shame people don't remember people like him. Hell, they don't even remember George Washington Carver, except once a year maybe."

"That's a lot of history for a small town. What do you mean he might be remembered once a year?" Chad asked.

"February, Black History Month."

"Well, maybe we can make more history here," Chad said. "All we have to do is get some questions answered and get the bad guys."

"I thought it was starting to bother you," Phillips said. "Well, it's bothering me too.

"Tonight I suddenly had the feeling that all the information was getting scrambled. I think what triggered it was the concise way Brock had given us the news of the last two days, it was so concise. I don't know, my head just suddenly said 'too much clutter'. We're getting information, but we really aren't processing it." Chad said as he headed for the room.

"I know what you're talking about," Phillips said. "At first we had nothing, then suddenly we had too many players, and too many questions. At least we know who most of the players are, now if we only knew what they doing. I doubt that Rogelio's dad knows what these guys are up to, if he did I think he would have said something already."

"I need to make those calls and I need Sanchez to call Bob when he gets back. Then maybe we can put something together," Chad said. "I would like you to call and see what is going on with the tracking. We need to know if all those little red dots are moving and in which direction. We also need to check and see if that van that blew in Virginia was on their map and I need to call the guys that had to turn around, I need know where they are."

As Phillips walked into the room behind Chad, his cell phone chimed followed by Chads' phone going off. They stood staring at each other as the same information was hurriedly given to both of them.

52

Brock and Sanchez came back to the room with bags of assorted fast food and piled it all on the table. Brock then reached into a grocery bag and pulled out two six packs of beer.

"Since I'm on vacation, I'm having a nightcap."

"We may need it before the nights over," Phillips said. "We got a call and two more vans exploded."

Brocks' demeanor darkened, "Interesting, where did it happen any fatalities?

"Don't know, it was just to alert us," Phillips said. "The Feds are on it and we'll get info later. Wonder why these guys are blowing up the vans, I'm sure there's a reason behind it. I must be missing something."

"That's just one of the things that's bothering me," Chad said. "I did get one question answered. I checked with the guys and the receivers have an auto alert. They used theirs in Beaumont and they said it was pretty loud. It went off when the van left the motel to get food."

"At least we know we can get some sleep," Sanchez said. "I'm going to take this food over to the guys, don't worry I'll try not to be seen."

"When you get back I need you to call Bob. I'll give you a list of the questions I have," Chad called after him.

Phillips opened a bag of food, "Brock and I will call and see what we can find out on any front. I want some answers on those vans, they need to tell us everything, not just a heads up. I want to know what these vans were carrying, it can't be anything major or the explosions would have been bigger. I bet that one we blew left a crater in the highway, not exactly what I wanted."

"I'm thinking that this is a diversion," Chad said. "If the cops are looking for vans then their attention is focused only in that direction. Maybe they'll put rental trucks on their radar since we left them one."

Phillips walked over and turned on the television, "Let's see if the news media has anything. We probably won't hear much since we'll be on the phones, but it's worth a try."

"I've got a guy I can call, who might be able to give us something," Brock said. "The only problem I think we're going to have with most people we call is no one is going to have anything different from we've already been given. The guy I'm going to call isn't in our normal loop and he might actually have something for us."

Phillips took a bite of his bacon cheeseburger, "If he isn't in….. ahh, never mind. Guess I'm not thinking."

"Not thinking, that's something I need more of," Sanchez said as he closed the door. "I need food, sleep and a mindless activity."

"Well, you walked into the wrong room for mindless anything." Brock said.

Chad put his burger down, grabbed a note pad and pen and started writing, "When you finish eating here are some questions I have for Bob. I'll leave the follow-up questions to you. Also, see if anything new has popped up."

Brock looked at his watch and stood, "I'll finish this in the other room. I'm going to give this guy a call now and see if I can catch him."

"Before you go," Chad said, "I called our people in Corpus, Port Arthur and Houston. I asked them to recheck the different sites for us on the off chance they slipped some type of explosive passed us. I also had them alert the refineries of a possible incident and to have their people keep an eye out for anything that looks like it doesn't belong and that includes cars and vans. I'll be getting call backs from everyone. This is all part of the uneasy feeling I have, I'm just covering the bases."

Brock turned as he reached the door, "If I can't reach him I'll be right back, otherwise this may take a while."

"I'm going to make a call out here," Chad said and followed him out the door.

Chad put his soda and fries on the hood of the car, leaned against it and dialed.

"Hey, anything new?"

"I don't know who came up with the saying 'no news is good news', but they obviously weren't in our business," Pepa said. "The Fed doesn't know anything. He's sticking to his story about being told it was just a way of keeping track of personnel. That's bullshit and if he fell for it he shouldn't be in the business. They've tried everything, so it must be what they told him. He's a newbie, so I guess it's possible. My house guests are doing well, but would like their son back."

"Tell them were still working on it. We want him back in one piece and breathing," Chad said. "Don't know if it will make any difference, but tell them that is one smart and brave kid they raised. From the clues he left us it appears he is taking control of his situation as best he can. Phillips did make eye contact with him on the drive from Houston. He looks tired, but he's alert. He seemed to stay calm when he saw Phillips, so he must know what he's up against. Don't tell the parents, but it appears they put a suicide vest on him."

"Oh crap, that's not good. Just another twist to make the job a bitch."

"Yeah, it makes extraction more difficult. Did you go through emergency procedure with your guests?"

"I've had them go through the drill a few times and I think they have it down. Won't really know until we need to use it. The perimeter is under guard and armed to the teeth. Very few people know about this place and I believe Mr. Older is one of them. Of course he doesn't know about the safety precautions I have."

"Do you think this guy can be flipped so we can use him? He's new and if he feels like they were using him for anti-American purposes, it might work to our advantage," Chad said.

"I'll talk to the guys and see what they say, I haven't been in on the questioning so I can't judge his reaction. As soon as I get an answer or if it works, I'll call you. If you get anything new call me," Pepa said.

"Got it." Chad put his phone down and looked back at the room then made his second call.

Three doors down from Chad's room Brock was waiting for his phone to ring. He had been successful in reaching his contact and was waiting for him to call back.

He grabbed the phone before it had finished the first ring.

"I'm here," Brock said.

"Hello my friend, sorry for the delay, but I had guests and didn't want to be rude," the man on the other end said.

"Mr. B., I hope my call won't cause you any problems," Brock said.

"No, no, no, this was only family. My sister–in–law, her husband and children, so many children. They were just leaving when your call came through, believe me I wish you had called an hour ago it would have made the last hour more tolerable. Tell me, how are your parents?"

"They are doing well and have been talking about taking a trip your way. Mother wants to go back to Italy, she fell in love with the coastal towns and villages. I personally think it is the wine and shopping, but I keep it to myself. How is your family and that beautiful daughter?" Brock asked.

"The family is as always and my daughter has decided to graduate early. She teases me about her really being your daughter since she is so smart. I tell her she is not as smart as she thinks, but she now wants to go to Harvard. So I may be calling you in six months and you are smart to keep your mouth closed when it comes to your mother," he chuckled. "You know in our business it is not very often we have the privilege of knowing one another's family. How is your friend Mr. Phillips, do you keep in touch?"

"Yes, as a matter of fact we are working together on a very curious case." Brock said.

"I knew you were not calling from half a world away just to speak of family. What can I do for you?"

Brock outlined what they had observed and the reports of vans exploding for no apparent reason. He also informed him of who they had identified as the Middle East players and asked him if he had heard of any operations that involved these people.

"Well," Mr. B. said, "a couple of months ago there was a rumor going around, but I didn't think anything ever came of it. Let me ask a few well-placed inquiries and I'll get back to you. It may take a few hours, but I'll call you no matter what I find."

"Don't put yourself in jeopardy for this, I thought maybe you might have heard something that would help," Brock said.

"If I had heard anything of significance I would have notified you or the other Mr. B., but there is always the chance that this is coming from someplace I'm not in touch with on a regular basis. Give me about three hours and I'll call you, in the mean time you take care of yourself. You are working within your own borders and that could be a problem for you, but you know that. Ciao."

Brock sat and looked down at his phone.

53

The four men made themselves comfortable, popped cold beers and waited to brief the group on their respective phone calls. No one in the room looked like they had good news to share.

Phillips looked at Brock, "I called the guys in the other room and told them to move their vehicle over here, then lay low and wait until the SUV and van leave. They're to call here after they've made sure it's clear and before they take up the tail. I want it to look like we've left, we're going to follow them by signal only. I hope by not having a visual on them we don't lose them, but that is why we have these devices, the signal should be good enough. I don't know whether they have spotted us or not, but I don't want to take any chances. We may stand a better chance of surprise if they think we're gone."

He looked down at a note pad, "I talked to the office and they don't have much on the vans that blew, the forensic teams are still going over them. They do know that there are no human remains in any of them, with the exception of the van in Virginia. They do know that arms were inside and they are trying to sort out what they were and if possible where they came from. As usual they will call when they have something."

Phillips leaned back in the chair, "I talked to the tech people watching the vans with the red dots on the map. Some of the vans are moving, others are not. The ones that are moving do not appear to be moving in any pattern, a few are moving together. They started this when they noticed fast dot movement, which indicated a vehicle, but when the movement slowed they marked it as being parked. The vans that are stationary will be turned over to AFT and the FBI within the next hour or so, glad I'm not the one breaking the news. It's possible that these vans are, for lack of a better word, the decoys and could be blown up at any time. The feeling at the office is that the vans are planted and then remotely detonated or they might be on a timer. They also feel that anything left in the van is purposely done. They leave just enough on board to make a significant explosion, of course no one has any idea why they are doing this. My thought is they are drawing attention to white vans and in the mean time they are changing their mode of transportation. It may be because of the van that was involved in the accident in Phoenix and the one in north Texas that was abandoned. Those two incidents were not on purpose and disrupted their original plan."

"The only information they would give me on the mess outside Phoenix probably isn't worth repeating, but I'll do it anyway. This is exactly what I was told, unusual flammable and explosive material residue was found. Still no sign of the two guys who ran or how they got away, no fingerprints in that SUV or van since they were burned down to metal."

"Now for the Falfurrias site." Phillips cleared his throat, "They tried for tire impressions, but either the sandy soil was too soft, tracks fell apart or too hard, no tracks. A lot of small animal activity across the tracks they did find, but they got some partials that matched tires used, surprise, surprise, on a Suburban."

"The prints on the bus came back to the driver, who is dead, and three unknowns. The unknowns will be our three hostages, but the way they are getting Jazmin's prints to compare and they are treating the mustard thumb print as Rogelio's. So the rest of our little group was wearing gloves. They also found fibers, which probably means nothing since it is a bus and I doubt they do a great job of keeping it clean. There was no brass found at the site where the tires were shot out, but they found .45's in the tires. Determination was a .45 revolver. The bus itself was stolen from a bus storage yard. It was parked near the back and was never missed, these guys just drove it out the gate like it was theirs."

Phillips put the notes aside, "That's it from me, I hope someone has something better than the crap I got. I don't think my people are going to do much more than monitor the situation now that the

Feds are on it, no reason for it except support. Brock, did you get your guy?"

Brock looked around, "I won't tell you anything about him, but I trust him and have for a long time. I only told him the basics of what we've got, I did not mention the kidnapping or any action we've taken. He had heard a rumor a few months ago about an operation in Mexico and Central America, but didn't think it amounted to anything. He's going to do some checking and get back to me in the next few hours. Since he knows who our players are, he'll know how and who to ask. Otherwise that's it from me for now."

Brock and Phillips both looked at Chad and Chad nodded to Sanchez.

"Okay," Sanchez took a deep breath, "I talked to Bob and things have been relatively quiet except they've had a number of boats coming in and unloading crates from the freezers into unmarked box trucks. It started with one boat and the next day they had three. He got curious and started taking a closer look and all he could see were wooden crates of various sizes and one time there was a heavy looking metal container. He kept a low profile and pretended to be checking nets and ropes on a boat nearby. I told him about the boat in Port Lavaca and he'll continue watching for it and see if he can get some plate numbers from the trucks. He offered to get photos next time one comes in, but I told it would be too risky and to hold off. He said his facial hair has reached the point where he feels he can go into Brownsville and do some investigating. I didn't try to dissuade him. He's pissed about the situation and wants these guys, all of them, in the ground."

Sanchez looked at Phillips, "I guess your idea about a change in transportation could mean box trucks. I also wondered how many small ports are getting these same type of boats offloading and Bob said he knew a couple of guys he would contact about it. That's it from my end."

Chad was leaning against the wall and moved toward the refrigerator for another beer. "I have Pepa working on something and I should hear back from her when and if it's set up. Next, the guys following the other two vans called and they didn't turn up this way, they're headed into Louisiana. I told them to call it in to the office and turn it over to the Feds, so they'll stay on the tail until the Feds catch up with them. That eliminates one of our distractions. I haven't heard back from the refinery detail, but their job is going to take a while."

Chad passed beer around and leaned against the wall again. "Our main objective should be to get this kid out of danger and if possible capture or kill the bad guys. Now that the Feds are involved we should turn any information we get on the arms beings transported over to them. All the business with the vans should be handled by the Feds and our tech personnel. I want to know what is going on, but not to the point of distraction. We can't afford to be distracted. I suggest that after we hear what Bob comes up with, we inform the office and let them pass the info to whoever is the lead with the FBI and ATF."

"I agree," Brock said. "Once we complete the extraction, then we can get more information. We'll have all their vehicles and cell phones, so we may be able track who they've been in contact with over the last few weeks. If I'm lucky this will lead directly back to the Middle East. I know the players are from that area, but I want to be sure that's who sent them."

Sanchez spoke up, "From my point of view that operation I ran across in Mexico is linked to this, otherwise I wouldn't have a dead friend and another who is hiding out. If Yolanda survives this, maybe we can get information from her too. See, damn it! This is why this thing gets so cluttered up." Sanchez started waving his arms, "It runs from Central America through Mexico and then here. It probably has its roots in the Middle East and who knows where else is involved. It's a cancer and it has its tentacles everywhere we look."

"Then let's just take it one step at a time." Chad said. "First Rogelio, then the rest of it. I can't speak for Phillips, but I'm willing to stay on this thing and help figure out your end of it. We'll let the Feds deal with everything else, but your end will stay with us, even if it overlaps."

"In for a penny in for a pound," Brock set his beer on the table. "I'm in, until I hear otherwise from my superiors. I'll also brief them on everything we find out about the overseas connection."

"I'm in too," Phillips said as he stood. "You're sticking your neck out for us, I can do the same. Now, if you'll excuse me, I want to call the office and give them the information Bob gave you, minus your idea about the other ports, so they can pass it on to whoever. I'll leave Bobs' name out of it, we don't want any attention brought to him. Brock, your info will stay between the four of us." Phillips pointed to everyone in the room, then turned and walked outside.

"I really appreciate what you are willing to do," Sanchez said.

"You have to remember this is for all of us and the country at large. I don't feel comfortable handing all we know to the people in D.C.," Brock replied. "Until we get this whole thing cleaned up, I'm not sure who to trust."

"Do you think we can keep the local cops out of this? I mean, when we go after Rogelio," Sanchez asked. "If we could figure out how to do it without gunfire it would be quieter."

"Oh no, there's going to be gun fire alright." Chad said. "I don't see any way around it unless you have some odorless gas in your back pocket."

"I'm going to have gas, but it ain't going to be in my back pocket," Sanchez chuckled.

"In that case maybe you should stay in Brock's room tonight."

Phillips came back into the room to the sound of laughter. "Okay, that's done. Now I suggest we try and get some sleep."

"Brock your guy is probably going to wake you up, don't stay up waiting for him," Chad said. "If I remember correctly a few hours over there could mean six. Operational efficiency is impaired by lack of sleep, so let's get some. Also, Sanchez and I are going to stay behind and check out the room over there and see if we have any more messages from Rogelio. As soon as we leave here I'll give you a call and get your position."

Phillips opened the door and looked back at Chad, "I appreciate that, but I don't know what he can write with, I doubt they let him have a hotel pen."

"He's resourceful," Brock said as he joined Phillips at the door, "He'll find a way."

54

Rogelio walked into yet another motel room, but this one was different. The two beds barely fit in the room, there was no room for him to have his own corner. The night stand that held the phone and lamp was tight against the beds, a second night stand was crammed into one of the corners. A small table and chairs sat under the window. Through the only other opening in the room he saw what looked like a closet, he walked toward it carrying his pillow and dragging a blanket, Yolanda followed him. When they reached the opening they found it was actually a small hallway that turned right and led the bathroom. There was a long closet along one wall with one end that faced the bed area, the other end was blocked by the opposite wall. Rogelio walked into the closet and dropped his bedding. He took off his jacket that had the sleeves cut off, reached for a hanger and hung up the heavy burden he had to wear. No one said anything, so he turned around and found on one behind him but Yolanda. He didn't go look for anyone, he just sat on his blanket and motioned for Yolanda to do the same.

He knew better than to go looking for his captors, they always knew where he was and anyway why go looking for trouble. He was more worried about Yolanda than anyone else, she had not said a word for over an hour. She just stared at the ceiling in the back of car, never looking right or left. Now she sat on her blanket, her knees pulled up and forehead resting on them. He knew she was hungry and thirsty, because he was. He still didn't understand why a person her age couldn't cope, or at least face the situation and help find a way out. Even with the way she was now, he couldn't bring himself to fully trust her. He looked up and saw the one called Jorge come through the door and walk toward them.

"Hey little guy, you don't have to sit in here, you and your girlfriend can have the other bed. I will be the only one sleeping in here tonight. Right now I am going to lock you guys inside while I go and get food, so take a shower and get comfortable. Of course I have no clean clothes for you, but at least you will be clean," he said as he walked to the door.

He turned around and looked at them, "Stay away from the window, there is no one to see or hear you and beside they will hear you in the other room. You don't want that, it might make them angry." He laughed as he closed the door behind him, then Rogelio heard him do something to the door. He knew you couldn't lock a motel door from the outside, so he must have done something else to it.

Rogelio turned to Yolanda, "We will wait a few minutes then you go take a very fast shower, I will take mine last."

While Yolanda was in the shower Rogelio walked the room looking for a place to leave a message. This was the perfect time to do it, but there was no place he felt safe in leaving it. He finally decided on his only option, took out his knife and got to work. He wasn't happy with where he had to put it, but he would have to take a chance. He finished as Yolanda came out of the bathroom. Her shirt was wet.

"Did you take a shower with your clothes on?" he asked.

"No, I only washed my shirt and panties. They are sticky wet but I don't care," she answered and sat in the closet.

Jorge came back with food and sodas, dropped them on the little table and left the room again saying he would be right next door. Rogelio and Yolanda devoured every crumb.

When Jorge returned he found them in the closet, "Hey," he said as he kicked the wall next to them, "Come sit on the bed, I need to talk to you."

They sat on the bed and Jorge sat at the little table.

"Tomorrow we are going to a house, a real house, not just a room," Jorge said. "It has a big yard and you can go outside, but of course you cannot go anywhere. There will be no neighbors for you to run to, but it is better than a motel every night. We will be there for a few days before we continue our journey. Mr. A. says it even has a big barn. It's only a short drive from here, but we couldn't go tonight because it will not be ready for us until tomorrow. Just think, very soon it will all be over. Soon you will be home."

Jorge smiled and patted Rogelio on the shoulder, "You have been very brave so far from home. Think of being home again."

Jorge opened the door, before he walked out he looked back at them, "Soon," was all he said as he closed the door.

"Yes, soon," Rogelio whispered.

Yolanda reached over and put her hand on his arm, "What do you mean?"

Rogelio put his finger to his lips and shook his head, "Shhh, wait." He walked over to the door and listened, then motioned for her to follow him.

She followed and sat beside him in the closet, "I'm afraid. They're going to kill us and bury us in that barn, I just know it."

"No, they won't kill us yet, their plan is not finished," Rogelio replied. "I think they're going to this house to fix their plan, I think something went wrong. I listen when they talk to each other and on the phone, they sound worried about something. If I could speak their language I would know what it is." He stopped speaking and just stared at the facing wall.

"Rogelio, Rogelio, what's wrong?" Yolanda asked bringing him back.

"Nothing, sorry. I was just lost in my own thoughts," he answered. "You must remember what I told you about having hope. You must also remember what I said about moving when I tell you. Even if you think what I tell you might get you killed, you do what I say because they will kill us anyway. When we get to this place look at everything you can without them noticing. Look at the doors, windows, stairs, notice where they go. Notice how far away the barn is from the house, remember everything."

"Now, we go to sleep in the big bed. We need to get a good, comfortable sleep," Rogelio said as he walked to the beds. "You sleep on the side next to the wall, I think it's safer."

They crawled beneath the covers and Yolanda closed her eyes and sighed.

"Trust me," Rogelio said to her. "Please trust me."

Then he closed his eyes and whispered to himself, "Soon."

55

Chad and Sanchez waited twenty minutes before heading over to the motel room where Rogelio had stayed. They wanted to be sure no one came back for some forgotten article. Chad went into the motel office, flashed his badge, ask for the room key and grabbed two cups of coffee. He told the desk clerk they would return the key in about thirty minutes.

They let themselves into the room, set their coffee down and began the search. Sanchez checked all the bathroom linens for any sign of a message, as well as every nook and cranny in the bathroom and hallway. He checked the closet, top and bottom, found only lint and dirt. He walked back to the beds and saw Chad sorting through the trash.

"I got nothing, even the bathroom trash can is empty."

"Same here so far," Chad said. "Check the dresser drawers for me and then we're out of here."

Sanchez did a visual on the top and bottom of the drawers, "I can't believe he didn't leave something. Like Brock said earlier, the kid has a brain he would have come with something."

"Unless he didn't have a chance," Chad replied. "Let's go."

Chad walked over to the television set, picked up the coffee he had set on top and checked behind it. As he was turning back around something caught his eye.

"Wait a minute, hit the lights for me."

Sanchez turned on the overhead light and walked over to Chad, "I'll be damned."

"The kid took a real chance, but maybe he knows his captors better than we do," Chad said as he dialed his phone.

"Hey, he did leave you something," Chad told Phillips. "I'll get a picture for your scrapbook. He scratched into the top of the television. It says, 'Aok' and second line reads, 'Imrdy'." Chad listened then said, "We're on our way."

They drove calmly out of town and when they hit the highway Chad turned on his flashers and pushed it way over the speed limit.

"Didn't know you had flashers on this thing." Sanchez laughed.

"I have everything, just wished I had room for all the equipment I need. This mess would have been a lot shorter if I had the right equipment," Chad said. "Brock and Phillips speak the language and what they didn't know the office could translate. We could've put them on live feed so the office would've heard it the same time we did."

"Evidently, Rogelio has a lot of confidence in us since he says he's ready," Sanchez said.

"I don't want to read too much into his message, but I think he's trying to tell us he's more than ready," Chad replied. "I think he has a plan of his own, I just hope it doesn't get in the way of what we need to do. Hold on exit coming up and I'm not slowing down."

The exit turned out to be a two lane country road with a canopy of green as the trees arched above them. Chad turned off the flashers and kept the speed slightly over the limit. The sun coming through the leaves above caused a strobe light affect as they passed beneath them.

Chad reached over and toggled the radio, but got no reply. He handed his phone to Sanchez, "Hit the 2 for me, that's Phillips, tell him where we are and find out where they want to meet us."

Sanchez got off the phone, "He said they're about eight clicks from the highway. We can't miss them, they pulled over to wait for us. So, we should be coming up on them soon."

"When we get there we'll go in and do a recon on the place, see what our options are and then do it. All you have to do is remember the codes I gave you and follow whatever plan we come up with," Chad said. "We all want to come out of this alive and with live hostages."

Sanchez nodded as they pulled in behind Brock and got out of the SUV.

Phillips saw them coming, got out of the car before Chad had come to a stop and leaned against the back of Brocks' car.

"The other guys are up ahead keeping an eye on the road to the house. The SUV turned down a driveway on the left, at least it looks like a driveway it's only one lane. When you're ready we can go meet them, but we are going to need a place to hide these cars. I figure we could go a bit further and see if there is another drive or a place to pull off that has cover. Then go in on foot, do a recon, lock and load, then move on them," Phillips said.

"Sounds good to me," Chad said handing his phone to Phillips. "Here's that picture of the message. What's with Brock?"

Phillips looked at the picture and absently said, "He's waiting for his guy to call and he's getting worried. Wish I knew what the hell Rogelio's thinking."

Brock got out of the car and looked over Phillips shoulder, "Told you the kid had a brain. We know he's ready for us so I don't think will have to tell him to stay low or run."

Brocks' cell rang, he looked at the number and walk away as he answered, "Hey, I was getting worried about you."

"Sorry for the delay, but I had to do some double checking," Mr. B. said. "The name you gave me, this Ali al-Souk, we have him as deceased. I take it you have a photo of him. May I ask where you got the identification?"

"Phillips office gave it to us, but I don't know where they got it. Hold on and I'll ask," Brock replied.

"Hey Jake, where did your office get the ID on the guy called Jorge, the Ali Souk?" Brock asked.

"I'm not sure, I can call and ask. Why"

"My contact says he was reported dead. Give your people a call."

Brock got back on his phone, "He's going to call now and see where they got the name. It shouldn't take long."

"While he is doing that I will tell you what I have," Mr. B. said. "According to our information Ali was killed in Syria several months ago while doing some work for ISIS. We are certain it was him because we were able to match finger prints, you see someone brought us his hand. Nasty business, but reliable. We also think that your person is Nasir al-Attar, they look much the same, but without your photo I have nothing to match our photo with, you see. Both of these men are psychotic, murderers, highly dangerous, but we consider Nasir as the worse of the two. Nasir and your other two players are well versed in American combat tactics, so however you decide to proceed they will probably be ready for you. I don't know if your people will have this in their dossier for Nasir, but he is a very capable sniper. It is rumored that Nasir had a thing going with Arel Shoukri, but that is just rumor. A cannot imagine anyone trusting her enough to get that close."

"When we are finished, I would like you to send me the photo you have and I will send you mine. Nasir has a scar on the left side of his neck, so if you get close enough you might be able to spot it. The scar runs from under his ear and curves toward the front of his throat, unfortunately not deep enough to kill him. You can clearly see it in our photo. My people like to joke that Arel gave him the souvenir when he failed to satisfy her. Obviously she must have had second thoughts because she didn't finish the job," Mr. B. chuckled.

"Now for the reason you called me last night. The story I have gotten is that an operation was planned in Mexico, sort of a training mission. It appears that it was supposed to be in Central America, then they moved it Mexico and now the rumor is that they want to do something eye catching in America. I have my little network searching for any information they can find, but I did find that arms were sent by various channels into Mexico and the U.S. The information on the arms shipments and Ali being erased was sent to our CIA contact, I'm surprised you weren't informed. For all intense and purposes this operation was planned in your part of the world, so unless we can find their contact here I cannot tell you what they specifically intend to do. I can tell you to be very careful because someone in your government is deeply involved or at least that is the rumor. When I get more from my people, I will inform you," Mr. B. finished.

"Do you have any idea if this is coming from one group or country?" Brock asked.

"I doubt it is coming from a country, it is more likely one of the terrorist groups they are all starting to blend together in our minds. One is just as bad as the other, well not really, I guess ISIS is the worse of the bunch," Mr. B. replied.

"Phillips just handed me a note, it seems that the information on Ali came from the CIA. I'll have to call our people and talk to them," Brock sighed. "In the meantime, thank you again and I will send the photo in the next five minutes."

"Be careful my friend, my daughter would be very disappointed if something should happen to you," Mr. B. said before he broke the connection.

Brock walked over to Chad, "I need that file with the photo of Ali. I need to send a copy of it for comparison purposes. Then I need to call my office."

While Brock messaged the photo he also briefed them on what his contact had told him. He walked back over to his car to make the call to his office.

"So, what difference does it make what this guy's name is?" Sanchez asked. "We have to go after him no matter who he is."

"We need to find out what our reports say about him, sometimes reports from overseas can be exaggerated and we need to know exactly what to expect from him. We don't want to go running in there and find explosives wired everywhere," Phillips said.

"I don't know," Chad said, "I think we can do this no matter who they are, of course they might have overwhelming fire power in there. I think if we handle this the right way we can do most of it from a distance, it all depends on what we find once we take a look. Right now we need to go, we're giving these guys too much time to set perimeters."

Brock walked back over to the group and leaned against his car.

"I called Bracken and asked him to look into the information I got. If this information was given to one of my people it should have been passed on to your office or we should have been directly informed. Now I'm worried about CIA offices being compromised and Bracken agrees. Bracken also confirmed that no one knows what I'm doing, but will double check," Brock sighed. "He is also going to set some of his secret minions loose and see if they can come up with anything within our offices.

"So you're saying any information going back and forth between our respective offices could be compromised as well. Isn't that just dandy," Phillips said.

"Okay then," Chad said, "we treat this as a possibly blown mission. We still go in, but with extreme caution. We don't do anything by the book. Since these folks know what usually happens, we will do what usually doesn't happen. The only thing we do by the book is expect the unexpected, use speed, surprise, and overwhelming violence. Now, let's go take a look at this house."

56

Brock and Sanchez were dropped off to keep an eye on the road, while the other two men followed Phillips and Chad to find a place to stash their vehicles. Less than an eighth of a mile from the house they found a slightly overgrown road on the right hand side. Chad led the way in with the big SUV and blazed his own trail to make a turnaround in the tall grass between the trees. The vehicles were dark so the shadows helped conceal them from the main road. Everyone put on a vest, checked their weapons, and locked the cars. Chad grabbed two extra vests and they started walking back to meet Brock and Sanchez. When they crossed the road Chad looked back to be sure the grass was springing back over the tire tracks, then crossed the ditch and walked near the tree line behind the other men.

As they walked, Chad looked past the tree line and noted the size of the trees that grew further from the road. He smelled the air and listened to movement around him, not human movement, but air, small animals and branches. If any of the men with him were talking he didn't hear them. He shut down, he heard nothing, had no thoughts, he was wiping the canvas clean getting ready to paint a new picture.

When they reached Sanchez and Brock, Sanchez opened his mouth to say something, caught a look from Phillips and closed it again. He watched as Phillips took an open legged stance and nodded at Chad. The two men from the Beaumont surveillance took the same stance and waited.

Chad handed Brock and Sanchez their vests. He then stood where he could make eye contact and talk to everyone.

"We're going in on recon only, don't engage unless it means your life," Chad said. "If you haven't already, turn off your phones, secure any keys or anything on your person that will make noise." No one moved. "Since there are so many of us we will probably sound like a heard of buffalo, so be as quiet and cautious as you can. Sorry we didn't have time to get aerial views, but we'll look them up when we get back to the vehicles. As soon as we catch site of the house we'll split up so we can observe all areas of the house and surroundings. I don't need to tell you what to look for, but while you're looking I need you to listen. Listen for animals, any heating, air conditioner or pump units that might switch on, we don't want something coming on and startling us. Remember animals can give you away, especially dogs and horses. No speaking, hand signals only, we'll use the mikes later. We'll break up into groups of three, when we reach the house. Phillips will take one group, I'll take the other and we'll go in opposite directions to surround the house. Brock and Sanchez will each take a side of the house, Phillips will meet up with me in the back. You two," he pointed at the two men from the Beaumont team, "will take the left and right front corners of the house. Once Phillips and I get to the back we will spend approximately fifteen minutes, when we're finished we'll swing back this way and pick you up. Stay on your station until we show up. Keep alert and remember to look up. I don't think they have enough people to put in the trees, but it only takes one. Are there any questions or concerns?"

No one spoke or shifted their positions. "Good, let's do this."

They walked down opposites sides of the road, watching the trees and ground for any signs of recent activity. Phillips and Chad saw the edge of the clearing at the same time and gave the signal to halt, they looked across the road at each other. Chad signaled that he was moving forward and for everyone else to stay put.

Chad edged his way down the tree line until the clearing was in full view. The tree line on his left went in a straight line passed the garage and then turned right and ran about ten feet until it ran against a large garden that was fifty feet from the back of the house. The tree line on his side of the road made a right and ran along the roadside as it turned in front of the house.

The long dirt driveway curved in front of an older two story farm house in need of fresh paint. At the present time it was a faded brown with off-white trim around the doors and windows. The screens over the windows were in good shape, same with the screen doors, no tears or rusted hinges. The upstairs had dormer windows in the front, no balcony or way down from the outside. There was a wraparound porch with a slanted, shingle roof, if you jumped from the window you would more than likely roll off or break a leg. A large chimney protruded from the roof. The window coverings on the inside were closed, but the faint sound of a television could be heard.

To the right at the rear of the house was a fairly large red barn with white trim, also in need of paint. It had the big double doors, which were pad locked and a people door to the left side. The loft door was also closed. Fencing ran from both sides of the barn almost to the tree line, with outside corrals that extended from the closed stall doors. The fencing ran back as far as the eye could see with cross fences and gates. The fences looked to be in good shape, no rotted wood and the paint was newer. Trees dotted the well-kept landscape around the house and barn, but no animals were in sight.

To the left of the house was a two car garage that matched the house, with windows on the side away from the house and a people door on the house side. The garage doors were closed, but with binoculars fresh tire tracks as well as foot prints could be seen in the dirt.

Chad turned and started back to the road to give Sanchez his new instructions.

Phillips saw Chad coming toward them, he and the rest of the men stood up. Chad walked over, huddled with Sanchez and walked across the road to Phillips.

"Long story, but I'm going with you," Chad said in a low whisper. "Sanchez is to wait twenty minutes at his spot before he heads back this way. You'll figure out why things changed once we get to the house. Let's go."

The trees were dense and the ground under foot was moist from the humidity, aside from staying low and having to move branches, their movement was quick and silent. Each man took his assigned post, settled in for the wait and began memorizing every missing paint chip.

Phillips and Chad moved cautiously through the trees behind the house and noticed the fence that ran from the barn was ten feet from the garden. Phillips used his binoculars to scan the ground around the corrals and could not find any sign that animals had been there recently. He didn't know much about ranching or farming, but it seemed to him that there should be some kind of animals around somewhere.

They started their move to a point that would put them at the center of the house. They both looked at the garden and were grateful for the rows of tall corn and dense vegetable foliage. As they made their way to the end of the garden Chad held up his fist and pointed. At the end of the garden, with an overgrowth of weeds and grass was an old tractor that almost touched the corner of the barn. Phillips was making mental notes about the house while Chad did the same to the barn.

The second floor had regular windows across the back, again no way down except a jump to the porch roof. There were two windows in what appeared to be the kitchen and two more to the right. The window in the back door was covered with a curtain and one that might be over the sink was also curtained. The two other windows were probably in a bedroom or dining room, but they had blinds covering them.

Chad looked at his watch, tapped Phillips on the shoulder and motioned they should be moving out.

Before they could move further than five feet the back door opened and Addison walked out on the porch. He look around and then headed toward the barn. Phillips and Chad flattened themselves on the ground.

Addison walked to the large barn doors, unlocked the padlock and went inside. Chad could hear him talking to someone or something inside. Addison's voice grew louder as he pushed a man through the doors. The man's hands were tied, his face was bruised and he had a slight limp. He appeared to be in his sixties, had on jeans and a T-shirt, both had fresh dirt on them.

"Gone on. We need you in the house, you have a call to make," Addison said. "Your phone has been ringing and we need you to call the sheriff and tell him you and the wife are taking a trip. You are also going to call whoever is calling here and tell them the same."

The older man made no move to go to the house. Addison took him by the front of his shirt, "Listen, if you don't make the calls your wife might have an accident. Her hand may get caught in the garbage disposal, now that would be nasty and messy. Better yet, maybe she's cleaning windows and falls from way up there. Why she could break her neck if that happened. Now moved it!" Addison said as he shoved the man toward the back door.

Chad and Phillips waited in the shadows of the corn. When they were sure no one else was coming outside they made their back to the tree line.

"Crap, just what we need, more hostages. Damn!" Phillips said.

57

No one spoke until they got back to the vehicles. Chad opened the back of the SUV, all interior lights had been disabled long ago, pulled out the laptop and looked at Phillips.

"I need you to call and have them send us the latest satellite pictures and I want the names and some background on the owners of the place. We already have a pretty good idea of the layout of the place, but I want to look at the immediate surrounding area." He looked around, "Everybody hold on while we get set up."

Brock passed around water until Phillips was off the phone. He looked at Sanchez, "You look a bit worried."

"Yeah, just a bit and you'll soon find out why," Sanchez said.

Phillips got off his phone, "We'll have the info within the next half hour, there's a delay because of background. Anybody get anything important?"

"I checked the garage windows with the glasses and there are two vehicles inside and I saw no movement inside," Brock said. "The other vehicles must be in the barn."

"The back has pretty good cover, but none of it near the house," Phillips said. "By near I mean about fifty feet from the house. The upstairs windows are not a good exit point, so if anyone is in there that's where they will stay until we get them out. Bad news is that we have two more hostages to worry about. Our pal Addison came out to the barn and exited with an older guy, he looks like they roughed him up a bit. From the conversation it sounds like the wife is in the barn too. Addison took him into the house to make some phone calls, one being to the Sheriff's Office. It sounded like they were trying to be sure they had privacy."

Sanchez shuffled his feet, "When Addison opened those barn doors I had a clear view inside. I didn't see the SUV and van, but there was a box truck parked just inside the door. The other two vehicles must be in front of it or off to the side. So whoever drove that box truck is either in the house or dead."

"If you're sure it was a box truck," Phillips said, "that's not good news. They could have enough firepower to ruin our plans for an easy take down. Of course the bigger question is, where did it come from?"

Chad was leaning against the back of his SUV, arms folded across his chest watching the computer.

"Since we now have two more hostages we go into stealth mode, in quickly and quietly", Chad said. "First order of business is to get that couple out of the barn, then check the truck. That will get two hostages out of the way and we might find out what else they have in the way of weapons. We need to do this with a minimal amount of damage, I'm sure these people didn't expect their home to be destroyed. We might even be able to keep the sheriff out of this.

"Sounds good, but those barn doors might be a problem. When you checked the outside stall doors, were they a viable entry point?" Phillips asked.

"Small padlocks on the doors, a lock-pick will handle that and the hinges look well oiled. We could get in and out fast if there's no injuries to the owners. You can hand them off, get them out of the area and then we can finish up. I'm going to check out the hay loft and see what kind of position I can get, but we probably won't need it. I figure there are seven guys, that's if there was only one in the truck, and our hostages in the house," Chad said.

"Odds are they are keeping the hostages close and they're all in a downstairs room," Brock added.

"Okay we'll plan as movements dictate," Chad said. "We all gear up with NVG's and communication devices. We won't need the NVG's until later, depending on when we get moving, but let's take them. Be sure and take extra clips, you don't want to be caught short. I have three packs to store the NVG's and a small medical kit, each group take one, also down a power bar it'll help." He turned to Phillips, "You got anything else?"

"Not right now," Phillips said. "Everybody relax until we get the info." With that he and Chad turned back to the computer.

Brock watched the guys from Beaumont walk toward their car, he and Sanchez started for his car. He turned again and watched as Phillips approached the Beaumont guys.

"I don't even know those guys names," Brock said to Sanchez.

"Stan and Mac, short for McDonald. Sorry I guess I should have introduced you, I met them when I delivered the food," Sanchez said.

"No problem, I'll go over when Phillips is finished with them. Are you doing okay?"

"Yeah, but I have a question."

"Go ahead and ask, I'll answer if I can," Brock said.

"I have a knife strapped to my ankle. Is that going to be a problem?" Sanchez asked.

"I wouldn't think so, not if you know how and when to use it. We all have a little something in reserve tucked away," Brock answered. "Mine is a gun strapped inside my left ankle."

"My knife is outside my right ankle, just in case you need it and I'm unable to retrieve it," Sanchez said. "I don't know how this is going to play out, but we need to have their backs when they go in that barn."

Brock turned on his phone to check messages and Sanchez started drawing in the dirt. "Look at this," Sanchez said and pointed to the drawing.

"This is the back of the house." He pointed to the side in the tree line, "This is where I was standing and I had a good angle on the barn and this end of the garden. Right here," he pointed to the left edge of the box that represented the barn, "this is where an old tractor is parked and there's a barrel sitting there next to it. Looks like it's used only for decoration, but on the outside edge behind the tire and barrel is a niche. I'm pretty sure I can get in there and with my darker skin color I might blend in with the shadows."

"That would put you closer to the barn and the backdoor with a direct route to both. Of course, a bullet would have a direct route to you," Brock said.

"Yeah, but they have to see me first and by the time they do it'll be too late."

Brock hunkered down next to Sanchez and picked up a stick. "Okay, if you have that covered then I'll do the outside stall doors. If I'm here," he drew a circle behind the garden, but closer to the fence, "I can see your position, the backdoor and the stalls. Once they get in and get the older couple, they will bring them out the same way, then I can shuttle them off to Stan and Mac."

"Then they can get them out of the area," Sanchez said. "Good idea."

"Yeah, now we just have to sell it to Phillips," Brock said. "I'll send him over and go introduce myself to the guys."

While Chad waited for the computer to alert him, he started working on the weapons he would be carrying. He spread an oil cloth in the back of the SUV, took apart the guns one at a time, reassembles them and worked the action. He then started retrieving clips, unloading and reloading. He looked over and saw Phillips had finished talking to Sanchez and Brock was back from talking to the Beaumont guys.

Phillips walked up, "Did you do mine? You can if you'd like, I trust you."

"I can after I do the long range weapons," Chad said.

"Thought you weren't going to use them," Phillips said.

"I'm taking one of them, but might as well do a couple of them."

"Brock and Sanchez have come up with a plan to keep us covered and I'm impressed. Evidently Sanchez started it and Brock thought it was so good that he finished it. Now we've just got to carry our end," Phillips said.

"Good, Sanchez is doing exactly what he should do. The more I'm with him the more I trust him with my back," Chad said.

"All we have to do is get in and out of that barn and Brock will take care of handing off the guy and his wife. Then we can go in and take care of the rest. I'd like to wait until at least dusk to do the barn. That time of day can play tricks with the eyes, plus if these guys know how we work, they won't be expecting trouble until early morning," Phillips said.

"Just don't hand them off too far, we need to debrief them and be sure they keep all this under wraps," Chad said.

Phillips started to walk away when a ding came from the computer.

Phillips looked at Chad, "I'll go round up the guys and we'll go over all of this together."

Chad opened the view of the property and it looked exactly as they had seen it on the ground with the exception of the property behind the barn. He pulled the view a bit further out and could find no neighbors within a mile.

"It looks like they have a pond way back behind the barn, but it looks to be for the back acreage. There is also another pond to the right of the house, but it's far enough away that we won't even see it. There doesn't appear to be any obstructions to worry about," Chad said.

"The run down on the owners is pretty simple," Phillips started. "He is a retired bank president and his wife is a retired teacher. They moved here from the Dallas area about five years ago and have been remodeling the house and barn. No priors except for a speeding ticket a few years back. No ties to any foreign influences. It does say that they have cattle and a couple of horse, but we saw no sign of them."

"I want to send two of you back to house to keep an eye on things," Phillips continued. "Sanchez, Mac, I'm sending you guys and Sanchez I want you back where you were before. I want you to mike-up so you can contact each other when necessary. If we had a sensor I'd have you set one up on the road that would at least give us a heads up in that area."

"I think I still have one in the back of our car," Mac said. "I'll go check."

Sanchez watched as Mac opened the false bottom of the trunk. He was amazed at the amount of fire power and devices stored there. Mac pulled a rectangular black box out and opened it, then they walked back over to Phillips.

"Yep," Mac said, "I have one. We'll set it up on the way in and try not to trip it on the way out."

Chad walked over and looked into the trunk, "You don't happen to have any subsonic rounds in there do you?"

"We might," Mac answered. "Have Stan check it out and see how many we have if any." He turned to Phillips, "How long do you want us out?"

"Give it about two hours. If it's too quiet make it an hour and a half, I just want to be sure they aren't burying any bodies and you might get a look a Rogelio. Put your radios on PTT – push to talk – and we'll monitor from here on the computer. If you run into trouble open your radios. Let's do a radio check and you're out of here.

58

Rogelio and Yolanda had been hustled out of the motel and into the SUV for a circuitous route out of town, Rogelio knew that the men were being sure no one was following them. After a drive down another highway they turned off onto a narrow road, all he could see was trees. They turned again onto a dirt road that was actually a driveway and arrived at a farm. They were made to stay in the car while Jorge and the man called Addison went to the front door. Rogelio could tell that whoever lived here was not expecting them, that meant Jorge had lied to him the night before. No one here was expecting them. Ignacio spent this time reassuring Rogelio that they would be here only a few days and then a few days later it would all be finished.

When Addison returned to the SUV, he took everyone inside the house. Rogelio could smell the jasmine that came from the flowers outside one of the windows somewhere, it reminded him of home, but it was the only thing that reminded him home.

The furniture was older, in good condition and comfortable, but you could tell it had been used for many years. The kitchen was newer and sparkled with stainless steel and marble, not a normal country kitchen. It smelled like bacon and eggs and made Rogelio's mouth water with the thought of bacon or pancakes with lots of syrup. He didn't realize how hungry he was.

Rogelio looked out the window in the kitchen door and saw a big barn and garden. He wanted to go out and play in the hay loft then run around the yard, just run around the outside of the house as many times as he could. He also wanted to go out and see his options for getting away. He would need to be sure that Yolanda could take advantage of the options as well. He was smaller than her and could hide or run through places that she couldn't. From what he could see through the window he thought a route through the garden to the woods would be good, but they would have to be really fast. If either one of them faltered on the run, they would be shot down and buried where they lay. The term 'pushing up daisy's' came to mind, but in their case it would be pushing up zucchini.

He felt a hand on his shoulder, looked up and saw Ignacio smiling at him. "Plenty of room to run around, yes? We will have something to eat and then maybe you and your friend can go out for a while."

They phone had been ringing when they walked in the front door and now it was ringing again. It was loud because there were phones in the kitchen, living room, dining room and some upstairs. Ignacio said something to Addison, they argued and the ringing finally stopped. Jorge was going through the refrigerator and pulling our food to cook. He looked over at Yolanda, shook his head and began cooking. The food was good, Rogelio ate too much and dozed on the couch, his head on Yolanda's shoulder.

He was awakened by someone shaking his arm, "Hey," Ignacio said, "you want to go outside? You may go out as long as you stay near the house, someone will sit on the outside and watch you."

Rogelio smiled, not about going outside, but at what Ignacio had said, because in his head he was thinking, *'sit on the porch and watch' is what you say shit head, 'on the porch'.*

They went out the front door with a man he hadn't seen before and sat on the porch steps. Yolanda took his hand, "Let's go for a walk, just around the house. I need to stretch my legs and clear my head."

They started to walk and the man followed them. They walked around the side of the house nearest the barn and went in that direction. As they got to the back corner of the house something off to the right caught Rogelio's attention. He casually looked over, but whatever it was he couldn't see it any longer. They walked toward the barn, the man stopped them, moved them across the back yard and back toward the front of the house.

They got back to the porch steps and Rogelio notice a swing hanging by a nail on the side of the big tree. He walked over and unhooked the ropes and it fell into position. He motioned for Yolanda to sit and began pushing her, she finally smiled again.

In a low voice he started talking to her, "I think they have the people who live here in the barn."

Still smiling Yolanda said through her teeth, "I think you're correct. They put them out there with the big truck. Do you think we can get away? There are places to hide out there, we just have to find them."

"I have been looking around and I see a few ways out, but it might get us killed. Maybe after dark we can get away, but which direction do we go? I need to think more, we would have to run away from the roads and hide in the woods," Rogelio said.

"Okay, my turn to push you," Yolanda said.

As they changed positions Yolanda said, "We run through the garden, into the woods, turn right and run behind the farm. Then we cut across the back and run in the opposite direction."

"We would have to stay low, move very fast and remember there are more of them to chase us. If they surround us and catch us it would be very bad," Rogelio said.

"They're going to kill us anyway, what difference does it make," Yolanda whispered. "What do you think they have in the van and truck and why do they hide them?"

"I heard that and you're right, there is no difference. I don't know what is in the truck, but I do know that it can't be good because..." he started to go on but something caught his attention again.

"What's wrong?" Yolanda asked.

"Nothing, I just thought I saw something," Rogelio replied. "It was probably just a deer."

"What about the stupid jacket they make you wear?" Yolanda asked. "You will have to take it off, it might get caught on something."

"Don't worry about the jacket, it will be gone," Rogelio answered.

Addison came outside and called for them to come into the house. As they walked inside Rogelio fought the urge to look over his shoulder, he crossed his fingers that the two legged deer he caught sight of could help them escape.

59

Chad watched as Mac and Sanchez disappeared down the road, he saw Phillips watching the computer so he walked over and asked Stan to check for subsonic loads, then went back to Phillips side.

"They'll give you a heads up when they get the motion sensor set up. I sure don't like this running back and forth in broad daylight," Chad said.

"I don't like it either," agreed Phillips. "But I see no other choice. We can't set up cameras so eyes on is what we've got. They'll have to be careful and stay low. I hope they see enough so we know exactly what we're walking into."

"Sanchez has a good eye for detail, or so I've noticed, but I wouldn't count on either one of them seeing too much. These guys aren't going to carry all their weapons around, we aren't in the Middle East. I'm sure they were briefed in that area, but maybe they don't give a shit. They may feel that they can carry, if no one can see them. They do love those weapons, but this is no time for a psychoanalysis."

"Yeah, the smaller the, ahem, brain, the bigger the gun. I hope they can confirm that Rogelio is still there. Maybe if we're really lucky someone will open that big barn door and then the back of that truck and Sanchez will get a peek inside," Phillips said.

"I've been thinking, remember when got that report from Bob Frank about the metal container that was offloaded? You don't think they could have brought in a nuke or dirty bomb do you?" Chad asked.

"I was hoping you wouldn't say that," Phillips said. "Yeah, I have given it some thought, but I was thinking suitcase nuke." He turned to face Chad, "I just don't know where they would have gotten one. When Sanchez gets back we can have him call Bob and see if we can get a better idea of the size of the container. I don't know about you, but I really don't want to be surprised by one of those."

Chad leaned against the back of the SUV, "Brock might be able to give us the viability of that."

"The viability of what?" Brock said as he walked up.

Phillips explained what he and Chad were thinking, "So, is it possible?"

"To use the tried and true phrase, yes, anything is possible. When my contact calls back I'll see what he knows. Now that we have some time, look at this photo he sent me of Nasir. In my opinion, this could be our guy Jorge. Let's compare it to your photo of Ali and see if you agree."

Phillips put his hand to his ear, "Confirmed." He turned to Chad and Brock, "That was Mac, the sensor is up and running. Now let's compare the photos."

Chad pulled out a section of a rear inside panel and took out the files he had at the motel in Corpus Christi. He found the file on Ali and pulled out the photos.

"It would be nice if we'd thought to get stills from that video tape at the facility, the one where Jorge/Ali takes off his shirt", Phillips said.

"I just want to see how much of a resemblance there is between to two," Brock said. "I thought you told Sanchez you had handed these files off."

"I lied," Chad said. "Well, here he is and I would say they could be brothers"

"Holy crap! Are you sure these are two different people? If it wasn't for that scar I would have a hard time telling them apart," Phillips said. "This needs to be called in, it should only take a minute or two. At least we'll have them updating their files. It'll really piss me off if they knew all about this and didn't bother to tell us."

"Yeah, but you'll be pissed if they didn't know," Brock added.

Brock leaned against the side of the SUV and motioned Stan to join them, "You might as well join us, no sense in us repeating everything three times."

By the time Stan joined Brock, Phillips was off the phone and Chad had downloaded the photo from Brock's phone to the computer.

"I wasn't treating your nuke idea loosely, I just wanted to get this photo business taken care of first," Brock said. "I don't think they would go through this much for a dirty bomb and it wouldn't give them the coverage they want. Not media coverage, but area and it would only contaminate the site for a week or for as long as it takes to clean up. A suitcase nuke would give them what they want, but I don't know where they would get the material unless they get from Iran and that would be pricy. Then again Iran wants to do us harm so they may just give it to them, hell they might even make it for them. It could come in any size, from a backpack to a footlocker and as long as the batteries are charging and they have the codes they could do it. Like I said before, I need to talk to my guy over there and see what he can find out for us. With the information we've given the FBI and both our groups, they are probably already on it. It think we should follow up just in case, nothing wrong with redundancy." Brock opened his phone, turned and walked away.

"Well, we just had to know did we?" Chad said. "Thinking you know is one thing, but having it confirmed is another."

"We don't really have confirmation," Stan said, "Yet."

"Hey, if it's in Brock's head that's good enough for me," Phillips said nodding in the direction Brock had walked.

"Ditto," Chad said.

Stan looked over at Brock then back at Phillips, "Wonder where they're planning to use it. I get why it came in down here, but this is a slow method of travel for something so potentially dangerous. Of course they did have plenty of diversions. Sorry, thinking out loud." Stan turned to walk back to this car, stopped and turned back to Chad.

"I have four subsonic loads if you want them. They're about three months old so they're still good," Stan said.

Phillips and Chad watched as he walked back to his car passing Brock on the way, Brock put his hand on Stan's shoulder, said something to him and proceed to walk their way.

"Mr. B. is not happy with everything we're finding. He especially didn't like the metal box that Bob saw. Now he thinks he's not getting all the information from his people," Brock said. "Maybe I should say the correct information. He tells me he has a guy on the Iranian side of things, but it might be dangerous to contact him right now, so I told him not to, that one of my guys will handle it. He also wants the information on the metal box when we get it. I then called Bracken, filled him in and he'll get back to me. I think we'll have the answer before either one of them calls back."

"If they have a suitcase nuke in that truck in the barn, all the more reason to do this as quickly and quietly as possible. I doubt they would set it off here, but they could let someone high up know they're in trouble and someone might be sent to pick it up."

"If they do that I have a feeling it will be a private jet that picks it up, then we lose track of it," Phillips said.

"Well, we can't have that happen," Chad added. "So, the only way anything leaves this State is with us or in a body bag." Chad looked at Phillips, "That isn't ego talking that's necessity talking."

"I agree," said Brock. "The only thing that bothers me now is if they did bring in nukes, I wonder how many there are. We may be raising an alert level we don't need, it still may be just hand weapons, but big ones. Obviously, we need to take everything into consideration and have all our alphabet agencies brought up to speed. I just don't want to tell them yet, at least not until we look in that truck. Can we all agree to that?"

Phillips put his hand to his ear so he could hear the transmission from Mac and Sanchez. He slowly looked up and said, "Do not, I repeat do not draw your weapons."

They slowly turned to see two men in black clothing, faces streaked with black dirt, standing twenty feet from them.

"Crap, we could have shot you," Phillips said.

"No, that's why we called. So you wouldn't shoot us," Sanchez said. "We waited to call so we could prove how quiet we are and how distracted you were."

"Guess we were distracted. Why did you decided to come this way?" Phillips asked.

Mac and Sanchez walked closer to the SUV and Stan joined them, "Well, we got worried about moving up and down that road so much, so before we split up to watch the house we decided to meet up at the far corner of the fence opposite the driveway," Sanchez said. "We cut through the woods parallel to the main road, crossed the road further down, cut back through the woods and came in here from the opposite direction. It took a bit longer, but it felt safer. If this had been west Texas it would have been so dry that you could have heard us coming a mile away."

"So, did you see anything helpful?" Chad asked.

"Not much, but we did see Rogelio and Yolanda," Sanchez said as the removed his gear. "They came out the front door and took a walk around the house and when they started for the barn, the guy with them steered them across the back of the house and back out front. Rogelio noticed the tree swing so they played on it for a while. The first thing I need to mention is the guy watching them was a new player, probably came in with the truck. The next thing is," Sanchez sighed, "I think Rogelio may have seen us."

"Hope on one else noticed," Phillips said.

"No, no one else noticed, Rogelio is really good at covering himself. He was walking around the side of the house and looked straight at me. I don't know if he actually saw me, but he thought he saw something," Sanchez finished.

"I think he might have caught site of my movements out front," Mac said. "All I did was shift my leg and he looked in my direction, but no one else, not even the girl, caught it."

"I think because he is shorter he gets a better angle on us, but nothing we can do about that now," Sanchez said. "We also think there is someone on the second floor."

"I caught movement of the blinds in one of the second floor windows. Couldn't tell who it was, but there was someone looking through the slats," Mac said.

"Okay, you guys take some down time. I think we'll be moving out of here in a couple of hours. Relax, but keep your edge," Phillips said.

"One more thing," Sanchez said. "I can't be sure, but I think Rogelio and Yolanda are planning something. When they were out on the swing we both caught them talking through their teeth. When I noticed a change in their attitude I moved around more to the front of the house. I was watching through the glasses and noticed that their teeth were showing constantly, then I caught some lip movement, but not much. There was something about the woods and running. Rogelio shook his head once and Yolanda suddenly looked sad. She changed places with Rogelio on the swing and as she passed him she said something that changed her whole demeanor. She seemed emphatic whatever it was. She doesn't act like the girl I knew before, but under the circumstances I guess she would be different."

Sanchez grabbed a bottle of water and sat on the edge of the SUV. After a long pull on the water he said, "These guys, these desert rats, are coloring outside the lines. They're using a Central American child to blackmail and hold at bay an agency of the US Government, if not the whole government. Before this night is over I intend to have blood on my hands."

60

The sun was starting it's decent in the east, the sky overhead was getting the sunset glow, as much as you could see of it, and Sanchez thought these last few hours were the longest he had ever spent. He had thrown himself down on a bed of leaves near the SUV and had spent time watching everyone and thinking. He found it interesting to see how each one of them prepared for battle, so to speak.

Chad had already cleaned his weapons and checked the ammo, but he did it again. He then cleaned out his vehicle, putting everything where it belonged or in his little wall safe. He saved the computer for last, because you never knew when something would arrive or need to be sent out. He and Phillips decided they would send a message to the office right before they left and when it was over if they had a cleanup to call in they'd use a phone. Chad was now sitting and staring out through the trees.

Phillips had joined Brock and they had spent time going over the upcoming effort and taking care of their weapons. Brock had made a call to his office to see if anything new had turned up and to shoot the breeze with his mentor. Phillips had gone over to help Chad load the packs they would carry and then lay across the back seat of the car with his eyes closed.

Mac and Stan cleaned and reloaded their weapons, put the receiver on charge, stored their phones in a rear compartment in their car and now lounged inside.

Sanchez stood up and tried to get some of the leaves and dirt off, but finally gave up and walked over to the SUV. He watched Chad, unmoving, as he approached the vehicle. He knew Chad was controlling his breathing and heart rate in preparation for the evening encounter. Sanchez silently took a few steps back, turned and walked to Brock's car.

Brock saw him coming and met him halfway, "I take it you're ready to go," he said. "I am, I want to get his thing going."

"I didn't want to bother Chad, it looks like he's doing his internal prep," Sanchez said.

"Yeah, Phillips is too. It's something the two of them do, or at least that's what Phillips said. What are Stan and Mac doing?"

"When I looked in on them it looked like they were asleep. Their breathing was normal, I mean they weren't doing controlled breathing. My prep is visual. I try to see all the possibilities and actions against those possibilities. Then I get myself ready for mayhem, I always expect the worse and pray for the best," Sanchez said.

"I do about the same thing, I don't try to get my breathing under control until I get where I'm going," Brock replied. "Everyone does it differently, some even have superstitions or rituals they go through. I guess with border work you don't see much of that."

"Some of the guys have different things they do if they are going into a dangerous area," Sanchez said. "I don't think they ever find themselves in this type of situation."

Brock did a chin jut in the direction of Chad, "Looks like we're getting ready to move."

Sanchez turned and saw Chad walking toward them, veer over to Mac and Stan and knock on the side of their vehicle. Brock walked back to his car and got Phillips.

Without preamble Chad said, "Be sure you have a minimum of thirty rounds each in your pack, first aid kit, and we've already discussed the rest. On top of everything else I'm taking an M16 because you can never be sure. I'm also taking the receiver for the SUV as I'm sure they have a plan and it probably contains an exit strategy. Stan take yours as well. Brock, Sanchez and I will take the back, Stan you and Mac cover the front."

"We're going to walk parallel the road, but heading back toward the highway. When we get passed the driveway we'll cross the road and double back," Chad continued. "We'll do a radio check before we get to the house. Once we get there I want open mics, we need to keep in constant contact. Remember we want this over quick, with as little damage to the property as possible. I'm not worried about blood spatter, its bullet holes that concern me, so make every shot count. If there are no question let's gear up and go.

Sanchez started to speak, but Chad read his mind, "Before you ask, they won't use the jacket Rogelio is wearing unless they're cornered. He's their insurance policy, they'll keep him close and that's why we need to be fast. The girl, unfortunately, in their eyes is expendable, but we'll get her cocooned and out of there. If what you and Mac saw holds up, those two will be waiting and prepared for us. Now, let's load up."

Chad turned to Phillips and the two of them took point, Mac and Stan brought up the rear with Brock and Sanchez in the saddle and took off east toward to main highway. When they were sure they had passed the driveway to the house they turned right and walked to the road. After crossing the road they turned right and walked in the direction of the house for another hundred yards. They stopped, turned on their mics and did another sound check.

The sky was darkening as they neared the house, they couldn't see any windows as the garage blocked their view, but they couldn't be seen either. Stan and Mac broke off, went right and moved to the front of the house. As they neared the house they split up, Stan was taking the left front of the house near the driveway and garage he would have the gap between the house and garage covered. Mac took the right front near the corner where he could see down the side of the house and cover the front door and barn. Once they were in position they confirmed it with a click of their radios.

Once they got confirmation Phillips led the way to the back of the house using wire cutters to get through the fence. One at a time they made for the cover of the garden and started for the barn. When they were three quarters of the way across the garden Phillips put up his fist in the stop gesture and motioned for Sanchez to move forward. As Sanchez passed Phillips, Phillips reached out and patted him on the back, Sanchez did not bother to look back or acknowledge him, but continued forward.

They watched as Sanchez crawled behind the last few feet of cover and disappeared in the corn stalks. Their gaze moved between Sanchez and the back of the house, all the interior lights were ablaze. Anyone looking out a window would not have seen any movement as no exterior lights were in use, but they watched for any sign of a door opening. All they could see of Sanchez was a slight movement of weeds or corn which mimicked a breeze, then no movement at all.

They waited then suddenly over their earpieces they heard, "I'm in the hole."

"How's it look?" Phillips said to him.

"Clear view of everything, except behind me. Good cover. Over," Sanchez said.

"It's a go," Phillips said.

Behind Phillips, Chad moved to his left at an angle, under the wood fence and crawled to the small corral. After clearing the open corral gate he headed to the stall door and removed his lock pick set from his top pocket. It took him three seconds to pick the small lock. He slowly opened the stall door, it didn't make a sound. He took a quick peek inside, it was dark except for a faint light probably from a lantern. He moved inside.

The stall he found himself in was clean with only a slight horse odor. He slowly made his way to the inside stall door which was open and moved so he had a view into the barn itself. An SUV was parked between him and the light, he could see the big box truck behind and to the side of the SUV, but could not see the source of the light. He move around the back of the SUV, which placed him near the front of the box truck, in front of the truck was a white van. He moved forward, behind the white van, worked his way to the right and up the passenger side of the van so he could see in the front window. Nothing but food wrappers and empty plastic cups. He took a step back and felt something jab him in the back, he froze.

Chad slowly turned and saw a shovel handle protruding from a tractor that was parked where a stall would be. He breathed again and chided himself for not seeing it before. He started moving across the front of the van, edged his head around a second tractor and saw two people tied up and chained to a barn post. Their mouths were not taped, this was going to be dicey he didn't want the woman to scream.

Chad stayed hidden and said, "Don't scream. I'm here to get you out."

Both the heads turned quickly toward the sound of his voice, the woman took in a sharp breath.

Chad slowly stepped out of the shadows, "I'm going to get you out of here, but we have to be quiet. Are either of you injured?"

He man shook his head, "Only a few bruises," he replied, "but my wife is pretty shook up."

Chad took out his lock pick again and opened the pad locks holding the chains, "We are going to go out the way I came in, through a stall door. Once we get outside stay as low as you can and move at an angle to the fence," he used his hand to show them the angle and direction, "go to the far corner of the garden. A guy will meet you there and get you to a safe place while we clean this up," he whispered.

The woman stood up, with the help of her husband and stretched, "If you'll give me a gun, I'll help you."

Chad smiled at her, "I appreciate that, but these are really bad guys and they have other hostages."

"Well, if you need us," the husband said, "we'll have your back. We're both better than average shots, actually she's the equivalent of Annie Oakley."

The husband walked over the tractor and pulled a .45 from under the seat, "Never know when you're going to run across a snake." He stuck the gun in the waist band at his back.

Chad shook his head and smiled, "Let's get out of here."

They were almost to the stall Chad used when the big barn door started to open. Chad pushed the couple down on the floor, motioned for them to stay put and moved toward the door. Over his ear piece he heard, "Coming in".

He got to the back of the box truck near the door when he saw two men coming through the entrance, one man dragging another. It was Sanchez.

61

As Sanchez had passed Phillips, he felt the pat on the back. No need to acknowledge it, he knew it was a pat of encouragement and 'go get 'em'. He smiled internally, he felt like he finally had a sign of approval. Not that he really needed one, but it still felt good.

He had worked his way through the weeds, garden plants and corn with no problems and he hoped no notice. When he slid under the tractor where he had seen the opening, he found it was actually a hole. It was easily big enough for him and must have been dug by some animal, the weeds across the front opening helped with this cover, but the weeds behind him were sparse. The bottom of the hole was beaten down and he hoped that whatever was sleeping here didn't show up for a nap. He confirmed with Phillips that he was in and gave him a quick report. He checked his immediate surroundings for quick egress, being sure that there was nothing around the old tractor that would snag his clothing or make noise. He peered over his left shoulder and got a glimpse of Chad moving low toward the barn, then he settled in to wait for the next phase.

Sanchez watched the men through the kitchen windows, never really sure which one he was looking at and watching their lips trying to catch part of the conversation. He thought how easy it would be to shoot one or two of them, but he was worried about deflection as the bullet passed through the glass. His orders were to wait and that is what he would do.

He heard Chad, over his ear piece, talking to the hostages in the barn and at the same time saw the back door open. He knew Phillips and Brock had seen it and Chad didn't need the distraction, so he didn't bother to relay the information, Phillips would take care of that if necessary. Whoever was coming outside didn't bother to turn on the porch light.

Sanchez slowly got into a crouch and watched as the man came down the porch steps smoking a cigarette and headed to the barn.

The man walked with a slight limp, was about a foot shorter than Sanchez and looked out of shape, considering the belly he carried. The man didn't look around, evidently comfortable in his surroundings, and unlocked the big sliding door. He removed the cigarette from his mouth and threw it on the ground, stepped on it and removed the lock.

Before he could turn and pull the door open Sanchez stepped up behind him, grabbed him across the top of the head and upper chest. The movement was quick and silent as the knife Sanchez carried went in through his lower jaw, behind his chin and up into his brain. Sanchez didn't even break a sweat, the man made no sound.

Sanchez pulled the door open, kicked dirt over the small amount of blood on the ground, hefted the body and as he was dragging it through the door he said, "Coming in." and hoped those listening knew what he meant.

Chad met him inside and they moved the body into a dark corner. "One down, I'm going back out. It won't be long now," Sanchez said over his mic.

Chad went back to the stall and moved the hostages outside and in Brocks direction, "Okay Brock, here they come. I'm not going into the loft, no time. I'll work with Sanchez from this position."

"Roger that," Phillips replied.

"I got them," they heard Brock say. "Taking them to the fence." They then heard Brock giving them their instructions and making a point that they stay clear of the action.

"If anyone else comes out to the barn, I got 'em," Chad said.

"Roger that," came back three replies.

Stan came in over their ear pieces, "I've got movement from the side door to the garage, someone's going inside." There was a pause, then "Garage door is open. Subject going back inside house."

"I've got movement at the back door," Sanchez said. "Watch yourselves."

A large man came down the porch steps. He was over six feet five inches tall and looked to weigh in at over three hundred pounds, bald head and a face for a horror movie. He had what looked to be burn scars down the left side of his face, Sanchez couldn't make out the right side because of shadows. He stopped and yelled to the barn, listened and then started forward again. Sanchez couldn't understand what he had yelled, maybe a warning so he wouldn't get shot.

He reached the double doors and pulled them both all the way open. The porch light lit up the man's back and the back of the box truck. He yelled again then climbed up on a ladder attached to the back of the truck and stood on the truck roof. The truck rocked on its' axle as the big man moved forward and was lost from sight. The truck continued to rock and then settled.

Sanchez relayed the information to Phillips and as he finished the truck started up and backed out of the barn.

They all heard Chad, "How the hell did he do that? They must have put a trap door in the roof of the truck. Shit! He didn't even look for his buddy."

The truck drove between the garden and the house, down the side of the garage and disappeared from Phillips view. What he did see was Chad flash through his peripheral vision running down the dark side of the house chasing the truck.

"I've got the truck," Stan said, "It stopped in the driveway near the garage. I've got a clear shot at the driver."

"No!" Chad yelled. "I got him."

The truck started moving again and the receiver Stan carried started flashing. He quickly put his hand over the light to block it from view, "Mac we gotta go the truck has a tracker on it, we have a signal."

Stan and Mac ran through the woods in the direction of their vehicle, not caring about any noise they made.

Phillips saw a shadowed shape rise off the ground near the fence, "Chad is that you near the fence?"

"Yeah, I had the extra tracking device. It's now on the truck. I had to jump in the brush to get out of sight. I've got the front now," Chad said. "I have movement at the front door."

A man came out the front door dragging Yolanda by the arm. She was screaming, pulling back and yelling Rogelio's name. The man jerked her and backhanded her across the face. He was only a foot taller than her, but muscular and spoke to her in Arabic. The lighting was good on the porch, but Chad didn't recognize him from any of the photos they had, dark hair, dark features and definitely Middle Eastern.

Chad was now positioned at the edge of the garage and as the man neared the garage door he fired, a hole appeared in the center of the man's head. Yolanda had collapsed to the ground. Chad rushed forward and grabbed her arm and pulled her around the corner of the garage just as another man came out the front door with a gun in his hand. Chad turned to see Brock behind him. Brock took the girl and ran for the fence and Chad turned to engage the gunman.

The man on the porch saw the body in front of the garage door and ran back inside, it was Addison.

"Addison was just outside," relayed Chad. "I guess we have the right address."

"I'm going in the back," came the reply from Phillips. "Sanchez you're with me."

Sanchez parted the weeds in front of the tractor and crawled part way out of the hole and watched as Phillips crawled out of garden. From his crouch Phillips held up two fingers to Sanchez and took off for the back door. Sanchez counted off two seconds and followed him. Over their ear pieces they heard Chad, "Garage walkway covered front and rear."

They eased up the steps to the back door and could hear noises from the front of the house. They had avoided the window in the door, but now Phillips took a quick peek, the room was empty. He eased the door open, visually cleared the room and motioned for

Sanchez to take the archway to the dining room while he went to the center door. Both men went into a crouch before taking a peek. Being in a lower position made the possibility of being seen less than at eye or shoulder level.

The dining room had an archway at the other end that opened into the living room. As Sanchez took a quick look he saw guns on the dining room table. He pulled back into the kitchen and held up two fingers to Phillips and mouthed Rogelio. Over the mic he whispered, "Door in dining, guns on table." Phillips nodded at him and started to move through the other door when they heard the men going into the dining room. Sanchez pulled quickly around the corner flat on the kitchen wall, knife in hand. Phillips crouched in the hall doorway and froze. Sanchez heard someone tell Rogelio to move and not be scared, then he heard the side door open.

The next thing Phillips and Sanchez heard was a heavily accented voice, "You shoot and your little friend here dies along with all of us."

Phillips and Sanchez moved to the side door, Wafiq turned in their direction, looked directly at Phillips and smiled, "It will do you no good, I push the button and we all die. You will never know what we have devised to bring your country to its knees. You will burn in hell while we go to our place in paradise."

Phillips noticed a blood smear on the side of Rogelio's face and in a split second Phillips was transported back to Afghanistan and the embattled hospital. The thick smoke and dust, the small fires and the cries of the injured. He could smell gun powder and charred flesh, he looked down at the body near his feet. It was the body of Rogelio. He felt a hand on his forearm.

Sanchez noticed that Phillips was no longer paying attention to the face off and when he looked in Phillips eyes he saw they were unfocused. He reached out and put his hand on Phillips arm. Phillips jerked and looked at him, gone was the hospital, he was back and looking into the eyes of his new friend.

Phillips made eye contact with Rogelio. Rogelio stared back at him and slightly nodded his head, looked around with his eyes only and nodded again. As Phillips watched him he thought he saw Rogelio mouth, "Do it."

Phillips and Sanchez took a step back into the house, Chad with his gun still up took a step back, but Brock did not. Phillips handed Sanchez a set of keys, "Go get Brocks car and hurry."

Sanchez tore through the house, out the front door, jumped over the porch rail, raced for the far corner of the fence and ran for the road.

The three men holding Rogelio moved into the garage closing the small door. After a few minutes they heard the engine of the SUV start. It exited the garage and fishtailed in the dirt.

"Son of a bitch, mother fuckers! What the hell just happened?" Chad yelled.

"It was bad timing, they were leaving anyway." A voice from the front of the garage said. "After they killed me they were leaving."

They all stood staring at Yolanda. She was cover in leaves and dirt, her shirt torn and a hard looking red bruise across her face. "Now Rogelio has no one. He wanted me to leave when I saw a chance, but I don't think he expected this. When they heard the shot it was supposed to be me, but it was too close to the house. That is why the name called Addison came outside, I was supposed to die in the woods."

The owners of the house walked up behind Yolanda, "I'm Kevin Lang and this is my wife Sue. Thanks, we probably would have been next. Do you want me to take care of those bodies? I can plant them in the back until you can get back to them, I know you have your hands full."

"Thanks that would be helpful. Aren't you curious as to what was going on?" Phillips asked.

"Nope don't want to know, the less we know the better and I'm sure we can't tell anyone about it, so why bother," Kevin said.

"Anyway, if it gets leaked out we'll hear all about it on the news," Sue added.

"We'll get a cleanup crew out here and try to get things back to normal, at least we didn't blow up the house," Phillips said.

"From what I gathered inside," Kevin pointed to the house, "it was a possibility.

Sanchez came down the driveway and pulled alongside them, "Let's go! Mr.," he nodded, "Mrs. You take care, but we gotta go."

The four men with Yolanda in the back seat drove back to get Chad's SUV.

Kevin with his arm around his wife walked back to the house, "Well Suz, get me the keys to the tractor and while you clean house I'll clean up the yard and barn. I guess someone will pick up those cars in the barn because I sure as hell don't want them.

62

Yolanda sat in back of Brock's car and could no longer hold it together, she sobbed heavily and watched as the men around her made phone calls and put their gear away. She had recognized the one they called Sanchez and wondered what he had to do with all of this, he must not have been who he said he was in Mexico because she did not know him as Sanchez. She wiped the tears off her cheeks when she saw Phillips walking toward the car.

"Are you going to be okay?" Phillips asked as he handed her a bottle of water, "Because I need to talk to you."

Yolanda nodded and heaved a sigh, "I'm worried about Rogelio, I'm afraid he might do something."

"What do you mean he might do something?"

"He had all these thoughts going through his head and he was no longer afraid of them. He kept giving me advice on what to do if certain things happened, but the main thing he said was for me to run, to get away," she said as the tears started again.

"I have someone coming to get you and take you someplace safe. You don't have to be afraid anymore, you're safe. I have to ask, do you know where they were going?" Phillips asked.

She shook her head, "I don't even know what they were doing, except killing people." She started crying again, "That poor lady on the bus, she didn't do anything but be a comfort to Rogelio and they killed her."

Phillips put his hand on her arm, "It's okay, we found her. She's going to be alright, she's in the hospital. Matter of fact she was worried about you and Rogelio. You stay right here and try not to worry."

Phillips walked over the Chad's SUV, Sanchez was in the passenger seat and Chad was standing with his door open. "I called Stan and told him not to wait for the Feds, just to turn the trucks location over and head back this way, we'll meet them on the road.

He said the helicopter had already picked up the tail and they were on their way. I'm sending Yolanda to Pepa, the professional and sympathetic ear. She'll be able to pull information out of her without any damage," Phillips said.

"Well, Sanchez and I are leaving. My receiver is still going off and I want to catch up with these guys. Call when you've handed her over and we'll give you our location, we can't do this without the two of you," Chad said.

Phillips and Brock watched them drive away, "We need to leave too," Phillips said.

"That Sanchez is definitely professional, he wouldn't even look at Yolanda," Brock said.

"Keeping that problem at a distance is the best thing to do in this situation. The last thing he needs on his mind is a woman," Phillips said.

"Preaching to the choir," Brock laughed

"Since we're sending her to Florida, it may be awhile before he gets to talk to her, if ever. I'm interested in finding out why she was here, she was bruised and cut in that photo from the border. Maybe she was kidnapped too, but I think she came willing to begin with and then things went bad. Pepa will find out for us."

Phillips reached for his phone, "The Feds sent a chopper from Shreveport to follow the truck and our people are sending a plane there to pick up Yolanda. Let's head back to the highway and I'll contact Stan, see exactly where they are and tell them where to meet us."

They walked back to the car to find Yolanda sitting in the back seat where they had left her. Brock started the car and Phillips looked over the seat at her, "We're leaving to meet the guys who will take you to an airport. From there you'll fly to a safe place in Florida. Do you understand?"

Yolanda looked up down at her hands, "You mean a jail in Florida."

"No, not a jail." Phillips said. "It's the home of a friend and I think you might like it there. She has a beautiful garden, no one will know where you are and even if they find out they can't get to you. She has quite a bit of company right now so you'll probably stay with her in the big house."

"What do you mean 'big house'?" Yolanda asked.

"She has her house, which is the big house and then she has a guest house which is smaller," Phillips replied.

"Why do you trust me, I could try to kill her and run away," Yolanda said.

"Well, I don't know if I can trust you, but if you try to kill this lady you'll get a big surprise. She can take care of herself, so don't try it," Phillips said trying for a matter of fact tone.

"These men you are taking me to, I'm afraid they will hurt me. Can you trust them?"

"With my life," Phillips said. "They were with us when we tried to rescue you and Rogelio. They are following the truck right now. Do you know what's in the truck?"

"No, the truck came to the house after we got there and they put it in the barn. Most of the talking they did was in Arabic or something like Arabic. At least that is what Rogelio said and he's smart so I believe him. Can I ask you a question?"

"Sure and I'll answer it if I can," replied Phillips.

"The other man who left in the SUV, he works for you too?" Yolanda asked.

Phillips looked over at Brock with a sideways glance. Brock smile, "Yes, he does. I can't tell you his name, but he always has his SUV and is there when we need him."

"No, not the driver, the other man," Yolanda sighed.

"Oh, him. Well, yes, right now he does. Again I can't tell you his name," Brock said. "Why do you ask?"

"No reason really, he just looked familiar to me," Yolanda answered.

Phillips and Brock both suppressed the urge to laugh.

Phillips turned and looked over the seat at her, "How did Rogelio get blood on his face? Did they hit him the way they hit you?"

Yolanda touched the side of her face, "No they never hit him, they treated him rough sometimes, but they never hit him. They make him wear that horrible bomb jacket and he always looks uncomfortable. Rogelio says it is just a threat and I shouldn't worry."

"So, how did he get blood on his face?" Phillips asked again.

"It was nothing, he tripped and fell in the front room and hit his head on the corner of the little table. He said it was a baby accident, that only babies do things like that. He laughed about it. He bled a lot, you can see the blood on his shirt when he doesn't have that jacket on."

"When was the last time you ate?" Brock asked her.

"Today," Yolanda said. "When we got to that house the one called Jorge cooked some food for all of us. I was surprised because he is a good cook."

"I'll see that you get something to eat before you get on the plane. It will be a short flight, but no sense in you being hungry. Unless, of course, you get air sick," Phillips said.

"I have never been on a plane, so I don't know if I get sick," Yolanda said.

Before Phillips could say anything else his phone went off, he answered and then spoke to Brock. "We're going to meet up with Stan at the entrance ramp up ahead where Hwy 74 meets I-20. There's a gas station and store there, we can grab some coffee and then Stan will only have a half hour drive to meet the plane."

"Is there somewhere I can go to clean up?" Yolanda asked. "I don't want people to see me looking like this, they will stare at me."

"No one's going to see you. It's a private airfield and the only people you will see are Stan, Mac and the three people on the plane," Phillips said.

"What three people, why three people?"

"You have a pilot, a co-pilot and a cabin person. The cabin person will see that you get cleaned up, get some medical attention and, don't count on it, but maybe clean clothes. If no clean clothes, then my friend in Florida will see that you get some when you get to her house," Phillips said.

Yolanda said nothing, just continued to look at her hands.

"Look Yolanda, I know you're probably still scared and you don't know us, but we're here to help you and get Rogelio back home safely. All you have to do is trust us, get on that plane and do what they tell you. Okay?" Phillips softly said.

"Are you the friend Rogelio talked about? The one who was going to save him?"

"Yes, and I am your friend too."

"Okay, then," Yolanda said. "I will trust you and your people, it has to be better than what awaited me with those other men."

"Hey," Brock said. "We're almost there, I'm turning off the flashers. No sense in calling attention to ourselves."

They pulled into the store parking lot and took turns going inside. Phillips bought drinks and snacks, Brock filled the gas tank and they settled in to wait for the other car to arrive. No one spoke until Stan's car pulled into the lot.

Phillips got out and opened the door for Yolanda, she hesitated, took a deep breath and got out of the car. Phillips walked her over to where Stan and Mac were getting out of their car. He introduced them, told Mac to be sure she ate before getting on the plane and stayed with her until Stan was ready to leave. He leaned down to the open rear window to reassure her one more time and then he and Brock watched as Stan took the onramp toward Shreveport.

"Those poor guys, they just came from that direction. Now that the truck's in Shreveport it could go in any direction and quickly. I hope the Feds stay with it and don't have some kind of strategy meeting before they stop them."

"I would say *if* they stop them, but with the cargo we think they may be carrying they'll stop them," Brock said.

"I'm glad we don't have to do it. If it was in the middle of the desert I wouldn't mind, but the logistic of having to clear the right area before you stop it is going to be a nightmare. Taking down Addison and getting Rogelio back is only the nightmare I want to face now." He took out his phone, "I'll call Chad and see where they are."

Sanchez picked up Chads phone, "How'd it go?"

"She'll be on the plane within an hour, they're sending one from Atlanta," Phillips said.

Chads voice came over the phone, "We have you on speaker. I take it the Feds are on the truck, hope they don't lose it. I need you to meet us and soon, I'm getting low on fuel. We are on I-20 coming up on the Marshall turnoff. How far away are you?"

"We're in front of you at the Hwy 74 exit, pull off here and give me the receiver and we'll take up the tail. As you come off the ramp stay right and there's gas and a store on your right, you can't miss it," Phillips said. "You're maybe fifteen minutes from us."

"You would not believe these guys," Chad said, "either they're afraid of a tail or they don't know what they're doing. They've been driving all over, backtracking on themselves, it's almost like they got themselves lost. So watch it, don't get to confident. We've been staying well behind them and just watching that little red dot move around. One more thing, be sure your toys are handy I don't trust these guys."

"We're ready for just about anything," Phillips said. "When you get here, let Sanchez fill the tank, I need you to pull that number on the farm and have them empty the pockets of our dead guys for cell phones, etc. Be sure to tell them to use their television forensic training to gather the evidence and no peeking either."

"Roger that," Sanchez said as he ended the connection

"Are you going to tell Phillips what Rogelio said?" Chad asked.

"Yeah, I should have told him at the time. That look on his face when he saw the kid," Sanchez paused, "it was like he went somewhere, was seeing something else. It worried me at first, but when he came back he was fine. I didn't think I should say anything because I figured he went back to that hospital and was seeing it all over again. It didn't seem to be the right time and he didn't need to second guess himself. If they had used that detonator we'd all be gone. I think he'd do just about anything to save that kid. The truth is I feel lucky to have caught his lips moving, just two words but I almost missed them. If it hadn't been for him rolling his eyes I probably would have."

"So, that's what caught your attention, rolling eyes," Chad said.

"Sure, when someone rolls their eyes, the mouth usually follows. Ask any parent about rolling eyes, they've all experienced it," Sanchez replied. "That kid's smart, there's a reason he wanted us to shoot."

"I guess we'll find out soon enough, but something's eating at me," Chad said.

"I know, me too," Sanchez agreed. "Why go to that farm?"

"They stored the vehicles in the barn, took the couple hostage, met up with the big truck, had breakfast and left. Why bother?" Chad said. "They could have met the truck anywhere. I think it was to get the van and the other SUV out of site and dispose of Yolanda. They would have killed the couple too and it would have taken time for them to be missed since they called the sheriff about leaving town. The bodies would have been left in the woods and the critters would have scattered the remains. The authorities would never have identified Yolanda, sorry I know you two have a history, but the fact is they were going to kill her."

"I think she was lucky to have lived as long as she did, I think they kept her for Rogelio" Sanchez said. "They would have killed her when they killed that bus driver, but Rogelio needed a distraction and Yolanda was it. They probably would have killed those other two guys if we hadn't."

"They had room in the two vehicles for them, but I think you're right. When that big guy left, he didn't wait for anyone to ride shotgun for him," Chad said. "Weak links and witnesses could be a problem for them. So, about the girl, you want to talk about it?"

"Nope, the history was brief and was part of an operation. As they say in the movies, she's in my rearview mirror," Sanchez replied. "I just want to know why she was with these guys."

"Then why he reaction to her name back in Corpus?" Chad asked.

"Aw, come on!" Sanchez sighed. "I almost made a mistake with a person of interest, who, by the way, I followed to some type of terrorist training camp. I was playing a role that got out of hand. Now, for some reason, she turns up with a bunch of bad guys. What would your reaction have been?"

"Point taken," Chad replied. "I just wanted to clear the air before we get into a tight situation. I wanted to be sure she wasn't going to interfere with your thinking process."

"The only thing that is sticking in my mind now is that she could have killed me, given the company she's keeping. Hell, she could be a killer too. I really don't know who or what she is and I didn't at the time, but for her to turn up here," Sanchez paused. "I guess it scared me a bit."

"At least you admit it, good for you," Chad said as he pulled down the exit ramp.

He drove straight to the gas pumps, got out and ran over to Brocks' car.

Chad handed the receiver to Phillips, "You're good to go," Chad said, "and so is Sanchez. No worries about the girl, he's fine."

Chad jogged over to the back of his SUV as Phillips and Brock took the ramp to I-20.

63

Jorge had grabbed Rogelio by the back of his neck and pushed him into the back seat of the SUV and laughed as they took off down the driveway and turned onto the road. Jorge watched through the back window to be sure no one was behind them. Ignacio had yelled something at Jorge, but Rogelio didn't know what it was. Jorge yelled something back and started to raise his fist, then suddenly changed his mind when Ignacio gave him a look that made Rogelio think of evil. The eyes that were already dark, turned darker and if this had been a movie they would have shot sparks. It made Rogelio shudder.

Jorge backed down, but slowly. He sat back and mumbled something that Ignacio couldn't hear. Rogelio heard it, didn't know what he said, but he knew that they might start fighting among themselves and this was in his favor.

When they were safely on the highway Ignacio looked over the front seat at Rogelio, "See I told you we needed you. Sorry your little girl friend got away, but she knows nothing and was a pain in my ass. Now they will torture her and she will probably die anyway and all for nothing." At this point Jorge and Ignacio laughed. Rogelio showed no reaction although he was seething on the inside.

Rogelio dropped his chin to his chest and leaned against the door. He couldn't believe how stupid these men were, Yolanda would not be tortured and killed. Addison should have told them they were in a civilized country and besides, they were going to kill her anyway. Who did they think they were fooling?

"If you are going to cry like a baby, get in the back," Ignacio yelled at him. "Do not take off that jacket. You will have to wear it all the time, until we are finished."

Rogelio climb over the seat and curled up in a ball in the back of the SUV trying to avoid eye contact with any of the men, especially Jorge. All of them were angry and started yelling at each other. He didn't know what they were saying, but he was pretty sure they were blaming each other. The big truck had left before all of the shooting started and the men seemed to be happy about that, which must mean it was almost over. Over for him anyway and over for anyone near the truck or its contents. Of course he was guessing, but he like guessing games and puzzles.

His next puzzle was why the doctor didn't shoot the men. Maybe, he didn't understand what he was trying to say, he tried to make it simple, or maybe the doctor was afraid they would really get blown up. Ignacio was not going to push the button, he still had things to do, that much Rogelio did know. Just like in the movies, it was a bluff. Ignacio still needed his hostage, at least for a while longer.

Rogelio tried to get comfortable, but the jacket was poking him all over and was uncomfortable, but he didn't care. He smiled, Yolanda had gotten away and she was safe. Now he was free to do what he had to do, he wasn't sure yet what that was, but he would know it when he saw it or felt it. He wouldn't have the help of Yolanda, but neither would he have the burden. He liked her, but sometimes she wouldn't listen or do what he said and he didn't want to have to worry about her when the time came.

He didn't want to move to look out the window, he knew they were driving around back roads because of the trees close to the road and all the turns, a highway was straight this wasn't. He could only hope that someone was following them because he thought the next time the car stopped he would die. By their hand or his he didn't know, all he knew was that it was almost over.

64

It didn't take Brock and Phillips long to catch up with the three men in the SUV, the signal staying steady on I-20 East. Traffic was light and Brock stayed well back of the SUV, both men settled in for a presumably long drive. As they arrived at the Monroe, Louisiana city limits Phillips finally received a call from Chad.

"Where are you?" Chad asked.

"Coming into Monroe. What's your location?" Phillips asked.

"Just leaving Shreveport, put us on speaker it makes it homey," Chad replied. "I called the Lang place and talked to Sue, she said Kevin was out digging holes and singing 'God Bless America'. She told me that she had taken pictures of everything inside the house and barn, including the bodies from several angles, just in case we needed them. She included pictures of the area where she and Kevin had been chained. Kevin took the big tractor out the back barn door so that the tire tracks of the big truck wouldn't be disturbed."

"They sound like they are up on forensic procedures," Brock said.

"That's just the beginning, you're going to love this," Chad said. "She put on rubber gloves and went around the house collecting anything they may have touched and putting each item in its' own bag, including the trash, then signed and dated each bag. Before she did all that she took a clean vacuum bag and vacuumed the whole house and then bagged the bag. She said she wanted to get it done before they, in her words, traipsed all over the house and compromised anything we might need. She kept the gloves on "as she cleaned up a bit", is how she put it. She doesn't want to do too much until after our people give her the go ahead."

"Well, she's thorough. We might get stuff we don't need, if there is such a thing," Phillips said. "Maybe we can hire her to run our evidence searches."

"Yeah, with Kevin singing behind her," Chad chuckled. "I promised Sanchez he could tell you the next part."

"I have news from Rogelio," Sanchez said. "When Sue went to check under the bathroom sink, she found someone had written something on the inside of the cabinet door. It was written in red, so I am assuming that it was blood since Rogelio had blood on his face. She took a photo of that too, the woman is a treasure."

"Well, what did it say?" Phillips almost yelled.

"Oh yeah," Sanchez chuckled, "D.C. and underneath that HRY".

"Now at least we have a destination," Brock said. "As soon as we find out which highway they take we can get more people and maybe stay ahead of them."

"You know, Yolanda told me and Brock that Rogelio had fallen and hit is head and had laughed about it," Phillips said. "Looks like he fell on purpose, wonder why he didn't use something from the kitchen."

"Probably because he was being watched closely and this was his only option," Sanchez said. "I also have something else for you. When we confronted Addison and crew outside the house, Rogelio tried to tell you something. Did you catch it?"

"I thought I saw his mouth move, but I thought I might be seeing things. It looked like he said "Do it", but it didn't make sense to me," Phillips said.

"That is exactly what he said," Sanchez said. "We can guess all day as to why he said it, but I think we should asked him. I don't think he has a death wish otherwise he wouldn't be leaving messages. You did the right thing back there as far as we're concerned. Those guys would've put a bullet in his brain no matter what."

Phillips sighed, "Well, glad that's cleared up, at least I know I wasn't losing my mind. Thanks for telling me."

Sanchez laughed, "Hey, that's why you signed me up, for my lip reading ability. I'm just living up to your expectations."

"What about the things from the dead guys' pockets," Brock said.

"They had already thought of that," Chad said. "They're wrapping the bodies in some old sheets, trying to keep the humidity to a minimum and putting any lint or anything they find in the pockets in plastic bags, one per body. The bags will be marked one and two to match the number they are putting on the body."

"I guess they have everything covered, I sure as hell can't think of anything else," Phillips said. "Our crew should be getting there before too long, they were sending people from Atlanta on the same plane that is making the trip to Florida. They won't be the heavy lifting crew, just the forensic people. They'll be picking up the things from Kevin and Sue and taking a statement, etc."

"So, what's the plan?" Chad asked.

"I think the only thing we can do is continue to follow until we know which highway they take to D.C," Phillips replied.

"I hope they don't decide to use side roads to get there. As it is we're about seventeen hours from D.C., if they take side roads it's going to take a lot longer. I imagine they will stop somewhere for the night, probably around midnight, they'll want to put some distance between themselves and that farm. If they do stop, we might be able to stop them for good. They know we are on them, they can't see us, but they know we're here," Brock said.

"They are probably looking over their shoulders as we speak," Chad said, "I'm trying to catch up with you guys, but I don't think I can without flashers. I'm going to contact LHP and let them know what's going on, I'll get back to you when we get closer," Chad said.

"I'll keep a light on for you," Phillips replied as he closed the connection.

"I know we need to stop these guys, but we also need some sleep," Phillips said to Brock.

"Push the seat back and take a nap, these guys aren't stopping anytime soon," Brock said.

Phillips pushed the seat back as far as it would go and tried to get comfortable. He closed his eyes, began to clear his mind and his phone buzzed.

"Uh-oh," Phillips said, "this can't be good." He listened, voiced a few expletives, asked a few questions and hung up. He looked over at Brock and toggled the radio.

"Chad," Phillips barked. "There's been an explosion in Seattle, one at the Los Angeles docks, and they picked up a van full of explosives outside the Valero Refinery in Corpus and that's just the good news. It appears the FBI did take that big box truck seriously, but they lost it."

"What the hell, how could they lose it? They were following it by air! Fucking idiots," Chad almost yelled as he hit the steering wheel.

"They lost it in Shreveport for a couple of minutes, then followed it toward Little Rock and somewhere in there, before Little Rock, it disappeared," Phillips sighed. "Our guys are trying to find the signal that you placed on it, but that's going to take some time. At least they have a place to start."

"How can you lose something on an open highway? Were they too busy on their iPhones? I can't fucking believe this, I gotta go," Chad said and ended the call.

"Maybe you should stop and shoot something, you know take the pressure off, vent your frustrations," Sanchez said.

"Not a bad idea," Chad said as he veered off the highway at the next exit. He stopped the vehicle on the side of the farm road, jumped out and started firing ahead and into the ditched. After seven shots he got back into the car, did a U-turn and got back on the highway.

"Thanks, Sanchez, I feel much better," Chad said.

"Actually I was joking, I thought it might break the tension," Sanchez said.

"It did break the tension, just not what you expected. Now I'm hungry, we need to eat."

Two exits later they stopped and got sloppy homemade burgers with the works and homemade fries. They sat in the parking lot making a mess of the SUV and not talking.

Sanchez finished his last bite, "I didn't realize how hungry I was, but I could use another coke."

"Make it two and I'll clean up this mess," Chad said.

Chad was wiping down the front seat when Sanchez returned with their drinks and a small brown paper bag.

"What's that?" Chad asked.

"The lady inside said we looked like such nice young men and she wanted us to have two of her special fried apple pies. Not wanting to be rude I accepted them," Sanchez said.

"We'll have to eat them on the road, we have a lot of time to make up," Chad said as the eased the SUV out of the parking lot and back onto the highway.

His phone rang five minutes later.

"They've stopped for the night and it's a busy place, we're near the airport outside Jackson, Mississippi. You can't miss it, we'll get two rooms, adjoining if possible. Can't figure why they are stopping here, we thought they'd drive most of the night," Phillips said.

"Only one reason I can think of," Sanchez said, "They're waiting for that truck to catch up with them."

"I think he's right," Brock said. "They were getting ready to leave when we confronted them, we messed up their plans."

"Right, so now they contact the driver and have him use a little misdirection. When he's sure he's safe, he meets them elsewhere and they continue with the original plan."

"What better place than an airport," Chad added, "Lots of delivery trucks coming and going."

"This whole case is two steps forward, one step back and I, for one, am getting really tired of it," Phillips said. "I'll call you back with the room numbers."

Chad glanced over at Sanchez and shrugged, "Guess we don't need the flashers."

65

Chad opened the door to the room and turned on the light, the room was nothing special, your typical motel room. Two beds, dresser, television, table, chairs, bathroom and the smell of disinfectant, granted that it was bigger than most and the interior was nicer, but still not home. He and Sanchez dragged the bags and themselves through the door, each took a bed and fell across it as Chads' phone chimed.

"Tell me lovely lady that you have captured the bad guys and rescued young Roger from certain death," Chad said into the phone.

"Wish I could tell you that, but I'm sworn to tell the truth, so, nope sorry big guy," Pepa replied.

"Did your new guest get there yet?"

"Not for another hour, but that's not the reason I'm calling. We have some information for you, Phillips is probably getting briefed right now," Pepa said.

"I'm putting you on speaker so Sanchez can hear, it's easier than repeating everything and I'm tired," Chad said.

"Before we get to the heavy stuff, I want you to know that when the girl gets here she'll be staying in the house with me. I'll get prints and the usual from her and see if we can get background on her, I'll start squeezing her before we get the prints back, we can't afford to wait. I talked to Mac and he said she is eager to talk to someone, so I'm not expecting any problems."

"We didn't spend any time with her, but Phillips did he might be able to give you some info on her. He didn't say anything to us about any conversations so he may have kept things low key, she was pretty scared," Chad said.

"I'll start from scratch, get her debriefed before I get to the heart of the matter," Pepa said. "Right now I have to give you what I do have."

"Before you get into that, how are your other house guests, especially Rogelio's parents, doing?" Chad asked.

"We have two agents staying with them, one male, one female, they aren't hanging on their every move, just close enough for protection. Theirs and ours, if you know what I mean. I've been spending time with them, as much as I can, and they really don't know anything. They are as much a pawn in this as poor Roger, I mean Rogelio. His mom spends the day in the garden, her husband is with her most of the time, but she cries so much that I worry about her. She has lost one son and may lose another, I don't blame her for crying. I have spent time with her alone trying to take her mind off of things and I have asked her to join me when our new guest arrives," Pepa said.

"I don't envy you this job, I can't handle tears. How's it going to work when Yolanda arrives?" Chad asked.

"I figure we'll be the welcome wagon, put Yolanda at ease or at least try. This might work to put both women in a better state of mind, especially since they have a common goal in helping Rogelio. Before I forget, we sent Mrs. De la Vegas' brother, Matt Haynes, and his family home and they're being heavily monitored by us. We put one of our guys in the house as a visiting family member and one in his office as a staff member. Believe it or not, this seemed to make everyone happy. I suppose they feel protected."

"I hope you have enough surveillance around your place, we don't need a repeat of what happened before," Chad said.

"I've got enough, no repeats please. That was a rough one to explain to neighbors. I can't believe Leigh told them it was a game of Gangland Hopscotch," Pepa laughed.

"Gangland Hopscotch?" Sanchez asked.

"Pepa is alluding to a previous case where upon closing it we got back to her home to find the driveway and fence perimeter littered with dead bodies. A group of twelve men had been sent with orders to kill her at any cost, they thought they had taken out her security system, but what they got instead was unexpected and life ending for all of them. The men were met by some people sent from security, who mowed them down. The only sign someone had been there were the chalks outlines. Pepas sister Leigh showed up after the bodies had been removed, at about the same time the neighbors showed up. She told them it was nothing to worry about, that a music video had been shot there called 'Gangland Hopscotch'. The neighbors kind of bought it, but Pepa still had some explaining to do," Chad explained.

"Well, down in Mexico they have Gangland Hopscotch, only it's not chalk outlines. How shall I put this, it's, well, more organic," Sanchez chuckled.

"Oh Man!" Chad groaned.

"Okay boys, now let's get down to the real reason I called," Pepa said.

"If Phillips is getting the same info, I guess I don't need a notebook," Chad yawned.

"Oh no, you'll remember this. Our research people have been looking into Addison and with the photo archives sent them they had some luck. They traced him back ten years when he entered the United States, but they couldn't get anything previous and what they did get was confusing. They called Carol in the basement, she got busy and came up with something interesting," Pepa said. "Our Mr. Older was over in the Middle East about twelve years ago doing some hush-hush work for Defense and recruited an asset, which he ran in Iraq and Afghanistan. He then sponsored this asset and got him a visitor's visa, then a permanent US visa, then the asset disappeared. Evidentially he and this asset became very close, because the asset went to work for him under a different name. Older even took him into the fold when he was given the White House job. We checked the first visa photo and it is a match to the photo you sent us and the one archives had. The assets name was Hakim Al-Addis. All he had to do was add the last two letters to get Addison. To be precise, Harris James Addison."

"Let me see if I have this straight," Sanchez said. "This asset, Al-Addis, gets the visas then disappears, changes his name and then reappears. I'll bet that Mr. Older gave him some help, like maybe false birth certificate, social security number and driver's license. So for all we know Older imported his own terrorist," Sanchez said.

"You're right on the money," Pepa said. "Carol pulled all the information you just mentioned, then crossed checked it. The birth certificate and social belong to a child that died in a small town in Idaho fourteen years ago. They tried to hide the trail, but Carol is much better than most. She said that when her red flag warning went off it just pushed her harder, she couldn't let go of it. If you don't need anything else from me, I need to go prepare for my new guest. I will leave the rest of the thinking to the four of you and don't trust anyone, I don't."

Chad looked over at Sanchez, "Another turn, Phillips is going to love this. I give it ten seconds before be knocks on that door."

It was more like twenty seconds, but the knock came on the adjoining door.

"I'm sure Pepa called you, so what do you think?" Phillips asked.

"Pepa called because she thought it would save time and I think we have enough to hang him when we catch up with him," Chad said.

"I know I'm not in the business like you guys, I'm just a lowly border agent, but I can't agree with what you just said," Sanchez said nodding at Chad.

"Why not? We have things going back ten years," Phillips said.

"Addison has the protection of someone very high up the chain, just think of the past," Sanchez said. "People with that kind of protection get away with it, the IRS twice, Clinton three times at least and for others the list goes on and on, even Presidents. So bringing him down using the information we have may not be that easy and we discussed Mr. Older a few days ago so I won't rehash that end."

"I'm with Sanchez here," Brock said. "We go with getting the kid back and if Addison gets killed in the operation, so be it. I could call my contact over there and see what else we can dig up, but I don't think it would help."

"So, do we know what room they're in?" Chad asked.

"Yeah, we had eyes on when they unloaded the car and made sure we got a room nearby," Phillips said. "This way we know the receiver will sound if they leave. Right now Brock and I are going to get something to eat." Phillips tossed the receiver to Chad. "Then I'm going to sleep for at least four hours."

"Don't worry I'm bringing back some beer," Brock said. "I'd prefer scotch, but beer will do for now."

Brock and Phillips walked out as Sanchez stifled a yawn. "I'll be asleep before they get back, but first I shower I smell like dirt."

"Okay, you shower and take the receiver with you, I'm going out for a quick run," Chad said. "It won't take long because I'm wearing boots and I'm already worn out. I just need to clear my head."

Twenty minutes later Sanchez came out of the shower with nothing on but a towel and fell across the bed. He groaned, buried his face in the pillow and let out a deep sigh as he began to drift into sleep, but it was short lived.

Chad came charging through the door, grabbed his phone and caught a look from Sanchez, "I left it here on purpose, didn't want any distractions," he said as he pushed his speed dial. "Hey, when you come back, be careful, I spotted a large white box truck in the lot parked near the target SUV. No, I'm not sure but it had that dark dirt on it. Call our guys and have them check for a signal."

He looked at Sanchez, "Stay awake I'll need you to answer this," he said as he tossed the phone. "I'm going to dive through the shower."

Sanchez leaned back on the pillows and thought about what Chad had just said about the truck possibly being at the motel. Mac and Stan had followed it to Shreveport, turned it over to the FBI and it was suddenly gone. That meant one of two things, either the guys in the chopper were on the wrong side or a decoy traded places with the actual truck. He preferred the latter for obvious reasons. A decoy would have given the truck plenty of time to get here, since it left the farm almost an hour before they did, but to happen to have a dirty FBI agent in the air was pushing it. Of course having a decoy truck in the right place was iffy, unless the guy in the truck figured he was being followed and called ahead. He kept turning it over in his head and it was the only two answers he could come with, besides it might be just another truck, "But who knows?" he said as he sat up.

"Who knows what?" Chad said as he walk across the room.

"Just thinking out loud again," Sanchez said.

"Well run it by me," Chad said.

It didn't take long for Sanchez to explain his thoughts on the arrival of the truck, He finished up and said, "If it isn't the right truck it's still not our fault, but we were right about one of the refineries in Corpus, our timing was just off."

"That makes twice our timing was off. At least we kept the sites in Corpus, Texas City and Port Arthur covered. I'm pretty sure they've doubled up on the coverage, the FBI is probably on it too," Chad said. "As far as the bad timing, I think to avoid it we hit fast and hard, do the recon as we go in, not first."

"Do you think Phillips will go for that?" Sanchez asked.

"He won't like it, but we have to do something. We've tried it his way, now it's my turn," Chad said.

A knock on the adjoining door interrupted them. Phillips walked in followed by Brock carrying a six pack of beer.

"He," Brock said pointing at Phillips, "wants to go to bed, while I just want to relax. So let's get everything covered and put it to bed for a couple of hours."

"I don't have much," Phillips said. "The guys tell me that's our truck out there. The explosion in Seattle killed two and injured four, thank God for badly placed bombs. At the L.A. port we weren't as lucky, they have ten dead so far and about one hundred injured. The area will be closed for about two weeks for the investigation and repairs. The Corpus van was carrying multiple explosives and a rocket launcher. It looks like they were going to explode the van then use the launcher to hit another area of the refinery. The men from the motel that were interviewed were not involved," Phillips stretch and got a beer from Brock. "What else did Pepa have to say?"

"Aside from the information on Addison, she's gearing up for Yolanda and is going to have Rogelio's mom help put her at ease. The Haynes family is back home and has our security at his office and their home. She'll let us know as soon as she gets anything from Yolanda," Chad said.

"On a different note," Chad continued. "I'm thinking that the next time we get a chance we hit these guys fast, no recon."

"Funny you should mention that," Phillips said, "Brock and I were just talking about the same thing. We tried it my way and that didn't work out to well, except we got a couple of hostages back. Now we do it the way you and Brock like it, down and dirty. Sanchez, are you okay with that?"

"I have no problem at all with it," Sanchez nodded.

Brock and Phillips stood to leave, Brock left two beers on the table and closed the door behind them.

Chad looked over at Sanchez, "Well, that was easier than I thought it would be.

"That's just the first step, it's the ones in the middle and end that I worry about," Sanchez yawned.

66

Chad woke to banging on the adjoining door, he looked at the bedside clock, 4am. He went over and opened the door to find Phillips standing there, at the same time Sanchez came rushing through the motel room door.

"Get dressed," Phillips and Sanchez said in unison.

Phillips turned and walked back into his room. "Just got a call from the office, the box truck is on the move."

"That's what I was getting ready to tell you. I went out to check on things and saw the big guy walk out to the truck. This time he used the regular door and not the roof. As soon as I was sure no one was going with him I came right back here," Sanchez said.

Phillips walked back into the room, "I want you guys to catch up with the truck, Brock and I will stay with the SUV. Since the receiver is with Mac, when you're ready call Dean at the office and find out where the truck is. Once you catch up with it give me a call."

Chad and Sanchez carried the bags back out to his SUV. "Before we call and get the location, we stop and get lots of coffee," Chad said.

"Good, I need it," Sanchez grumbled.

Chad pulled out of the parking lot and turned into an all-night diner, Sanchez ran in for coffee and Chad secured the bags they had thrown in the back. As soon as Sanchez got in the car, Chad made the call.

"Dean, where's the truck? Chad said. "I've got you on speaker."

"Boy aren't we cheerful this morning, not even a hello, how are ya, no nothing," Dean said. "I see how you are. Who's with you, Phillips?"

"No, it's Sanchez. Sorry about being abrupt," Chad said, "how about I take you out to dinner later this month?"

"That's my boy, always the charmer, you're on," Dean replied. "Sanchez, I heard about you, I heard you got a pair. You have to have them to work with this guy. Now, Chad did they put the new GPS system in that tank you're driving?"

"Yeah, but I haven't used it yet," Chad said.

"Turn it on and I'll get you what you need."

The GPS lit up and showed a street map with a blinking light on it. They watched as it suddenly moved.

"What, a tracking system?" Chad asked.

"You didn't read the book in the glove box did ya, well when you get back home read the one in your usual ride. This new system allows us to feed the tracking information we get straight to your GPS. All our big SUV's have them and we are in the process of equipping all our vehicles with them. The next thing is we'll be using the screen in the center of your dash to send you messages."

"Isn't it going to be dangerous, reading a screen and driving?" Chad asked.

"Nope," Dean said, "You'll have a button that will active voice only and, before you ask, after the message is delivered it will automatically delete itself. Don't think it's replacing us, you still need us to input the information."

"Does Phillips have one of these yet," Chad asked.

"Nope, I don't even think he knows about it, he has his personal vehicle, we only install on company vehicles. If he ever decides to change his mode of transport to one of ours then he'll have it. Of course it doesn't help if you leave your vehicle, then you still need the handheld receiver to pick up movement. Point of interest, since you guys have two vehicles that you're tracking, both will show up on your screen if they get within ten miles of each other. If you want more than a ten mile view, you need to fiddle with it and it will give you a broader view. Read your book, it'll explain it."

"Wish I had known about this earlier," Chad said.

"It wouldn't have helped you, because we weren't tracking it until Phillips called and requested it. Honey, we don't have time to track everyone. This case of yours has us running all over the country," Dean laughed.

"What do you mean all over the country? We only have a couple of devices working," Chad said.

"We have three in Florida, two on the Haynes vehicles in Virginia, two on Mr. Older, and a couple out west that they felt should be watched. We had one on one of those white vans and we got to watch it blow up in real time. First there's a little dot, then it gets bigger and poof, it's gone," Dean laughed again. "Wish we had sound."

"You're an evil person," Chad laughed.

"I disagree," Dean said, "Not evil, I think of it as patriotic. These are bad guys trying to hurt my country and its citizens. Blow 'em all up!"

"Remind me to stay on your good side," Chad said.

"Honey, you are always on my good side. See you when you get back," Dean was gone.

Sanchez stared at him. "Dean is a woman?"

"Of course. What, you thought that she was a he? Did you think...," Chad paused and started laughing. "I guess the start of that conversation would confuse you. No, Dean is all female. DeeAnna Dean is a piece of work and damn good at her job. I'd introduce you, but Dean is an acquired taste, she takes a while to get used to. Hell, I know a couple of guys that won't go near her."

Chad looked at the GPS, "That's a pretty wide view, the truck must be twenty miles from here."

Sanchez reached in the glove box and got the manual, "Let me see if I can figure out how to get this thing to tell us what we need." He reached over, found a button, read more pages and looked at Chad, "I'm putting the street name display on and the twenty mile radius, do you want the sound on or just a flashing light?"

"The light is fine, but how do we know if we get to close?" Chad said.

"We'll see the truck," Sanchez said.

"Very funny,"

"When we get within a mile our red dot will show up, also as we get closer the screen will drop from the twenty mile radius to fifteen to ten, etc., then when get a visual we can turn it off," Sanchez said. "And, right here on the bottom right we have a mileage display so you know how far away your target is and that can be turned off as well. Pretty nifty." Sanchez smiled.

"Nifty?" Chad chuckled.

"Yeah, nifty. My dad uses it all the time, it's something that's cool, but also useful. Why you never heard that before?" Sanchez asked.

"Of course I've heard it before, I just didn't expect you to know it." Chad smiled, "Being so young," he added.

"Hey I'm not that young and call Phillips," Sanchez spouted.

Chad got off the phone and saw that Sanchez was holding a bag. "What's that?"

"These are those fried pies that lady gave us last night. Want one?"

"Are you sure they safe to eat?" Chad asked.

"Why not, they're cooked and they're pies, I'm having one," Sanchez said as he opened the bag. "Umm, good," he said around a mouthful, handing one to Chad. "Consider it breakfast."

"So, why were you downstairs when the truck left?" Chad asked.

"Couldn't sleep so I figured I would go down and keep an eye on things," Sanchez said. "I was afraid that they'd leave and we wouldn't know who was in the truck. Anyone one of them could have driven off and we'd have no idea if a couple of them got in the back. They could leave the SUV here and just use the truck, too many variables running through my head, so I did something about it."

"Did you stop to think that maybe Phillips or Brock were watching it?" Chad asked.

"Phillips said he was going to bed and Brock would have said something if he was going out. So, yeah, I thought about it. Now I have questions," Sanchez said. "Did you tell Pepa about my history with Yolanda?"

"No, she doesn't need to know. It has nothing to do with her interviewing Yolanda," Chad said.

"Okay, next. What did Dean mean about me having a pair?"

"Oh, she probably read Phillips report on the farm fiasco and saw the part about you taking out that guy in front of the barn," Chad said.

"He's already filed a report?" Sanchez asked.

"Yep, he has to file one at the end of each day. He calls in, records the report, then it gets transcribed," Chad replied. "Dean likes men of action, she says she lives vicariously through the transcripts since she's stuck in an office, therefore she reads a report if she hears of a good one."

"Isn't that a breach of your security?" Sanchez asked.

"It would be if all of the employees didn't have top clearance." Chad glanced at the GPS, "Looks like we're catching up, I want to get a visual before we hit Birmingham. I don't think they want to go through Atlanta, too much traffic, I figure Chattanooga."

"I don't know about that," Sanchez said. "The information Ignacio, aka Wafiq, gave was they had an uncle in Atlanta. Maybe they really do have a contact there."

"I wasn't aware of that. Of course it may have been something they picked up and used, but we can't ignore it. We'll know which way they go as soon as we get to the interchange in Birmingham, they can still get to D.C. from Atlanta," Chad said.

"It looks like he's stopped, the dot isn't moving. If we catch up with him do we take him or wait for Phillips?" Sanchez asked.

"Personally I'd like to take him now and turn the truck over to the Feds, but we should wait until they're all together. Anyway I'm pretty sure this guy is in contact with Addison and I don't think we can bluff our way through a phone call. Plus we run the risk of wasting time talking to cops, answering questions and leaving Phillips and Brock out there on their own."

"I'm just saying we could do a drive-by on him, but you're right, if they can't reach him it could be bad," Sanchez said. "We're within five miles of him and he hasn't moved, so be careful we don't want to run over him."

"How can we be within five miles of him? He must be driving in the slow lane and stopping a lot. It bothers me that he didn't wait and leave with the SUV, especially if he's driving slowly to waiting for the others, it makes no sense," Chad said.

"Unless it's a trap, they do know that we're on to them," Sanchez said.

Chad quickly pulled off onto the side of the highway, "Crap, you could be right and I'm driving headlong right into it. I better call Phillips in case they have something planned for him."

Sanchez watched the dot on the GPS map while Chad spoke with Phillips, it still hadn't moved. He pushed the button for a daylight satellite view of the area, the red dot stayed on the map. He zoomed in enough to see where the truck had stopped and the area surrounding it. He felt in the pit of his stomach that they shouldn't go near the truck. They needed to stay where they were and wait. Sanchez reached over and poked Chad in the arm and gave the time out sign.

"Put us on speaker, I need to talk to him," Sanchez said.

"Phillips I'm putting you on speaker. Go ahead Sanchez."

"I don't have a good feeling about this. I took a good look at where this guy is stopped, it looks like a rest stop and it's surrounded by woods. He's been there longer than a normal stop and there is no restaurant or gas station in the area. Either they are thinking we'll follow him there, or he's going to blow the truck like they did with those vans or he's waiting for them to catch up and waiting for them doesn't seem right. If you want us to go in, I would do it on foot and armed because unless this guy had a heart attacked his waiting for something."

"If there is an exit ramp close, but not passed the rest stop, take it and wait for us. Don't go near that truck. We are on I-20 and headed your way," Phillips said.

"Pass them. Pass the SUV." Sanchez said.

"What? Are you crazy?" Phillips shouted.

"Call Dean and have her track it, Sanchez is right, pass them," Chad said. "Trust us, I'll explain when you get here. Right now I need to get to that exit and call you back with the exit number."

Phillips called Dean while Brock notified the State police that he would be moving down I-20 with lights, gave them his government plate number and hung up. He looked over at Phillips, "You going to be okay with this?"

"I don't like not having eyes on that SUV, but Dean will track it and I trust Chad. If he says Sanchez is right then I believe him, they've got something going on that they are confident with and we need to be there."

While they were talking Brock had fallen back from the SUV, it was no longer in sight.

"Ok, let's do this," Brock said. He pulled into the passing lane and hit the lights.

In the SUV, Rogelio was asleep in the back and didn't see when Phillips and Brock passed them, nor did he hear the surprise in the voices of the men in the front.

67

Chad and Sanchez stared at the GPS, the dot hadn't moved. "I say we get closer, pull off the road and go take a look," Sanchez said.

"Well, I say you drop me off close to the rest stop, turn around, park on the opposite side of the highway then cross the highway on foot," Chad said. "That way, we'll be pointed in the right direction for a quick getaway."

"Think we can do this before they get here?" Sanchez asked.

"Sure even with lights it's going to take them forty-five minutes at least. We can do it, we're just going to take a look," Chad said.

"Can't do it, too much traffic. Horns will be honking and I might get killed, plus there's too much light, he'll see me," Sanchez said.

"Aw, come on, it won't be that bad," Chad said.

"If it's so easy, you run across the highway."

"Okay, we'll do it your way," Chad sighed. "I'll pull off and we can cut through the woods, take a look then come back here. Check your side arm, grabbed the binocs, we're leaving."

As soon as they saw the sign for the rest stop they slowed, pulled off the highway well passed the sign and into the grass. They double checked their side arms and cut through the underbrush and entered the woods. They angled their way through the trees, a wire fence and slowly approached the rest stop. One hundred yards from the parking lot the underbrush got denser, Chad halted, looked up and eyed the height of the trees.

"Keep watch I'm going up there." Chad pointed up at the tree and hoisted himself up onto the lowest branch, "I think I can get a look at the truck from here. Hand me the glasses."

Sanchez handed him the glasses and watched as Chad climb higher.

"Perfect," Chad called in a low voice. Through the tops of the other trees he could make out the truck. It was parked in the truck area of the lot and was facing the amenities. There was a slight breeze moving the tree tops, but he could see a man on top of the truck. He started down the tree.

"I can see the truck from here," Chad said. "The big guy is prone on the top. I'm coming down."

"Can we get him from here?" Sanchez asked as Chad started down.

"Sure we could, he's got a gun up there with him so we would be justified. It looks like you might have been right, it's a trap, but we don't shoot him," Chad said handing the glasses back to Sanchez. "Someone would hear the shot and I don't want to leave ballistics behind."

"Yeah and Phillips will want to do one big clean up on these guys," Sanchez.

"Speaking of which," Chad said, "we better get back before they get here."

After flipping an illegal U-turn in the median, they made it back to their exit and settled in to wait.

"You know that's a pretty big guy, we probably should have shot him," Chad said. "I have a rifle, it's not too late we can go back."

"Thought you didn't want to leave any trace behind," Sanchez said.

"I've got some older ammo and a mystery gun, they couldn't trace it," Chad said.

"I've never heard of a street buy referred to as a mystery gun," Sanchez said.

"It's not a street buy," Chad said. "I call it a mystery gun because I can't remember where it came from. I've been meaning to dump it, but I keep thinking it might come in handy someday. Then it becomes a sewer gun. We don't have time anyway"

"Phillips is probably biting his nails trying to figure out why we told him to pass those guys." Sanchez stretch and yawned.

"Well, he's about to find out. Here they are," Chad sat up.

Brock parked behind Chads' SUV and Phillips walked up to the passenger door. "What's this all about?"

"Get Brock and we'll explain," Chad said.

Brock and Phillips climbed in the back of the SUV and Chad filled them in on the GPS system. Chad relayed to Phillips the information Dean had given him about his personal car.

"Guess I'm going to have to start using one of the office vehicles. I'm not sure I like the idea of them sending messages on the center screen, there are times when I don't want to be bothered," Phillips said.

"Then just ignore it, they're not asking for a conversation. If they need to talk to you, they'll let you know," Sanchez said. "According to the book they only use that to send you information you requested or is in reference to the request and only if you are in transit. The factory installed screen shows until you turn on the direct screen, in other words, if you get compromised and you're in your vehicle nothing will pop up on the screen. The cool part is if you're a hostage in your own vehicle, you can push a button and the conversation in the car is relayed directly to your office. As Dean says, read the book."

Phillips looked over at Chad, "Looks like I need to get a new car."

"You need to go see Uncle Sal, he'll give you a choice of vehicles and get it ready for you."

"Who's Uncle Sal?" Sanchez asked.

"He's in charge of all our vehicles, sort of a motor pool or car lot," Chad replied. "You go in find a car you like and he takes it from there. We get a lot of our field cars from government seizures, the office personnel drive the fleet cars. Oh, why we call him Uncle Sal will be obvious when you meet him."

"So, you have tactical vehicles like this, you didn't outfit this on your own," Brock said.

"No, I went in to grab an SUV, told Sal how I wanted it outfitted and it worked so well for me that we did ten more. Then those six were placed around the country near major airports. When I fly in someone meets with one or leaves it in the lot. Other operatives use them as well, not just me. The original one is sitting in Florida in my garage. I usually have a chance to get more prepared, but this case just kept changing and what I needed I didn't have. We may have to do some tweaking on the SUV's when I get back."

"I'll go talk to Sal when we finish up with this mess. Now, why the big hurry and why have us leave those guys behind?" Phillips asked.

"Because Sanchez was right, I didn't know it at the time, but he's right," Chad said. "It's a trap. When Sanchez told me how he felt about the truck leaving ahead of the SUV and we found out about the GPS, it just seemed logical and safer for you to get your asses ahead of them. I bet you really surprised them by blowing past them, now they should be confused."

"How do you know for sure it was a trap?" Phillips asked.

Chad pointed out the red dot which still had not moved. "We took a look and the big guy was on the roof of the truck with a gun and I think he was waiting for us. I did see the outline of the trap door he used, it drops into the cargo area. There must be an opening for him to get from the cargo area into the driver area, which means he can get to whatever is in the back of that truck if need be."

"I don't like the sound of that and I thought I told you not to go near the truck," Phillips said.

"We didn't go near the truck, we were about a hundred yards out and I was up a tree." Chad said. "There was no way we wanted this guy to know we were around. As far as they are concerned, they don't know where we are and now with this GPS we don't have to get close."

"I'd still like to stay within a mile of them," Phillips sighed.

"We will once the other guys show up and collect the truck. Why don't you guys relax for a while and let the GPS do its job,"

Chad sighed and slouched down in the seat. "Then we can follow them to the inevitable end."

Sanchez leaned forward, "I'm going to pull the view out on this GPS to ten miles so we can see when that SUV gets close." He started to say something else when Phillips phone chimed.

Phillips listened to the caller, thanked them and looked around the car. "That was Dean, the SUV made a twenty minute stop near Tuscaloosa and is continuing this way. She also passed us another message," He sighed and bent forward looking at the floor, "Another white van blew up, this time near the Government Center in Sacramento."

"This time of day, that can't be good," Brock said. "They have barriers, right?"

"The van was an office delivery van and he was expected. The driver is legit, he got out, loaded a dolly, went into the building and the van blew." Phillips looked back up, "The van was sabotaged. Nothing is known yet about victims, but damage is extensive. Needless to say the Feds are on it, they have an office near the site. What we know so far is that the driver told officials the van was handling strangely, not taking corners as smoothly as it should. He called the problem into his office and was told to take it to the shop after his deliveries."

"Sounds to me like things might be changing, except they are still using vans," Brock said. "I think we can expect to see box trucks next, I don't think we'll see many suicide bombers. If they were using radicals we might, but they are using illegals and I can't see them giving up their lives. They could drug up some homeless people and use them, it's a bit farfetched but I wouldn't put it passed them."

"Why Sacramento, why not a bigger statement?" Sanchez asked.

"Trial run," Brock said. "See if they can do it, see how good our security is in these areas. Plus, if they keep hitting places in the west they take the focus off the east coast. Think about it, they've only had one explosion in the east and they don't know which direction that van was heading."

"We turned this truck over to the Feds, so they know there is one running around on this side of the Mississippi. That should alert someone," Sanchez said.

"True, but they lost the truck and we don't know if the information was passed on to someone higher up," Brock answered. "Remember we really don't know who to trust right now, we don't know how far up this goes in these departments."

"I think we stay with these guys and take this truck out of the equation, it might put a dent in their plans. Once we get the kid back they won't have a hold on anyone and we might get more answers. I still think Haynes knows more than he's telling and he won't talk as long as the kids in danger," Chad said.

They heard a strange ring tone come from under the front seat. Sanchez scrambled to answer it.

"That's my other phone, it must be Bob or my sister," Sanchez said picking up the phone. He look at the caller ID, "I'm putting you on speaker."

"That's good because I don't want to repeat this more than four or five times," Bob sounded out of breath. "Another one of those boats came in early this morning and I watched them unload it, I even helped. I figured if I did some of the lifting I could get a better idea of what they were transporting. Once I had a few minutes alone I took a few cell pictures, which I'll send to you. This stuff they're bringing in can't be good, I had a really bad feeling about it."

"They left you alone with the cargo?" Sanchez asked.

"Not without some diversions," Bob replied. "Some of my buddies have been filled in on the curious stuff coming in and I don't mean fish. So I recruited them to help me keep an eye on things, I even have two of them doing some work on the Brownsville thing. Anyway I had them create a diversion so I could get pictures."

"That's taking a chance, I don't want you to get yourself killed," Sanchez said.

"Don't worry, these are not new friends, we go way back," Bob laughed. "Back to the shipment. We unloaded two large metal containers and a couple of long crates. As soon as they were unloaded the boat took off, no refuel, just up and left. As soon as the truck started moving I called the State cops, gave them the plate number and described what we had unloaded. Since we are a fishing town and these weren't fish, they took me seriously. I know I should probably have cleared it with you guys first, but I didn't want them to get away. Like I said before, I had a really bad feeling."

"We haven't gotten a call on this from my office. Are you sure they took you seriously?" Phillips asked.

"Oh yeah, they did," Bob laughed again. "They picked up the truck once it got close to Robstown, outside Corpus Christi. They had followed it in the air and once it got passed the Sarita check point the cops moved in to follow them. They waited for a violation, so that they had just cause and the cop noticed a badly damaged right front tire, so he pulled him over."

"Two questions," Phillips said. "How did they get passed the check point and how did the cop get inside?"

"From what I can gather, once they left here they loaded other stuff in the back to cover the cargo and there was nothing for the dogs to hit on, so they got the all clear. As far as getting into the back of the truck, that was the easy part," Bob snickered. "State cops had another car coming from the opposite direction and when the first cop stopped the truck the second cop used lights and sirens to get to him. The first cop had the driver and passenger exit the vehicle and when they saw the second cop coming their way, they took off running. I would have loved to have seen that. I bet they're back across the border now."

"You think they were illegals?" Phillips asked.

"Yeah, they kept to themselves while we loaded the truck, no eye contact whatsoever. The guys from the boat directed the loading and didn't speak to the driver. They just closed the back of the truck, waved at the driver and got back on the boat. The driver walked over, locked the back of the truck, spoke to the passenger in Spanish and they left," Bob said.

"Did you find out what they were carrying?" Sanchez asked.

"Yeah, the one cop came by with a Fed and asked some questions and once the Fed left I got the scoop. The cop, Rick Granly, you remember him, he's the one who helped out on that mule run a year ago, "Bob said.

"I remember him, he's the one who puts peanuts in his beer. What'd he say?" Sanchez said.

"The Feds swooped in as soon Rick radioed in about the crates. They came in by helicopter and opened the crates on the spot," Bob said. "The crates contained RPG's and the metal boxes were dirty bombs, unarmed I might add. Rick said they really started to scramble once they opened that first metal case. I would have liked to have seen that, I wonder what a Fed scrambling looks like, that's a rarity."

"Are you going to be okay with this?" Sanchez asked.

"No problem, we're leaving town for a while. The four of us may head to Galveston or maybe Dallas. I told the guys in Brownsville to back off for a bit, in case things heat up after this bust. For the last few days I've been spreading it around that we were planning a trip, just in case we needed to leave. Nothing wrong with being prepared."

"Hey, Bob, Phillips here. Thanks for all your work and I suggest you continue to watch your back."

"I here ya, you guys do the same. I'm gone," with that Bob ended the connection.

"Well," Chad said, "That puts a spotlight on things, at least we now know what may be in that truck."

"I'm afraid if things don't start moving for us, we may get called off," Phillips said.

The GPS made a hollow 'bloop' sound and all four men looked up as the second red dot blinked on the screen.

68

The two red dots on the GPS stayed steady at the rest stop for almost twenty minutes. When they did move it was together and toward Atlanta. They drove slightly over the speed limit, exited I-20 and drove into an older residential area. The houses were of the cookie cutter variety, identical but flip-flopped. Most were in need of painting, the yards, both fenced and unfenced, were fairly modest and well-kept except for the obligatory one or two.

When the dots became stationary, Chad drove to within a block of the house, Brock parked a block away in the opposite direction. Three pairs of eyes watched not only the house, but the houses around them, watching for anything unusual. The fourth pair of eyes was Phillips and he could not take his eyes off the target house and the two vehicles parked in front of it. He waited to see if a curtain would be pulled aside to check the street outside, but it didn't. The longer he looked at the curtains he realized they weren't curtains but what looked like sheets put haphazardly over the windows. They hung at odd angles and weren't smooth, but wrinkled and folded over themselves and they didn't match.

The house was a plain looking faded blue with chipped white trim and a small porch reached by two concrete steps. A picture window, where the living room would be, faced the street, two smaller windows also faced the street and only one on the side of the house near the front. Phillips decided there must be another one on the side toward the back, as well as back windows and a back door. The driveway ran down the side of the house to a detached garage, which he couldn't see. A single car sat in the driveway, new and way too expensive for the neighborhood.

Phillips toggled the radio, "Have you seen any movement from your side?"

"No, nothing," Chad replied.

"I wish we had been able to see who got out of that fancy car and who answered the door," Phillips said.

"You'll see them when they come out, I don't think they will leave anyone behind. If anything they'll have extra," Chad said. "As soon as that front door opens, we'll back out of here. I don't want them to see this vehicle."

"What and you don't think they'll recognize this one?" Brock asked.

"I'm thinking they'll come back this way, but if they don't just duck down," Chad chuckled.

"Very funny. Maybe I'll put on a pair of nose glasses, that'll fool them," Phillips said as his phone chimed. "That's my phone, I'll get back to you."

Chad turned the volume down on the radio and looked out the windshield. "I'm just thinking out loud here, but if you were offered a job would you go to work for us?

Sanchez looked over at him and then back out the window, "I like working the border. It's just that this mess has really put a kink in the job, especially if I have a target on my back. Bobs' idea of getting a fishing boat was really tempting, but people that know the score need to be on the border and I'm one of them."

"Phillips does two jobs, I don't know why you couldn't," Chad said. "We could use someone on the border whether Phillips stays there or not. You know, to keep an eye on things. There's just too much shit going on with foreign nationals crossing or trying to anyway. If the powers that be okay it, would you be interested?"

"Have you talked to Phillips about this?" Sanchez asked.

"I don't need to talk to Phillips about it," Chad replied.

Before Sanchez could say anything else they heard the radio come on again. Chad reached over and turned up the volume, "We're still here."

"I've got some news," Phillips said. "They tracked Arel to L.A. and had a team following her movements until she disappeared into the Latino community. Then when the explosion happened at the

L.A. port our people started searching the security videos from the area and she popped up on three of them."

"What was she doing or do I already know" Chad asked.

"She was seen on two separate feeds doing what looks like recon, so yeah, it's what you would expect. The other feed is after the explosion and it looks like she's taking photos." Phillips answered. "She's dressed like a dock worker, jeans, t-shirt, boots, and a ball cap. I haven't seen the feed, but that's what they are telling me."

"We don't need the feed, she's FBI meat now," Chad said.

"At least we know where she..," Phillips stopped speaking. The front door of the house had opened.

They watched as three men and Rogelio walked to the SUV and truck. Rogelio shuffled down the walkway looking at the ground and got into the back of the SUV. He big man got into the truck and waited. A fourth man came out of the house, locked the front door and got in the car that was parked in the driveway.

"Where the hell is Addison?" Phillips almost yelled.

"I don't see him either and if that guy locked the door, he must not be inside," Chad said.

"Unless he's dead," Brock said.

Chad started backing up. Phillips voice came over the radio again, "We're going to take a look inside, stay with these guys. I'll contact you when we clear the house."

"Roger that," Chad said as he pulled around the corner and got out of site in a driveway.

Chad and Sanchez watched as the three vehicles passed the end of the street, the red dots on the GPS flashing. When the vehicles were a few blocks away he toggled Phillips on the radio, "We're on them. If they decide to turn back I'll give you a call."

"Thanks, we're moving now," Phillips replied.

Chad picked up his sped, "Sanchez I need you to get the plate number on that other car and the only way we are going to get is to see if he turns off. Watch from your side and if he turns right let me know, I'll watch from this side. If the other vehicles don't turn with him we'll turn and follow him until you can get the number then we'll get back on Rogelio. We need to know who that guy is, not necessarily where he's going."

"I guess you know that Addison isn't in that house," Sanchez said. "They dropped him off during that twenty minute stop in Tuscaloosa. Whatever instructions he gave were passed on to the truck driver at the rest stop."

"I was thinking the same thing and I think you're right," Chad said. "I don't think they would've kill him, but you never know with radials like Wafiq. They wake up on the wrong side of the bed and people die."

Sanchez leaned toward the passenger door, "Okay, the car just turn right at the red and white sign."

"Got it," Chad hit his blinker and quickly followed almost catching the car.

Sanchez picked up the glasses and started repeating the plate number to himself as he reached for his notebook. "I've got it, let's get out of here."

Chad looked at the GPS, took the next left, reached for this phone and handed it to Sanchez, "Hit the seven, a phone will ring on the other end, when it stops ringing you'll hear two tones. After the tones say 'plate' then read what you got, don't say anything else, it will read them back to you, if they are correct just hang up, if not repeat them."

Sanchez gave the plate number to the anonymous voice on the other end and closed the connection. "That's all there is to it, you never talk to anyone?"

"Only when they call back," Chad replied. "And only when they get something."

They got in position a half mile behind the SUV when they heard Phillips over the radio. They gave him their position and slowed to give Brock time to catch up.

"What was in the house?" Chad asked.

"Nothing but a few pieces of furniture and a TV. No food, refrigerator was empty, it could be a drop or even a safe house of some kind. Addison must have disappeared at that stop they made," Phillips replied.

"Yeah, we figured that." Chad said. "We got the plate number on the other vehicle and called it in, we should hear something shortly. I'm thinking it's a rental."

"We need to make a gas stop, I'm almost on fumes," Brock said. "Now that we have your GPS system it shouldn't be a problem."

"Good, we'll top off and I need to get some gear ready in the back and let me guess. Brock needs food," Chad did his best imitation of Cookie Monster.

"Nothing heavy, something tells me I don't want a full stomach," Brock replied. "I have you in sight, we're about six cars back."

"Let's just make it quick, I want eyes on from now on," Phillips said.

They stopped and while Phillips and Chad filled the vehicles Brock and Sanchez went inside the store. As Brock was leaving the store his phone rang, he looked at the caller I.D. and held his breath. Sanchez noticed the sudden change and looked at him. Brock motioned for Sanchez to go ahead, he needed privacy for the call.

"I didn't expect to hear from you again. I hope all is well," Brock said as he answered the call.

"Hello my friend, yes everything is fine now. I'm sitting in the mountains looking at the children playing in half melted snow. Now they will track mud through the house and my wife will be, as you say, at wits end, until it is cleaned up." the voice replied.

"So you left the country I assume," Brock said.

"You assume correctly. Considering the state of the world it seemed like a good idea, but that is not the reason for my call. I received some interesting information about an hour ago that I need to pass on to you."

"That sounds ominous," Brock replied.

"It is. Please be most careful with your case and I know you are still on the chase because there has been nothing in your American news broadcasts to tell me differently. I have gotten credible information on one of the suitcase nukes we discussed. Our man in Iraq was finally able to make it out of the country, he has been in hiding and was unable to send us any information for well over a month. He came straight to me with the information because of its importance. This nuke was purchased by a group that Wafiq worked for previously and had been seen meeting with several months ago. This group moves freely to and from Iraq, it basically knows no borders. We paid no attention to him meeting with them, as he meets with many people, but with this information it seemed expedient that I inform you."

Brock swallowed hard, "So, you're tell me..."

"Yes," the voice interrupted, "the nuke was sent to the United States. The other information he passed to me confirmed that the operation we spoke of was most definitely moved to Central America and was heading to your country. Their orders were to create confusion by attacking smaller targets, staging unexplained explosions, then hitting the larger target. They were to recruit those who wanted to cross into the United States, they were told to use the most expendable people they could find."

"Didn't they think we would raise the alert level once the explosions happened?" Brock asked. "Don't answer that, I already know the answer."

"Yes you do, when you have the right people looking out for you," the voice said, "that can be avoided. Maybe not completely but for a period of time. After all, they haven't raised the level yet. If they have, they are keeping it quiet."

"I thank you for getting this to me, maybe we can stop them," Brock said.

"I must tell you that they sent RPG's and C4 your way as well as a couple of dirty bombs. They were assembled here because no one traces what you buy or asks any questions. So be on the lookout for them. I don't need to tell you that we would like these people taken off the face of the earth. Be safe and call me," with that the connection was broken.

Brock walked over to the vehicles and gave them the news he had just been given. "I didn't tell him about the dirty bombs that were found, I didn't see the need to impart that info," Brock sighed as the four men stood looking at the ground, deep in their own thoughts.

Chad was the first to speak, "Well, I can't say we didn't expect this news, it just feels different when it's been confirmed."

"Something else to think about," Sanchez said. "Since they are using illegals and they seem to be the only ones being spotted, it looks like cartel activity. There's no suspicion thrown on Middle East types. Smart on their part, or it would have been if you guys hadn't been on your toes."

"A lot of that credit goes to those photos you took and your codes on the back. If you want more credit, let's take care of these guys," Phillips said as he got back into the car.

Chad looked at Brock, "This may get bad, but we won't know until we catch up with them. We're going to stay as close as we can without them spotting us. Don't let Phillips talk you into doing something we might all regret."

69

When Rogelio awoke in the back of the SUV he sat watching out the back window. He couldn't find the car the doctor was riding in or the SUV he had seen with it. The doctors car had been behind them in the distance for a long time and he felt secure in the knowledge that it was there watching their every move. He was so tired, but with the doctor watching them he felt safe, he didn't have to think for a while, he could sleep. Now, without his watchers, it was back to the same fear.

He felt the car slow and watched as they pulled into a store with gas pumps, a restaurant and some other buildings. Addison turned from the front seat and motioned for him to get out. He and Addison walked into the store and Addison bought him some snacks, a soda and had him pick out some comic books and magazines. He had the store clerk hold their purchases as they walked to the bathrooms. When the door closed behind them Addison knelt down and placed a big hand on his shoulder.

"I won't be going with you the rest of the way. I have things that I need to do," Addison said. "When this is over I will be sure you are returned home to your parents, but the only way I can do this is if you do exactly what you are told. I'll be seeing your Uncle Matt in a few days, I will let him know that you are alright. All you have to do is stay out of the way of these men and do what they ask of you. Do you understand?"

Rogelio nodded and the two of them walked back out to the car.

Addison spoke to Ignacio and Jorge in that strange language and then walked away. Rogelio watched him go into another building, then he heard the one called Ignacio speaking to him and pointing toward the car.

They drove for a long time and Rogelio still did not see the car he was looking for in the many behind them. They stopped at a rest stop and met the big man with the truck. There was a lot of yelling and head shaking, he didn't know what the problem was and really didn't care. The next leg of their journey was shorter and ended at another house.

The house was nothing much to look at, no flowers, weeds for grass and a broken fence. The inside was much the same, not much furniture and it looked like no one had ever lived there. Another man in a suit was waiting for them, he too seemed angry. They turned on the television and made him sit on the couch while they talked in the kitchen. He heard nothing that was said, he was too busy with his own thoughts.

He felt himself moving in the direction of not caring if he lived, only that these men didn't. Mentally he had made several plans and now that he didn't have Yolanda to worry about he could move on any one of them at any time, just not in this house. He looked down at his hands and ran his fingers along the edge of the jacket he now never took off. He started running his ideas through his head one more time looking for a flaw, looking for other options.

He jumped when the television was turned off. He looked up and Jorge was standing over him, "It's time to go little man. You need to know that we have very powerful friends here, more powerful than the men who have been following us. Don't think they are going to stop us or rescue you, because they can't. They have been given new orders and those orders are to leave us alone."

Ignacio walked out of the kitchen smiling and looked at Rogelio. "Now that we are not being followed there is nothing in our way, we can finish this and you can go home. Good news, yes?"

Rogelio nodded, walked out the door and shuffled to the SUV, he didn't look up or down the street, only at the ground. He knew the only way they wanted to send him home was in a coffin. He climbed in the back of the SUV and sat there wondering if they knew he was aware of the men who had been following. Better question was why they felt the need to tell him any of this?

As the SUV pulled away from the house he climbed over the seat, into the cargo area and once again put his head on the old pillow. He felt a tear roll down his cheek. He quickly sat up, wiped it away, and shook head to clear it. He stared out the rear window and the eyes that were only moments ago soft, childlike and scared had turned cold.

70

Chad stayed a mile behind the target vehicle, Phillips wanted to be closer, but Chad and Brock agreed that they needed to stay out of sight for a while. Once they got onto I-85 pointing toward Charlotte, North Carolina, they settled in for the possible long drive. Brock and Phillips made calls to their respective offices, Phillips to his case handler and Brock called Bracken. Neither of the call recipients took it well.

Bracken told Brock to remain on the fringes and if the Feds showed up to disappear. Brock gave him the information he had received from his Middle East contact and informed him that it had been called in directly. Phillips on the other hand was told to turn everything over to the Feds, that it was getting too dangerous for his little band of merry men. Phillips explained about the truck the Feds had lost and he really didn't trust anyone right now. He insisted that they stay on it, using the excuse that whoever took over would get the kid killed. He was sure they could handle it and when the dust cleared they would call in DHS and the Feds to take over.

"I don't think anyone knows where we are anyway," Phillips told his contact.

"Don't be so sure of that," was the reply he got.

"What are you talking about?" Philips asked.

"We got a call from the Feds. They got a call from someone telling them to call off the guys following the SUV. The person who took the call told them they didn't have anyone following anybody. They in turn told her to check with somebody higher up and see that the dogs were called off and if they didn't back off things could get real bad. Then they broke the connection. So our contact up there called us to let us know and pass it on to you if necessary."

"How long ago was this call made?" Phillips asked.

"They got the call about an hour ago and I got the info about fifteen minutes before your call."

Phillips bit back an angry reply and instead said, "Good, that means we have them worried or we're getting to close. I'll fill Chad in and don't worry, if we can't handle it I'll make the call."

"I hate to see those guys called in as much as you do, but one way or the other I know you'll take care of it. Watch yourself." The line went dead.

Before Phillips could put his phone down it chimed again. He answered, listened, asked no questions, confirmed he understood and put the phone down.

He filled Brock in on the warning phone call, then shook his head, "Where do they get these people? He should have called me before I called him."

"I believe you had the same sentiment a few days ago when Jazmin was in the hospital," Brock said.

"Well, if I survive this and before our fishing trip, some heads are going to roll in that department. If I lose my job over it no big deal, at least I'll be alive."

"Then you can open that private practice you've always wanted. You know, dealing with insurance paperwork and of course all that government medical coverage. Ahh, nothing more satisfying," Brock said sarcastically.

"No, no insurance, cash or credit card only and I'll make house calls. Seeing how a person lives can influence their illness and recovery," Phillips said.

"Well, before you hang out your shingle you have to survive this. So get Chad on the radio and give him the news, he and Sanchez might want to know when to duck," Brock said.

Chad took the news unflinchingly, "That's nice to know, nothing like the possibly of getting your head blown off when you least expect it."

Sanchez only sighed as he pulled his weapon from under the front seat and checked the chamber. "I wonder if aluminum foil hats would help."

"They won't deflect a bullet," Chad said.

"No, but then we would look like just a bunch of idiots playing spy games. You know a disguise of sorts," Sanchez laughed.

"That would look great, silver cone heads driving around the country," Chad chuckled.

"If you guys are finished with your comedy routine, I have more. I received a second call and I was asked to pass the plate information on to you. It seems the car was a rental and was rented by a Frank Smith from D.C. The phone number and address are bogus and it was paid for in cash," Phillips said.

"Can't say we're surprised," Chad replied. "And there will be no prints in the car since when the guy left that house he had on gloves and I bet he never took them off."

"I have more," Phillips said. "Those red dots we had the guys watching, well more have shown up. A few of them disappeared, probably from the bombs that went off, but they have been watching more come across the border. They had ten come across in Arizona, and six come across the Canadian border. Of those six three were in the northeast and three in the east. While I was getting this information five more dots popped up at JFK Airport and two at Dulles in D.C., all at different areas of the airports. They think it was at different arrival gates. They are going to stay on the airport signals and see where they go, they are especially worried about the D.C. signals. By the way, our signals from Ignacio and Jorge, I hate calling them that, are showing up back at that house. Maybe our mysterious Frank Smith was down here to remove them. Anyway, our guys in Atlanta are going over to find them, the signal is still inside so it should be easier to find than if they had thrown it out the back door."

"I guess they still haven't homed in on the signal track. They need to get on that," Chad said.

"They have Reed on it and if anyone can do it he can," Phillips said. "Once he gets a fix on it and after we get this cleaned up, they'll make a move on the site. The powers that be want to get to the top of the chain."

"Yeah and what are they going to do once they get there. There's too many ways out of that one," Chad said as his cell rang. "That's me, I'll get back to you."

Chad hit speaker on his phone, "You're on speaker, what ya got?"

"I only have a minute, but I got something from Yolanda that I thought you would want to know about," Pepas' voice came over the phone. "I had asked her if she ever overheard any of them talking about what their mission was and she said they always talked in a language she didn't understand, she said it was the same language most of the men at the camp in Mexico spoke."

"Wait," Chad said, "they spoke to her at the camp?"

"No one ever spoke to her except the people she was with, it was just what she heard while there. But that is not why I called, she told me that she thought an older man was in charge of things. When I pressed her on why she thought that, she said the men always called him the older. Wait, don't say it, I asked her if they called him 'the older' or just 'older'. She thought for a few moments and said it was just 'older' and it was usually the man Addison speaking," Pepa waited for her words to sink in.

"Well, that isn't enough proof for a court of law, but it's enough for me," Chad said. "That will probably cinch it for Phillips too."

"I've already pushed the information upstairs and they are going to work on getting something more definitive. She's a nice girl, but she's holding something back. I'll work on her some more and get all of it from her and I haven't heard what our Mexico contact has come up with on her. I need to go, just wanted to pass that on. Take care."

"That confirms two things," Sanchez said. "It was a training camp and it is Mr. Older."

Chad got Phillips on the radio and filled him in on what Pepa had said. "It's coming together, I don't know what it is but it's tying up."

"We need something harder than her word, I hope our people can come up with more. At least it's something," Phillips said.

Phillips turned down the radio and looked over at Brock, "You sure have been quiet. No opinions or input, you're off your game. What's wrong? Are you seeing something I'm not?"

"No and I have put in my two cents now and then."

"At the beginning of this you had a lot more to say and you were more amped," Phillips said.

"I'm doing as ordered, staying on the fringe. I'm just a hired gun doing pro bono work," Brock said.

"Aw, Jeez! Are you going to pout too?" Phillips said.

"I'm not pouting, I'm pissed. On the fringes, what a crock." Brock said through his teeth.

"You're not really on the fringe of this thing and you know it. This is your case as much as mine, maybe even more so. If it wasn't for you we probably wouldn't be this far," Phillips said.

"I know, it's just something I keep telling myself to keep the nerves down. It's been a while since I have been in this position," Brock said running his hand through his hair. "We're getting ready to walk into something big and people are going to die and with luck it will only be them. I don't know how many things like this you have taken part in, but this is probably the most dangerous one you will undertake. These aren't just bad guys, these are terrorists and they have no other agenda than to destroy or die trying. They want to do nothing but kill and cause mayhem. They will kill anyone for any reason, you, me, the kid, all of us and whatever they have in that truck will definitely do it. There are no rules of engagement here, for them or us. We're walking into this with no up armored vehicles, unless you consider Chads' SUV enough. We have to get rid of these guys and secure that truck with what we have available."

"Now that's the Brock I know and love," Phillips said.

"It's a scary thing to take on in the middle of a foreign desert, but worse on your home soil. I just want you to know that what you see once this thing starts, is a different me. The person you saw at the farm was me on the fringe, but when this goes down I'll be right in the thick of it, because you're going to need me. That is why Bracken told me to disappear if and when the Feds show up."

"So, you're coming up from the deep," Phillips said

"You bet your ass I am!" Brock half laughed.

71

For Phillips time was dragging by since all they could do was drive, but at the same time it was moving too fast to act. The closer they got to Charlotte the more he worried. From Charlotte it would only be slightly over six hours to D.C. and they wanted to secure Rogelio and the truck before they got into highly populated areas. He tried to put himself in the minds of these men, he didn't think they would stop at another motel, with the route they had taken it looked like they had a destination in mind and that worried him even more.

He shifted in the front seat and reached for this phone, "Kathy, I just want to give you our position and be sure you keep an open line for us."

"Already on it, Mr. Phillips. We've had an open line for you since last night, those were orders from Pepa," Kathy replied. "So just push the button and we'll have you."

"Thanks," Phillips said and put his phone down.

"I've been thinking about a money trail and we can't even start looking for that since we don't have a starting point. This thing has to be costing a lot of money," Phillips said.

"It could be funded directly from the Middle East, but you're right we do need a starting point and I don't think our pal in D.C. is taking it out of his personal account," Brock said. "The heavy weapons have been brought in, but they had to have bought the lighter weapons here. I'm thinking hand guns and some long guns, those can be bought off the street. We also don't know for sure where the explosives came from. Did they bring all those in or purchase them here?"

"I'm wondering if some of this stuff was carried across the border, Sanchez said he did find out that human mules were carrying something across." Phillips said. "I'm going to get someone started on finding out if our pal has an offshore account."

Phillips reached over to toggle the radio. "Wait on that," Brock quickly said, "we've got two white vans coming in behind us." He nodded at the rearview mirror, "Let's be sure they're legit."

Phillips waited and when they had passed Chads vehicle he toggled the radio.

"Did you catch that?" Phillips asked. "Do you think they're part of this?"

"Yeah and I saw them coming. They have paper plates, it makes them look they are headed to a buyer. Good cover," Chad said. "Heads up we've got more coming in behind you." He told Sanchez, "Slump down."

Sanchez slumped down in his seat so he could barely see over the dash and tried to pick up numbers on the plates. When the four vans cleared them, Sanchez sat up and wrote down a number. "I got the numbers and they're all the same number, but I got them."

Phillips came over the radio, "Just for drill, call it in. I don't think all those numbers should be the same."

Brock said, "Here come two more. We need to stay close to these vans, there's an exit for I-77 coming up."

"Okay," Chad came back, "pass me and keep them in sight until we know where they turn off. We'll stay with the target."

The two white vans passed Brock and before he could pull out behind them another van pulled out of traffic and into the fast lane. Brock shouted into the radio, "Sanchez, Get the plate number, it was a regular plate."

Chad watched Brock pass them then toggled the radio, "Sanchez called in the plates, we should hear something soon. He told them it was urgent."

"Roger that," Brock came back.

Brock followed the vans until they took an exit right before hitting Charlotte. As soon as all the vans had taken the exit, Phillips put his phone on speaker and called the tracking unit back at the active case facility. "I need to know where a line of nine white vans is headed. They just passed us the other side of Gastonia and turned onto I-77 toward Winston-Salem."

"We'll get them on satellite. Piece of cake," a voice came back.

"Why do you say that?" Phillips asked.

"Because the plate number that Chad just called in is the same plate as one of the vehicles you placed a tracking device on a few days ago. We lost it for a few days, must have been in a fortified garage of some sort, but we've got him now. Greg just gave Chad the same info," the voice informed him.

"Holy shit!" Phillips said.

"No kidding," the voice replied. "We're good. We'll call you when we get the info on that other plate number."

"Interesting that this other van should show up," Brock said. "I thought it was headed in the other direction or it could be the one we turned over to the Feds when it went into Louisiana. Which means they lost it. Is there some way you can check and see what happened to both of those?"

Phillips picked up his phone again as Brock toggled Chad, "Can you see us and how far behind the target are we?"

"I'm trying to catch up with you now and you're about a quarter mile behind the target," Chad said.

"I'm going as slow as I dare in this traffic and I don't want to pull over," Brock said.

"Just keep doing what you're doing and stay on I-85, our target is going through Charlotte and has not changed highways," Chad said.

"I just called in and checked on that last van that just went by us and it's the van we turned over to the Feds," Phillips said. "They lost it in New Orleans, they had two cars and CCTV looking for it, but it just disappeared."

"Well, if it went into a shielded garage, I can't fault the Feds. New Orleans can be a tough place to tail someone, even if you know where they're going," Chad said. "When they were ready all they had to do was jump on I-10 and then jump on Highway 65. Pretty easy drive to here."

"Where is that second van the guys were following?" Chad heard Brock ask.

"They have it headed to St. Louis, how that happened I'll never know, this whole thing is unpredictable," Phillips replied.

"That's just the way they want it," Chad interjected.

Phillips phone rang again, "Go," was all he said, then listened for a few minutes.

"We've had another explosion," he said when the call ended. "Bay Bridge in California. Two white vans were crossing the bridge when one stalled, the other one pulled up behind it, obviously traveling together. The drivers got out to check the stalled van when both of them blew, killed both drivers and put cars in the water and a lot of twisted metal on the bridge."

"So they're remotely detonating them," Brock said. "Another reason to be able to track the personal tracking devices."

"The bridge is listing and has a big hole in it. They must have stopped near one of those faulty pillars and took advantage of it," Phillips finished.

"Any idea on the loss of life?" Sanchez asked.

"All they gave me was the info on the drivers. We'll have to turn on the radio to get the ongoing news," Phillips said.

"Well, let's do it," Sanchez said smiling and rubbing his hands together. "I haven't had my news fix in days." He found the news station, sighed deeply and closed his eyes.

"I swear I have never seen anything like it." Chad laughed. "You're like a dog getting his belly scratched."

"Say what you will," Sanchez said, "at least you get to find out what is going on in the world, even when they get their facts back asswards."

They had tuned into the report as a reporter was interviewing a witness who had passed the stopped vans and had barely cleared the blast area when the vans were detonated. The witness was talking about the damage done to his car by flying debris and his voice was shaky. The reporter asked him what he remembered seeing, "I'll tell you what I told the police," the man said. "These two vans, panel vans, were in front of me about two cars ahead. The brake lights on the van in back came on and traffic stopped in my lane, now I didn't know it was two vans until I passed them, anyway the last I saw they had pushed the one van off to the side of the lane. The other driver pulled his van behind it, I guess they were traveling together, otherwise why would he stop. Man, when my wife sees this car she is not going to be happy, we have insurance, but I don't know if it will cover this. Anyway, I don't know how far I had gone when there was this huge whomp sound, the bridge shook, there was a blast of wind that pushed me forward a little and then all this stuff started coming down on the car. I knew it wasn't an earthquake because of the falling debris. I mean I'm on a bridge dude, what's to fall on me, the sky?"

Sanchez laughed, "Now where else can you hear that kind of stuff and live of all things. Ya gotta love it."

The news broadcaster went on to give the death toll at ten with an unknown amount missing and thirty-five injured. The police were attempting to clear the bridge of all people, but some would not leave their cars on the bridge unattended. The police were having difficulty assuring them that no one would be able to get near them but the authorities and that when possible they would all be towed. In the background a man could be heard yelling that the police couldn't be trusted either. They were speculating that one of the vans must have been carrying explosives and were calling it a horrible accident.

"Boy do they have a surprise coming," Brock said over the open radio.

"Sorry, I thought I had turned you off," Sanchez said.

"It's more fun listening to it this way, plus we don't have to mess with finding the station," Phillips added.

"The Feds and DHS are going to be very busy, I think this is just another one of many to come," Chad said.

"You're right and until they start taking us seriously and start tracking down those transmitters a lot of people are going to die," Brock said.

"Once the Feds get all the forensics on that explosion I think they'll take it seriously," Chad said. "Okay, I can see you now and I'll be passing you in less than five minutes. I'm turning the radio down."

Brock looked in the mirror, spotted Chad and as Chad passed them Sanchez gave them at little salute. Brock gave a little chuckle, "I think Sanchez proved is worthiness back there at that farm. That nine inch blade of his came in handy."

"When he said he had it, he really meant it," Phillips said as his phone chimed.

"What ya got?" Phillips sighed as he listened, "Shit, okay we're on it, thanks and keep us on your radar we are right behind Chad."

He didn't break the connection, but toggled the radio. When he heard Sanchez answer he said, "We got a problem. That van with the tracking system on it is behind us. Get off somewhere, but keep us going in the same direction and I'll explain the rest."

"Roger that, we have an exit coming up," Chad said.

Into the phone Phillips said, "Let me know if that van follows us."

Chad followed the exit off the highway and into a restaurant parking lot, drove down two parking lanes and as he pulled back onto the service road he asked, "What's going on?"

"Hell if I know, but I got a call that two of the vans turned around and came back this way. One of them being the missing van. I didn't like the idea of them being behind us," Phillips said. "We also got the information on that plate number that was on all those other vans. It's bogus."

"Follow me," Chad said and took a sharp right into a tire shop. He pulled right up to an empty bay, jump out and started talking to one of the mechanics. Then walked back to Brock's car.

"What, you have a tire problem?" Phillips asked.

"No, but I don't think it's a coincidence that we have those vans behind us, Chad said. "Either they have a device on one of us, they recognized one of our vehicles or they're just being extra cautious that we're not behind them. We're here so I can check under the vehicles."

Chad walked back over to his SUV, opened the back and pulled out a small black box. He had Sanchez pull the SUV into the garage, had the mechanic raise the rack, held up a device and started scanning the undercarriage. When he finished, Sanchez backed out of the bay. Chad then motion Brock to pull his car up.

"We're clean," Chad said after Brock pulled out of the bay. He turned, handed the mechanic a twenty, thanked him and got back in his car.

"Let's catch up with these guys, they really are pissing me off," Chad said over the radio.

Phillips got back on his phone, "Stay on those vans."

"We are and they didn't turn off, they're still ahead of you. The other seven vans are still being watched and they're on I-77," the voice came back. "If there is any change we'll notify you."

"Roger that," Phillips said.

"I'm thinking we should put the Feds or somebody on those vans," Brock said.

"What so they can lose them? Phillips replied. "I think if we can keep the satellite on them we should be okay for now."

"Keep your guys watching them and call the Feds anyway. You need to cover your ass and the public," Brock said.

"We really don't know what's in those vans and I sure don't want to make a mistake," Phillips said.

"Do it anyway, this is not the time to have doubts," Brock prodded.

Before Phillips could make the call the radio came on, "Hey," Chad said. "Call and have the guys track our target. I want to try and get off their radar, just in case."

"No, I want to try and keep them in site," Phillips said.

"Listen to me Jake," Chad insisted. "If they think or know we are following them, they can kill the kid right there in that car, dump the body where we'll be sure to see it. They're close enough to D.C., if that's their target, that while we are standing over a body they get the job done. With us using the GPS and the guys tracking the van, we won't lose them. I thought we were trying to save Rogelio's life. If they know we're here and we back off maybe they'll think that threat they called in worked and they'll drop their guard."

"They need him, they won't kill him," Phillips said in a low voice.

"I don't hear much conviction in that statement," Chad said.

"I'm not here to take sides," Brock said, "but Chads' right, they don't really need him anymore. We're now less than six hours from D.C and there are a lot of possible targets between here and there. I'm just saying, if they don't have the kid to assure a hit on their original destination they can pick another one." Brock paused and glanced over at Phillips, "Make the call Jake and have them notify the Feds and watch both sets of vehicles. Tell them what we're doing and why. Actually, have them plug in the other transponder to Chads' GPS and we'll have two sets of eyes on them"

"Okay Chad, we'll do it your way," Phillips said and turned down the radio. He made the call and tried to relax.

"Don't worry," Brock said, "we'll get them."

72

Brock ran everything through his head, he wanted to be sure he had covered everything. While Phillips was watching Chad scan their vehicles, he had made a quick call to Bracken to update him. In turn Bracken had updated Brock.

Bracken had his best investigators and his men on the inside, check on the Director of the FBI to insure that he was not compromised by the ongoing events. When the Director had been cleared, Bracken invited him to dinner explaining that he had some sensitive information he wanted to turn over. They arranged to have dinner at Brackens' home and when the Director arrived Bracken checked his arms for the scar and explained why. Over dinner Bracken told the Director what had been uncovered and the names of those in the government who were suspected of being involved.

"I didn't give him any of your names and he understood why I wanted to keep it to myself," Bracken said. "I also told him that only a select few of my people knew what was happening and asked him not to interfere with what was going on in the field until they got a call. He told me was going to start his own covert investigation in his offices as well as looking into other areas. Before he left I handed him a thumb drive with a time line of the events and the information we had. With him working his end and Philips on the operational end, I think we have it covered. Philips boss was apprised of what I was doing and in the long run agreed that it should be done. Now, I'm asking you not to say anything to Phillips about any of this, he needs to work it his way. I don't want him to think someone is watching over his shoulder."

Brock agreed and asked, "Does the Director know you have someone on this?"

"No, I told him the information came from an independent team. He knew who I was talking about and was aware that something was going on, just not exactly what it was. We also discussed the truck that had been followed and lost by his people and the explosions across the country. I'm going to keep him up to date whenever I have something," Bracken replied.

"What was his reaction?" Brock asked.

"I would say surprised. I really don't think he was aware of how bad it is," Bracken said. "I think that since they have been spoon fed the information they haven't put it together yet, if anyone has, they haven't informed him."

"They may have been spoon fed, but it was in big bites. Someone is holding out on him," Brock said.

"I believe that is why he is starting an investigation, but I don't want to assume anything," Bracken said. "I'm going to have my men keep an eye on things over there, but from a distance. I don't want them blown."

Brock wanted to tell Phillips about the call, but knew he should wait until later, when he had to tell him. He started to go over the conversation again when he heard the radio beep.

Phillips turned the volume up, "What's up?"

"Our little caravan has stopped," Chad said. "I'm going to try and get closer, but I don't want to be seen so keep your eyes open, they might try to flank us again."

They drove northeast of Greensboro toward Raleigh following the GSP signature. Before reaching Raleigh they turned north, took the service road and slowly neared an area of dense trees and underbrush. The GSP showed they were within a quarter mile of the van, truck and SUV. They came to a road on the right, on the corner was a large sign that read, For Sale or Lease, Office and Warehouse. The sign was old and weather worn, parts of it pocked with bullet holes.

Chad eased around the corner and proceeded slowly down the road. As soon as Chad saw the open gate through the trees, he stopped and toggled the radio again, "We don't want to go in any further with the vehicles. Let's back out and we'll go in on foot."

They went back to the main road and found a deep, accessible grove of trees and bushes. They backed the cars in and pulled brush over the front of the lead car.

Chad opened the back of the SUV, called the tracking unit and requested a satellite image of the surrounding area, then turned on the laptop. Phillips and Brock joined him at the rear door. Sanchez was pulling things out of a duffle bag in the rear seat.

"I want to get an idea of what we are walking into, then we need to find out how many of those vans came in here," Chad said. "Let's gear up like we're not coming back, I want to try and end this here. Brock, I want you to secure your issued weapon and use one of ours. We want plausible deniability for you and we can't if your ballistics match up."

The computer signaled that the map was up, Chad reach over and zoomed in in the area. "This isn't much help, it only shows three buildings. It looks like an office, what appears to be the warehouse and another small building in the rear. This must have been a pass over before these guys arrived and I'm not waiting for another fly over. We'll just go in and see for ourselves."

After securing their gear they skirted the road and neared the gate. Before them sprawled the vast parking lot and vacant buildings. Staying low and using the dense brush for cover they moved left down the perimeter of the fence until they found where a large section of the fence had collapsed. The far end of the collapsed section was on the blind side of the buildings. The front building looked like the office, the windows and doors were boarded up and had not been disturbed. The entire area around the buildings was concrete, no landscaping unless you considered the weeds growing through the cracks. Bottles, cans and paper littered the edges of the fence and buildings. Behind the office they could see the top of the warehouse and its rows of windows.

Brock spoke into his mic, "This looks familiar, same layout as an operation in Iraq. Let's get up next to that office."

They moved two at a time across the cracked concrete and flatten themselves against the block wall of the office. Chad used his Cornershot to look between the office and warehouse. He watched for some time then pulled back.

"Our big truck driver and Wafiq were standing out there," Chad said. They heard a car leave and Chad continued, "Wafiq gave him a large envelope and they shook hands before the big guy got into that car that just left."

"Well, at least we won't have to deal with him," Sanchez said, "but we need to get a look in that warehouse."

Chad peeked around the corner again and signaled them to run for the side of the warehouse. When they were clear, Chad followed. They kept a foot away from the sides of the building and eased to the corner where Chad again took point and looked around the corner.

Sanchez covered the rear and the corner behind them, if anyone walked around that corner all they would find was the end of his knife. He turned to look back at the others and scanned the back of the building, when he looked up he noticed a ladder that went up to a catwalk.

"Hey, look," Sanchez said into his mic. When they turned around he pointed up and walked back so he was positioned under it.

"Wonder why it's so high up, it must be seven feet off the ground," Phillips said.

Sanchez was busy examining the wall and the ground under the ladder. He moved a few feet left of the ladder and looked around, knelt on the ground and pulled up a handful of weeds then examined the ground under them. He stood and ran his hand over the wall behind Brock then back to the section nearest the ladder.

"I think there was a loading dock here. The cinder blocks are a bit uneven and a couple of them were broken to fit the space and if you look at the weed pattern it's almost a straight line with right angles coming back to the wall. Plus the weeds are growing through rotten wood. If there was a dock here then the ladder would have to be that high. I'm going up."

Sanchez reached up but his fingers were just shy of reaching the bottom rung. Brock laced his fingers together and boosted Sanchez high enough to get a good purchase on the rungs. He tested the ladder, it was stable so he started to climb. When he reached the catwalk he reach out and gave it a tug, it too was stable. He crawled onto the walkway and stayed low to avoid the windows, they were covered with a gritty film, but would show shadows. He made his way to the door and stood to check the hinges, took a small canister out of his pocket and sprayed them.

"What's he spraying them with?" Brock asked.

"A graphite spray. It works quickly and penetrates without having to move the hinge," Chad answered.

"Good. While he's up there I'm going over to the back of that other building. I think I can get a good look at the garage doors and maybe get an idea of what we have in there," Brock said. "Cover me and I'll give you a call when I'm coming back."

Brock took a peek around the corner, then made the run across the thirty-five feet of open concrete to the back of the next building. The building was one story with high windows and one back door, Brock checked the door, locked. He watched the ground for broken glass or any object that would give his position away as he also kept an eye on the opposite corner of the building. He reached the far corner and took a quick look, it was clear so he eased around the corner and out of site.

The far side of the building was the same as the back, but there was no side door. He looked through one of the dirty windows. "I'm okay so far" Brock said into his mic. "This looks like a mechanic or machine shop. There's some big racks in there and what looks like oil stains on the floor. Hard to tell through these windows. I'm moving forward."

"Roger," Chad said.

Brock stayed under the windows and watched for any shadow he might cast. Five feet from the front corner he pulled a small pair of binoculars from his front pocket and got flat of the ground. He crawled to the corner, held his pistol across his chest and leaned out to get a good look. By keeping on the ground he wouldn't be spotted quickly. No one would be looking for someone that low, most people look for things at chest level, three feet and lower is unexpected.

He stayed still letting his eyes adjust to the distance and the shadows beyond the bay doors. "I've got one van outside, left of the doors," Brock whispered. "I can make out another van inside as well as the SUV. I can't see the interior, the vehicles are blocking my view so I can't see the truck. The van doors are open and one guy just threw his cigarette out the bay door. There is probably a small office in there. If so, then they could be using it. Over."

"Roger that," Chad came back. "Do you want to sit tight and see what else you can pick out? Over."

"Yeah," Brock said. "The longer I'm here the clearer it gets. I'll give it five more, then I'll start back. Over"

Brock saw someone move to the side of the van and remove a grocery bag and a jug of water. As the man moved back into the interior another man passed him and came out the open bay door, it was Jorge/Nasir. Brock stayed perfectly still and then he heard it, the sound of another vehicle approaching.

As Nasir turned in the direction of the oncoming vehicle, Brock pulled back behind the corner. "We have company,"

73

Brock watched the left side of the building as a black sedan turned the corner, pulled passed the bay doors and blocked the space between the warehouse and the third building. Two men, one wore a jacket and both looking uncomfortable in jeans, got out of the car and walked back to the doors where Wafiq had joined Nasir. Brock could still hear an oncoming vehicle as he passed the information to Chad and suggested that one of them get the plate number on the sedan.

Phillips voice came over his ear piece, "I'm coming to you and Chad is going up with Sanchez. He doesn't like being in the open."

"Make it quick, another vehicle is coming," Brock said.

A small box truck pulled around the corner of the warehouse as Phillips said, "I'm in back, coming around."

"We have a second box truck," Brock said.

"Roger that," Chad came back. "We're trying the door."

The box truck pulled up next to the van, two men exited the cab and walked toward Wafiq. From the physical greeting that was given, Brock figured them for old friends.

Phillips crawled up next to Brock as he relayed the info to Chad. Brock pulled back and looked at Phillips. "The odds just keep increasing," he said then covered the mic with his hand, Phillips did the same. "I hope Sanchez is a good shot," Brock said quietly to Phillips. "I think this is going to get ugly."

"I wish we had better cover, so I could see what's going on out there," Phillips said. "Two pairs of eyes are better." He looked to his left toward the fence. "The ground slopes down before it reaches the fence, I'm going to back up and take a look."

Phillips eased his way toward the fence and down the slope. Before he got even with Brock he drop down and belly crawled forward until he could see the bay doors. There was a small pile of broken concrete near the top of the incline. He slowly scooped debris and leaves and pushed them up in front of him. He carefully pushed them around the concrete to give him more cover. He left a small cleft in the pile so he would have a clear view of their target.

"Okay, I'm in position for now," Phillips said, "and I have a straight view into the warehouse."

"Roger," came a reply from Chad. "We made it through the door and are on the inside catwalk. Everyone was too busy with the new arrivals to notice us. It's fairly dark in here, once our eyes adjust we're going to see if we can spot the kid. We have one white van on either side of the doors, the big box truck is parked at an angle next to the van on your right. The office is on our left, your right, in the far corner, can't see inside. Big place, we'll take the long shots from up here and it looks like we have two vans parked on your left, not one. Repeat, two vans on your left. Opposite end has a people access door. Over,"

"Good luck," Phillips said. "Oh shit, we've got a sheriffs car coming around the corner."

"Probably noticed all the activity and that means he has cause. In turn that means the locals are aware." Chad said. "These guys won't let him leave. This is going to be a cluster fuck." Chad covered his mic and looked at Sanchez, "Things may get hot in a hurry. Use your side arm only when necessary, you'll be more accurate with the scope. If conditions put us in close gun play, I want you to think of your weapon as part of your hand, as if you were throwing a punch. Only instead of a fist it's a bullet and instead of throwing a punch, you pull the trigger. If you find yourself in the open, isolated and outnumbered, just start firing at them. The first shot can be anywhere on their body, the second shot is the kill shot. Once you start firing first you have the upper hand. Right now we'll have the added problem of not knowing the positions of Brock and Phillips once they get inside. When this starts Wafiq or Nasir is going to go for the kid. Oh, and stay near my six as much as possible when we get below."

Into his mic Chad said, "We're going to try and pick them off from up here if possible, so drive them our way if they make a move on the officer."

"Roger," said Phillips. "Brock is watching them through the binocs. There is quite a conversation going on out there."

"I think the cop asked for ID's," Brock said. "The two guys from the car handed theirs over, but no one else has made a move to comply. The driver from the truck is turning his over now, but Wafiq and Nasir are walking back inside. The cop just took a few steps to follow them, but one of the guys from the car said something to him."

Brock and Phillips watched as the deputy turned back to face the man who had spoken to him. As they watched, the man in the jacket pulled a gun and fired. At the same time the deputy hit the ground Phillips fired and put down the man in the jacket.

"Cop down, one bad guy down," Brock said.

"We're in it now, drive them our way," Chad replied.

The men standing outside were confused as to the direction of the second shot, but they all had guns drawn. They started backing toward the bay doors as Phillips fired again and hit one of the guys from the second truck. The driver of the car ran and took cover between the car and the warehouse, the rest of the men moved into the warehouse.

Brock and Phillips quickly moved to the back of the building they were using for cover, Brock dropped to a crouch and eased down the side near the sedan. He moved to the front of the car, stood and called out to the man hiding beside it then ducked down. The man stood and fired in the direction of Brocks voice. Phillips fired from the corner of the building, over Brock and watched the man fall. Brock moved around the side of the car, checked the body and gave Phillips the thumbs up before moving down the wall toward the doors. They could hear gunfire from inside the warehouse.

"Another one down out here, we're coming in," Brock said.

"Wait," they heard Sanchez say. "Let me clear the doors."

Sanchez moved left down the interior catwalk with the M16 to get a better line of sight on the doors, as a bullet hit the wall behind him. There were two guys behind a van, one of them brought a gun up to fire again. Sanchez fired first, wounding one and driving them further to the interior. He caught movement at the opposite end of the building and fired as the small door opened.

"Go," Sanchez said and watched as Brock and Phillips edged into the warehouse. "The small door at the front end, somebody opened it. Couldn't see who it was or if they got out."

"Roger," came three replies.

Brock and Phillips moved inside the warehouse doors on opposite sides using the vans parked on either side for cover. They cautiously cleared the interior of the vans and started moving forward.

Chads voice came over the ear piece, "Four stay where you are, keep them inside. Don't let anyone near that box truck."

"Roger," Sanchez said. He kept his eyes moving, sweeping the area below him for signs of movement. As he watched a man in a white t-shirt moved to the back of the truck on his right. He pulled his sidearm and fired twice, head and chest.

Sanchez caught movement and saw a man move to the small front door. Chad took the shot and the man was thrown forward into the wall, as he bounced back he grabbed a tool trolley and it rolled with his body and both blocked the door way.

"We should be down to three," Phillips voice came over the earpiece. "Anyone have eyes on the kid?"

"Negative," came the replies.

"We're on our way down," Chad said.

There was a slight shuffle behind the van on Brocks right, he and Phillips turned at the same time. Brock fired first. While Phillips covered him he walked over and found the guy still alive, but his collar bone had shattered and the hole in him would take more than a few stitches. Phillips threw him handcuffs and Brock cuffed him to the bay door rail.

"If these guys are going to take on a project like his they need to put on more weight. Hell, the bullet was bigger than that little guy," Brock said.

They all heard a door open. Chad and Sanchez sighted on the office door and watched as it opened wider. Brock and Phillips dropped into a crouch and looked in the direction of the office.

"Office door," Chad confirmed. Brock and Phillips moved to the back corner behind a van and near the office. Sanchez moved closer to Chad behind the box truck. Chad motioned him to go around to the other side of the white van and help cover Phillips.

"Do not shoot, I have to boy. Stand where I can see you, both of you," the voice echoed in the quiet.

"Come out," Phillips said as he and Brock moved from behind the van. "We won't shoot, we want to see the boy."

"There will be no negotiations. I will walk out of here with the boy, we will get into the car and drive away," the voice stepped from the office with Rogelio in front of him. It was Nasir aka Jorge.

"We'll let you leave, but the boy stays here," Phillips said.

Nasir pushed Rogelio in front of him as they left the office, keeping his hand on the back of Rogelio's neck. He pulled Rogelio as he moved to the SUV.

Phillips took a step forward. Nasir stopped, smiled and put the gun to Rogelio's head. With his left hand he reached into his pocket, "If you come any closer," he held up his left hand, "I will push this button and we will all die and this building will be nothing but rubble."

Rogelio moved slightly to the left of Nasir and stood staring at Phillips. He slowly moved his right arm and a small smile appeared on his face. Before Phillips or anyone could move Rogelio was a blur of movement as he plunged the knife into the upper thigh of his captor. Blood immediately shot out of the wound as Nasir screamed and grabbed his leg, but he did not let go of the phone in his hand.

He cursed and screamed at Rogelio, then he pushed the button. Nothing happened. He continued to push the button and curse until Phillips reached down and wrenched the phone from his hand. The gun Nasir had carried was on the floor behind Rogelio, Brock went over and secured it.

Rogelio stood over Nasir and smiled at him. Then in perfect English he said, "Not only is your Spanish the worse I have ever heard, but you are very stupid."

Rogelio took off the jacket and turned the inside so Nasir could see it. The lining had been cut and Rogelio ripped the rest of it free. The lining now hung from the jacket showing that each connecting wire had been cut. Rogelio took the other cell phone out of its pocket and turned it around so it could be clearly seen, the back of the cell phone was gone, as well as the sim card and battery.

"As they would say in the movies, you had no back-up. You should have checked your work every day. Now you are going to die because your God forgot to give you a brain." Rogelio turned and walked away.

Chad and Sanchez were walking passed the van and Sanchez stepped into Rogelio's path. Rogelio looked up at him, wrapped his arms around Sanchez and very quietly thanked him before he passed out.

Phillips got down on the floor next to Nasir and grabbed him by the front of his shirt, "Nasir al-Attar taken down by a seven year old, they will tell stories about you and laugh. Unfortunately your wound is not life threatening."

Nasir looked at him and laughed, "You think you have beaten us. I am but one, there are more to come and you will die. Your country will be in pieces when we are through and I will die a martyr."

Over his ear piece Phillips heard Chad's voice, "We've cleared the vehicles and bodies, but no Wafiq."

"Where is Wafiq?" Phillips said.

"He is gone," Nasir said. "You will not find him, we will both be martyrs."

"No you won't," said Phillips. "No virgins for you."

Phillips reached into his pocket and pulled out a plastic baggie. He opened it and smeared it all over Nasir's mouth. Nasir licked his lips, "This is sweet. Why you are giving me candy?"

"No," said Phillips. He smiled down at Nasir, "Not candy that is bacon grease from my breakfast. I don't believe they give virgins to those who have been tainted with pork." Phillips twisted the front of the shirt tighter as panic crossed Nasir's face, "You see you crossed some lines. First you kidnapped a child, then you illegally crossed the border," Phillips got right in Nasir's face, tightened his grip on the shirt and said in a low voice through clinched teeth, "But the biggest line you crossed was when you tried to fuck with my country." As he was saying this he slowly reached down and placed his gun over Nasir's heart and pulled the trigger.

Brock walked over to Phillips, whipped down Nasir's gun, pressed the dead man's hand around it and let it fall to the ground.

"Good thing you shot him," Brock said, "he was going to kill one of us with that thing."

Chad walked up, putting his phone back in his pocket, "Cleanup is on the way. The deputy is unconscious, but will make it from what I can tell. It needs to be called it in after our crew gets here. At least we have a matched to that photo of Nasir. Nice scar, bet that hurt. Brock you need to get the hell away from here, the Feds are on their way too. They said they will handle the locals. Keep the gun, you may need it if Wafiq is out there."

Brock took his phone out and snapped a picture of Nasir. "I need to send this to my contact. I'll let him know we'll send fingerprint confirmation later. This will make his day."

Sanchez carried the still unconscious Rogelio as they left the warehouse. On the way out they passed the wounded man cuffed to the door rail. Phillips checked him and found he was still breathing, they walked outside. Phillips went to the deputy, still on the ground in front of the second truck.

Phillips stood up, "Either that guy was a bad shot or they didn't shoot to kill, because I don't know how that guy could've missed at almost point blank range. It's a shoulder wound, but I think the deputy must have cracked his head on the concrete when he fell. It's a through and through and I need something to stop the bleeding."

Phillips found a shirt in the back of the sedan, checked the front pocket and then used it on the deputy. As he finished, the cleanup team pulled around the corner. Brock patted Phillips on the back and disappeared around the back of the warehouse.

"You got here fast," Chad said to the lead tech.

"Yeah, they were watching. When the beacon stopped and you asked for the image they knew. So they moved us closer," the tech said.

"Before anyone else gets here, you need to remove and replace a body near the office in there. It's a contact wound and we need to keep the body for a while," Chad said. "The deputy here needs to get to the hospital. Okay, we'll leave you to it."

Another sedan, white this time, pulled around the corner and the woman in it got out. "I'm Emma and I understand you have a package for me."

74

Phillips took Rogelio from Sanchez and turned to Emma, "I need some time with him. I want to check him over and explain things to him. He doesn't need any more trauma right now."

Rogelio stirred in his arms and opened his eyes, "I thought I was dreaming, but you really are here. Thank you, I knew you would come," he said as he threw his arms around Phillips neck.

Phillips walked to the back of Emma's car and opened the back door, "I need to talk to you and be sure you're alright. Do you have any injuries?" he asked as Rogelio climbed into the car.

"No, I'm fine. They didn't hit me or anything like that. Where is Yolanda, is she okay?" Rogelio asked. "The lady from the bus they killed her, I should never have spoken to her."

"Yolanda's just fine," Phillips said. "We found the lady from the bus, they didn't kill her. Her actions probably saved her life. She's still in the hospital, but she's going to be okay and she was very worried about you. Rogelio, I have to ask you a few questions, but first I want to tell you that the lady out there, Emma, is going to take you to see your parents. They are in Florida staying with a friend of mine, Yolanda is there too. You and Emma are going to fly there in a private plane and she'll take good care of you and keep you safe."

"The first thing I need to know is where did you get the knife?" Phillips asked.

"You don't have to call me Rogelio, I am really Roger. Rogelio is what they call me at home, it's Spanish for Roger. I found the knife under the television thing in the motel. It was just a steak knife, but I sharpened it. Most of the places we stayed had metal pipes under the sink and I rubbed the blade on them. Then the mean girl that was with us was using a stone on her knife and I saw how sharp it was. I saw her drop the stone in one of the motel rooms near the bed, she didn't know she had dropped it, so when they left me alone a grabbed it. I was surprised she didn't see it because nothing goes very far under those beds. It was a good thing I kept it because the rest of the places we stayed had plastic pipes. I kept the knife in my shoe next to my ankle. In there, in the office, I took it out and put it in my pants."

"How did you know what to do to that jacket? You could have killed yourself," Phillips said.

"I watch a lot of television and movies. I thought if I took the phone apart and cut all of those wires it wouldn't work anymore. I knew it was the only choice I had. They were going to kill me anyway, so if I accidentally it blew up they would die too. I had nothing to lose. When I started to cut the wires I noticed that one of them was no longer connected so I checked the others ones and found one more. Luck for me he wasn't paying attention to what he was doing, they were busy laughing and talking. Is the man called Jorge dead? I wanted him to die, he was a very evil man. The one who pretended to be my brother wasn't so bad, he protected me, but they were all mean to Yolanda," Rogelio said.

"Yes," said Phillips, "he's dead, but you didn't kill him. You, my young friend are very smart and inventive. I'm proud to know you." Phillips ruffled Rogelio's hair and laughed. "When you get to Florida my friend will have a lot of questions for you, she will need to know everything that you saw or heard. While you're there you and your mother will have a beautiful garden to enjoy. Now, I want you to meet Emma and go get on that plane. I will see you in a few days."

"Do you promise?" Rogelio asked.

"I promise," Phillips replied.

Phillips started to get out of the car, "Wait," said Rogelio. "The other men, the ones from the border that helped you. Will you tell them thank you, that I owe them much and will never forget."

"I'll tell them," Phillips said.

Phillips rejoined Chad and Sanchez. "Our team is almost finished. I told them they needed to hurry and that the body was my main concern," Chad said.

A man in a white jumpsuit joined them. Handed them each a blue cloth and asked them to clean the palms of their hand and put each cloth in a separate plastic bag.

"Don't want you guys walking around with gun residue and blood on your hands. We have what we need so we're out of here." He collected the bags and walked away.

The three tech team vehicles drove passed the four incoming FBI vehicles as they left.

"That was cutting it close," Phillips said. "I wouldn't want to have to explain a body in the back of one of our vehicles."

Phillips, Chad and Sanchez walked over to the FBI team as they exited their vehicles and Phillips spoke to the head of the FBI team. His men got busy taking photos of all the vehicles, dusting for prints and attempting to take an inventory. The man handcuffed to the bay door was going to be moved to a secure medical facility.

"When you get a statement from the kid, I would like a copy of it," the Agent said. "I hope your people didn't take away too much of my evidence."

"You will get his statement, plus a statement of another hostage they were holding and the woman they shot in west Texas," Phillips said. "As far as evidence, our people only come in to take their own photos, check us out and remove any weapons we used. You'll get a report from them too."

"I take it you will be available if I have any questions after your debriefing," the Agent said.

"Of course," Phillips answered.

They left the FBI team, rounded the corner of the building and started walking back to their hidden SUV. They waved as Emma and Rogelio passed them on the road and breathed a collective sigh of relief. They continued walking in silence.

"I hope the Feds don't realize that a body is missing," Sanchez finally broke the silence.

"I don't think they will, this isn't the first time we've done this and probably won't be the last," Phillips replied. "Anyway some of those bodies were moved when we searched them and of course the one was moved so we could cuff him."

"You know this isn't over," Chad said.

"Yeah, but at least we have the kid back," was Phillips reply.

"The family is going to have to go into hiding for a while. Maybe we can relocate them here in the States until the heat is off. I'm afraid these guys may retaliate," Chad said. "We also need to find Wafiq, it didn't take him long to disappear."

"Plus," Phillips said, "We need to help Sanchez clear up the mess in Mexico."

"I've been thinking about that," Sanchez said. "I think me and the boys can take care of that ourselves. I've got a few ideas I'll run by them and we'll pick one. No sense in you guys getting involved. If we find we can't handle it, I'll give you a call."

"Talk to Ray before you go home, he may have some ideas for you," Chad said.

"As long as you're sure you don't need us, then I'm fine with it. It might get messy dealing with those guys after what we've seen here," Phillips said.

All three men stopped in their tracks in the middle of the road. "Shit!" Chad yelled.

They all turned and started running back to the warehouse. A containment truck was heading straight for them.

Phillips yelled, "You guys keep going, just go, go!" He flagged down the truck with his ID in his hand. Out of breath and talking as fast as could and still make sense, he said to the driver. "Radio, do you have a radio?"

"Yeah, why?" the driver said.

"Call the warehouse, get them all out of the warehouse now. Hurry," Phillips said.

The guy in the passenger seat handed the driver the radio. When someone answered the radio he delivered the message, but the guy on the other end was hesitating. Phillips yelled toward the radio, "Remote detonation. Get them out, hurry."

Phillips heard the guy on the other end yelling for everyone to clear the area. He looked at the driver, "I hope they run far enough away. What are you hauling away?"

"We've got those two big metal containers," the driver said.

Phillips gave a sigh of relief, "Go, get away from here, hurry and keep your side arms handy."

He stepped off the drivers step and started for the warehouse again. Chad, Sanchez and six guys were running toward him, he stopped and waited for them. As he watched the ground behind them erupt.

Later Phillips tried to recall what he saw first, but there was no first. It was an ear splitting blast followed by debris, fire, smoke, all shooting into the sky, the ground moving beneath his feet. He felt himself falling and watched as the men running toward him were thrown off their feet and forward. Then the debris started to fall. Chunks of concrete blocks, tires, metal and he was sure there were seared body parts. All they could do was cover their heads and pray the main debris field would stay behind them.

When it seemed clear Phillips sat up, then started walking toward the scattered men. They were all moving and checking themselves for injuries, they all had scrapes and cuts, but nothing was broken. Sanchez had a cut on the side of his head that was bleeding and he was dazed. Phillips suggested they to get to the side of the road and get off their feet, that their equilibrium was going to be off and walking around was not a good idea. No one would listen, they wanted to get back and see the damage.

They worked their way through the debris back to where the warehouse complex once stood. There were a few small fires and the concrete dust had dissipated in the breeze. There was a good sized crater filled with concrete and smoldering debris. The FBI vehicles had been tossed onto their sides or flipped over, the one that had been parked nearest the warehouse doors was no longer visible

"Well, at least this tells us there was no bomb aboard any of those vans or trucks. This looks like an ammo dump exploded," Chad said.

They could hear sirens in the distance as the lead FBI agent looked around, "This is going to take a bigger crew to go through this than what I have here and I'm going to need two more cars."

The fire department and emergency vehicles turned the corner and headed toward them.

"This is going to be fun to explain," Sanchez said.

"I got it," the FBI Agent said as the lead emergency vehicle stopped next to him. He flashed his badge, spoke one sentence, turned around and shrugged his shoulders.

"Okay, why doesn't one of you tell me how you knew there was going to be an explosion," the Agent said.

"We didn't know for sure," Phillips said. He then proceeded to go over the recent explosions, the tracking chips and anything else he felt would clear things up. "At least those two metal containers were removed before the explosion. If what we think was in there had gone up, we wouldn't be standing here. I hope the photos you took weren't damaged, you're going to need them." Everyone looked over to a guy examining his camera.

Forty-five minutes later Chad, Phillips and Sanchez walked into a diner and found Brock drinking iced tea and writing in a note book. "I hear there was an explosion in your area, something about an old warehouse complex. I was twenty minutes away when I thought about those remote detonations. I knew you'd figure it out."

They took turns telling him about the explosion, Rogelio and how slow they all felt not remembering the other detonations sooner. They ate and discussed the events that might be coming down the road while the ends of case were tied together and about possible prosecutions and cover-ups.

Brock looked at Phillips, "Was that really bacon grease you put in Nasir's mouth and where did you get it?"

"Now where would I get bacon grease?" Phillips laughed. "That was a couple of those syrup packets from the motel with salt added to them. I figured if I had a chance I would use it. Hell, he wasn't going to know what bacon grease tasted like. I just had to be sure he believed me."

Phillips looked over at Sanchez, "You're going to go with us and be debriefed then we'll fly you home with a fat check in your pocket. Brock will go with us too and a report will be sent to Bracken."

"Where are we going to be debriefed?" Sanchez asked.

"If I tell you that, I'll have to kill you," Phillips said, then burst out laughing. "We're going to find a hotel in Raleigh, I'll call our people and they'll come to us." Phillips started laughing again, "You should have seen the expression on your face. Goes to show you how tired we are. I do bad jokes and you believe them. I'm really going to miss you."

75

In the four months that had passed since the explosion that almost caused an FBI team to lose their lives, nothing had happened. There had been no progress to bring those responsible or those implicated, to justice. The President, in his true fashion, gave a speech which poked fun at the charges against government officials. The Attorney General gave a statement denying that he or his office had anything to do with the recent events, but they would do their utmost to find the guilty parties. Senators and Congressman took turns both condemning the charges and demanding answers. One side ridiculed the charges and the other side wanted a congressional committee to investigate. The public knew this was politics as usual and nothing would ever come of the investigation and no one would be held responsible.

The man known as Mr. Addison, had disappeared. He was last seen by neighbors, putting a suitcase in the back of his car. The search of security tapes at airports and other venues showed no trace of him. When asked, the AG's Office said that he was on extended leave for personal reason.

Most of the evidence had been destroyed in the explosion and the ensuing fire. The photos and the two metal cargo crates were not enough to bring charges against anyone and those who had been in possession of the crates had been blown to pieces. The finger prints on the containers had belonged to the men in Port Mansfield who had unloaded them. The one man who survived was a Mexican National who spoke little English, had only been hired as a driver and bore no scar indicating he had a chip implanted. He had explained how a solid wall was between the cab and the rear of the van. The van doors were locked and he had no key for them. The men who hired him were paying him good money, so he asked no questions.

The contents of the two metal crates were not made public, but teams were taking everything apart. Their job was to disable them and discover where they had been put together. Everything and everyone had been moved to an underground facility, but no one was saying where. This move in itself was a good indication of how lethal the contents were.

Within eight hours of the explosion all of the red lights indicating the personal tracking chips had winked out. The techs monitoring the lights said they were there and then they were gone. At first they thought something had gone wrong with the computers, but then they realized it wasn't the computers. It was if someone had flipped a switch, they simple disappeared.

Law enforcement across the country was notified about the white vans, but the consensus was that you couldn't stop and check every white van. It turned out that is wasn't necessary. Abandoned vans started turning up in parks and parking lots. Forensic teams were called in and most of them showed traces of explosives or ammunition. Even small splinters from crates had been retrieved and in one vehicle a torn piece of an inventory list had been found. As reported by the injured driver, there was a wall between the cab and the back of the vans. Of the seventeen abandoned vans, only two had been cleared as not being suspect vehicles. The question on official minds was where the contents were and what exactly was missing?

The reunion of Rogelio with his parents brought tears to the eyes of everyone present. Yolanda waited a few hours before she came forward to greet him, she wanted him to have time with only his parents. She had a bandage on her upper arm where they had removed the tracking chip and worried about him questioning it, so she chose clothing that would cover it. When they did reunite he was surprised by what he saw. He commented on the fact that her bruises were going away and she was clean, she laughed, but he could see something in her eyes that he was sure showed in his eyes as well. It wasn't fear, it was a wariness, an acute sense of being hunted.

Pepa had taken her time debriefing him and with the help of his mother the process went smoothly. There were times during the interview when Pepa noticed a change in him, his eyes would darken or become vacant and he would become hesitant to speak. His mother noticed it too. Pepa suggested that with time it should pass, if not, counseling might be necessary. Rogelio knew he had changed and he doubted he would ever be the same. He would have to watch what he talked about and try to hide the hate that he felt for the man who stole his brother and his brothers' name.

Rogelio and his family would be temporarily relocated, but Yolanda wouldn't be going home until they could clear her background. There were questions about her that had not been answered and until they were she was basically under house arrest.

After being debriefed, Sanchez flew home and Brock drove to D.C. to meet with Bracken. Chad and Phillips drove to Florida, Chad went home and Phillips went to see Rogelio. After hugs of thanks, Phillips and Rogelio took a private walk in the garden.

"I really don't know how to thank you for what you did," Rogelio said. "You and your friends could have died saving me, but you did it anyway."

"If it wasn't for you," Phillips said looking down at him, "we would not have known that you had been kidnapped or what these guys had planned. I think we should be thanking you."

Phillips sat on a bench near the pond and motioned for Rogelio to join him. "You've been through a lot, it's changed you and that will never go away. You grew up quickly because of what happened. You've seen and done things that most people only read about or see in movies. What you do with the experience is up to you. You are very intelligent and I think you'll turn this into something good. Don't dwell on the bad things that happened, it's okay to remember them, just not all the time. Do you understand what I'm trying to say?"

"I think so," Rogelio answered. "Don't worry, I won't go around killing people because they make me angry," he smiled. "I had to do what I did, I had to help you."

Phillips smiled back at him and nodded. He reached in his pocket and handed Rogelio a card. "This is my phone number. If you need to call me for any reason, you call. Even if it's just to talk. Okay?"

Rogelio nodded, took the card and they shared a manly handshake before returning to the house.

Matt Haynes was reluctant to give a statement to the FBI or DOJ for fear of the repercussions, he knew giving information that implicated the AG was futile and dangerous. The information he and his wife had already given, when the tracking device was removed, was not official enough for either of the department heads, they wanted him under oath. His brother-in-law pointed out to him that his job and life were probably already in jeopardy. He should retire early, move his family and then give the requested statement. They could open a fishing camp on the southern coast of Costa Rica or the Yucatan, fly tourist around and enjoy life. The children agreed and said they could go to boarding school together and spend vacations on the coast. Matts' eldest daughter reminded him that she only had two years of high school to finish and they could all use fake names. Rogelio, who now only wanted to be called Roger, was very excited about going to school with his cousins.

Yolanda was finally cleared to go home to Mexico. The day she was to leave she sat in the garden with Pepa and told her about the man she had met in Mexico and then had seen again with the men who saved her. She wanted to know his real name, but Pepa wouldn't give it up. Yolanda assured Pepa that she wasn't a whore and that she really liked the man and wanted to see him again. Pepa stood her ground. As Yolanda was walking out to get in the agency car that would take her to the airport, she turned to Pepa and told her that the reason they could find very little in her background was because it had been scrubbed. That she worked with a secret group that was trying to stop the training camps in Mexico and her job was to infiltrate these groups and retrieve information. Her previous job had been to gather information on the drug cartels. Before Pepa could say anything, Yolanda turned and got into the car.

A few weeks later Matthew Haynes resigned from his position citing personal reasons and made his official statement to the FBI.

Around the same time Haynes was giving his statement, a news story came across from Mexico. There had been a terrible accident at a survival training camp in the mountain area not far from Nuevo Laredo. It was reported that there had been a series of explosions that caused landslides in the area. There was speculation as to the cause for the explosions, ranging from the gas reserves they kept on hand for the vehicles, the large amounts of propane used for the mess hall, to the possibility that unstable dynamite from an old mining operation had been disturbed. The number of dead was unknown, but thankfully, no tourists had been hiking in the area. Rescue and recovery efforts were underway, but hope was dwindling for survivors.

Chad read the article and laughed at the idea of gas reserves and a mess hall at a survival camp. He reached over, picked up his phone and called Sanchez.

"So, how goes it on the border?" was the first thing out of Chads' mouth.

"Hello to you too," replied Sanchez. "The border is still here and in good hands."

They chatted and joked for a while before Chad said, "That thing that we talked about before you left, I suspect that it has been resolved."

"Yeah, it wasn't as big a problem as we thought. Piece of cake," Sanchez replied.

"While I have you on the phone, I just read about a bad accident in the mountains near Nuevo Laredo. Anything new on that?" Chad asked.

"I don't know much about it," Sanchez replied. "I had been on patrol all day and then I was in the office catching up on paperwork when it came over our radio. It sounds like the whole side of a mountain fell into that valley. We may never know the death toll."

Chad asked, "So I guess Ray and my guys give you some ideas when you were here, you know, about his little toys?"

"Actually he did and tell him thank you the next time you see him," Sanchez said.

"Will do, glad he could be of assistance. Listen we need to get together and soon, I want to hear about your latest endeavors. Can you get some time off again?"

"For you anything," Sanchez said. "Are we going fishing?"

"Yeah, I need some down time," Chad replied.

76

The sleek black Mercedes with dark tinted windows and no headlights drove up the driveway and stopped in front of the stately two story home. The house was situated on twenty acres of gently rolling, cross fenced Virginia countryside. The nearest neighbor was far enough away that the house couldn't be seen, much less the driveway, but never assume anything.

The driver got out and walked to the front door, punched in the code to unlock the door and used the security code to turn off the alarm system and security cameras. The passenger brought in two large cases from the car. The front door was closed and locked before they proceeded upstairs. They didn't need interior lights, they wore night vision goggles. They were both dressed in black clothing, black gloves, their heads and faces were covered and they wore black shoes covers.

The entryway was marble, as were the stairs and connecting hallways. The only carpet they had to cross was in the bedroom they were now entering. They carefully stepped in each other's steps to minimize the prints. They passed through the French doors and walked out onto an oversized balcony. They had arrived early to allow themselves time to set up and get ready for the night ahead. The area had been scouted, this house and balcony had been chosen for its strategic placement, this was not the first time they had entered this house and stood on this spot.

There was no moon or lights, they would be setting up using only their NVG's. A one inch thick slip proof ground cover was put down, then came two L115A3's. They replaced their black gloves with surgical gloves and loaded their weapons with .338 Lapua's, each bullet was polished before being loaded, two for each weapon. Next came the sand bags that actually held oats, wheat and peas, these would give their weapons the stability they needed, but without the weight and with the added benefit of easy disposal. The men lay prone with their weapons, sighting them in and doing the last minute adjustments. They had a clear unimpeded view of the brick colonial house with a dozen cars parked in front. It was a bit over a half mile away as the crow flies. Both men were thinking the same thing, "Please let our intel be correct." They knew that their targets always traveled together, but whether they would walk out the door at the same time was a question that couldn't be answered.

It was 10pm, the dinner party should be breaking up at any time. Now it was just wait and watch.

At 10:45pm guests started leaving, both men tensed for the briefest of moments, then relaxed. They watched cars leave until there were only three left, and only one of those would be leaving.

One of the men said, "No wind, barely a breeze, perfect." These would be the only words spoken between the two men since arriving at the house.

They both started controlled breathing and slowed their heart rates. They had practiced this shot together over a thousand times, in every scenario they could think possible. In wind, rain, blowing dust, uphill and down, with and without trees. They could complete the shot in their sleep.

The two men now worked as one. Like musicians who had played together for thirty years, they used peripheral awareness and knew instinctively what the other was going to do.

They watched the front doors open and two body guards exit the house, then AG Older and Mr. Addison emerged. They stood on the front porch laughing over something one of them had said.

The two men on the balcony pulled the trigger at the same time and in less than five seconds there were two bright red spots on the front doors. The targets were down, clean shots to the head. They watched only long enough for confirmation.

The two men then casually replaced all their gear, put on their gloves, double checked for any evidence that might have been left behind and left the house. While one replaced their gear in the hidden air tight compartment in the back of the car, the other reset the alarm and cameras. The car, weapons and clothing would later disappear until needed again.

Their head coverings came off, the headlights remained off and navigating with their NVG's they entered the country lane. The headlights wouldn't be turned on until they left the area. They didn't see any emergency vehicles until they reached the highway. They pulled off they highway thirty-five miles later where they changed their clothing and placed everything in separate plastic bags and stored them with the other gear. Both men breathed a sigh of relief as they headed south.

Neither man spoke.

At 7pm local time, 3800 miles away a cell phone chirped. Chad took the phone out of his pocket, read the message, typed in a response, took out the sim card broke it in half and dropped it overboard into the water. He reached into his pack took out a new card and slipped it in his phone.

He looked over at the man rigging fishing poles, "That was a message telling me that someone finished our job for us. It appears that Mr. Older and Mr. Addison were shot and killed tonight as they left a dinner party in Virginia."

"Who did it? Anybody we know?" Sanchez asked.

"They have no idea," Chad said. "Right now they're not even sure where the shots came from, it's still too early and they'll have to wait for daylight to find anything. They'll get the prelims done before that, but they won't find anything."

"Why did you change sim cards?" Sanchez asked. "You're on vacation, almost four thousand miles away."

"Partly out of habit and there is no reason anyone should inform us, Chad replied. "I know it was our case, but to inform us that quickly looks hinky. One thing you learn in this business is to always cover your ass. Phillips and Brock probably got the same message."

"Think we'll win the bet?" Sanchez asked.

"Yeah, I do, if Phillips doesn't cheat," Chad laughed, "and drinks too much beer. Being in the Bahamas they are going to have too many diversions and rum. I have a feeling they will forget why they're there."

Sanchez reached over and hit the lights that illuminated the water, "Well we can't win if we don't bait the hook. Let's go fishing."

Acknowledgements

I would like to thank Angela Hoy and Todd Engel for putting this book together and bringing it to market. A big thank you to two Sheriff's Department Deputy's for their time in explaining certain procedures.

A special thank you to Bonnie Stockton-Gilbert for her Prologue and keeping me on track and Don Wible for urging me forward.

CPSIA information can be obtained
at www.ICGtesting.com
Printed in the USA
LVOW12s2147101116

512530LV00001B/74/P